*"Jeff Edwards has created a superb t.\
beginning to end. A truly spellbind\
executed."*

— **CLIVE CUSSLER**, Internation.\
and *'RAISE THE TITANIC'*

*"A taut, exciting story by an author who knows his Navy — guaranteed to\
keep you turning pages well into the night!"*

— **GREG BEAR**, New York Times bestselling author of\
'MARIPOSA,' and *'DARWIN'S RADIO'*

*"Jeff Edwards takes his readers to the brink of Armageddon and beyond!\
THE SEVENTH ANGEL is a remarkably-sophisticated, breathlessly-paced\
naval drama, with the unique mastery of ruthless geopolitics that is fast\
becoming the distinct signature of this Veteran-turned-novelist!"*

— **JOE BUFF**, Bestselling author of *'SEAS OF CRISIS,'* and\
'CRUSH DEPTH'

*"Artfully conceived and beautifully written, THE SEVENTH ANGEL by\
Jeff Edwards is a riveting tale chock full of adventure, thrilling action, and\
rich characters. Anyone who has ever loved the sea will love this one!"*

— **GAYLE LYNDS**, New York Times bestselling author of *'BOOK\
OF SPIES,'* and *'THE LAST SPYMASTER'*

*"Brilliant and spellbinding... THE SEVENTH ANGEL took me back to\
sea, and into the fury of life-or-death combat. I could not put this book\
down.*

— **REAR ADMIRAL JOHN J. WAICKWICZ, USN (Retired)**,\
Former Commander, Naval Mine and Anti-Submarine Warfare\
Command

*"A harrowing tale of nuclear blackmail that races towards the\
unthinkable with frightening realism."*

— **DIRK CUSSLER**, Bestselling author of *'CRESCENT DAWN,'*\
and *'BLACK WIND'*

*"A page turning, sip-from-a-fire-hose thriller in the world of underwater\
ballistic missiles and rogue former Soviet states."*

— **JAMES W. HUSTON**, New York Times bestselling author of\
'FALCON SEVEN,' and *'SECRET JUSTICE'*

THE SEVENTH ANGEL

THE SEVENTH ANGEL

Jeff Edwards

STEALTH BOOKS

THE SEVENTH ANGEL

Copyright © 2010 by Jeff Edwards

Stealth Books

www.stealthbooks.com

ISBN-13: 978-0-9830085-1-4

Printed in the United States of America

To Vailia Dennis

For a lifetime of friendship, love, and shared wisdom
— all squeezed into a few short years.

ACKNOWLEDGMENTS

I would like to thank the following people for their assistance in making this book a reality:

Rear Admiral John J. Waickwicz, USN (Retired), former Commander Naval Mine and Anti-Submarine Warfare Command—for his invaluable technical advice and sharp editorial eye; Lieutenant (junior grade) Bryan Wagonseller of the National/Naval Ice Center for his help in understanding ice formations in the Sea of Okhotsk; Bill St. Lawrence for sharing his extensive knowledge of ice-drilling technologies; Peter Bordokoff, Liza Pariser, and Ian Kharitonov for their exceptional Russian language skills; Captain Valery Grigoriev, Russian Navy (Retired), for his help with Russian naval language and Russian Navy procedures; novelist and former Trident submarine officer John Hindinger for giving me a basic unclassified understanding of ballistic missile trajectories; Master Gunnery Sergeant (EOD) Samuel A. Larter, USMC (Retired) and Sergeant Major R. A. "Skip" Paradine, Jr., USMC (Retired), for answering my questions about Explosive Ordnance Disposal as conducted by the U.S. Marine Corps; Master Modeler Richard Melillo of The Modeler's Art (TheModelersArt.com) for building me an extraordinary model of the DMA-37 torpedo; Staff Sergeant Justin Schafer, U.S. Army, for help with small arms and the M-4 carbine; Brenda Collins for her diligent assistance in locating map resources and her excellent editorial advice; Robert MacDougall for his help with ballistic missile defense; OS2 Rob Andrews of the U.S. Coast Guard Navigation Center for refreshing my memory on matters of ship navigation; Kenneth R. Gerhart of the Defense Intelligence Agency for answering my questions about defense intelligence, and Maria Edwards, for her impeccable research, skilled editing, and tireless promotion of my novels.

There were other contributors who are not named here, by their own request, or through oversight on my part. In every case, the information I received from these people was superb. Any inaccuracies found here are either the product of artistic license, or my own mistakes. Such errors are in no way the fault of my contributors.

Finally, I would like to thank my editor and friend, Don Gerrard, for knowing when to encourage me, when to challenge me, when to kick me into shape, and when to get the hell out of the way and let me run.

"…we witness today, in the power of nuclear weapons, a new and deadly dimension to the ancient horror of war. Humanity has now achieved, for the first time in its history, the power to end its history."

President Dwight D. Eisenhower
September 19, 1956

"And there came a seventh angel, his robe hemmed with fire and the sword of doom in his hand. Written upon his brow was the name of death."

Jashar 10:21
(*Sefer haYashar*)*
Lost book of the Old Testament

* Translation circa 1552, from the private archives of Giovanni del Monte.

PROLOGUE

The deck gun fired again, sending another ninety-six pound naval artillery round thundering into the night. For an instant, the muzzle flash from the big gun stripped away the concealing darkness, revealing the low angular profile of a U.S. Navy destroyer.

The vessel revealed in that microsecond of illumination was strange-looking. The squat pyramid shapes of her superstructure and the steep angle of her mast gave the destroyer very little resemblance to any previous generation of warships.

The flare of light was as brief as a camera flash, gone almost the instant it appeared, and the ship was once again hidden against the dark waves of the Northern Arabian Gulf.

The ship's name was USS *Towers*, and she was the fourth (and last) of the Flight III *Arleigh Burke* Class destroyers. She was a blend of superb naval engineering and cutting-edge military stealth technology, a combination that had caused a great deal of hype and wild speculation.

News magazines had taken to calling her a 'ghost ship,' and a growing body of Internet mythology credited the destroyer with capabilities that could only be managed by Hollywood special effects wizards. The reality was impressive enough, but it was considerably short of the myth, and well within the boundaries of known physics.

The vessel's radar cross-section, infrared profile, and acoustic and magnetic signatures were all severely minimized, and a layer of phototropic camouflage made the ship difficult to detect and track visually. Even so, the *Towers* was far from invisible, despite the ever-growing body of myth that surrounded her name.

But hype didn't matter now, and neither did speculation. USS *Towers* was wounded, and she was running for her life.

Three-thousand yards aft of the ship, hidden beneath a dark blanket of seawater, a second torpedo was coming to finish the job that the first had begun. No amount of myth or hype could stop it, or even slow its approach.

The deck gun fired again, and the strange-looking warship was again silhouetted against black water for an instant. The gun barrel was at maximum elevation, and the firing charge was reduced, making the trajectory very high and extremely short. The round crashed into the wave tops a few hundred yards ahead of the ship.

To either side of the bow, the ship's smaller guns followed with their own lesser furies, hammering .50-caliber machine gun bullets and 25mm chain-gun rounds into the waves just forward of the vessel. It was a tactic of purest desperation.

The ship was surrounded by a field of naval mines, their numbers and locations hidden by black water. Any one of those mines could crack the hull of a warship like an eggshell. The guided-missile frigate USS *Samuel B. Roberts* had learned that lesson the hard way two decades earlier, in this very same body of water, just a few hundred nautical miles to the south. The *Samuel B. Roberts* had nearly been blown in half. Whether or not *Towers* was about to repeat that lesson was still yet to be seen.

Under any other circumstances, the proper tactic would have been to maneuver at two or three knots, locating each mine with the ship's Kingfisher sonar, and mapping a safe route to the edge of the minefield. But moving slowly was not an option now. The torpedo was getting closer by the second. It was locked on to the ship's acoustic signature like a cybernetic bloodhound, and the deadly machine was following the trail with a ruthless precision that no living creature could equal.

The *Towers* needed every ounce of speed that her engineers could squeeze out of their wounded vessel. Every fifty yards of forward motion was another second of life. But it wasn't going to be enough. The torpedo was faster, and—unlike its target—it was not slowed by damage. The weapon was rapidly overtaking the destroyer. The seconds were beginning to run out.

Standing behind the Tactical Action Officer's chair in the air-conditioned semi-darkness of Combat Information Center, Captain Bowie watched the chase rushing toward its conclusion on the giant Aegis display screens. The fingers of his left hand gripped a steel crossbeam in the overhead, steadying his body against the motion of the ship. His right hand rested casually on the back of the TAO's chair. His posture was carefully-relaxed, and he concentrated on keeping the tension out of his facial expression.

He knew without looking that the men and women of his CIC team were watching him out of the corners of their eyes. They were measuring his reactions, drawing confidence and hope from the calm assurance of his demeanor.

His crew needed hope right now. They were scared, and they had every reason to be. They were exhausted, and their bodies were bruised and bloodied. More than a few of their shipmates were already dead. Their ship was grievously damaged, and the fight was not over yet.

Bowie ran a hand through his short black hair, and relaxed the set of his shoulders. He looked more like an accountant than a naval officer, and he knew it. His long face and narrow cheekbones gave him an air of clean efficiency, and the slight downturn of his mouth tended to make him look pensive, even in the most relaxed of circumstances. The effect was usually offset by his quick brown eyes and his easy laugh, but there was nothing to laugh about tonight. Nothing at all.

This was the craziest tactical situation Bowie had ever heard of. Even the worst-case everybody-dies training scenarios weren't this bad. His plan for dealing with the situation was even crazier, if such a thing was possible.

It was not a good plan; Bowie knew that. Maybe it wasn't even an entirely sane plan, but what the hell else could he do? If there were other options, he hadn't been able to think of them.

There was no time to sniff out a safe path through the minefield. If they reduced speed enough for sonar to detect the mines, the torpedo would catch them and kill them. If they tried to run without seeing the mines, they were nearly certain to hit one. That would kill them just as quickly.

On the big display screen, the *Towers* appeared as a small green cross, enclosed by a circle. A single green speed vector protruded from the center of the symbol, like the stick of a lollipop. The symbol was pointed southwest now, inching toward the irregular red boundary that represented the edge of the minefield. They were moving in the right direction—toward safe water—but the flashing red torpedo symbol was less than 2,500 yards behind now, and moving a lot faster as it continued to close the gap.

The mines didn't appear on the tactical display at all, except the general outline showing the boundaries of the minefield. That information had come from COM Fifth Fleet, via the Special Warfare unit attached to U.S. Navy Central Command. But there were no coordinates for the mines themselves: no clues to their locations, or even how many were there. It might be a hundred, or five hundred, or five thousand.

The *Towers* couldn't map a safe route through the minefield, and the ship could not survive without one. The only choice was to create their own path through the mines, clear a safe route where none existed.

Out on the darkened forecastle, the deck gun continued to pound the water with naval artillery shells every two and a half seconds. The forward machine guns and the two chain-guns continued to hammer their own projectiles into the wave tops. The ship was pumping a tremendous amount of mechanical force and shrapnel into the sea. Theoretically, some of that brute kinetic force should penetrate far enough down to reach the mines. That was the plan: to pulverize the water hard enough to trigger the mines at a distance, clearing the way ahead of the ship.

But it wasn't working. Bowie's crazy plan, which had seemed at least distantly feasible when he'd given the order, did not seem to be bearing fruit. There were no answering explosions to show that the guns were finding targets. For all of the racket and thunder, the guns had not yet triggered a single mine.

Bowie felt a hand on his left shoulder. He turned to find his second in command, Lieutenant Commander Peter Tyler, standing behind him. Pete was a good man, and a damned fine executive officer. Just the kind of guy you'd want in your corner if things got ugly.

He leaned in close, and spoke quietly into his captain's ear. "Do you think this'll work?"

Bowie shrugged. "Frankly, I have no idea. I just know that it's better than sitting around waiting to die."

His last word seemed to echo in the chilled air of CIC, and Bowie wished instantly that he hadn't said it.

He opened his mouth to add something else—*anything*—to wipe that dreadful word out of the air. Before he could speak, a thundering boom shook the entire ship.

For a half-second, Bowie thought they'd been hit, but the Officer of the Deck's voice came over the Tactical Action Officer's communications net. "TAO—Bridge. Close-aboard explosion off the port bow!"

The TAO keyed the microphone of his headset to acknowledge the report, but his voice was drowned out by a second explosion.

"TAO—Bridge. Close-aboard explosion dead off the bow!"

All around him, the members of Bowie's CIC team began exchanging glances. He knew what they were thinking. Maybe the skipper's crazy plan was going to work. Maybe ... just *maybe*, they were not all going to die tonight.

On the Aegis display screen, the symbol for *Towers* was moving toward the boundary of the minefield. The torpedo had closed within 2,000 yards and was gaining fast, but it looked like the ship might be clear of the minefield before the weapon struck. If the ship could make it that far, they could maneuver without fear of mines. They could *crack the whip*—run the tricky evasion maneuvers designed to throw pursuing torpedoes off the scent. They might have a chance.

"I think this is working," a voice behind him said. "Looks like you might still pull the fat out of the fire, sir."

Bowie turned, expecting to see his XO. Instead, he found himself staring into the eyes of Lieutenant Clinton Brody, the pilot of the USS *Towers* helicopter, *Firewalker Two-Six*.

A prickle ran down the back of Bowie's neck. Something wasn't right here. He felt a stirring in his gut: an indefinable certainty that some crucial element of reality had suddenly veered off in an unexpected direction.

The gun roared again. The sound had a different character to it—muted, with a sort of weirdly-metallic echo. A report blared from one of the overhead speakers, but the voice was tinny, and too garbled to understand.

Bowie's gaze was still locked on the young pilot's face. Lieutenant Brody was not supposed to be here. No, that wasn't right. He *couldn't* be here. It wasn't possible.

The realization came instantly, and it brought another abrupt shift in the fabric of reality. The world seemed to stutter and then freeze in place, like a film break in an old-fashioned movie projector, the last frame of broken celluloid still trapped behind the lens. All action had stopped, but that last image persisted, Combat Information Center and its crew held motionless in an instance of frozen time.

Lieutenant Clinton Brody could not here, because the man was *dead*. His body had been burned and cut to ribbons by the Siraji missile that had ripped his helicopter from the sky.

He couldn't be here. But here he was, staring back at Bowie.

The world had gone eerily silent. The pounding of the guns, the murmur of the CIC crew, the whisper of cooling fans, the surge of the ship through the water, were all gone. The sound of Bowie's own breathing suddenly seemed almost painfully loud.

"You're dead," he said softly. It was somehow both a statement of fact, and an accusation.

The dead helicopter pilot nodded, and a long slice opened in the flesh of his left cheek—skin parting almost magically—blood spilling down the side of his face as the cut widened and the ivory-yellow of the man's cheekbone was revealed. "Yes, sir," he said. "I *am*."

He squared his shoulders and saluted, as though presenting himself for inspection. As he lowered his hand, it fell limply at his side, injuries manifesting instantly, leaving the pilot's arm mangled and fractured in numerous places. "My crew are dead too. Both of them."

The other two members of the helicopter aircrew were suddenly standing behind the dead officer: his copilot, Lieutenant (junior grade)

Julie Schramm, her brown hair singed and twisted, her once pretty face scorched and nearly black with bruising and blood; and the aircraft's Sensor Operator, Petty Officer Second Class Daniel Gilford, his right leg missing from the hip, the side of his head a mass of ragged tissue and splintered bone.

Bowie had only a second to register this hideous sight before more of the grisly figures began appearing. Commander Rachel Vargas. Lieutenant (junior grade) Alex Sherman. Seaman Terrence Archer. Petty Officer Gerald Blake. Fireman Apprentice Thomas James Keiler. Each of their bodies burned, or bleeding, or broken.

The gathering of corpses continued to grow, and Bowie recognized every one of their faces.

This was the accounting of souls. Every man and woman in that growing crowd had died under Bowie's command.

His chest tightened until he could barely breathe. He had tried to protect them. He had done his best to lead them well. He had tried to keep them safe from harm. But they were dead, despite his intentions.

Every one of them was dead, and there was nothing Bowie could do about it.

The thought seemed to break the spell. The transition from dream to wakefulness was instantaneous. Combat Information Center vanished, and the bodies of the dead Sailors were gone with the flicker of an eyelid.

Bowie lay in the bunk of his at-sea cabin, staring up into the darkness and feeling the pounding of his heart and the gentle rolling of the ship. The sheets had gotten themselves twisted around his legs, the way they always did when he had the dream. He knew without checking that his cheeks were damp with tears.

He made no move to wipe them away. The commanding officer of a warship is not supposed to cry, but Bowie thought—as he always did after the dream—that his tears were an honest tribute to Rachel Vargas, and Alex Sherman, and Clint Brody, and the rest of them. They deserved his tears. And, like it or not, Bowie knew that he deserved the dream.

He supposed that it was technically a nightmare, but he rarely thought of it that way. In his mind, it was something different. It was a reckoning. It was a balancing of karma: a none-too-subtle reminder that human lives depended on his actions and his orders, and that he did not always wield that power with perfect judgment.

He fumbled for his watch in the darkness, found it, and pushed buttons until the dial lit up. It took him a couple of seconds to focus his eyes well enough to read the time. It was 02:07, just a few minutes after two AM.

Bowie tugged the sheets away from his legs and groaned. Two in the morning. Damn.

He could have used more rest than that, but he knew from past experience that it was no good to try again. Once it got started, the dream was with him for the night. If he went back to sleep now, the dream would come again. And again.

He climbed out of his bunk. Better to get up now, and make a long day of it. He'd grab a cup of coffee and head over to CIC. Maybe one of the civilian engineers would be up already, and he could get some more information on this *Mouse* unit they were supposed to be testing.

His fingers located the light switch. He flicked it on, blinking in the sudden illumination. He yawned hard, and reached for his coveralls.

The dead deserved to have their say. He couldn't begrudge them that, no matter how much sleep it cost him. They could haunt his dreams as often as they wanted. They had earned that right. But Bowie's waking hours belonged to the world of the living. He planned to keep it that way.

CHAPTER 1

MANILA, REPUBLIC OF THE PHILIPPINES
FRIDAY; 22 FEBRUARY
0302 hours (3:02 AM)
TIME ZONE +8 'HOTEL'

Oleg Grigoriev should not have been alive. The part of his mind still capable of rational thought was aware of that. By all rights, he should have died back there in that alley, where those Chinese bastards had dumped his body with the rest of the garbage.

But he was not dead. Not *yet*.

He staggered down the darkened sidewalk, following the pools of feeble yellow light cast by the street lamps. The dim circles of illumination had become his mile posts—the only method of measuring progress toward his destination.

The Americans… He had to reach the Americans.

His senses were playing tricks now. He could hear the whine of distant traffic, but not the scrape of his shoes on the cement. He could feel the damp of the sweat on his cheeks, but not the hot flow of blood down his ribs. Even his sense of distance had become weirdly distorted. His courier duties had brought him to Manila many times, and he had driven down this stretch of Roxas Boulevard more than once. It was only a few city blocks. But it had somehow stretched itself into an impossibly-long tunnel of darkness, punctuated by widely-spaced glows of sickly yellow.

His left knee buckled, and he tottered sideways, slumping against the windows of a car for support. He drew a long breath, doing his best to ignore the rattling gurgle in his chest.

It was getting harder to breathe, but at least the pain was gone. Most of it, anyway. The white-hot agony in his ribs had faded to a distant ache—disconnected—as though it belonged to someone else.

He wondered dimly if the lack of pain might be a bad sign. Was he in shock? Or was his nervous system shutting down as his bodily functions began to fail? Certainly his mind seemed to be slipping. He could no longer remember how many times the bastards had shot him.

8

That last thought brought a grim smile to his lips. They obviously hadn't shot him *enough* times. Not enough to kill a rangy old Russian bear like Oleg Grigoriev. A few Chinese bullets would kill an ordinary man perhaps, but not a former Sergeant in the Tamanskaya Guards. Not an old Soldier of the Iron Saber brigade.

Grigoriev took another gurgling breath, and forced his eyes to focus. He could see it now in the distance, the brighter white glow of the security lights that surrounded the American Embassy.

He pushed himself upright, and swayed back to a full standing position. His knees would have to hold out a little longer. Keep walking. He had to keep walking. He had to reach the Americans.

His own people had betrayed him; that much he knew. The Chinese would not have dared to harm him without authorization from Zhukov. The bastards wanted the warheads too badly. They'd never risk blowing the deal by killing Zhukov's courier. That could only mean that Zhukov had authorized the hit. And then he'd sent Grigoriev to Manila, to a rendezvous in a deserted alley, in this cesspool of a country where life was cheap. Straight into the hands of the Chinese killers.

Grigoriev coughed, sending a spasm of pain through his chest. He lurched forward, stumbling toward the lights of the embassy one faltering step at a time.

They wanted to throw him out with the garbage, did they? Leave him dying among the broken beer bottles and the cat piss? Trying to protect their precious secrets. Hide their plans from the Americans.

Grigoriev could taste blood in his mouth now, but the tough old Russian grinned anyway. He'd show the bastards. The Chinese. Zhukov. All of them. He'd tell the Americans *everything*, and then he'd sit back with a fat bottle of Moskovskaya and watch the whole thing go to hell.

CHAPTER 2

ICE PACK — NORTHERN SEA OF OKHOTSK
LATITUDE 58.29N / LONGITUDE 155.20E
FRIDAY; 22 FEBRUARY
1421 hours (2:21 PM)
TIME ZONE +11 'LIMA'

The helicopter came to a hover less than a meter above the ice. It hung there for nearly a minute as the downwash from its rotors blasted snow from the rugged icescape below. The roaring vortex of mechanically-induced wind created an instant blizzard around the aircraft, reducing effective visibility to almost zero. But there wasn't enough snow to cause a true whiteout. Within seconds, the light accumulation of powder had been blown away, revealing a circle of dirty gray ice a little larger than the sweep of the rotor blades.

This was not the smooth ice sheet of the Arctic. The ice pack in the Sea of Okhotsk was strained and twisted by the collision of two opposing ocean currents, and the relentless hammering of the Siberian wind. The ice was pocked with hillocks, ridges, and fractures—a frozen diorama of unreleased pressure.

The helicopter made no attempt to land on the torturous surface. It maintained position, while doors slid open on either side of the fuselage. Three men made the short jump to the ice, and began unloading equipment through the open doors of the aircraft. As soon as the equipment was unloaded, the helicopter lifted away, climbing to an altitude of a thousand meters where it circled while the others carried out their mission down below.

The men moved quickly and smoothly, despite the roughness of the terrain. They worked without speaking, communicating via hand signals when required, but even that was rarely necessary.

They were a well-oiled team, and they had already performed this operation four times before at other locations on the Okhotsk ice pack. This would be the fifth and final time.

Their cold weather gear was ex-Soviet military issue. The dappled grays and dingy whites of the snow camouflage were a near-perfect match for the surrounding ice. From a few hundred meters away, they would be all but invisible, not that visibility particularly mattered out here. They were the only living souls for at least two hundred kilometers.

In forty minutes, the job was done; the team was back aboard the helicopter and thundering away through the frigid Russian sky.

Already the winds were beginning to hide the evidence of their work beneath a thin layer of grubby snow. The seven new holes in the ice were rapidly disappearing, as was the network of thin wires that cross-connected the holes like a spider web.

A scrap of torn plastic fluttered and skidded across the ice, sticking for a moment against the slope of a pressure ridge. For the briefest of seconds, a single word was visible—black Cyrillic lettering stenciled against gray plastic. The word was *vzryvchatka*. Explosive. And then the wind caught the scrap and snatched it away, leaving no visible trace that man had ever set foot on this forbidding stretch of ice.

CHAPTER 3

It was like falling into night. The deepwater submersible *Nereus* continued its descent into the Aleutian trench—passing from the midwater zone, where blue wavelengths of light were still visible—into the aphotic zone, where no light penetrated at all.

Charlie Sweigart stared through the *Nereus's* forward view port as the last traces of light deepened from twilight blue to a shade of black that few human eyes had ever seen. A half mile above, the *Nereus's* tender, the Research Vessel *Otis Barton*, was enjoying the bright morning sunshine. But down here, the only light came from the mini-sub's interior lights, and the glowing faces of the instrument clusters.

"Bottom coming up in fifty meters," Gabriella said.

Her voice sent a tiny shiver down Charlie Sweigart's spine. Gabriella's English was flawless, but her voice carried a musical French-Canadian lilt that never failed to give Charlie a tingle.

Charlie nodded without looking back. "Thanks."

The cabin of the submersible was as cramped as the cockpit of the space shuttle. Charlie sat in the pilot's seat, nearest the bow of the little submarine, surrounded by gauges, digital readouts, and equipment status lights. Gabriella's seat at the sensor console was behind Charlie and to his left, so he couldn't see her without turning almost completely around in his chair. That would be a bit *too* obvious, so Charlie made do with glimpses of her reflection in the ten-inch thick plate of curved lexan that formed the forward view port.

The reflections weren't perfect. The curvature of the surface brought some distortion to the images. But Charlie could look at Gabriella in that imperfect mirror as often as he wanted.

Who was he kidding, anyway? What would a tall, willowy blonde want with a pudgy little sub-jockey like Charlie? A tall, willowy, *smart* blonde. *Doctor* Gabriella Marchand—on loan to NOAA from *Centre océanographique de Rimouski*, in Quebec—had PhDs in Oceanography, Geochemistry, and Marine Geophysics. She didn't like for Charlie to call her *doctor*, but doctor she was. She was one very smart lady, and she was rapidly becoming one of the world's leading experts on methane hydrate deposits, whatever *those* were.

Charlie had read the research proposals and goals for this project. He'd been to the pre-dive briefings, and studied the mission plans carefully. This was their seventh dive, so he knew the plan inside and out. He had the navigational waypoints all programmed into the *Nereus's* computers. He knew the currents in the Aleutian trench, and he knew how to compensate for the drift they'd try to put on his boat. He could put the submersible within inches of every sampling site on the Dive Plan. But the real work on this project was up to Gabriella. Charlie was just the bus driver.

He glanced at the glide angle indicator, and eased back on the control yoke to slow the boat's rate of descent. Outside of the pressure hull, the submersible's four propulsor pods rotated slightly, canceling some of the vessel's negative buoyancy with vectored jets of water.

"Forty meters to bottom," Gabriella said.

Charlie suppressed another shiver. Gabriella's bottom was considerably closer than forty meters, but it was not a good idea to think about *that*.

Charlie nodded again. "Forty meters. Thanks."

He was just sneaking another peek at Gabriella's reflection when a different voice came from behind him.

"So, what color is it?"

Charlie flinched. He'd almost forgotten that Steve was even there.

Steve Harper, the other permanent member of the *Nereus* crew, sat at the engineering station, behind Charlie and to his right. Steve was a good guy. He could be a jackass when the mood struck him, but he was usually pretty easy to be around. He was also a skilled technician and an excellent button masher. Charlie liked working with him, at least when Steve wasn't startling the hell out of him.

Charlie cocked his head. "Huh?"

"I asked you what color it is," Steve said.

"What color is *what*?" Charlie asked.

"The Porsche," Steve said. "Didn't you just buy a new Porsche?"

"Oh, yeah," Charlie said. "Well, it's not new. But it's in really good shape."

"You've got a Porsche?" That was Gabriella.

"Yeah," Charlie said. "It's a ninety-eight Turbo Carrera. Low mileage. It's pretty nice. Good paint. Nice interior. Excellent mechanical condition."

"I like the nineties-models better too," Gabriella said. "I think they changed the suspension in the new ones. I don't like the way they handle as much." She seemed to be taking it for granted that Charlie's decision to buy a used model was a matter of preference rather than finance.

"What color is it?" Steve asked again.

Charlie grimaced. "It's – uh, red. Sort of a light red."

Steve whistled through his teeth. "Dude, you got a red Porsche turbo? You are sooooo set!"

"What's our distance to bottom?" Charlie asked. It was time to derail this conversation. He did *not* want to talk about the Porsche.

"Thirty-two meters to bottom," Gabriella said.

Charlie nodded. "Thanks." He eased back on the yoke a little more. They were still a little too far away from the bottom to see anything, but this was as good a time as any to heat up the exterior lights. "Floods coming on," he said, and he flipped three switches near the top of his console.

Outside the hull, three banks of sealed halogen floodlights flared to life, casting a sphere of light around the little submersible. The darkness was not banished; it hung just beyond the reach of the floods, like an impenetrable curtain of blackness. This was where night lived. On the surface, the sun ruled half of the planet at any given time. But down here, night was *always* master.

The thought gave Charlie a mild case of the creeps, despite the fact that it had occurred to him a hundred times before. It *was* a little creepy. But it was also cool. Because this was Charlie's domain. Anywhere else in the world, he was just a geeky looking guy with a spare tire around his waist. But down *here*, Charlie flew like Icarus through the secret realms of darkness. He'd had *that* thought before too, but it never failed to bring a smile to his lips.

He dimmed the cabin lights, to make it easier to see through the view port. Gabriella's reflection faded with the interior illumination.

Steve snorted. "What exactly is a *light* red? Is it like a candy apple red? Or a fire engine red?"

Damn it. He wasn't going to let it drop. "No," Charlie said with a sigh. "It's more of a *whitish* red."

"A *whitish* red?" Steve's voice was incredulous. "You mean like a *pink?*"

"It's not pink!" Charlie snapped. He stopped and corrected himself. "I don't like to think of it as pink, okay?"

Steve's laugh sounded like the cackle of a hen. "Dude! You bought a pink Porsche?"

Charlie tapped a pressure gauge with unnecessary force. "Will you kindly shut the hell up?"

"Aye-aye, sir!" Steve said it in a theatrically-formal voice. "Shutting the hell up as ordered, sir!"

If past behavior was anything to judge by, it was a fair guess that Steve had accompanied the words with a brisk simulation of a salute, pointed in the direction of Charlie's back.

A laugh from Gabriella confirmed the suspicion.

Charlie opened his mouth to call Steve an asshole, when the control yoke gave a strange twitch. All thoughts of playful banter vanished instantly from his mind. "Steve, did you feel that?"

"Did I feel what, Porsche Boy?"

"I just felt some kind of a jerk in the control yoke," Charlie said.

"Yeah, yeah … Let me guess, it was me, right? I'm the jerk?"

"Knock it off," Charlie snapped. "I'm not joking!"

The control yoke twitched again, harder this time—an abrupt twist to the right that nearly wrenched the pistol-shaped grips out of his hands. The submersible rolled about ten degrees to starboard, in instant response to the movement of the controls.

Charlie snatched the yoke back to the left, and then centered up quickly, compensating for the sudden roll. The sub righted itself, but he could feel a definite starboard drag.

"I've got some kind of steering casualty," Charlie said. "Switch me to backup, now!"

"I'm on it," Steve said. "Switching to backup steering now!" He punched a button and relays clicked softly.

"Thanks," Charlie said. The drag on the control yoke vanished as the backup steering circuits kicked in. For a half-second, he considered trying to finish the dive on backup steering. But the deep ocean is unforgiving. When something went wrong a half mile under water, the smart thing to do was head for the surface before a *little* problem could become a *big* problem.

He checked the dive clock on the instrument panel above his head. "I'm declaring a *mission abort* at time zero-nine-five-seven. Call it in."

"Got it," Steve said. "Mission abort, time zero-nine-five-seven. Is this an *emergency* abort, or a deliberate abort?"

Charlie thought about that for a few seconds. An emergency abort meant releasing the fifteen hundred pound lead ballast plate built into the bottom of the submersible. The boat would instantly gain three-quarters of a ton of positive buoyancy. They'd shoot for the surface like a cork. Their assent would not be easily controllable, and there was the possibility of ramming into their tender ship as they broke the surface. Charlie was a good pilot, and he was pretty certain that he could steer clear of the *Otis Barton*, but there was a degree of risk.

A deliberate abort would allow him to control the *Nereus's* assent. It would also save the expense of the lead ballast plate; those things were custom-manufactured to excruciatingly fine technical tolerances, and they were *not* cheap. A deliberate abort also meant a lot less hassle once they got to the surface.

If he declared an emergency, formal investigations would follow. They would be required by law. Everyone associated with the project would be interviewed within an inch of their lives. Every nut and bolt on the submersible would be removed and inspected. The *Nereus* would be decertified for diving operations for weeks, or even months. Gabriella's research project would be over the second Charlie spoke the word 'emergency.'

If he called for a deliberate abort due to minor technical issues, the troubleshooting and repair of the steering problem would go down in the logs as routine corrective maintenance. They might be able to resume the diving schedule tomorrow, or the day after.

His fingers tightened on the controls. "Deliberate abort," he said. "I am not declaring an emergency."

"Understood," Steve said. "Deliberate abort."

Charlie heard him lift the handset for the underwater telephone. Like all other forms of electromagnetic energy, radio waves are rapidly absorbed by water. Within a hundred feet of the surface, they could talk to their mother ship, the Research Vessel *Otis Barton*, by radio. But even the most powerful radios can't penetrate a thousand feet of water. When the *Nereus* was this deep, all communications had to be carried out via the underwater telephone, a two-way acoustic transponder system that could transmit and receive amplified voice signals.

Steve began his report. "*Otis Barton*, this is *Nereus*. We are declaring a deliberate mission abort. I say again—deliberate mission abort." He spoke slowly, pronouncing each syllable with great deliberation. Amplified acoustic voice signals had a tendency to become garbled as they propagated through the water. He paused to give his message time to stop reverberating through the water.

Charlie pulled back on the yoke, bringing the nose of the submersible up. "Let's go, old girl. Time to head back toward fresh air and sunshine."

"I'm not that old," Gabriella said softly.

It was obviously intended as humor, but her words gave Charlie a chill. This was not the pleasant tingle of attraction, but the cold realization that his decision to avoid an emergency abort might be putting Gabriella's life at risk. He'd gotten so locked up in weighing the technical issues of the decision that he'd forgotten to factor in Gabriella. Charlie and Steve were accustomed to the risks. This was what they trained for. This was their *job*. But to Gabriella, this was a scientific expedition. She probably hadn't considered how badly things could go wrong at the bottom of a three thousand foot tall column of water.

At this depth, the water pressure on the hull was over 1,300 pounds per square inch. Suddenly, Charlie could almost feel the ocean squeezing his little submarine, pressing in the way that the darkness tried to crush the sphere of light cast by the flood lamps.

From somewhere near the rear of the cabin came a rapid metallic chattering. Electrical relays were clicking on and off many times a second, making electrical connections, breaking them, and then making them again. The exterior floodlights dimmed, brightened, dimmed again, and then went out.

"Holy shit!" Steve shouted. "I'm losing the main electrical bus! I've got breakers tripping all over the board, and I'm showing low volts on the auxiliary bus!"

Charlie lifted his right hand from the control yoke to fumble for the emergency ballast release. The hot ozone smell of burning electrical insulation filled the air. His fingers wrapped around the handle, but— before he could release the safety latch—the control yoke darted hard to the right. Charlie couldn't hold it steady with only one hand. It twisted out of his grasp, rolling the sub almost ninety-degrees, onto its starboard side.

Charlie was thrown against his safety belts. His head slammed into something. Neon colors exploded in his brain, smearing bright streaks of pain on the insides of his eyelids. Far away, he could hear someone screaming. He wanted to turn and find the screaming person, to help if he could, but his body didn't seem to be obeying his commands.

Like Icarus, his magic wings had failed him. They folded uselessly and tore away from his body. And Charlie Sweigart tumbled helplessly into the heart of darkness.

CHAPTER 4

ICBM: A COLD WAR SAILOR'S MUSINGS ON THE ULTIMATE WEAPONS OF MASS DESTRUCTION

(Reprinted by permission of the author, Retired Master Chief Sonar Technician David M. Hardy, USN)

In the years since the fall of the Warsaw Pact, the word *bomb* has come to be associated with terrorism. We use the term to describe car bombs, roadside bombs, improvised explosive devices, and the feared — but never seen — *dirty* bomb. When we think of bombs, we think of wounded American Soldiers, dead or injured Middle Eastern civilians, and innocent victims in European train stations. But for the last half of the twentieth-century, the word meant something altogether different.

I was a child of the Cold War. I was born in the shadow of Sputnik, when America's nuclear adversary, the USSR, dominated the strategic high ground of outer space. I took my first steps at just about the time a Soviet surface-to-air missile blasted Francis Gary Powers and his U-2 spy plane out of the sky over Sverdlovsk. I was learning to brush my own teeth right about the time the Cuban Missile Crisis had the world teetering on the brink of nuclear holocaust. John F. Kennedy and Nikita Khrushchev managed to drag us back from the edge of destruction, but it was nearly a foregone conclusion that, sooner or later, the Cold War was going to go hot.

Back then *the bomb* was the *big one*: the A-bomb. The term didn't refer to any individual weapon. Outside of James Bond movies and the pages of *Dr. Strangelove*, there was no ultra-secret doomsday device waiting to bring nuclear annihilation to the human species. The bomb was the label we gave to the collective nuclear arsenals of the world. It was cultural shorthand for our bombs, and China's bombs, and the bombs of the Soviet Union. And, in carefully unspoken subtext, the term signified the eventual extermination of man by his own hand.

That was the world I grew up in. A world in which it was taken for granted that we would see Armageddon within our lifetimes. When I enlisted in the Navy that was the world I served in. We didn't look forward to it. We certainly didn't want it. And, despite what you may have seen in movies or political commentaries, the militaries on both sides went to extraordinary lengths to prevent it. But many of us labored under the mortal certainty that a nuclear showdown was inevitable. The United States and the Soviet Union were going to unleash their nuclear arsenals upon each other and the world. It wasn't a matter of *if*, it was a matter of *when*.

Now, so long after the fall of the Berlin wall, those fears seem distant and even a bit foolish. We've refocused our worries on terrorism at home and abroad. We're concerned about the stability of the Middle East. We're nervous about the threat of nuclear weapons in the hands of Iran and North Korea. But the specter of the Russian bomb has been laid to rest. The apocalypse will not arrive riding on the shoulders of a Soviet-built ICBM. Or will it?

The Russian military, under-funded at the best of times, is having trouble paying its own people. According to the U.S. National Intelligence Counsel, Russian Strategic Rocket Forces are suffering from wage arrears, food shortages, and housing shortages. Put simply, the Russian military is having difficulty paying, housing, and even feeding the very people entrusted with safeguarding their strategic nuclear weapons.

In 1997, the 12th GUMO (Main Directorate of the Ministry of Defense) was forced to close a nuclear weapons storage site due to hunger strikes by its workers. In 1998, the families of Russian nuclear workers organized protests to recover back pay and benefits. The Russian media reports that the pay problems have been ironed out, and that most Russian military personnel are now paid regularly. But even on full pay, many members of the Russian military cannot afford to feed their families. Russian officers rarely receive more than $70.00 a month, and their enlisted personnel are paid considerably less than that.

Contrary to the reassurances of the Russian press, the problem hasn't gone away, and it doesn't stop at pay shortages. The U.S. intelligence community believes that weapons-grade plutonium, seized in Bulgaria in 1999, originated in Russia. Some time between 2001 and 2002, Chechen rebels stole radioactive materials from the Volgodonskaya nuclear power station near the Russian city of Rostov-on-Don. Control over the material at the site in question was so lax that the date of the theft can only be estimated to within about 12 months. This is not the plot of a bad science fiction movie; it's an ongoing state of affairs.

In 2000, sailors aboard a Russian submarine in Kamchatka stole nine radioactive catalyst tubes used for igniting the nuclear reactor. The tubes contained palladium, which is more valuable than gold. Not realizing that the stolen tubes were radioactive, the sailors hoped to sell them to a local scrap metal dealer. Following the incident, the Kamchatkan newspaper *Vesti* reported that the thieves had nearly caused a nuclear disaster when they attempted to lift the control rods out of the reactor. The *Vesti* article claimed that an accident was only averted because an unidentified Russian submarine engineer had the foresight to weld the handle of the control mechanism down, so that the thieves couldn't lift it.

Two senior Russian submarine officers were relieved of duty after the incident came to light, and two Russian admirals and ten other officers were penalized for negligence. The deputy head of the Russian North East Army Group's press center accused the media of exaggerating the danger.

The crime rate in the Russian military is skyrocketing, with theft, criminal assault, drug dealing, and illegal weapons trafficking as the most persistent problems. Desertions and suicides are both on the rise among the enlisted ranks. The problem, in other words, appears to be getting worse rather than better.

If the difficulties were confined to the conventional Russian military, I'd call it an internal problem. After all, the crime rate in the Russian Federation and the readiness of their military are their business, not ours. But the incidents mentioned above and many more like them make it clear that the integrity of the Russian nuclear forces is being affected. Men guard Russian nuclear stockpiles. And the mounting evidence tells us that those men are in serious trouble.

As a veteran of the Cold War, I feared the former strength of the Russian military. Now, in the wake of its virtual collapse, I'm beginning to fear its weakness even more. In other words, the danger of nuclear attack may not be as remote as we'd like to believe. Our margin of safety may be narrower than ever. To the eyes of this old Sailor, it appears to be eroding by the second.

How did we arrive at this precarious state of affairs? Is it possible to trace the chain of events that led us here?

If we hope to gain any true degree of insight, we must understand the weapons themselves. What are these engines of destruction that cast the shadows of annihilation over our very planet? Where did intercontinental ballistic missiles come from? How were they developed? And, perhaps more importantly, *why*?

Any study of ICBMs must begin with the history of rocketry. And that takes us back to ancient China.

CHAPTER 5

WHITE HOUSE
WASHINGTON, DC
MONDAY; 25 FEBRUARY
6:30 PM EST

At six foot four, President Francis '*Frank*' Chandler was taller than both of the Secret Service agents who escorted him through the double doors into the White House Situation Room. In truth, there probably wasn't much more than an inch of height difference between Frank and the shorter of the two agents. Both agents were large men in superb physical condition, but something about the president's long-boned frame and shambling walk made him seem larger than he really was.

The impression was further exaggerated by some indefinable element of presence. The agents looked sharp and professional in the conservative business suits that were the de facto uniform of the plainclothes branch of the Secret Service. Their suits were probably off the rack, with only the amount of alteration needed to make them fit properly. Frank's suit was a masterpiece of single needle tailoring in blue-gray Hunt & Winterbotham wool, and he still came off looking like a farm hand dressed in someone else's clothes. Even the legendary Georges de Paris, tailor for every American president since Lyndon Johnson, could not make Frank Chandler look at home in a necktie.

Back during Frank's now famous underdog bid for Governor of Iowa, Jenny had started calling it the *Jethro* factor. His wife had only used the term in private, but Frank's campaign manager had come unglued at the first mention of Jenny's secret joke.

The man had very nearly shouted into Jenny's face. "The *Beverly Hillbillies*? I'm trying to get the media to treat the son of a corn farmer like an honest-to-god political heavyweight, and you're coming out with the Beverly-*frickin'*-Hillbillies? If word of this gets around, it's going to make the front page of every newspaper in the state."

Jenny hadn't been the least bit intimidated by the man's outburst. "It's a joke," she'd said calmly. "Lighten up."

21

The campaign manager's nostrils had flared visibly. "I *know* it's a joke. And that's exactly what your husband's campaign is going to become when the media gets a hold of it." He'd crammed his hands into his pockets with a force approaching violence. "What are you going to say when some reporter shoves a microphone in your face and asks you why your private nickname for your husband is Jethro?"

Jenny had rewarded the campaign manager with a mischievous little smile. "When he played the role of Jethro Bodine, Max Baer Jr. was six feet-four inches of strapping young stud. And—from what I've heard—the man is hung like a plow horse. So I guess I'll tell the reporters that it's an utterly natural comparison to make."

She'd turned up the wattage on her wicked little smile. "Let's see them run *that* on the front page of the papers."

Frank nearly grinned at the memory. He knew perfectly well that Jenny would have made good on her threat if the Jethro question had ever come up at a press conference. She would have pointed her blue eyes directly into the camera lenses, and happily informed the assembled reporters and a few million television viewers that her husband was hung like a plow horse.

It wasn't true, of course. But after sixteen years of marriage and two children, Jenny still seemed to be under the happy delusion that it *was* true. Sometimes she still called him *Jethro* in private moments, unless she had a couple of vodka martinis in her, in which case she might substitute the words *plow horse*.

Frank covered his mouth and faked a cough to hide the dopey smile that threatened to seize control of his face. He used the half second of respite to compose himself. He wasn't twenty-five years old any more, or even forty-five. It was time to act his age and get his mind back on the job. It was time to be the President of the United States.

He covered the last few steps to his chair at the head of the long mahogany table, and turned to face the four members of his national security short staff. Per the dictates of protocol, everyone had come to their feet as their president had entered the room. He sat down, and motioned for the others to take their seats.

At the left side of the table sat White House Chief of Staff Veronica Doyle, and National Security Advisor Gregory Brenthoven. To the right sat the Chairman of the Joint Chiefs of Staff, Army General Horace Gilmore, and the newly-appointed Secretary of Homeland Security, Becka Solomon—brought in after a third heart attack had forced her predecessor to retire from public service.

Most of the chairs at the long table were vacant. The small gathering formed the core group of regular attendees of the President's Daily Security Brief: the so-called 'short' staff.

For a full-fledged meeting of the National Security Council, the vice president would have also been present, along with the secretaries of State, Defense, and Treasury. In that case, the Director of Central Intelligence would have probably conducted the briefing himself, in his role as statutory intelligence advisor to the NSC. But this was a routine daily briefing, and the point man was a solemn-faced young analyst from CIA's Directorate of Intelligence.

The president flipped open the blue-jacketed briefing folder and looked up at the analyst. The man was in his mid-twenties, probably not long out of college. Were they really getting younger? More than likely not, but it certainly *seemed* that way.

The analyst nodded, "Good evening, Mr. President." He pointed a small remote toward the oversized flat screen plasma television at the far end of the table. The screen flared to life, showing the Presidential Seal against a blue background. The analyst pressed a button and the famous emblem vanished, replaced by a passport-style photo of a stocky middle aged man with heavy Slavic cheekbones and graying whiskers.

The analyst nodded toward the screen. "At approximately three AM local time on Friday the twenty-second of February, this man—a Russian citizen named Oleg Yurievich Grigoriev—approached the front gate of the U.S. Embassy in the Republic of the Philippines and asked for asylum. The Marine guards called for the embassy's emergency medical team, because it was obvious that Grigoriev had been shot several times."

"That's not standard procedure, Mr. President," the national security advisor said. "Grigoriev is not a U.S. citizen or a member of the embassy staff. By the book, the guards should have contacted Manila emergency services and let the locals handle things. But the man was in shock, and losing blood fast. The guards figured he would bleed to death before the locals could get a medical team to the scene."

Veronica Doyle jotted a note on the cover page of her briefing folder. "We should give State a heads-up on this," she said. "We're going to take some heat from the government of the Philippines for not following diplomatic procedure. They may want you to make a formal apology, Mr. President."

"I don't mind taking a punch in the nose over this," The president said. "Human life outweighs political protocol. Period. End of sentence. If the Republic of the Philippines wants to make a ruckus over this, we'll turn it back on them. I'll do a press conference, and publicly ask President

Layumas if she thinks our embassy guards should stand around and watch gunshot victims bleed to death in order to satisfy the niceties of diplomatic procedure."

"I … uh … I don't think there's going to be a diplomatic issue, Mr. President," the analyst said. "I don't believe the locals even know that Mr. Grigoriev is in our custody. And the Operations Directorate doesn't think we should tell them, sir."

"Hold it," The president said. "This hasn't been reported to the Philippine locals?"

The analyst swallowed visibly. "Uh … no, Mr. President."

Becka Solomon, the Secretary of Homeland Security, closed her briefing folder with a thump. "Why the hell *not*?"

"I'd like to take a crack at that question," Brenthoven said. He pulled a small leather-bound notebook from the pocket of his jacket, flipped it open, and read for a few seconds. His eyes were still on the notebook when he resumed speaking. "The CIA has been interested in Mr. Grigoriev for several years, now. He was a soldier in the Red Army before the collapse of the Soviet Union, and a tank commander with the Soviet Iron Saber Brigade during the last eighteen months of the Soviet occupation of Afghanistan. His highest rank was *Stárshiy Serdzhánt*, or Senior Sergeant—roughly equivalent to Sergeant First Class in the U.S. Army. You'll find a short dossier on the man in your briefing packages."

Everyone except for the DI analyst and Brenthoven stopped to thumb through the blue folders on the table in front of them.

The national security advisor continued. "Mr. President, the CIA has fairly conclusive evidence that Grigoriev is a covert international operative."

Doyle's eyebrows narrowed. "You mean a spy?"

"More of a bag man," Brenthoven said. "A courier, who hand carries sensitive documents and information back and forth between his sponsor nation and foreign countries they want to communicate with."

"Isn't that kind of thing usually handled by diplomats?" the president asked. "Wasn't that the whole point of the 1961 Vienna Convention on Diplomatic Relations? Governments send sensitive documents by diplomatic courier, because it's illegal to detain a diplomatic pouch, or search its contents."

"You're quite correct, Mr. President," the analyst said. "But there are cases in which a particular government might not want even its diplomatic corps to know what it's up to. Circumstances that call for a higher-than-normal level of secrecy, or circumstances where a country's leaders want to maintain maximum deniability."

The secretary of homeland security looked at the analyst. "So that's this man's job? To bypass the Russian government's legitimate diplomatic channels of communication?"

The analyst nodded. "Yes, Madam Secretary. That's Langley's assessment. Except we don't think Grigoriev is working for the Russian government."

General Gilmore stared over the tops of his black-framed glasses at the analyst. "If it's not his own government, then who does our Russian friend work for?"

The general's voice was quiet and even-toned. Like his round pleasantly-featured face, his voice seemed out of place in a professional warrior. He looked and sounded more like a librarian than a fighting man. But, appearances aside, he was a combat Soldier, from his boot laces to his regulation Army hair cut. The rack of ribbons above the left pocket of his uniform jacket included the Bronze Star medal, with the affixed "V" insignia for valor under enemy fire.

The analyst shifted his gaze to the general. "The ... uh ... The Operations Directorate thinks that Mr. Grigoriev works for Sergiei Mikhailovich Zhukov, the governor of the Kamchatka kray, on the Kamchatka peninsula in southeastern Russia." The analyst paused for a second to let this strange pronouncement sink in. Then he continued. "Analysis of Grigoriev's travel and spending patterns over the past year suggests strongly that he has been acting as the go-between for confidential negotiations between Governor Zhukov and certain elements of the government and military of the People's Republic of China."

The last word caught the president's attention. "China? What does the Chinese government want with the governor of an obscure Russian province?"

"We don't know for certain," Brenthoven said. "We have very little hard evidence, but what we *do* have is frankly scaring the hell out of us, Mr. President."

The president nodded. "Alright, Greg. Enough pussyfooting around. You've set us up for the bad news. Now, go ahead and deliver the knockout punch."

Brenthoven closed his notebook and looked directly into the president's eyes. "Sir, due to the extent of his injuries, Mr. Grigoriev has only been conscious for short periods of time since he came into our custody. It may be several days before we can interview him properly. However, during his brief periods of lucidity, he's managed to let us know that he wants to negotiate a trade. He'll tell us what he knows in exchange for political asylum."

The president cocked an eyebrow. "If he crawled into our embassy with a bunch of bullet holes in him, there's a good chance that this man qualifies for asylum whether he knows anything useful or not. What do we think he can tell us?"

"We're not sure yet, sir," the analyst said. "But he's already revealed one piece of information that we didn't have before."

"And what would that be?" the general asked.

The analyst took a breath. "Most of the top positions in the government of Kamchatka are held by former officials of the Soviet communist regime. Sergiei Zhukov is no exception. In the eighties, he was a mid-level apparatchik in the communist party. That's pretty much common knowledge in the intelligence community. But we *didn't* know that Zhukov used to be senior security officer for KB-11."

Veronica Doyle frowned. "KB-11 ... Where do I know that from?"

"KB-11 was the old Soviet designation for Design Bureau Number 11," General Gilmore said quietly. "It was the main laboratory at a Soviet military research city called *Arzamas-16*. After the collapse of the USSR, the facility was renamed the *Russian Federal Nuclear Center*. Back in the bad old days, that's where the Cold War got started. Design Bureau Number 11 designed and assembled the nuclear weapons for the Soviet military arsenals. That's where the Russians first built the atomic bomb."

The president looked at the analyst. "You've followed up on this?"

The analyst nodded. "Yes, sir. We don't have much to go on yet, but the few pieces we know about all appear to confirm Grigoriev's story. The Ops Directorate has verified that Sergiei Zhukov *was* the senior security officer at Design Bureau Number 11."

"You still haven't told us how this all connects to China," The president said.

Brenthoven looked at the president. "Sir, Mr. Grigoriev claims to have been the middle man for a deal between Zhukov and the Chinese Politburo. Russian nuclear technology in exchange for some kind of Chinese military intervention."

Doyle brushed a speck of lint from the lapel of her gray silk business suit. "That doesn't make any sense," she said. "China already *has* the bomb. They don't *need* to get it from Russia, and certainly not from a Podunk province like Kamchatka."

"It's not that simple," the national security advisor said. "China *does* have the bomb. But not the kind of bomb they *want*. Their nuclear weapons are all single warhead configurations; each missile carries one nuclear warhead. But they've been trying since the eighties to develop *MIRV* technology, or *multiple independently-targeted reentry vehicles.*

One missile can carry multiple nuclear warheads, and strike several different targets at the same time. The People's Republic of China has poured a lot of time and money into MIRV research, but they haven't been able to make it work. Remember the big stink at the Los Alamos National Laboratory in the late nineties? One of our scientists was caught trying to pass nuclear secrets to China. *That's* what the Chinese were after. MIRVs."

General Gilmore smiled ruefully. "In the minds of a lot of the minor nuclear powers, MIRV technology has become the admission ticket to the grown up table. The United States has MIRVs. Russia, Great Britain, and France have them. But Israel doesn't. India, Pakistan, and North Korea don't. And neither does China."

"Okay, the Russians have this MIRV technology, and the Chinese want it," Doyle said. "Does it necessarily follow that the governor of Kamchatka can deliver it to them?"

"We don't know yet, ma'am," the analyst said. "But it's possible. He *did* work in close proximity to the technology at Arzamas-16. And he's got a fairly significant slice of the Russian Navy's nuclear arsenal right in his own back yard."

The analyst clicked his remote, and the photo of Oleg Grigoriev was replaced by a map of the Russian Federation. Near the right edge of the map, the Kamchatka peninsula dangled from the southeastern edge of Siberia. The shape of Kamchatka was vaguely like that of Florida, narrow at the northern edge where it connected to the mainland, bulging broadly in the middle, and then tapering to a dagger point at the southern end.

The analyst pressed another button and his remote became a laser pointer. He directed the beam toward the video screen. The red dot of the laser pointer flitted across the map of Kamchatka, and came to rest on a black dot labeled *Petropavlosk-Kamchatkskiy*.

"This is Petropavlosk, the capital city of Kamchatka." Another click of the remote brought up a pop-up window to the left of the Kamchatka peninsula. The new window contained a grainy black and white photo of a naval base. A trio of submarines were visible, each moored to a battered concrete pier. "Petropavlosk also happens to be the home port for the Russian Pacific Fleet's nuclear missile submarines. Based on the latest threat assessments, there are three Delta III class nuclear ballistic missile submarines based in Kamchatka. Each of the Delta III submarines carries sixteen Russian R-29R ballistic missiles, better known to NATO countries as the SS-N-18 Stingray. And each of these missiles is armed with three nuclear weapons, in a MIRV configuration. That works out to 48 nuclear warheads per submarine."

He paused for a second to let his words sink in; then he looked at the White House chief of staff. "To answer your question more clearly, ma'am, we think there's a very good chance that Sergiei Zhukov can deliver MIRV technology to China, if that is indeed his intention."

Veronica Doyle frowned. "Those submarines aren't under Zhukov's control, are they? I mean, the Russian military isn't going to hand command authority for strategic nuclear weapons over to a local politician, right?"

"No," said Brenthoven. "Ultimate control of those subs rests in Moscow, with the Russian Ministry of Defense. Local command authority flows through the senior naval officer in Petropavlosk, who takes his orders from Moscow. Provided the Russian command structure remains intact, Zhukov shouldn't be able to touch those submarines."

"Do we have any reason to expect a disruption of the Russian command structure?" the president asked.

Brenthoven rubbed his chin. "We don't have any specific intelligence about an external threat, Mr. President, if that's what you mean. But the Russian Navy is having a rough time right now. They're drastically under-funded. Their sailors are underpaid to begin with, sir. And it's not at all unusual for them to go months without being paid."

"This has been going on for a while, sir," General Gilmore said. "It's a problem in all branches of the Russian military, but it's especially bad in their Navy. The crime rate among their officers is spiraling out of control, and it's even worse among their enlisted sailors. Extortion, theft, robbery, you name it. Sailors are stealing parts and supplies from their own ships and submarines, and selling them to feed their families."

The president looked at his national security advisor. "So the deteriorating state of the Russian military could make it vulnerable to destabilization?"

Brenthoven nodded. "That's a possibility, sir."

"It's a very *real* possibility," General Gilmore said. "Not so much in places like Moscow, or Vladivostok. The Russians pour a lot more effort and resources into maintaining their military units stationed in high-visibility areas. But some of the obscure bases in Siberia, the Urals, and Kamchatka get little or nothing these days. When people get hungry enough, and desperate enough, the system starts to break down."

"This is the twenty-first century," said the White House chief of staff. "Russia may not be the great Soviet Empire any more, but it's still a major industrial nation. Conditions can't possibly be as bad as all that."

"Yes they can," the secretary of homeland security said quietly. "Look at how quickly and utterly our own infrastructures broke down when Hurricane Katrina wiped out New Orleans. Evacuation systems failed; communications failed; emergency relief efforts were overwhelmed; police officers deserted their posts. Hell, in some parishes, the police were looting and shooting right alongside the nut jobs and the criminals."

She shook her head. "We tell ourselves that we're beyond such things, but we're not. The fabric of civilization is much thinner and more fragile than we'd like to believe. And, if the system can break down in the most powerful and prosperous nation on the planet, it can certainly happen to the Russians."

The president stared at the video screen—the Russian nuclear missile submarines superimposed over the map of the Kamchatka peninsula. "Do we have any reason, beyond oblique hints by Mr. Grigoriev, to suspect a legitimate connection between China and the Governor of Kamchatka?"

"What little evidence we have is almost entirely circumstantial," the national security advisor said. "But the medical team at the embassy in Manila pulled a half-dozen 5.8mm military rounds out of Oleg Grigoriev. Ballistic analysis tells us that the bullets were fired from a short-barreled Type 95 assault rifle, the same configuration favored by the Special Operations Forces of the Chinese People's Liberation Army." Brenthoven closed his leather-bound notebook and tucked it into the pocket of his jacket. "That doesn't *prove* that the shooters were Chinese military, but it certainly seems to fit the scenario. If Grigoriev is telling the truth, it makes sense that the Chinese would try to shut him up."

The president scanned the faces of the people gathered around the table. "We're smelling a lot of smoke, but I don't see any fire. I'm not saying that it's not there, but I can't see it yet. If one of you can connect the dots on this Kamchatka-China thing, now is the time to speak up."

No one spoke.

"Okay," the president said. "Keep on this, Greg. Maybe it's nothing, but I'm not ready to make that call yet." He nodded to the analyst. "Let's move on. What's next?"

The analyst keyed his remote, and the pictures on the video screen were replaced by an image of a small submarine hanging from a launch and recovery crane on the fantail of a white-hulled oceanographic research ship. "Mr. President, this is the deepwater submersible *Nereus*..."

The president sighed. Submarines. *Why* did it always have to be submarines?

CHAPTER 6

USS TOWERS (DDG-103)
NORTHERN PACIFIC OCEAN (SOUTH OF THE ALEUTIAN ISLANDS)
TUESDAY; 26 FEBRUARY
0947 hours (9:47 AM)
TIME ZONE -10 'WHISKEY'

"How much oxygen have they got left?" The voice came from one of the half-dozen or so khaki-clad men and women milling around near the ship's boat deck. Ann Roark made a point of ignoring them as she worked through the list of pre-launch procedures to get *Mouse* ready to go into the water.

Some of the onlookers were probably chiefs and some of them were probably officers, but Ann couldn't tell the difference. It had been a man's voice, but beyond that, Ann didn't make any effort to figure out which of the Navy types had spoken. As far as she was concerned, they were all pretty much interchangeable.

The pattern was fairly set now; one of the uniforms would toss out some variation of that question every minute or so, always delivered in hushed tones, and always unanswered. "Do you think they've still got air?" "Are they alive?" "How did it happen?" "How bad is the damage?" "Why aren't they communicating?"

The Navy types weren't really talking to Ann. They probably weren't even talking to each other. The whispered questions seemed to be a kind of conversational defense mechanism. By recycling the same unanswerable queries, it was somehow possible to imagine that the crew of the *Nereus* was still alive. When the questions stopped, the mental images began to filter in: two men and one woman lying dead in the darkened confines of the tiny submarine.

Ann didn't indulge in the useless string of unanswerable questions. She had her own mindless litany: a statement, not a question. "This is not supposed to be a rescue," she said through her teeth. Her breath came out like smoke in the cold Alaskan air. "This is not supposed to be a rescue. This is not supposed to be a freaking rescue!" She had repeated those

31

words to herself at least fifty times, as though blind repetition could alter the situation.

She moved carefully as she worked. There was frost on the deck, and she didn't want to slip and fall on her ass in front of all these Navy yahoos. They'd laugh about *that* for forty years, wouldn't they?

Mouse hung from the heavy steel arm of the boat davit, swinging gently from the cable that was ordinarily used to raise and lower the ship's two Rigid-Hulled Inflatable Boats. The robot was bright yellow, disk-shaped, and about seven feet in diameter. A pair of large multi-jointed manipulator arms protruded from the leading edge of the disk, and three pump-jet propulsion pods were mounted to the trailing edge in a triangular formation. The forward end of the robot was arrayed with clusters of camera lenses, sonar transducers, and other sensors.

The curve of the machine's yellow carapace was stamped with the words NORTON DEEP WATER SYSTEMS, and the streamlined black 'N' of the Norton corporate logo. It was the company's mark of ownership, there for all the world to see. For all of Ann's personal sense of ownership, Mouse belonged to Norton, not to her.

She unscrewed a waterproof pressure cap from the ventral data port, and plugged a length of fiber-optic into the narrow connecting jack beneath. She plugged the other end of the cable into a hand-held test module about the size of a brick, and began to punch buttons and watch the results on the built-in digital display. The readouts were all in hexadecimal, but Mouse was Ann's baby. She knew every status code by heart.

Officially, the machine's name was *Multi-purpose Autonomous Underwater System Mark-I*. Usually, that was shortened to M-A-U-S, or *Mouse*. By classification, it was an Unmanned Underwater Vehicle, *not* a robot. The United States Navy didn't care for the word *robot*, with its science fiction movie connotations. Consequently, that word was never officially used, and even unofficial use of the *R-word* was discouraged. The machine was either referred to as *Mouse*, or by one of several more generic designations: the *unit*, the *package*, the *system*, the *equipment*, or even the *UUV*. Never the *robot*.

To Ann, the controversy over that one word was a perfect example of the warped logic at the heart of the military value system. Military types had no problem launching missiles at people they'd never even met, but they practically wet their pants if you called a piece of equipment by the wrong name.

Ann's coworker, Sheldon Miggs, attributed that particular fixation to *improved communications*. According to Sheldon, standardizing the names for equipment, tactics, and supplies went a long way toward making sure that someone didn't launch the wrong missile at the wrong time, shoot the wrong target, or pour the wrong kind of chemical extinguishing agent onto a raging fire. When Sheldon told it, the whole thing made a certain twisted degree of sense. Then again, Sheldon bought off on too much of that whole 'defense of freedom' shtick. To him, these military types represented something heroic. Ann saw them for what they really were—robots in starched uniforms, responding to programs written by greedy politicians and the military industrial complex.

And *that*, come to think of it, might explain why the Navy didn't care for the *R-word*. Maybe they didn't like the competition—one group of robots to another.

Screw the Navy. Not one of their acceptable terms came as close to describing Mouse's nature and abilities as the dreaded *R-word*. Mouse *was* a robot, and Ann was damned well going to *call* it a robot.

She sequenced through the test readouts one at a time, verifying that every one of Mouse's components was operating within design specifications. She paid particular attention to the error-checking routines for the robot's command code. She'd put in a brand new patch in the software last night, and she wasn't entirely sure that it was stable. But no errors were showing up this morning, so maybe she was worrying for nothing.

Just for good measure, she sequenced through every test readout again. Again, every test passed without error. The robot was purring like a kitten.

Ann disconnected the test cable and replaced the pressure cap on the data port. She was careful to check the o-ring seals, and to make sure that the threads of the cap were properly seated. Like all of the other external fixtures, the data ports were waterproof, and rated to withstand the pressure at the robot's maximum operating depth. She could have theoretically left the cap off entirely without affecting the robot's performance, but there was no point in taking unnecessary chances.

When she was satisfied that the port was properly covered, she checked the seals and alignments on every other external fitting. Finally, she looked up at the burly Navy man standing by the controls for the boat davit. She knew from earlier introductions that he was a second class petty officer, but she couldn't remember what it was about his uniform or rank insignia that was supposed to tell her that.

She had forgotten the man's real name, but she knew that the Navy types all called him *Boats*. Maybe that was because he was in charge of the boat deck. Ann didn't know, and she didn't particularly care. As long

as he handled her equipment with respect, the man could call himself the
Queen of Sheba.

Ann caught his eye and nodded. "Let's do this thing."

Boats gave her a thumbs-up, then he glanced around the boat deck and
spoke in a loud voice. "All hands stand clear of the boat davit while
conducting over-the-side operations."

The crowd of khaki onlookers was well clear of the work area, but they
all shuffled backwards a few steps anyway. Their murmuring trailed off as
the angled arm of the boat davit pivoted smoothly to the left, swinging
Mouse out over the lifelines, where the robot dangled twenty feet above
the wave tops.

Boats checked the alignment of the davit, made a minor adjustment,
and then punched the control for the winch motor. With a muted hydraulic
rumble, the winch began to reel out cable, and Mouse descended toward
the water.

This was what the looky-loos had come to see: the weird yellow
machine, embarking on the great rescue mission. What a bunch of
freaking idiots.

The davit operator was good. At the last second, he reduced the speed
of the winch, and Mouse settled into the water with barely a splash.

Boats caught Ann's eye, and waited for her signal.

Ann looked over the side of the ship. Mouse was trailing at the end of
the cable, his bright yellow hull about three-quarters submerged in the cold
slate-gray waves.

This was always the scary part. As long as Mouse was hooked to the
cable, they couldn't lose him. But the second they let him off the leash,
the robot would be on his own—beyond human control.

In some places, the Aleutian trench went down more than 25,000 feet.
If something went wrong in water this deep, Mouse could be lost forever.

But they couldn't keep the robot on the leash. He couldn't do his job
with the cable attached, and even if he could, that went against the entire
purpose of an autonomous machine. Ann had devoted years of hard work
to making sure that Mouse could operate safely without human
intervention. Why was it always so difficult to turn him loose?

She took in a deep lungful of the startlingly cold Alaskan air, and
exhaled, her breath coming out as a cloud of vapor. She gave Boats a nod.
"Let him go."

The Sailor manipulated the davit controls, and the clamp at the end of
the cable disengaged itself with a metallic thump. Hydraulics moaned
again, and the winch began reeling in the cable.

Free of his tether, Mouse floated just below the waves for a couple of seconds, bobbing gently with the swells, as though gathering his wits or getting his bearings. And then the robot's propulsion pods came to life, driving the machine forward, and down.

For a second or so, Ann could see the robot's yellow form through the water, and then it disappeared into the depths. For better or for worse, Mouse was on his own.

⚓ ⚓ ⚓

Twenty minutes later, Ann sat in the ship's Combat Information Center, and stared at the screen of the ruggedized laptop computer that served as the display and control interface for Mouse. Somewhere out there, across two miles of ocean and three thousand feet under water, Mouse was approaching the downed mini-sub. The robot was due to transmit a final updated position report before beginning its survey of the accident site.

The khaki-brigade had followed her inside. They were lingering around CIC, keeping mostly out of Ann's way, but sticking close enough to see the action—if there was any.

Jesus. Didn't these people have jobs?

A flashing status indicator on the laptop screen grabbed Ann's attention. Personal feelings aside, she had a job to do. Part of that job meant swallowing her distaste for these military yahoos, and simulating a degree of courtesy that she didn't really feel. But the other part of her job—the *important* part—was making sure the robot did what it was supposed to do. That part Ann was very good at.

Her eyes stayed fixed on the screen. If something was going to go wrong, *this* was when it would probably happen.

Mouse's onboard computer sometimes failed to transition properly from *directed transit mode* to *autonomous mission mode*. The robot had no problem following programmed navigational waypoints from one set of geographic coordinates to the next. It also operated pretty reliably under full autonomy, using the situational-response algorithms built into its core programming to make decisions, and its maneuvering motors, sensors, and manipulator arms to take whatever actions were dictated by the results of those decisions. It even made good decisions, the majority of the time. *That* was supposed to be the tricky part: getting a self-directed machine to assess complicated problems without human intervention, and then plan and carry out appropriate corrective actions.

Mouse could *do* all that. But sometimes the damned thing went crazy during the transition from one mode to the other. During two out of the last five test runs, the robot had completed transit mode without a hitch, and then promptly abandoned its mission and returned to its launch point, where it had driven itself to the surface and steered in circles until it was captured and shut down.

In Ann's technical log, the unplanned excursions were written up as Unpredicted Vehicle Behavior. That was geek-speak for '*the robot did something freaky and I don't know why.*'

Ann had been up most of the night, working on a software fix to patch the mode transition problem. She'd located a bug in the command code, but she had no idea if correcting it would fix the problem. The patch looked pretty good on paper, but she needed a week or so of testing to be sure. Not that there'd been any time for tests. Mouse had gone back into the water just minutes after she'd uploaded the new code—orders of the ship's commanding officer—Captain *Bogie*, or whatever his name was.

It wasn't fair, damn it! This was just supposed to be an Advanced Technology Demonstration. They were here to put the Mouse prototype through its paces, find out what worked and what didn't, in an actual shipboard environment. What the hell was the Navy thinking, trying to turn it into a rescue? For that matter, why were those idiots at corporate going along with it? Until the Navy signed off on the final contracts, Mouse was still the property of Norton. The company could have said, 'no.' They *should* have said, 'no.' Why hadn't they?

Ann knew the answer to that question. She just didn't like it. The International Submarine Escape and Rescue Liaison Office was rushing people and equipment to the scene as quickly as possible, but the nearest submarine rescue equipment was still at least eight hours away. Unfortunately, the men and women aboard the *Nereus* might not *have* eight hours. For all anyone knew, they might not even have eight minutes.

Finding the submersible wasn't an issue. Like most manned underwater vessels, the *Nereus* was equipped with an emergency transponder. The little black box was working just fine. It had been transmitting an emergency locator beacon every six minutes since the accident had occurred.

The real problem was depth. The *Nereus* was nearly three thousand feet down. Much too deep for divers. Even the advanced hardsuit dive rigs couldn't withstand the water pressure that far down. At this particular moment in time, one Navy destroyer and one crazy-assed underwater robot were the only hope of rescue.

That was so wrong that it was nearly perverse. The lives of human beings should not be allowed to hang by so thin a thread.

The software wasn't ready. The hardware wasn't ready. And Ann sure as *hell* wasn't ready.

This whole situation had disaster written all over it. The people on that submarine were going to die, and Ann and Sheldon were going to get the blame.

Where *was* Sheldon, anyway? Ann risked a quick look over her shoulder. No sign of Sheldon. Nobody back there but the gaggle of Navy officers and chiefs, watching over her shoulder. Waiting for Ann to either pull a miracle out of her ass, or make a mistake that would kill the people on that submarine.

She swallowed, took a deep breath, and tried to will her body to relax. *Forget about the Navy boneheads. They don't matter. Watch the screen. Do the job. Pretend they're not even here.*

The cool semi-darkness of CIC made it a little easier to ignore the unwanted onlookers. As long as they remained relatively quiet, she could mostly tune them out.

Someone tapped Ann on the left shoulder. She flinched at the unexpected contact, and whipped her head around see the newcomer. It was that captain guy, Brodie, or whatever.

The man held out a ceramic mug and smiled. "Coffee?"

Ann took the offered cup. "Thanks." She turned back to the screen. Still no sign of Mouse's updated position report. Had the robot stopped communicating altogether? Could her program patch have caused some unexpected side-effect that made the mode transition problem worse rather than better?

"I'm Captain Bowie," the man said, apparently oblivious to the fact that Ann was attempting to ignore him. "We met briefly when you came on board, but I haven't really gotten around to chatting with you yet. It's Ms. Roark, right?"

Ann nodded. "Just Ann, sir."

She kept her voice carefully polite. It was a simple matter of self preservation. There were not exactly an infinite number of job opportunities in the robotics industry, and fewer still in Ann's area of specialty: *underwater* robotics. If she wanted to keep paying the rent, she had to be civil to the uniforms.

Anything beyond courtesy was Sheldon's responsibility. Sheldon was the talker. It was his job to shake hands, answer stupid questions, and generally keep people too busy to bother Ann. A job at which he was failing miserably at the moment.

The captain stepped closer and leaned over to look at the screen. "How are things looking?"

Ann suppressed a sigh. This guy wanted to make small talk.

"I'm waiting for an updated position report," she said. "Mouse is coming up on his last navigational waypoint. We should be getting a fix on his position any time now." She paused for a second, and decided to be honest. "He's actually a little bit overdue. I expected to hear from him almost a minute ago."

"Is there a problem?"

Of course not, Ann thought. *Everything is just fine. I've got three lives depending on an untested code patch that I wrote at three in the morning, when I was practically cross-eyed from sleep depravation. But everything is peachy here, Mr. Captain, Sir. Just freaking peachy.*

She glanced up at Captain What's-his-name, and wondered for a second if she had said some of that last bit out loud. More than likely not, because he didn't seem to be ramping up to indignation. His brown eyes looked tired, but not angry.

Ann returned his stare with one of her own. From a strictly physical perspective, she liked what she saw. He was in his late thirties or early forties, about six feet tall, and almost good looking in a nerdy clean-cut sort of way. His black hair was too short to have any real character to it, and his narrow face seemed slightly out of proportion to his neck and body. Still, the overall package wasn't bad, if you were into overgrown Eagle Scouts.

Looking beyond the physical was another matter. Whatever points he picked up in the looks category were far outweighed by his non-physical deficits. The man obviously bought into that whole bullshit warrior-Zen thing. Ann could see it in everything about him, from his body language to the starched creases in his uniform. He was a card carrying member of the 'Defenders of Freedom Club,' just like Ann's father had been.

She caught herself and mentally shifted gears before she could say anything stupid. This was not the time for a drive down that particular stretch of Memory Lane. "Where's Sheldon?" she asked.

The captain shifted his gaze to the laptop screen. "I believe he's up in the wardroom, talking to your company on the satellite phone. COMPACFLEET is busy signing promissory waivers, to make sure that you guys get paid in case we break your Mouse prototype, or lose it somehow in the rescue attempt."

Ann nodded and turned back to the laptop.

"You didn't sign on for any of this," the captain said. "We understand that. You come out here to run some tests, and the Navy shoves a rescue mission in your face. We know you're not ready, and we know that your equipment isn't ready either." He took a deep breath and let it out. "But, right now, your Mouse Mark-I is the only game in town."

Ann nodded absently. "I understand, Captain."

"I'm sure you do," said the captain. "But I'd like to hit one more quick point before you get too far into this."

Ann looked up and found that he was staring at her again.

"I know you'll do your best," he said. "But there are a lot of ways that this operation could go sour. There hadn't been any communication with the *Nereus* for hours. The guys on that submarine might already be dead."

Ann nodded slowly. This was not quite turning into the Go-Navy pep talk she'd been expecting.

"We don't know what kind of damage that submersible has taken," the captain said. "They could be flooding, or running out of breathable air. If their electrical system has failed, they could die from hypothermia. The ocean temperature at three thousand feet is just a hair above freezing. Twenty four hours is a long time to go without heat, especially when your only clothes are light duty coveralls."

He looked back to the laptop screen. "If they had an electrical fire, they might even have burned to death, or died from smoke inhalation."

Ann rubbed her eyes and blinked several times. "Are you trying to cheer me up, Captain?"

The corners of his mouth turned up—the ghost of a rueful smile. "No. I'm just telling you that the odds of success are not in our favor. Everyone in the chain of command knows that. The Navy will take the heat if things don't work out. You're not going to be left holding the bag."

Ann nodded. "Thank you, Captain. I appreciate that."

She turned back to the laptop. Yeah, right. For all of his noble words, Captain Eagle Scout would throw Ann and Sheldon to the wolves about two milliseconds after the shit hit the fan. That was the way these guys worked. When something went wrong, they went hunting for a scapegoat.

She scanned the screen. Mouse still hadn't reported in. She'd give it another minute or so, just to be sure. But she was grasping at straws. This rescue, if you could even call it that, was over.

CHAPTER 7

The flashlight shook in Charlie Sweigart's hand, the dull circle of yellowish light bobbing and jittering spasmodically as another uncontrollable wave of shivers wracked his body. He tried to thumb the *off* switch, to conserve the little remaining battery power until the worst of the spasms had passed. But his hands were too numb from the cold to properly obey his commands.

The batteries rattled inside the body of the flashlight. The light grew marginally brighter for a few seconds, and then dimmed again. The glow seemed pitifully small and weak in the tomblike blackness of the submersible. The *Nereus* carried three emergency flashlights, and this was the last of them. Charlie had already worn out the batteries in the other two, fruitlessly searching for the electrical fault that had robbed the submersible of power.

The submersible lay on its starboard side, heeled over about thirty degrees, its bow slightly elevated by the rising slope of the Aleutian trench. The odd tilt put the chairs at the wrong angle for sitting. The only stable position was sort of a leaning crouch, with feet braced against the deck for support.

The angle of the deck wasn't just a matter of discomfort. The fifteen hundred pound lead ballast plate built into the bottom of the submersible was designed to drop vertically from a form-fitted recess in the keel. But the canted deck pushed the weight of the ballast plate to one side, putting some massive amount of lateral torque on the emergency release mechanism.

Charlie had fought with the release handle until his hands were raw. The latches were too far out of alignment. The release mechanism was

40

hopelessly jammed, and—along with it—their chances of getting the *Nereus* back to the surface.

The shakes running through Charlie's body were nearly convulsive now. His teeth were chattering so hard that he thought they might shatter. He clamped his jaw shut and forced himself to override the tremors in his muscles.

When he had regained a measure of control, he pointed the dwindling beam of the flashlight toward the open faceplate of the secondary electrical bus. Like every other surface in the cockpit of the little submarine, the open doors of the access panel were beaded with moisture—water vapor from their breaths, condensed out of the air by the cold.

That was how they were going to die. Charlie knew that now. The cold. Of all the ways they could die down here … drowning … asphyxiation … implosion … they were going to freeze to death. He would never have predicted that.

At the current rate of consumption, the emergency air flasks would probably last another two days. The hull was holding pressure. There were no leaks, and no escaping air. But the heaters had died along with the electrical system. Without the heaters, the cold water surrounding the *Nereus* had gradually leached away all the warmth in the submersible. The temperature of the air in the cockpit had reached equilibrium with the temperature of the water outside the hull: just a couple of degrees above freezing.

There was irony in that too. The cold was going to kill them, but they weren't technically going to freeze to death. The core temperatures of their bodies were well down into the range of hypothermia now, more than cold enough to kill them. But they wouldn't quite freeze. When the cold had sucked the last of the life from their bodies, they would hover in a lethally refrigerated state just a few degrees warmer than the temperature of ice. Not quite popsicles. More like …

Charlie shook his head, sending throbs of pain through his bruised cheek and battered forehead—both still tender from their collision with one of the instrument clusters during the accident. He was losing focus again, his mind wandering down blind alleys; another symptom of hypothermia.

He forced his eyes to focus on the relay panel below the electrical bus, trying to locate the bundle of wires that he'd just been tracing with his eyes.

"Turn off the light." It was Steve's voice, floating out of the darkness somewhere behind Charlie.

"I can … fix this," Charlie said. His speech felt halting and strange. "Just give me … another few … minutes. I can find … the problem."

"Turn off the damned light," Steve said again. "And get that stupid dog out of here."

Charlie didn't turn off the flashlight. He could feel another round of tremors coming on. "Dog? What … dog?"

"The one in your pocket," Steve said. "And don't think I can't hear you. I've got your ass set for speed-dial."

Charlie's eyes lost focus on the wires. He blinked several times and tried to will them to work properly. "What … What in the hell … are you … talking about?"

"He's hallucinating," Gabriella said. It was the first time she had spoken in over an hour. She was shivering so violently that it was difficult to understand her words. Charlie could hear her teeth chattering.

"Late… stage… hypothermia," she said. "His… brain is starting to… shut down."

"I better not catch that dog using my phone again," Steve said. "I'll kill him. Him and his damned motorcycle."

Steve's voice was muffled and strange, but it didn't have the stuttering hitch that was present in Charlie and Gabriella's speech. Steve wasn't shivering any more. That meant something, but Charlie couldn't remember what. When a cold victim stopped shivering, something bad was happening. Was Steve already dying?

The flashlight gave one final flicker and died. Damn it! He'd let his attention wander again, and now the last flashlight was dead.

No more light. No more heat, and no more light. Just darkness. And cold.

"I should have done an emergency abort," he said. "This is my fault."

Listening to his own words, Charlie realized that the hitch in his voice was gone. He wasn't shivering anymore. He wasn't even all that cold. His feet were beginning to feel warm. So were his hands.

This wasn't a good sign either. He was aware of that in a detached sort of way. "I should have dropped the ballast the second I knew we had a problem." He was talking to himself now. "This is my fault. This is all my fault."

The cold was receding now. He knew that the growing warmth in his body was an illusion, maybe a sign that he was sliding into some deeper and more languorous stage of existence. He didn't care. The cold wasn't as painful down here. In fact, it was kind of pleasant.

He closed his eyes, not that it mattered much in the pitch darkness that had taken command of the submarine. He could sleep now. Just for a few minutes. And, while he was sleeping, he could trace the wiring harnesses in his mind. When he woke up, he would fix the broken whatever it was, and they would get back to the ship in time for lunch.

Everything was going to be fine now. Charlie knew that. Everything was going to be just fine.

"You never asked me out."

The words caught him as he was dozing off. "What?"

"You never asked me out," Gabriella said again. "I kept waiting for you to ask me out, but you never did."

Charlie smiled languidly. "Now *I'm* hallucinating."

Gabriella's French-Canadian accent was like birdsong in his ears. She wasn't shivering any more either.

"No you're not," she said. "You may be dying, but you are not hallucinating."

"This is my fault," Charlie said softly.

"Yes" Gabriella said. "It *is* your fault. You've had plenty of chances, but you've never asked me out."

"That's not what I meant," Charlie said. "We're going to die here. We're *already* dying. And it's my fault." He was getting sleepy now.

Gabriella sighed, the sound echoing off of unseen surfaces in the darkness. "If you don't ask me out, I'm going to kill you before the cold does."

"And that damned dog," Steve said feebly.

"Right," Gabriella said. Her voice was getting sleepy too. "You *and* that damned dog."

Charlie nodded, although no one could see him. This was all part of the hallucination; that much he knew. But what better time to do the impossible? The unthinkable …

"Would you like to go out to dinner with me?" He winced at the sound of his words. Even in this dying world of frozen dreams, he was terrified of what Gabriella might say.

"That's the best you can do?" she asked. "You're in your dying moments, and possibly hallucinating, and you ask me out to *dinner?*" She snorted. "If this was *my* hallucination, I'd go straight to the sex."

Charlie felt himself grin. "Can we go straight to the sex?"

"Of course not," Gabriella said. "You have to buy me dinner first."

And with those words, Charlie suddenly knew that it was okay to die. He opened his eyes and stared into the darkness, still smiling. He could feel sleep tugging at him. But he wanted to be awake for another minute or two, to savor the amazing idea that Gabriella actually wanted to go out with him, even if it was only the delusion of a dying brain.

It took him a few seconds to notice the light. It started small, a tiny glowing pinprick moving through the curtain of black water outside the view port. He watched it idly as it grew, moving closer in a series of looping zigzags that reminded him vaguely of a bloodhound sniffing out a trail. Still it moved closer, the light growing to the size of a golf ball, and then a basketball.

Charlie lifted his head to get a better look at it. The thing, whatever it was, came to a stop about ten feet from the nose of the *Nereus*, and hovered there. Charlie raised a cold-numbed hand to shield his eyes against the light. He squinted into the hallucinatory brightness.

He could see something behind the light now: some sort of bizarre machine, perhaps a quarter the size of the *Nereus*. It was vaguely disk-shaped, with a pair of heavy-looking mechanical arms, flanked by clusters of lenses. To Charlie's foggy brain, it looked like a crab riding a Frisbee.

The strange machine turned to the side, revealing a yellow-painted stretch of hull marked with large black lettering. Charlie struggled to force his blurry eyes to focus on the words. 'Something-or-other DEEP WATER SYSTEMS.'

Then, the machine moved again, curving to the left until it had disappeared from the viewport's line of sight.

Charlie's eyes remained locked on the place where the machine had been. Could he have imagined it? He was still trying to figure that out, when the water outside the viewport lit up with an eerie blue-green light. For about a second, the light seemed to strobe and pulse rapidly. Then it was gone, leaving behind only the blackness of the ocean bottom.

"I think I'm having another hallucination," Charlie said.

Gabriella was almost asleep now. "I already told you," she muttered. "Dinner first."

CHAPTER 8

ICBM: A COLD WAR SAILOR'S MUSINGS ON THE ULTIMATE WEAPONS OF MASS DESTRUCTION

(Reprinted by permission of the author, Retired Master Chief Sonar Technician David M. Hardy, USN)

In tracing the roots of modern rocketry, some historians prefer to begin with the ancient Greeks. According to the writings of Roman author and grammarian Aulus Gellius, a Greek philosopher named Archytas built a steam-powered rocket device in approximately 400 B.C. Cast from clay and shaped like a pigeon, this device reportedly flew about 200 yards. The pigeon was attached to a guide wire during its flight, which may have supported the device's weight, so there is some dispute as to whether or not it was powerful enough to fly without external assistance. Very few details of the flight are known, so it's difficult to gauge the significance of the Archytas pigeon, beyond the basic fact of its existence.

About three centuries later, a Greek mathematician and engineer named Hero (or *Heron*) of Alexandria invented another steam-propelled device with rocket-like characteristics. Known as an *aeolipile*, Hero's invention consisted of a rotating sphere, driven by steam from a heated kettle of water.

History generally remembers Hero's aeolipile as the first operational steam engine, but it can (arguably) be classified as a rocket-type reaction engine.

Like the work of Archytas, the direct impact of Hero's invention on the history of rocketry is difficult to assess. It's therefore understandable that many historians have opted to discount the earliest attempts of the Greeks, and begin the timeline of rocketry with the Chinese.

Some time prior to the 10th century A.D., alchemists in China stumbled across the formula for gunpowder, possibly while attempting to create the legendary elixir of immortality. Although the combination of sulfur, saltpeter, and charcoal dust did not have mystical life-extending properties, the unknown alchemists quickly discovered that their new compound would flare and burn vigorously when exposed to flame.

The timing of this momentous discovery is a matter of contention, with some historians fixing the date as early as the 1st century, and others arguing that it may have occurred as recently as the 9th century. Regardless of the precise date, there is no doubt that the invention of gunpowder transformed the nature of warfare, and ultimately altered the path of human history.

The first people to utilize the mysterious new compound may have been religious Mandarins, who filled bamboo tubes with the volatile mixture, and threw them into fires to frighten away demons during religious festivals. The results were predictably loud and impressive, and it was probably only a matter of time until one of the bamboo tubes failed to explode, and shot out of the fire on a trail of burning gas.

These crude bamboo rockets were almost certainly the product of accident rather than design, but it was an accident that many Chinese experimenters were eager to repeat. Some resourceful soldier, whose name has been lost to history, began attaching bamboo rockets to arrows. When lit and fired from a bow, these *fire arrows* streaked through the air, to drop like flaming meteors on the armies of China's enemies.

Eventually, as Chinese rockets became more powerful and more reliable, the arrows became an unnecessary component. The rockets became viable weapons without arrows attached. By the mid 11th century, gunpowder rockets were one of the deadliest weapons in China's military arsenal.

In 1232 A.D., the armies of the Sung Dynasty used rockets to repel Mongol invaders at the battle of Kai-Keng. The Mongol hoards, which were legendary for their ferocity in battle, broke and ran before this devilish device that rained fire and death from the sky.

Historical accounts of the period indicate that the Chinese rockets were large in scale, and there is evidence that the military engineers of the Sung Dynasty developed new ways to magnify the lethality of their weapons. Where previous generations of rockets had relied on unaugmented gunpowder explosives, these new rockets were armed with iron shrapnel and incendiary materials, in what may have been the first application of advanced warhead technology.

During the same period, the Chinese military made similar advancements in rocket propulsion techniques. Simple cylindrical exhaust tubes gave way to 'iron pot' combustion chambers, that shaped and directed the thrust of the rocket exhaust.

The cumulative effect of these advances was dramatic. Thirteenth century documents reported a Chinese rocket so massive that the sound of its launch was heard fifteen miles away. Everything within a half-mile of the weapon's point of impact was flattened or destroyed.

The destructive potential of the Chinese rockets was not lost on the Mongols. Following the battle of Kai-Keng, the Mongols began producing their own rocket weapons. It's not clear if the early Mongol rockets were the product of independent development, reverse engineering, or espionage.

Regardless of the source of their knowledge, the Mongols introduced rocket warfare to the battlefields of Europe and the Middle East, where they blasted the unsuspecting armies of their enemies without warning, and without mercy. The famously ruthless Mongol leader Genghis Khan, and his third son, Ögedei Khan, used rockets with devastating effect when they conquered parts of Russia, Eastern Europe, and Central Europe. Descriptions of rocket attacks also appear in literature detailing the Mongol siege of Baghdad in 1258.

The enemies of the Mongol hordes were at first stunned by the unexpected appearance of this frightening weapon. But like the Mongols themselves, the armies of these other nations were quick to copy this new form of warfare.   The proliferation of rocket technology began to accelerate rapidly.

There is evidence that Arabian warriors used rockets in 1268, to attack the French armies of Louis IX during the 7th Crusade. The writings of Syrian military historian Al-Hasan al-Rammah suggest that the Arabs were routinely using combat rockets to attack their enemies by the year 1285.

It didn't stop there. At the close of the 13th century, Japan, Korea, India, and Java had all begun to integrate rockets into their military strategies. Rocket warfare was quickly spreading through Asia and Eastern Europe.

This strange and lethal weapon was no longer confined to the borders of China. It had been unleashed upon the nations of the earth.

The ancient Chinese alchemists had begun with the search for eternal life. Instead, they had given birth to a massively-lethal engine of war, and perhaps even planted the seeds of the destruction of mankind. But the rocket's legacy of devastation was just beginning. The true and terrible power of China's creation had yet to be felt. The world had seen barely a hint of the carnage that was yet to come.

CHAPTER 9

KAMCHATKA KRAY ADMINISTRATION BUILDING
#1 PLOSHAD LENINA (LENIN SQUARE)
PETROPAVLOVSK-KAMCHATSKI, RUSSIA
WEDNESDAY; 27 FEBRUARY
0817 hours (8:17 AM)
TIME ZONE +12 'MIKE'

The edges of the windows were frosted with ice crystals, but the center of each pane was clear enough to see through. Sergiei Mikhailovich Zhukov, Governor of the Kamchatka kray, stared through one of these ovals of transparency at the park across the street. It was snowing again, but Zhukov's eyes looked past the falling flakes to the statue of Lenin.

Nearly ten meters tall, the enormous bronze statue stood atop a red marble obelisk of nearly equal height. It was a majestic thing, the father of the modern communist ideal towering like a god above the heads of ordinary men.

But the statue was an anachronism. Lenin's magnificent dream of a world ruled and managed by common workers had crumbled along with the Warsaw Pact. His teachings had been abandoned and then reviled by his own people. The workers complained that their god had failed them, or worse yet, that Vladimir Ilyich Lenin had been a false god all along.

Zhukov's jaw muscles tightened. The god had not failed his people. Instead, the people had failed their god.

A door opened behind him, but his eyes never left the statue.

"Governor Zhukov?" It was the voice of his chief assistant, Maxim Ivanovitch Ustanov. "The latest satellite imagery is in, and we have updated position reports on the Chinese ships. Both ships are moving exactly according to the schedule. In a little less than an hour, they will turn north out of the shipping lanes and divert toward Petropavlovsk."

Zhukov nodded. "Thank you, Maxim Ivanovitch."

Ustanov paused for a few seconds before speaking again. "We're approaching the point of no return, sir. When those Chinese ships tie up at our piers, there will be no turning back."

Zhukov smiled slightly without looking up. "Are you getting cold feet, my old friend?"

Ustanov coughed. "Not at all, sir. I ... ah ... I just wanted to keep you advised of the status of the plan."

Zhukov nodded again. "We were masters of the world," he said softly. "We were the great Soviet Empire: the Russian bear who crushed everything in its path. When we roared, the earth trembled."

He sighed. "*Now* look at us. Look at what we have become, what we have been reduced to. We are a toothless old dog. We cower in the corner and hope that no one throws a boot at us."

Zhukov looked up for the first time, making eye contact with his assistant. "No, my old friend, we cannot stop. We must do this thing. We owe it to Mother Russia. We owe it to the future."

Ustanov made an uncertain face. "But the risk ..."

"It is worth the risk," Zhukov said. "It is better to seek greatness and fail, than to strive for mediocrity and succeed."

He checked his watch. "Wait another hour, then have the militia begin rounding up the tourists and the foreign business executives. All personal electronics must be confiscated, including wristwatches, calculators, cameras, and music players. This new technology is too difficult to keep track of. Nearly anything might be used to send an email message or make a phone call."

He shifted his eyes back to the park. The snow was falling faster now, nearly obscuring his vision of Lenin's statue. In another day, maybe less, the secret would be out. All eyes would turn to this obscure little smudge on the face of the globe, and the world would rediscover the true power of Russia. But the secret must keep for a few more hours.

The world had taught itself to fear little men, with little bombs, and the insignificant dreams of insects. This they had labeled *terror*. The very word brought a mirthless smile to Sergiei Zhukov's lips. The world had forgotten what terror really was. But it was about to remember.

CHAPTER 10

MOUSE (MULTI-PURPOSE AUTONOMOUS UNDERWATER SYSTEM)
NORTHERN PACIFIC OCEAN (SOUTH OF THE ALEUTIAN ISLANDS)
TUESDAY; 26 FEBRUARY
1021 hours (10:21 AM)
TIME ZONE -10 'WHISKEY'

In technical terms, Mouse was experiencing a *third-order heuristic non-parity as a function of suboptimal iterative taxonomic indexing.* In plain English, the robot was confused. It had reached the designated navigational coordinates, performed a detailed sensor survey of the area as specified by its current mission program, and located an object that closely matched the identification criteria for its target.

The object under examination was approximately the correct shape (nominally ellipsoid with dorsal and ventral protrusions), approximately the correct size (7.924 meters in the major axis, and 2.438 meters in the minor axis), and closely located to the center of the designated search grid (31.626 meters from grid reference zero). Based upon these factors, and the lack of any other remotely qualifying objects within the perimeter of the search grid, Mouse's onboard computer had labeled the object as *"Presumptive Target #1,"* and assigned a confidence factor of 98.2%. Mouse was 98.2% certain that Presumptive Target #1 was the object that it had been sent to locate.

None of this had been difficult for Mouse. These were exactly the sorts of evaluations and decisions that the robot made best. The problem was *mud.* Mouse didn't know anything about mud, and that lack of knowledge was interfering with the robot's ability to make a critical decision.

The next phase of the mission required Mouse to identify a loop-shaped fixture on the upper surface of Presumptive Target #1. Mouse had located a fixture near the designated area of the object. Using physical location as a primary criterion, the fixture was a high-confidence match, after correcting for variations in spatial orientation. Presumptive Target #1 had approximately 12.5 degrees of y-axis rotation and 30.0 degrees of z-axis rotation, but—corrected for that—the candidate fixture had a location confidence factor of 99.8%.

The problem lay in the *shape* of the fixture. Mouse's mission program queue contained a detailed digital model of the fixture the robot was programmed to identify. And the fixture at the specified location was not a good match for the model, only 41.2%. It was in the correct place and was roughly the correct size, but it was not the correct shape.

The fixture had a name. It was a lifting shackle. And, as Mouse had been advised, it was loop-shaped. Unfortunately, the lifting shackle was packed with mud, compliments of its encounter with the sticky sediments of the Aleutian Island slope during the accident that had put the submersible *Nereus* on the bottom of the ocean.

Had Mouse known about the mud, the robot could have completed its identification of the lifting shackle, and moved on to the next phase of its mission: locating the lifting cable that the Research Vessel *Otis Barton* had lowered into the ocean. The phase after that, connecting the *Otis Barton's* cable to the *Nereus's* lifting shackle, would not be difficult at all. But to get there, Mouse had to correctly identify the lifting shackle, hiding under several layers of Aleutian Island mud.

Mouse wasn't aware of any of these things. It had not been told that the fixture had a name. It didn't know that Presumptive Target #1 was the deep water submersible *Nereus*, or that the three human beings inside the submersible were either dead or dying. Mouse didn't even know what a deep water submersible *was*. The robot only knew that it was at the correct geographic coordinates, hovering five meters away from an object that closely matched its search criteria, evaluating a candidate fixture that was not the correct physical shape.

The situational-response algorithms built into Mouse's core programming decided to examine the puzzling fixture from another position. With measured surges from its maneuvering thrusters, the robot moved ten meters to the East, and swung its nose a corresponding amount to the left, so that it faced the object from a different angle.

When the maneuver was complete, the candidate fixture was once again centered in the cone of light cast by Mouse's sealed Halogen lamps. Satisfied with its new position, the robot studied the illuminated fixture through a pair of high-resolution video cameras. The results were no more satisfactory. The fixture was still the wrong shape.

Once again, the situational-response algorithms did their work. The computer shut off the robot's Halogen lamps to minimize optical interference, and triggered its *LIDAR* scanner for a more detailed look at the improperly-shaped object. Short for *Light Imaging Detection And*

Ranging, LIDAR was similar to radar, except that it transmitted and received low-intensity laser light instead of microwaves. The LIDAR scanner mounted on the upper leading edge of the robot's hull directed a burst of laser light toward the presumptive target. In the space of one second, the scanner emitted 400 pulses of high-frequency laser light in a clockwise reticulated-rosette scanning pattern, and recorded and evaluated the resulting reflections.

The wavelength of the laser was tuned to 495 nanometers, in the blue-green band of the optical spectrum, the frequencies least likely to be refracted and absorbed by water. The individual laser transmissions were timed so closely together that a human eye could not have distinguished them as discrete events. A human observer—had one been present—would have seen only a second of flickering blue-green light.

The LIDAR scanner completed its transmission sequence. The laser went dark, and the Halogen lamps snapped back on to provide illumination for the video cameras as the robot processed and assembled images from the laser scan.

The detailed LIDAR images revealed nothing new. The candidate fixture was still the wrong shape.

The cognitive architecture that formed the core of Mouse's operating program was designed to continue functioning in the event of one or more logical failures. In computer-speak, this concept was called fault tolerance, or graceful degradation. Had the graceful degradation software been correctly coded, Mouse would have been able to override the programming conflict and continue its mission. But there was a bug in the program code. When the graceful degradation loop was triggered by an error, it was supposed to activate a subroutine to record the nature of the mistake for future correction, and then bypass the error to continue functioning. Instead, the faulty program activated the emergency maintenance subroutine, erroneously informing the robot that it had sustained critical damage, and ordering it to return to the surface for repair. *This* was the software bug that Mouse's programmer, Ann Roark, had been chasing, and it wasn't corrected yet.

Faced with an insolvable logical conflict—this fixture on the upper surface of Presumptive Target #1 *must* be the one specified, but this fixture *cannot* be the one specified—Mouse's core program activated the graceful degradation routine. The faulty software responded by triggering the emergency maintenance subroutine.

The robot's computer immediately noted the damage signal and prepared to abandon its mission and head for the coordinates it had been launched from.

Without Ann Roark's middle-of-the-night tinkering, the rescue of *Nereus* would have ended there. But Ann, in a burst of desperate and bleary-eyed wisdom, had crafted a slight modification in Mouse's program code. The patch didn't *fix* the problem because Ann Roark still hadn't found the bug that was *causing* the problem. This was a different type of programming. This was a *workaround*.

In the lingo of programmers, a workaround is a temporary and usually imperfect way of forcing a computer to operate in spite of an uncorrected malfunction. A workaround does not repair a broken piece of program code, it merely tricks the computer into pretending that the problem doesn't exist.

The workaround Ann Roark had patched into Mouse's program had four simple elements: one conditional statement, and three commands:

> **(1) <<<< IF [emergency_maintenance_routine = active]**
> **(2) CANCEL [emergency_maintenance_routine]**
> **(3) RESUME [normal_operation]**
> **(4) INVERT [last_logical_conflict] >>>>**

The first line of the patch triggered the workaround as soon as Mouse's computer went into emergency maintenance mode. The second and third lines of the patch canceled the call for emergency maintenance mode, and ordered the robot to continue operating as if no error had been received. The last line of the patch did the important work; it inverted the results of the logical conflict that had caused the error in the first place.

Mouse had been stymied by the fact that the fixture it had located did not match the shape of the digital model stored in computer memory. The code patch inverted that logical state, changing "INCORRECT SHAPE" to "CORRECT SHAPE" in Mouse's memory.

The logical conflict was resolved. Mouse's computer determined that all conditions had now been met for this phase of the mission. The robot moved on to the next phase and began searching for the *Otis Barton's* lifting cable.

⚓ ⚓ ⚓

USS *Towers*:

Fifteen minutes later, three thousand feet above Mouse's position and two miles to the south, a small triangular green icon appeared on the screen of Ann Roark's laptop computer. Ann yawned so hard that her ears popped, and she thumbed the trackball, scrolling the computer's pointer over the new symbol. A tight block of letters and numbers appeared next to the icon.

It took a few seconds for her tired eyes to focus on the tiny status report. She read it, and then she read it again. And then she screamed at the top of her lungs.

She jumped out of her chair and clasped her hands over her head like a prizefighter celebrating a victory by knockout. "Yes!" she shrieked. "Yes, damn it! *YES!*"

She turned around and locked eyes with the first of the Navy geeks who caught her attention. "Call the *Otis Barton*," she said. "Tell them to start hauling in their cable!"

The Navy guy, whatever his name was, looked stunned. "Does this mean ..."

"Yes!" Ann shouted again. "It means that mama's little mouse is bringing home the cheese!"

⚓ ⚓ ⚓

Otis Barton:

The Research Vessel *Otis Barton* rode easily on the waves, the white paint of her hull and superstructure gleaming in the midday sun. Originally constructed as a *Victorious* Class acoustic surveillance ship for the United States Navy, the squat little vessel had been retired from military service and reconfigured for marine research by NOAA, the National Oceanic and Atmospheric Administration.

On the ship's fantail, a large hydraulic winch turned steadily, reeling in a long cable of braided steel at the painfully slow rate of fifty feet per minute. The winch had been designed to launch and retrieve a towed acoustic sensor array known as SURTASS. But the object hanging from the end of the submerged cable was not an underwater listening device. It was the deep water submersible *Nereus*, and within its pressure hull were three human beings.

No one knew the nature of the accident that had trapped the submersible on the slope of the Aleutian trench, under three thousand feet of water. There had been no communication with the *Nereus* since the little submarine had declared a mission abort more than twenty-four hours earlier. No one knew whether the crew of the *Nereus* were alive, or dead. This might be a rescue operation, or it might be nothing more than the recovery of three bodies.

The retrieval crew was composed of five workers: a winch operator, two riggers to attach tag-lines to the miniature submarine and guide it onto the deck of the ship, and a pair of divers in insulated wetsuits — standing by to go into the water if anything went wrong. In warm weather, there would sometimes be a few spectators, out on deck to enjoy the sunshine and watch the mini-sub come out of the water. When the weather was cold or the seas were rough, the spectators tended to stay inside the ship, where they could keep warm and dry.

This close to Alaska, the weather was much too cold for casual onlookers. If this had been a routine operation, no one but the retrieval crew would have turned out to watch. But this was not a routine retrieval operation, and there were nearly twenty people on the fantail. Two of them were medical personnel, ready to render emergency treatment if required. The rest of the crowd were there to watch, and to add their silent moral support.

Every man and woman not actively engaged in the safety and navigation of the ship was present. No one had called for them. There had been no announcement over the ship's public address system. They had been drawn to the fantail by instinct, and by unspoken common consent.

At fifty feet per minute, the slowly-turning winch had taken almost exactly an hour to haul in three-thousand feet of cable. The onlookers had stood the entire time, braving the cutting cold of the Aleutian wind as foot-after-foot of dripping steel cable was reeled in.

They were coming to the end now. The damaged submersible was nearing the surface. In a minute or so, the Nereus would break through the wave tops — hauled unceremoniously back from the dark ocean depths.

The winch operator watched the cable meter on his control console scroll slowly, like the odometer of a car. "One hundred feet!" His words seemed to hang in the cold bright air. No one else made a sound.

"Fifty feet." His voice was softer this time, as if he were a little unnerved by the oddly persistent ring of his own words.

"Twenty feet." It was the last depth report he gave.

The water surrounding the cable was beginning to bubble and churn. The crowd held its collective breath as the water heaved and frothed. Almost without warning, the *Nereus* broke the surface.

The winch continued to turn, lifting the little submarine free of the water. The hull of the submersible was streaked with the sticky dark silt of the sea bottom. The orange and blue paint scheme of her hull looked almost toy-like, as if this were the plaything of some spoiled child. It suddenly seemed ludicrous to entrust human lives to such a frail and silly machine.

The riggers moved forward, attaching their tag-lines, and swinging the submersible into her cradle. The divers were moving almost before the sub was firmly seated, scrambling up the curved silt-covered sides of the hull to the hatch at the top. They spun the handle furiously, and the pressure seal relaxed with an audible hiss.

The hatch swung up and open, and one of the black-suited divers lowered himself through the opening immediately. His head and shoulders reappeared through the hatch a few seconds later. He raised his hands into the air, and pointed both of his thumbs toward the sky. "They're alive!"

He said something else, but his words were lost in a roar of shouts and laughter.

They were *alive*!

CHAPTER 11

21ST SPACE OPERATIONS CENTER
ONIZUKA AIR FORCE STATION
SUNNYVALE, CALIFORNIA
TUESDAY; 26 FEBRUARY
1238 hours (12:38 PM)
TIME ZONE -8 'UNIFORM'

Technical Sergeant George Kaulana looked at the two oblong smears of video on the display screen of his SAWS console and raised his eyebrows. "Where are *you* guys going?" The SAWS console—short for *Satellite Analyst Workstation*—was receiving an imagery download from *Forager 715*, a U.S. Air Force Oracle III series surveillance satellite currently passing over southeastern Russia. *Forager's* primary surveillance mission was the nuclear reactor facility in Brushehr, Iran, so the perigee of the satellite's elliptical orbit was designed to bring it to an altitude of only about 280 kilometers during passes over the Middle East. The digital cameras built into the satellite's 2.4 meter mirror telescope were designed to take their best pictures from that altitude.

At the moment, *Forager* was on the outbound leg of its transit, heading toward apogee, the farthest reach of its orbit, 1,005 kilometers above the earth. The altitude of the satellite as it passed over southeastern Russia was about 500 kilometers and increasing steadily. Its camera's were still functional at that altitude, but they were operating well outside of their optimum focal length. The images scrolling across the screen of Technical Sergeant Kaulana's console were of significantly lower resolution than images shot from *Forager's* preferred altitude, but the satellite analyst had no trouble identifying the two blurred oblongs as ships.

Kaulana's job for this particular satellite pass was to count the number of submarines tied to the pier at the Russian naval base at Petropavlosk, Kamchatka. The ballistic missile submarines based in Petropavlosk represented a sizeable fraction of Russia's nuclear strike capability. The movement of those subs was an ongoing concern. The United States and

Russia might not be enemies anymore, but it wasn't smart to lose track of another country's nuclear arsenal if you could avoid it.

The two blurry shapes on Kaulana's screen were obviously not submarines and the Russian Navy didn't maintain surface warships in Kamchatka, so the two unidentified ships were probably nothing to worry about. If they'd been following the shipping lanes toward the West Coast of the U.S., he wouldn't have given them a second look. But both of the unidentified ships were well north of the shipping lanes, and based on the orientation of their hulls, it looked like they were heading toward Petropavlosk. There wasn't necessarily anything unusual about that. Avacha Bay, the harbor at Petropavlosk, got quite a bit of merchant shipping. But the destination of the ships was cause enough to give them a closer inspection, just to verify that they weren't military vessels. If Kaulana let a couple of warships slip unnoticed into Petro on his watch, the Lieutenant would skin him alive. Better to check them out.

He used his trackball to pull a wireframe cursor around one of the shapes and keyed the SAWS console for image enlargement and digital enhancement. The video display flickered briefly as it reacted to the increased demand for processing power. A few seconds later, the enhanced image appeared on Kaulana's screen.

He looked at the blocky white superstructure that ran most of the length of the ship. It wasn't a tanker or a container ship, but it was definitely some kind of merchant vessel.

He shifted his cursor to the other shape on his screen and repeated the enlarge and enhance process. A few seconds later he was looking at another merchant vessel with the same sort of blocky white superstructure, an apparent duplicate of the first ship.

He increased the image contrast to make the details of the ship's structure stand out more clearly, and then spent nearly a minute using his cursor to carefully tag points along the outline of the hull and the corners of all visible topside features. When he thought he had given his console's computer enough clues about the shape of the vessel, he pressed a key to activate a silhouette recognition module in the system's software.

He got a match in seconds. His unknown ships were 20,000-ton Ro-Ro vessels, built by HuangHai Shipyard in China.

Kaulana drummed his fingers on the gray steel shelf that housed the SAWS console's keyboard. He could identify nearly every class of warship in the world by sight, but he wasn't very well versed when it came to merchant ships. What in the heck was a *Ro-Ro*?

He punched a few keys to query the computer, and was rewarded with a brief explanation. *Ro-Ro* was the common abbreviation for *Roll-on/Roll-

off. Ro-Ro ships were vehicle carriers, designed to transport cars or other vehicles from one seaport to another. The *Roll-on/Roll-off* designation referred to built-in hydraulic ramps that could be lowered to allow a vessel's cargo of vehicles to drive onto the ship at loading, and drive off when the ship reached its destination. According to the computer summary, the two Ro-Ros on Kaulana's screen were capable of carrying about 2,000 cars each.

He whistled through his teeth. That was a lot of cars. He shrugged and released the images from his console's processing queue. As long as the ships weren't military, it didn't really matter where they were going. The destinations of a couple of Chinese car carriers could hardly be considered a matter of national security.

⚓ ⚓ ⚓

Kaulana would repeat that line of reasoning at his court martial a little over a year later. The officers of the court would ultimately give him the benefit of the doubt and find that—based upon the information available to him at the time— Technical Sergeant George Kaulana had *not* been derelict in the execution of his duties when he'd declined to investigate the Ro-Ro vessels further. But the military court would also remind Kaulana that all of the death and destruction that came after might have been averted if he'd paid more attention to that harmless looking pair of Chinese merchant ships.

CHAPTER 12

KUZBASS (K-419)
NORTH PACIFIC OCEAN (SOUTH OF THE KURIL ISLAND CHAIN)
WEDNESDAY; 27 FEBRUARY
1402 hours (2:02 PM)
TIME ZONE +11 'LIMA'

Kapitan Igor Albinovich Kharitonov of the Russian Navy stood to the left of #1 periscope and glanced at the spot above the ballast control panel where the master dive clock should have been. He felt a familiar stab of annoyance as his eyes found the gaping rectangular hole where the oversized digital clock had been pried from its mounting.

They had *stolen* the master dive clock. His fists tightened unconsciously. The *Kuzbass* was a front-line nuclear attack submarine, and some *svoloch* had stolen the master dive clock. The very thought made Kharitonov want to punch someone repeatedly in the head. He was kapitan of the boat, and such behavior was not permitted in senior naval officers. But regulations wouldn't keep him from beating the thieving bastard to death if they ever caught him.

The theft had occurred at *Pavlovskoye* submarine base, the submarine's home port near Vladivostok. The *Kuzbass* had been moored to a guarded pier in the naval station's security area, and *still* someone had managed to get into the control room and make off with the damned dive clock. How was such a thing even possible?

The base militia was investigating the theft, which meant precisely nothing. It had probably been one of their guards who had let the thief on board to begin with, no doubt in exchange for a couple of hundred rubles, or a few American dollars. Unless, of course, the thief was a member of Kharitonov's own crew. He couldn't rule that out. A man could barely feed himself on what the junior Sailors got paid. It was impossible to provide for a family on wages that low, and some of the junior men *did* have families.

Kharitonov sighed and shifted his gaze to the clunky analog clock that had been borrowed from the Officer's Mess and strapped to a pipe as a temporary replacement for the missing dive clock.

Temporary, of course, was a relative term. The Supply Officer had requisitioned a replacement part. But there were no master dive clocks to be had in the navy warehouses. The inventory records showed eleven clocks available for requisition, but none could actually be located. Officially, the missing clocks had been misplaced, which likely meant that they were sitting alongside the clock from *Kuzbass* in the back room of some dealer in stolen property.

The temporary clock said fourteen-oh-three. It was nearly time.

Kharitonov checked his wristwatch a half-second later: a habit born out of a career's worth of training and personal experience. A nuclear submarine Sailor could afford to take nothing for granted. Every cross-check was an opportunity to catch a mistake or malfunction before it killed you.

The watch was a relic of the Cold War: a stainless steel *Vostok Komandirskie*, with brushed steel hands, and a featureless black dial with large white machine-stamped numerals. The only ornamentation on the watch was the red star of the Soviet Union, embossed above the 6 o'clock position near the bottom of the dial.

Kharitonov noted with satisfaction that his watch matched the time on the temporary master clock to the second. Not that he'd expected otherwise, but expectations and certainties were not quite the same things.

He gave the stem three twists to keep the mainspring taut. The steel gears clicked solidly, oddly loud sounds that spoke of both mechanical precision and overkill craftsmanship. According to popular rumor, the old Komandirskie models were supposed to be bulletproof: an assertion which Kharitonov had never felt the slightest desire to test. But the watch's rugged construction did seem to lend credence to the idea.

He lowered his wrist and scanned the control room, his eyes carefully avoiding the empty spot that marked the theft—instead taking in the oversized gauges, clumsy electrical switches, and heavy-duty pipes and valves that formed the submarine's control systems. Like the heavy old watch, his submarine, the *Kuzbass*, was a masterpiece of Soviet brute force engineering. And, like his watch, the *Kuzbass* had out-lasted the old Soviet Union, and now lived on in the service of *Rossiyskaya Federatsiya*, the Russian Federation.

The Americans called this class of submarines the *Akulas*, akula being the Russian word for *shark*. The official Russian Navy designation was *Schuka-B*, after a highly aggressive breed of freshwater pike. Kharitonov preferred the American term. The image of a shark was more dangerous and glamorous than that of any fish, but—far more significantly—the term conveyed a compliment of the highest order. The Americans were the most lethal nuclear submarine Sailors on the planet, and the *Schuka/Akula* class were the first Russian-built attack subs that scared the hell out of them.

Although they bore many of the unwieldy earmarks of Soviet Cold War engineering, the *Akula* subs were extremely fast, and exceptionally quiet. Not as silent as the new American *Virginia* or *Seawolf* class boats, but quieter than the vaunted *Los Angeles* class nuclear attack subs that were the backbone of the US Navy's submarine fleet. In any case, the *Akulas* were nearly undetectable to most types of sonar.

Armed with a combination of 65 centimeter and 53 centimeter torpedoes, RPK-255 Granat strategic cruise missiles, and an impressive array of mines and antisubmarine missiles, *Akula* class submarines were far more deadly than any shark that had ever prowled the ocean depths.

Kapitan Kharitonov was proud of his boat. Despite the heavy hands of her designers and the light fingers of the unidentified asshole who had stolen the dive clock, *Kuzbass* was 110 meters of lethal black steel.

Kharitonov himself looked like he might have been designed by the same brute force engineers who had laid the plans for his submarine. Exactly two meters tall, he was within centimeters of the maximum allowable height for Russian submarine Sailors. His shoulders were broad enough to force him to go through hatches at an angle, and his arms were so thick that even the heavy steel Komandirskie looked like a child's watch against the wide bones of his wrist.

His dark hair and eyebrows were a near perfect match for the black serge of his winter uniform. Thanks to some skillful needlework on the part of his wife, the uniform did a bit to disguise his oversized frame, as did the speed and agility of his movements. In his youth, Kharitonov had been a fencer. Although he hadn't touched a saber or a foil in nearly a decade, he'd never lost the quickness and balance he had learned on the fencing floor at Pogosov.

What had happened to the Russia of his youth? A few short years before, the formidable Soviet military had been undefeatable. The vision of worldwide communism had been a foregone conclusion. Now the great Russian military couldn't even keep the riff-raff from stealing its submarines a piece at a time. How had the mighty Soviet empire fallen so far and so quickly?

Kharitonov checked the temporary dive clock again. Fourteen-oh-five. It was time. He tapped the Watch Officer on the shoulder. "Take the boat to periscope depth."

The *Kuzbass* had been ordered to rendezvous with a Tupolev TU-142 anti-submarine warfare aircraft based out of Yelizovo air station on Kamchatka. Upon establishing contact, the submarine and aircraft were to conduct a detect and evade exercise. For three hours, the big lumbering bomber-turned-submarine-hunter would pepper the ocean with sonobuoys and crisscross the waves with its magnetic detection equipment in an attempt to locate and track *Kuzbass*. All the while, the submarine would be doing its best to avoid detection by the sensors of the searching aircraft.

The Watch Officer glanced back at Kharitonov and nodded. "Sir, take the boat to periscope depth, aye!" He turned toward the Diving Officer. "Make your depth forty meters."

The Diving Officer acknowledged the order and repeated it back. Not more than two seconds later, he issued his own order to the Stern Planesman. "Five degree up bubble. Make your new depth four-zero meters."

The Stern Planesman, Seaman Viktor Petrovich Ermakov, repeated back his orders and pulled back slowly on the steering wheel shaped control yoke. Eyes locked on the plane angle indicator, he leaned slightly closer to the Helmsman seated to his right. "I'm sick of this recycled air," he said quietly. "In a few moments, I'll be topside with the kapitan, breathing *real* air for a change!"

Before the official start of the exercise, the *Kuzbass* was scheduled to surface in order to give the sensor operators on board the TU-142 an opportunity to practice using their video cameras and infrared cameras to detect and track a *real* submarine.

Once the boat was on the surface, depth control would be handled by the controlled flooding and pumping of the trim and drain tanks, leaving the Stern Planesman with nothing to do. Aboard the *Kuzbass*, as aboard most Russian submarines, the Stern Planesman became the topside lookout when the sub was on the surface. Which meant that Viktor would soon be up in the conning tower with his commanding officer, enjoying sunshine and non-recycled air.

"Don't talk nonsense," the Helmsman said. "We aren't more than twenty kilometers from the ice pack. It's nice and warm down here, but the air up topside will be colder than a Siberian whore." He chuckled. "Your *sosiska* will freeze and fall off!" A *sosiska* was a thin Russian sausage.

Viktor elbowed his friend in the ribs. "You've been drinking the water from the reactor again, haven't you? You're hallucinating. My *sardelka* is fat and juicy! It is a man's sausage!"

The Helmsman snorted. "You'll see how fat and juicy it is when that cold air hits it."

Viktor laughed, but kept his eye on the depth readout. He cleared his throat. "Passing sixty meters."

The Diving Officer nodded. "Very well. Zero your bubble. Take all planes to horizontal. Level off at four-zero meters."

The Watch Officer pulled a communications microphone from its cradle in the overhead angle irons. "Sonar—Watch Officer, coming shallow in preparation for going to periscope depth. Report all contacts."

The answer came from an overhead speaker a few seconds later. "Watch Officer—Sonar, we hold three contacts at this time, all evaluated as fishing boats, and all bearing to the South. Target number one, surface, bearing 176 degrees with slow left bearing drift. Target number two, surface, bearing 194 degrees with moderate left bearing drift. Target number three, surface, bearing 212 degrees with slow left bearing drift."

"Watch Officer, aye."

The Watch Officer reached up and grasped the hydraulic control ring that encircled the upper hull penetration for number one periscope. He rotated the control ring about ten degrees to the right. With a muffled thump, the scope hydraulics engaged, and the periscope began to rise from its form-fitting well beneath the deck.

As soon as the optics module slid clear of the deck, the Watch Officer leaned over and flipped the periscope grips into place. A second or so later, when the scope had risen about a meter, the Watch Officer crouched and placed his left eye against the black rubber collar surrounding the eye piece. He followed the still rising optics module, starting from a crouch and turning the scope as he duck-walked his way through an entire 360 degree revolution.

Kapitan Kharitonov observed his Watch Officer's periscope procedures without speaking, noting with silent approval that the young lieutenant managed to complete a full visual sweep by the time the eyepiece had reached eye-level above the deck and he could stand normally.

The Watch Officer thumbed a control button, increasing the optical magnification of the scope and began a second visual sweep. At forty meters, the head of the periscope was still well submerged, but enough sunlight filtered down to that depth to backlight any sizeable object on the surface of the ocean. The lieutenant was checking for *shapes and shadows*: the telltale silhouettes of any ships or boats floating on the surface.

In a perfect world, sonar would detect any surface vessels well ahead of time, allowing the sub to steer clear, but it's nearly impossible to hear a boat or ship drifting with its engines cut. In the past, more than a few submarines had collided with quiet surface craft, usually with devastating consequences to both vessels. A little extra caution during this procedure could easily make the difference between safety and disaster.

The Watch Officer increased the magnification of the scope again and conducted a third sweep. When he was finally satisfied that the surface near the submarine was clear of collision hazards, he pulled his face away from the periscope. "Diving Officer, make your depth twenty meters."

The Diving Officer nodded. "Make my depth twenty meters, aye!" He turned and began issuing orders to the individual watch stations. Five minutes later, he had the boat holding steady at its new depth and trimmed to his satisfaction. "Sir, my depth is two-zero meters."

Kapitan Kharitonov nodded. "Raise the radio mast."

The Watch Officer acknowledged the order and flipped a switch on an overhead panel. The muffled whine of hydraulics announced the raising of the radio antenna mast. A green status light illuminated on the panel. The Watch Officer looked at his kapitan. "Sir, the radio mast is deployed and locked."

Kharitonov nodded. "Very well." He lifted a radio microphone from its cradle and verified that the channel selector was set to the designated frequency for the exercise. He held the mike to his lips, pressed the transmit key, and spoke. "*Volk-shentnadtsatiy,* this is *Kuzbass.*"

Volk-shentnadtsatiy, Wolf-sixteenth, was the call sign of the Tupolev TU-142 anti-submarine warfare aircraft that would be attempting to track the *Kuzbass* for the next few hours.

The radio speaker rumbled with static, but there was no reply.

After about a minute, he keyed the mike and tried again. "*Volk-shentnadtsatiy,* this is *Kuzbass.*"

Again there was no answer.

"We are at the proper coordinates, at the correct time, and on the designated frequency," Kharitonov said. "Perhaps our esteemed shipmates in naval aviation have forgotten how to locate the ocean."

Most of the members of the control room crew chuckled.

Kharitonov looked over at the hole where his master dive clock should have been. "Or it could be that some gutless idiot has stolen their clock and they don't know what time it is."

There were fewer laughs this time. His men knew that, joking aside, their kapitan was still torqued over the missing clock.

Kharitonov keyed the mike again. *"Volk-shentnadtsatiy,* this is *Kuzbass.* Do you read me?"

This time, there was a response. *"Kuzbass,* this is *Volk-shentnadtsatiy.* I read you clearly."

Kharitonov's eyebrows went up. *"Volk-shentnadtsatiy,* this is *Kuzbass.* I am at periscope depth and preparing to surface for your camera and infrared sensor runs. Do you read?"

The reply came almost immediately. *"Kuzbass,* this is *Volk-shentnadtsatiy.* Understand you are at periscope depth. Can you mark your position with a smoke float?"

Kharitonov frowned. A smoke float? If those flying idiots were any good at their job, they wouldn't *need* a smoke float to locate a submarine.

He sighed. "Watch Officer, launch a smoke float for our cloud-hopping shipmates."

The young lieutenant repeated the order and carried it out. "Smoke float deployed, Kapitan." He grinned. "I used an orange one so they won't have any trouble finding us."

Kharitonov returned the grin. "Good thinking, Lieutenant." He started to key the microphone when an ear-splitting squeal erupted from the radio speaker. He grabbed the gain control and cranked the speaker down to minimum volume. The painful sound was diminished but still audible.

He was about to call for a technician when one of the radiomen stuck his head into the control room. "Sir! Our communications are being jammed!"

Kharitonov's ears were still ringing, but he heard the man without difficulty. "Are you certain?"

"Positive, sir," the radioman said. "We're getting broad spectrum jamming on all naval communications frequencies."

"Understood," Kharitonov said.

The air crew of that plane really *were* idiots. Obviously one of the operators had hit the wrong button by mistake. No doubt they'd realize the error before long and shut down their jammers.

An intercom speaker crackled in the overhead. "Control—Sonar, torpedo in the water! Repeat, torpedo in the water, bearing zero-four-four! Recommend immediate evasive maneuvers!"

Kharitonov's brain went into high gear immediately. The torpedo report *had* to be a mistake, but he couldn't take that chance. "I have the deck," he shouted. "All ahead flank! Left full rudder!"

The boat heeled over instantly as the Helmsman executed his orders. "Sir, my rudder is full left! All ahead flank!"

"Very well," Kharitonov said. "Launch countermeasures!" He paused for a half-second. At flank speed, hydrodynamic force would mangle the periscope and the radio antenna. "Down scope! Retract the antenna mast!"

The deck began to vibrate as the turbines brought the screw up to maximum speed. Something *had* to be wrong with the sonar equipment. The torpedo *had* to be a mistake. But no ... he could hear it now, right through the hull, the unmistakable dental drill whine of high-speed propellers. It wasn't a sonar error. It really *was* an incoming torpedo. The sound was quickly growing to a howl.

"Countermeasures away!" the Watch Officer shouted.

The intercom speaker flared again. "Control—Sonar, we have startup on a second torpedo! Repeat, we have two inbound torpedoes! Classify both torpedoes as 400 millimeter type UMGT-1!"

Those were Russian torpedoes, air launched. They had to have come from *Volk-shentnadtsatiy*. Why was their *own* aircraft shooting at them?

"Emergency dive!" Kharitonov said. "Full down bubble on all planes!"

Before the Diving Officer could acknowledge the order, the intercom speaker crackled again. "Control—Sonar, no takers on the countermeasures. Both torpedoes have acquired.

Outside the hull, the howl of approaching torpedo screws rose to a deafening shriek.

Kharitonov opened his mouth to order an emergency rudder change, but his voice was drowned out by the explosion of the first torpedo. He couldn't tell where it hit, but the shock of the impact slammed into him like a speeding car, lifting him off the deck and throwing him sideways against the housing for #2 periscope. He felt several of his ribs break.

The submarine heeled well over to port in response to the explosion. Kharitonov tumbled to the deck where he lay in a haze of shock and confusion, his body too stunned to even draw breath.

His left wrist was turned at such an angle that his old watch, the Vostok Komandirskie, was positioned just a few centimeters from his face. He stared stupidly at the heavy stainless steel timepiece, his addled mind not really registering its presence. Slowly his eyes slid back into focus and his brain began to process information again. Somewhere beyond the numbing silence of his damaged eardrums, he thought he could hear the thunder of rushing water.

He blinked, and his body began to think about moving again. He could dimly perceive the first ghostly twinges of pain, and he realized that he had been temporarily shielded from the reality of his injuries by shock. It would all come back to him; he knew that. His body's defense mechanisms could delay the inevitable for a little while, but they could not prevent it.

He couldn't stay down here any longer. He needed to get to his feet, get his brain working, regain command of the situation. He had to save his boat.

But something caught his attention. It was his wristwatch. The second hand was frozen in place. The watch had stopped. The all-powerful bulletproof masterpiece of Soviet craftsmanship had given up the fight. It was almost funny if one only knew when to laugh.

Then the second torpedo struck, and the world disappeared in a fury of fire and water.

CHAPTER 13

ICBM: A COLD WAR SAILOR'S MUSINGS ON THE ULTIMATE WEAPONS OF MASS DESTRUCTION

(Reprinted by permission of the author, Retired Master Chief Sonar Technician David M. Hardy, USN)

The 14th and 15th centuries were periods of great experimentation in the field of rocketry, and several major advances came about as a result. An English monk named Roger Bacon developed improved formulas for gunpowder, greatly increasing rocket flight ranges. In France, poet, historian, and inventor Jean Froissart discovered that the accuracy of a rocket's trajectory could be improved by launching it through a straight length of pipe, or tube. His idea became the precursor of the modern bazooka.

Meanwhile, rockets continued to become more common on the battlefield. French troops led by Joan of Arc used rockets in the defense of the city of Orleans in the year 1429. The French also used rockets during the siege of Pont-Andemer in 1449, and at the assault on the city of Ghent in 1453.

By the 1500s, rocket warfare began to fall into disfavor. Advances in artillery made the smoothbore cannon an increasingly attractive alternative for the armies of Europe and Asia. Nevertheless, the 16th century brought a new development to rocketry: one that would ultimately open the door to both space travel, and nuclear warfare.

In 1591, a German fireworks maker named Johann Schmidlap began building 'step rockets' in order to lift his fireworks to greater altitudes. Schmidlap's earliest step rockets had two stages, consisting of a large sky rocket (first stage), which carried a smaller sky rocket (second stage). The larger first stage would propel the rocket as high as it could go before its engine burned out. The engine of the smaller rocket would then ignite, and the second stage would separate from the husk of the first, and continue to climb to higher altitude.

Schmidlap's goal was simply to build more impressive fireworks, but his multi-stage rockets would become the foundation for manned spacecraft, and nuclear missiles.

It should be noted that the idea of multi-stage rockets may have originated with Conrad Haas, an Austrian artillery officer who described the concept in a manuscript written between 1529 and 1569. Johann Schmidlap may or may not have been aware of the works of Conrad Haas, but—regardless of his possible influences—Schmidlap was the first to put the concept into practical use.

The next great breakthrough in rocketry occurred in 1687, when Sir Isaac Newton published '*Philosophiae Naturalis Principia Mathematica*' (Mathematical Principles of Natural Philosophy). Although the text was not geared specifically toward rockets, *Principia Mathematica* outlined 'Newton's Laws of Motion,' and described the natural principles that allow rockets to function. This work has been credited with elevating rocketry from blind trial and error into the realm of science.

Thanks in part to the work of Sir Isaac Newton, rocket warfare experienced a revival in the 18th and 19th centuries.

After a series of successful Indian rocket attacks against the British Army in the late 1700s, artillery expert Colonel William Congreve began designing rockets for the British military. Congreve's rockets proved to be highly effective weapons. British ships used Congreve rockets to bombard Fort McHenry during the War of 1812.

Francis Scott Key, who witnessed the assault from the deck of a British warship, was inspired to write the poem that became America's national anthem: *The Star Spangled Banner*. When he penned the famous line about *the rockets' red glare*, Francis Scott Key was referring to the British Congreve rockets that were pounding the besieged American fort.

In 1903, a Russian schoolteacher by the name of Konstantin Tsiolkovsky published a report in which he suggested the switch from traditional solid rocket fuel to liquid rocket propellants. Tsiolkovsky theorized that the range and speed of a rocket are controlled by the velocity of its exhaust gasses, and he calculated that liquid rocket fuels would provide higher gas velocities than solid rocket fuels.

Tsiolkovsky's writings influenced the research of Robert Goddard, who began building liquid fuel rockets in the early 20th century.

Unlike solid fuel rockets, which require few (if any) moving parts, a liquid fuel rocket is a highly-complex machine. In place of a simple combustion cylinder and exhaust nozzle, a liquid fuel rocket requires feed-pumps, turbines, oxygen tanks, and an intricate network of piping to connect them all. And where a solid fuel rocket needs only an ignition source, a liquid fuel rocket requires precise control mechanisms.

The task before Goddard was daunting, but he believed that the potential benefit was worth the difficulty and risk.

On March 16, 1926, after a long string of failed attempts, Robert Goddard managed to successfully launch a liquid fuel rocket. Powered by gasoline and liquid oxygen, his rocket flew for about two and a half seconds, reaching an altitude of 41 feet before landing in a cabbage patch about 180 feet from the launch pad.

By current standards, it was not much of a flight. It didn't even approach the performance of the least successful solid fuel rockets in history. But a liquid fuel rocket had flown. Like the Wright Brothers, with their first faltering airplane flight at Kitty Hawk, Robert Goddard had proven that his strange machine could fly.

While Goddard was still struggling to get a liquid fuel rocket into the air, on the other side of the Atlantic Ocean, another great rocket pioneer was making his own mark upon the face of history. In 1922, a German/Romanian physicist named Hermann Oberth submitted a 92-page doctoral dissertation on rocket science. His dissertation was rejected as 'utopian,' and his doctoral degree was withheld.

Oberth responded by publishing his dissertation in 1923, under the title '*Die Rakete zu den Planetenräumen*' ("By Rocket into Planetary Space"). Oberth went on to expand the work to 429 pages, re-publishing it as '*Wege zur Raumschiffahrt*' ("Ways to Spaceflight") in 1929.

Oberth's writings inspired scientifically-minded people of many nations. Rocket clubs and associations began springing up all over the world.

Of particular note was a German rocket association, called '*Verein fur Raumschiffahrt*,' the Society for Space Travel. The club's membership included Wernher von Braun, Hermann Oberth, and Arthur Rudolph, and many others who would go on to play major roles in the field of rocket science.

After purchasing a plot of land near the city of Berlin, the club members built a '*Raketenflugplatz*' (rocket airfield), and began launching rockets of their own design. The earliest of these, the *Mirak* series, were largely failures. But the club's *Repulsor* series was highly-successful. Some of the Repulsor rockets reached altitudes of over 3,000 feet.

In 1932, the club approached the German army for funding. Club officers arranged a demonstration launch for the army. The rocket failed, but Captain Walter Dornberger—who was in charge of the German army's rocket program—was impressed with the knowledge, skill, and dedication of the club members. He offered to fund the club's experiments if the members would agree to operate under conditions of secrecy, and focus their efforts toward developing military rockets.

Some of the members voted to accept Dornberger's offer, and others voted to reject it. The ensuing argument, coupled with a continued lack of funding, caused the club to dissolve in 1933. Even so, the impact of Verein fur Raumschiffahrt was far from over.

Following the death of German President Paul von Hindenburg in 1934, Chancellor Adolf Hitler combined his office with the office of President, and declared himself to be the *Führer*. Under his command, the National Socialist German Workers Party (better known to history as the *Nazi Party*) began a massive campaign to build up the German military. Hitler's goal was nothing less than the conquest of Europe, and— ultimately—the subjugation of every nation on earth.

To achieve the Führer's objectives, the German military began a number of aggressive research programs, all aimed at creating the kind of super-weapons needed to conquer an entire planet. Among these secret projects was the German rocket program, and several members of the Verein fur Raumschiffahrt rocket club, including Wernher von Braun and Arthur Rudolph, were seduced or coerced into joining the Nazi quest to build super rockets.

One of the most successful developments of the Nazi rocket program was the *Vergeltungswaffe 1*, or V-1 rocket. Also known as the *buzz bomb* or *doodlebug*, the V-1 was powered by a pulse jet engine, and guided by a gyro-magnetic autopilot system. The first test flights occurred in late 1941 or early 1942. After some initial guidance problems were ironed out, the V-1 proved to be an incredibly powerful weapon. Many military historians classify it as the first cruise missile.

By 1944, Germany was launching V-1 rockets at England, literally by the thousands. According to a report written by American General Clayton Bissell in December of 1944, about 8,025 self-guided V-1 rockets were launched at targets in England during a nine-week period of that year. As a result of this unrelenting barrage of rockets, more than a million houses and other buildings were destroyed or damaged, and tens of thousands of people were killed.

The rocket, which had been a formidable engine of war almost from the outset, was becoming the first weapon of mass destruction.

The V-2 rocket program (*Vergeltungswaffe 2*) ran concurrently with the V-1 project, but the V-2s were much more technologically advanced. Under the engineering expertise of Wernher von Braun and Arthur

Rudolph, the V-2 rocket became the first true ballistic missile, and the first man-made object to reach sub-orbital space.

After climbing to the fringes of outer space, a V-2 rocket would tip over and drop back down into the atmosphere, diving toward its target at four times the speed of sound with a 2,150 pound warhead of highly-explosive Amatol. The combination of extreme altitude and supersonic speed made the rockets invulnerable to anti-aircraft guns and fighter planes, and the enormous warheads made the rockets exceptionally powerful. A single V-2 rocket could reduce an entire city block to ankle-high rubble.

In terms of technological achievement, the V-2 was a quantum leap forward. In terms of tactical effectiveness, it was somewhat less impressive. Despite its speed, range, and warhead capacity, the V-2 was not very accurate. Also, the V-2 became operational too late in the war to have much impact on the outcome of the fighting. Of the more than 6,000 V-2 rockets built, only about half were ever launched as weapons. The remainder were destroyed, expended by testing, or captured by the Allies at the end of World War II.

The war in Europe came to an end on May 7, 1945, when Generaloberst Alfred Jodl signed the documents of unconditional surrender on behalf of the German High Command. Adolf Hitler lay dead by his own hand, and his beloved Berlin was in flames. Hitler's dream of world domination had fallen to ashes, along with much of his erstwhile Nazi empire.

Hitler's super rockets had come too late to turn the tide of the war, but no one could deny that the V-1 and V-2 really *were* the super rockets that he had threatened to build.

On the other side of the world, the war in the Pacific was entering its bloodiest phase. The defeat of Imperial Japan was considered a certainty, but the Japanese were preparing to fight to the very last man, woman, or child. Japan would *not* surrender.

But everything changed in August of 1945. On the sixth day of that month, an American B-29 bomber obliterated the Japanese city of Hiroshima with a single atomic bomb. More than 70,000 people were killed instantly, and nearly a quarter of a million more would die from the effects of nuclear radiation over the next few years.

Three days after the destruction of Hiroshima, while Japan was still reeling from the shock of losing an entire city to a single bomb, America followed up with a second nuclear attack on the Japanese city of Nagasaki. Once again, a single atomic bomb was used, and once again the devastation was complete. Somewhere between 40,000 and 75,000 people were killed by the direct effects of the explosion. And—as with Hiroshima—tens of thousands more would die over the following years.

Representatives of the Japanese Emperor formally signed the documents of surrender on September 2, 1945, aboard the battleship USS *Missouri*, at anchor in Tokyo Bay. The Second World War was officially over. The nations of the earth were ready to turn towards peace. But the threat was not ended.

Germany's rocket scientists had shown the world how to build missiles and rockets capable of reaching space, and spanning the distances between nations. America's own scientists had discovered the secret to building nuclear weapons. It was only a matter of time before the two deadliest technologies in history merged to become a single weapon with unimaginable destructive power.

The weapons of World War II had given rise to the weapons of World War III. For the first time, mankind had the knowledge and the ability to destroy all life on planet earth.

CHAPTER 14

AVACHA BAY COMMERCIAL SEA PORT FACILITY (OJSC)
PETROPAVLOVSK-KAMCHATSKI, RUSSIA
WEDNESDAY; 27 FEBRUARY
1814 hours (6:14 PM)
TIME ZONE +12 'MIKE'

The sun was just beginning to dip below the volcanic peaks to the west of the city, when Customs Officer Evgeny Petrov spotted the militia car. The big black Volga squeaked to a stop near the head of the pier, about thirty meters from where the customs man was standing.

Arms wrapped around himself for warmth, Petrov hunkered farther down into his heavy wool greatcoat, and trudged toward the car, his boots crunching through the layer of rime ice and snow that covered the cement quay. He had called for militia backup nearly two hours ago, and the idiots were just now getting here.

A car door opened and a man climbed out and tightened his own coat, as Petrov covered the remaining distance to the car. The driver wore the uniform and insignia of a major in the militia.

A major? That much was good, at least. The militia man was going to need some clout to handle this situation. But where were his men? Had the fool come alone?

The militia officer straightened his hat and turned up the collar of his coat against the wind. "I am Major Noviko," he said. "Are you Petrov?"

Petrov nodded. "Yes." He looked around. "Where are your men?"

"A truck is coming behind me," Noviko said. "It should be along in a minute or two. In the meantime, why don't you tell me what the problem is?"

Petrov pointed toward the pier. "*There* is the problem," he said.

Moored to the pier were two ships: enormous boxy vessels, the size of skyscrapers laid on their sides. The ships were car carriers, both of the same design, with blue-painted hulls and white superstructures.

The vessel closest to the head of the pier had the name *Shunfeng* lettered on the hull near the bow. The second ship had the name *Jifeng* painted in the same location.

Both ships had large open cargo doors, and steel ramps extended down to the pier. As the two men watched, strange-looking six-wheeled vehicles drove down the ramps of both ships, and fell into line behind long rows of similar vehicles that were already parked on the pier.

There were perhaps a hundred vehicles on the pier already, their motors all running as they sat idling on the snow-encrusted concrete. They were all painted dark green, and they all had angular profiles and heavy construction. Some were relatively featureless. Others bristled with antennas, or were topped by what were unmistakably guns. They were obviously military vehicles.

"These ships have no authorization," Petrov said. "We have spoken to the masters of both vessels, and they claim that these vehicles are for delivery to the naval base at Rybachiy. But they have produced no proof of clearance, no manifest transfers, no delivery authorization of any kind."

Petrov nodded toward the still growing ranks of military vehicles. "I have formally notified both masters that it is against the law to offload their cargoes without customs clearance." He scowled. "As you can see, they ignore our warnings."

The major nodded gravely. "Yes, I see. And how many men do you have in your charge, here?"

"Three," Petrov said. "Myself, and two other customs agents." As he watched, another pair of the angular six-wheeled vehicles rolled onto the pier. These were topped by what seemed to be rocket launchers.

"So far, they are remaining inside the fence of the customs area," Petrov said. "But we can't keep them here if they decide to leave. That's why I called the militia for reinforcements."

"A prudent move," Major Noviko said. He checked his watch and frowned. "My men should be here by now."

"Perhaps you should call them, to check," Petrov said.

"I will," Noviko agreed. "But first, please summon your other two agents." He surveyed the lines of military vehicles. "We're going to need a much larger response force to contain this. I want to have more information before I call in the request."

Petrov nodded and unclipped a tape-swaddled radio from his belt. The pier lights were flickering on now, and the sun was nearly gone behind the peak of Koryaksky mountain.

As he summoned his men by radio, Petrov noted that the stream of vehicles had finally halted. They sat idling on the pier, clouds of vapor rising from their exhaust pipes.

Shubin arrived almost immediately. Borodin took a couple of minutes longer. He'd been down at the far end of the pier, and he was breathing heavily when he stumped over to stand near his supervisor and the militia officer.

Major Noviko nodded. "Is this everyone?"

"Yes," Petrov said. "At least until our reliefs show up in about an hour."

"Good," Noviko said. His right hand came out of the pocket of his greatcoat, and Petrov had barely registered the presence of the automatic pistol when he heard the crack of the first bullet.

Borodin dropped to the frozen concrete like a sack of potatoes. Shubin raised his hands and took a rapid step toward the militia officer, but the gun whipped around quickly, and a bullet hammered through his forehead. His body collapsed beside Borodin, blood spilling among the ice and snow.

Stunned by the suddenness of the attacks, Petrov's only thought was to run. He turned, his boot heels slipping on ice, but Noviko's pistol barked again.

He felt himself slammed forward, as though someone had punched him in the spine. He pitched forward, and fell to the pier. The impact with the frost-covered concrete was somehow more painful than the bullet.

He lay in the ice and snow, his faced turned toward the nearer ship. Men were coming down the cargo ramp now. A *lot* of men. Soldiers. In black uniforms.

Petrov's vision was failing by the time the first squad of soldiers came near. He couldn't turn his head for a better look, and he couldn't see them clearly. But as his brain processed his very last rational thought, he wondered why the strangers were speaking Chinese.

CHAPTER 15

WHITE HOUSE
WASHINGTON, DC
WEDNESDAY; 27 FEBRUARY
3:12 AM EST

President Chandler nearly dropped the phone before his sleep-numbed fingers managed to fumble the receiver to his ear. "Yes?"

"Mr. President, this is Lieutenant Colonel Briggs, the Situation Room Watch Officer. I'm sorry to wake you at this hour, but we have a developing situation that requires your attention, sir."

The president muffled the mouthpiece of the phone with one hand and yawned heavily. When the worst of it was past, he uncovered the receiver. "Situation room?"

"No, sir," the lieutenant colonel said. "This is a National Command Authority issue. The Secret Service is going to want you in the bunker, Mr. President. And the National Military Command Center is requesting permission to initiate COG protocols."

The president sat upright in bed, the sudden movement jerking the phone to the edge of the bedside table, where it teetered precariously. *COG* was short for Continuity of Government. COG protocols were rapid action plans for moving designated cabinet secretaries and members of Congress to secure locations outside of the Washington, DC area, to protect the succession of national leadership in situations that directly threatened the survival of the American government. In theory, COG protocols were intended to react to unknown threats as well as known. In practice, that was understood to mean one of three things: extraordinary natural disasters, terrorist acts of nearly unimaginable scope, or impending nuclear attack.

The thought drove the last vestiges of sleep from President Chandler's brain. "Are we under attack?"

"No, sir," Lieutenant Colonel Briggs said. "Fighting has broken out in Kamchatka. We don't have many details yet, but it appears to be some kind of revolution or military coup. There are a relatively large number of

Russian long-range nuclear missiles stationed in Kamchatka, and we don't know who has control of them at this time." He paused for a few seconds. "I can't go into details over a non-secure phone, Mr. President. We should have more information for you when you get down to the bunker."

As if on cue, there was a light knock on the door. A second later, it opened to reveal a pair of Secret Service agents. "Mr. President? We have orders to escort you down to the bunker."

The president hung up the phone and looked over at Jenny, still snoring softly beside him. He peeled the blankets off his legs and turned to put his feet on the carpet. "I'll wake up Jenny," he said. "Make sure the agents assigned to Susan and Nicole get them down to the bunker, and try not to frighten them any more than necessary." He lifted his robe from the back of a chair and began pulling it on.

The nearer agent nodded. "We'll wake up your family if you'd like, sir. But Command Post is online with the National Military Command Center, NORAD, the National Reconnaissance Office, and the 21st Space Operations Center. If there's a launch, missile flight-time from Kamchatka will give us about thirty minutes warning. In the event of a nuclear launch alert, we can evacuate your family to the bunker in under five minutes. If I may offer a suggestion, Mr. President, it would probably be less frightening to let them sleep, for the moment at least."

The president shook his head and opened his mouth to repeat the order to wake his family. Then, he caught himself. His own concern for his family's safety grew out of the love he felt for his wife and daughters. The Secret Service's motivations were professional rather than emotional, but they were at least as powerful. He had no doubt that any member of his protection detail would willingly step in front of a bullet to protect his wife and children. It was their profession, their sworn duty, and the central tenet of their entire way of life. Reminding them to consider his family's safety was entirely unnecessary, and probably insulting.

He checked his head shake and turned it into a nod. "Fair enough," he said. Then the father-husband instinct made a last quick attempt to override logic. "Don't let anything ... I mean, if there's any doubt about their safety ..."

The agent nodded. "You have my solemn word, Mr. President. If there's any doubt at all, we won't waste a *second* in moving your family."

President Chandler pulled the belt of his robe tight and took one more look at the sleeping form of his wife. "All right," he said. "Let's go."

Three levels below the East Wing of the White House was a tube-shaped citadel known officially as the *Presidential Emergency Operations Center*, or *PEOC*. Unofficially, the shelter was called the *bunker*, a nickname that had emerged during the Reagan administration when nuclear war with the Soviet Union had seemed like a very real possibility. Protected by a forty foot blast shield of high-tensile ferroconcrete, Kevlar, and armored steel plating, the bunker housed office facilities, sleeping quarters, computer systems, communications equipment, and a command center that duplicated the functions of the West Wing's Situation Room.

According to popular rumor, the bunker was designed to survive a direct nuclear blast. But despite its extraordinarily reinforced architecture and multiply-redundant life support systems, no engineer familiar with the physics of nuclear warfare had ever made such a claim. In the evaluation of most experts, the bunker could provide a high-degree of survivability against a near-miss. Where nuclear weapons were concerned, that was as good as things got. Even the massively protected NORAD facility, tunneled deep into the hard Colorado rock of Cheyenne Mountain, was only estimated to have a 70 percent probability of surviving a multiple-megaton nuclear strike. Against high-yield nuclear warheads, words like 'bomb proof' and 'impenetrable' lost all meaning.

Conspiracy buffs had long conjectured that the bunker contained enough food, water, and bottled air to last three years. In reality, the size of the facility limited the provision stockpiles to *months*, not *years*. Despite the claims of the supermarket tabloids, there *were* no secret preparations to keep the president, his family, friends, and cabinet members alive for decades following the nuclear annihilation of the American people. In the event of a full scale nuclear attack, it was hoped that the bunker and similar emergency preparations would keep the president alive long enough to coordinate retaliatory strikes and the last ditch defense of the country. But if America died—the president, his family, and all of his friends and political allies—died right along with it.

When President Chandler walked through the heavy blast doors, he bypassed the entrance to the operations room, detouring to his emergency sleeping quarters for just long enough to throw on some clothes. He chose simply: khaki trousers, a pullover shirt embroidered with the University of Iowa logo, and loafers. He didn't want to waste time on a suit and tie, but neither was he willing to preside over an emerging nuclear crisis in his bathrobe and slippers. He dressed quickly, and was sliding into his chair at the head of the conference table within two minutes.

A tall dark-haired woman in a white U.S. Navy uniform came to attention until he was well seated. "Good morning, Mr. President. I'm

Commander Kathryn Giamatti, the Deputy Situation Room Watch Officer. Lieutenant Colonel Briggs is engaged in a secure conference call with the Secretaries of State, Defense, Treasury, and Homeland Security, so I'll be handling your initial briefing, sir."

The president nodded. "Thank you, Commander. Has the national security advisor been notified?"

The commander nodded. "Affirmative, sir. Mr. Brenthoven is on his way to the White House. We're expecting him any time now."

"Correction," said a voice from the other side of the room. "Mr. Brenthoven has *arrived*."

National Security Advisor Gregory Brenthoven stood in the doorway. His suit was rumpled and there were dark circles under his eyes, but his gaze was focused and alert. He nodded toward the president. "Good morning, sir. Sorry I'm late. I was in Foggy Bottom when I got the call."

"No problem, Greg," the president said. "Are you planning to take over this briefing?"

"Not unless you want me to, sir," Brenthoven said. "I got the basics over secure phone during the drive in, but I'm sure the commander here is more up to speed than I am. With your permission, Mr. President, I'd rather sit in and maybe ask a few questions."

"Of course," the president said. "Pull up a chair."

The national security advisor did so, retrieving a small leather-bound notebook from the inside breast pocket of his jacket.

The president turned back to Commander Giamatti. "Proceed."

The commander pointed a remote toward a large flat screen display built into the wall opposite the president's chair. The Presidential Seal appeared, set against a blue background. "Sir, this will be a preliminary briefing. With your approval, we'd like to schedule a full meeting of the National Security Council for nine AM."

The president nodded.

Commander Giamatti thumbed a button on the remote, and the Presidential Seal was replaced on the screen by a map of southeastern Siberia and the Kamchatka peninsula. Another click of the remote, and a window popped up, displaying a fairly high-resolution satellite image of a city.

"About two hours ago," the commander said, "major fighting broke out in the Kamchatkan capital city of Petropavlovsk. Our most current satellite imagery of Petropavlovsk is more than ten hours old, well before the apparent onset of hostilities, and we don't have any airborne surveillance assets in position for an immediate look. One of our destroyers, USS *Albert D. Kaplan*, is equipped with Sea Shrike unmanned reconnaissance drones, but they'll have to violate Russian airspace to get close enough to see anything. The Air Force has already initiated orbital burns on two surveillance satellites to maneuver their footprints to cover Kamchatka. For the moment, we're relying on HUMINT reports, and feedback from the Russian government. And frankly, Mr. President, there's not a lot of either at the moment."

HUMINT was the military acronym for <u>Hum</u>an <u>Int</u>elligence: information gathered and reported by people, rather than surveillance hardware.

"Understood," the president said impatiently. "We can't *see* anything; we don't *know* anything, and we're reduced to reading *tea leaves* and staring at the entrails of goats. I've got that. But somebody woke up half the government for a *reason*. I'd like to know what the damned tea leaves *say*."

Commander Giamatti's cheeks reddened. "Yes, sir." She swallowed before continuing. "Mr. President, we have indications that the Russian military is ramping up to an advanced state of combat readiness. Intelligence sources in Moscow and Vladivostok confirm that Russian nuclear forces have been ordered to an increased alert status. Analysis of Russian Command and Control message traffic is consistent with a rapid escalation of nuclear and conventional readiness. We haven't seen this level of activity since the worst days of the Cold War. Almost half of the Russian Pacific Fleet is putting out to sea."

"Why half?" the president asked.

The commander paused. "Pardon me, sir?"

"Why half?" the president asked again. "If the Russians are gearing up as heavily as we think they are, why are they only putting half of their Pacific Fleet to sea?"

Brenthoven looked up from his notebook. "That's probably the best they can manage, Mr. President. The Russian Federal Navy is in bad shape. I'll be surprised if they actually manage to get *half* their units to sea in any sort of realistic fighting condition."

The president waved a hand. "Continue."

"Initial indications from Petropavlovsk suggest that the fighting there is military in nature, rather than insurgent," Commander Giamatti said. "A rough assessment of the scale indicates major combat operations. There's some fighting scattered through the city itself, but most of the activity appears to be concentrated in the vicinity of Rybachiy naval station."

President Chandler pursed his lips. "I haven't memorized the name of every Russian military base, but we're sitting in the bunker, the Russians are peeing their pants, and the National Military Command Center wants to initiate Continuity-of-Government protocols. So I'm assuming that this Rybachiy naval station is home to part of the Russian nuclear arsenal."

"Yes, sir," the commander said. She thumbed her remote again, and a pop-up window appeared on the screen to the left of the Kamchatka peninsula. Inside the new window was a grainy black and white photo of a naval base. Three submarines were moored to battered concrete piers.

The president realized that he'd seen this exact same slide just a couple of days earlier, during the briefing about that Russian courier who claimed to be the middleman in some back-channel deal between the Chinese military and ... the president frowned ... the Governor of Kamchatka.

"Rybachiy naval station, at Petropavlovsk, is the home port for the Russian Pacific Fleet's ballistic missile submarines," Commander Giamatti said. "According to the most recent threat assessments, at least three Delta III class nuclear ballistic missile submarines are based at Rybachiy. Each Delta III submarine carries sixteen Russian R-29R missiles ..."

"Also known by the NATO designation of SS-N-18 Stingray," the president said. "And each missile is armed with three nuclear warheads, for a total of 48 nuclear warheads per submarine."

The commander nodded. "You're up on your Russian missile subs, Mr. President."

"Not really," the president said. "But I got some of this during an intelligence brief a couple of days ago." He frowned. "Tell me, Commander, is the Chinese military involved in this somehow?"

The naval officer looked puzzled. "Mr. President, how did you ..."

"The intelligence brief I mentioned. I'm just playing connect-the-dots."

"We *do* have uncorroborated reports from Petropavlovsk, suggesting that Chinese soldiers—or military personnel who appear to be Asian—are present in large numbers, and appear to be heavily engaged in the fighting."

"Is this the HUMINT you spoke of?"

"Part of it, sir," the commander said. "But the source is unofficial and unconfirmed. A twenty-two year-old American college student on an ecotourism vacation to Kamchatka. Her name is Janeane Whitaker. She claims she's been hiding in an attic above a café since the militia, the local police, began rounding up all visitors and foreigners about twelve hours ago."

Brenthoven paused in his note-taking and looked up at the commander. "Why did it take us twelve hours to find out about this?"

"Ms. Whitaker's mobile phone is apparently not compatible with the cellular networks in Russia. Her only means of communication is a palmtop computer or a PDA; we're not sure which. She tapped into the café's wireless internet signal and began firing off emails. She's an ordinary citizen, without any particular connections in the military or government, so she didn't have any fast-track method of communicating with anyone in positions of authority. She ended up sending emails to the 'Contact Us' links on every government website she could think of. The White House, the State Department, the Department of Homeland Security, the FBI, and the Pentagon."

"That doesn't sound like a very efficient process," the president said.

"It's not, Mr. President," the national security advisor said. "Every agency in the government receives thousands of crackpot emails every day. I know who shot JFK; my neighbor is running a secret al-Qaeda training camp in his basement, and brain-sucking aliens have taken over the local television studio. Don't get me wrong, sir. There are some useful suggestions buried in all of that junk, and occasionally even some bona fide intelligence tips, but it's not easy to separate the wheat from the chaff. An uncorroborated email from a foreign internet café about secret police activity in Kamchatka? Frankly, it's a miracle that anybody followed up on it at all."

"They didn't at first," Commander Giamatti said. "Until the Russian military went into overdrive."

"Do we still have contact with this woman? Janeane Whitaker?" the president asked.

"Uh … No sir. She reached her daily spending limit."

"Her *what*?"

"Her daily spending limit," the commander said. "The wireless internet provider charges by the minute, and apparently Ms. Whitaker's credit card has a low daily spending limit. They cut her off and we lost contact."

The president stared up at the ceiling. "I don't believe this. We have a multi-billion-dollar intelligence apparatus and the one person in the entire world who can tell us what's going on has maxed out her credit card?" He turned to his national security advisor. "Can't we do something about this? Every agency in the government has at least a few thousand dollars of discretionary funds. Can't someone get on the phone to the bank and deposit some money into this woman's account?"

Brenthoven sighed. "The State Department has people working on that right now, sir. Ms. Whitaker's bank is based out of California, and it doesn't offer twenty-four hour customer service. State is on the phone to California, waking people up. It's after midnight out there."

The president looked down at the table and shook his head. "If we weren't sitting on the brink of a nuclear emergency, this might actually be funny. Can we just forget about Kamchatka, and launch some missiles at the damned bank?"

The door opened, and an Air Force lieutenant colonel walked in, carrying a white folder bordered with red diagonal stripes. He moved quickly to the national security advisor, whispered into his ear and handed him the red and white folder.

Brenthoven opened the folder and scanned the document inside as the Air Force officer quietly made his report. After a few seconds, Brenthoven looked up. "Mr. President, we have updated satellite imagery of Petropavlovsk. One of the Delta III nuclear missile submarines has gotten underway, and is currently unlocated. As far as we can determine, it's carrying a full loadout of nuclear ballistic missiles."

"Jesus Christ," the president said.

The Air Force Officer faced the president and came to attention. "Sir, I'm Lieutenant Colonel Briggs, the Situation Room Watch Officer. I've just been on the phone to the Joint Chiefs. The National Military Command Center is still waiting for permission to initiate Continuity-of-Government protocols, and CINCNORAD is recommending DEFCON 2." The lieutenant colonel paused and took a breath. "Mr. President, the Joint Chiefs concur with CINCNORAD's recommendation. They are also recommending DEFCON 2, sir."

President Chandler felt his stomach tighten. DEFCON 2, or Defensive Readiness Condition 2, was the highest level nuclear alert for American military forces. The United States hadn't been to DEFCON 2 since the Cuban Missile Crisis, when the world had come within *days*—perhaps *hours*—of World War III. The only higher readiness level was DEFCON 1, full preparation to launch nuclear war.

He frowned. "No. From what we can see, the Russians are already jumpy as hell over this. If we hike up our own nuclear alert levels, we're only going to make them more nervous than they already are. And the spookier they get, the more likely they are to do something stupid. We don't have enough information to justify that sort of risk."

He looked at his national security advisor. "The Russians have definitely got themselves a problem, but I don't see any reason to believe that it involves us. For all we know, that submarine put out to sea to safeguard its missiles, to keep them out of the wrong hands. No one has shown me any evidence that the intentions of that sub are hostile to the U.S."

"Mr. President," the Air Force officer said, "with all due respect, anything that affects the stability of the Russian nuclear arsenal involves us. That submarine has enough firepower to incinerate every major city in the western United States."

The president shook his head. "We're over reacting. We can't let things move this fast."

"I understand your caution, sir," the lieutenant colonel said. "And I understand that I'm just a light colonel and you're the Commander-in-Chief. But I've been doing this all my *life*, sir. If this escalates into a nuclear engagement, it's *all* going to happen fast. Nuclear warfare follows a completely different timeline than conventional war, Mr. President. Our reaction window won't be measured in weeks, or even hours. We'll have minutes. And if we get caught with our pants down, we won't have any time at *all*."

The president nodded gravely. "I understand, Colonel. I'll keep that in mind."

He turned to his national security advisor. "This is what that courier was talking about. We were briefed about him a couple of days ago, remember? The Russian bagman who staggered into our embassy in Manila, bleeding to death from five or six bullet wounds. Gregorovitch? Is that his name?"

Brenthoven laid the folder on the table. "Grigoriev, sir. Oleg Yurievich Grigoriev."

The president nodded. "That's the guy. He was claiming to have information about a deal between the governor of Kamchatka and the Chinese Politburo. Something about trading Russian nuclear missile technology for Chinese military intervention."

The president looked at the screen. The black and white photo of the Russian submarine base stood out next to the map of Kamchatka. "I didn't put much stock in Mr. Grigoriev's claims at the time, but it looks like he might have the inside track on this. Let's see if we can find out what that gentleman has to tell us."

"We've been trying, sir," Brenthoven said. "We've got agents by Mr. Grigoriev's bedside around the clock, but he's in pretty bad shape. His doctors don't know when he'll be stable enough to talk to us."

"Let's hope it doesn't take too long," the president said. "We may not have a lot of time."

CHAPTER 16

National Security Advisor Gregory Brenthoven opened a door, and ushered the tall Russian man into the Roosevelt Room. A pair of tucked-leather Kittinger armchairs had been drawn up near the fireplace at the center of the curved east wall. The chairs created a small and informal meeting area, away from the long conference table.

Brenthoven nodded toward the chair on the right. "Please, Mr. Ambassador, make yourself comfortable."

"Thank you," Ambassador Aleksandr Vladimirovich Kolesnik said. His English was only slightly accented. He sat in the offered chair, and ran a long-fingered hand through his thick white hair.

Brenthoven took the other chair. Before he could begin with the traditional diplomatic pleasantries, the Russian Ambassador cut directly to the point of the meeting.

"My government thanks you for your generous offer," Kolesnik said. "But we do not require military assistance at the present time."

The national security advisor watched the man for several seconds without speaking. In appearance, Kolesnik was as far removed from the stereotypical Russian bear as it was possible to be. He was thin and fastidious, with deep-set eyes and a triangular face that made his bushy white eyebrows look as though they belonged to someone else.

Brenthoven thought about allowing the pause in conversation to stretch a few seconds longer. In matters of diplomatic exchange, Ambassador Kolesnik was not comfortable with silence, a trait that could sometimes be taken advantage of. But now was not the time for gamesmanship. The Russians were already climbing the walls; there was nothing to be gained by intentionally putting their senior diplomat on the defensive. Better to get to the hard part quickly, and hope that open discussion could somehow allow them to work past more than a half-century of mutual distrust.

Brenthoven raised his eyebrows. "Mr. Ambassador, at the very *least* you have what appears to be a military coup on your hands," he said. "Your own news services are openly describing it as a *civil war*."

"It is not civil war," Kolesnik said. "It is a minor local struggle. Nothing more. An insignificant uprising."

Brenthoven fished his small leather notebook from the pocket of his jacket, and held it without opening it. "The entire Russian military has been moved to a state of high alert, *including* your strategic nuclear missile forces. You've mobilized nearly every available naval vessel in your Pacific Fleet. There are foreign combat troops on your soil. From the perspective of the U.S. government, that doesn't sound insignificant."

"It does not involve the United States." Kolesnik said. "We appreciate your concern, but this is an internal matter."

"My government does not agree," Brenthoven said. "We have reason to believe that the insurgents have managed to deploy one of the ballistic missile submarines that was stationed in Kamchatka, along with its arsenal of 48 nuclear warheads. Mr. Ambassador, that's more destructive force than the entire human race has unleashed in the history of this planet."

The ambassador nodded gravely. "It is the K-506, the *Zelenograd*."

Brenthoven jotted the name and hull number of the submarine in his notebook. "Has the sub been located yet? Have your naval units detected her?"

"*Him*."

"I'm sorry?"

"You asked if our naval units have detected *her*. But *Zelenograd*, submarine 'K-506,' is a *he*, not a *she*."

The national security advisor smiled weakly. "I've never been much of a Sailor, sir. It was my understanding that seagoing vessels are *always* presumed to be female."

The Russian Ambassador returned the thin smile with an equally weak smile of his own. "American ships, yes. Russian ships, *no*. Russian vessels are *always* male. The tradition goes back at least to *Pyotr Alekseyevich Romanov*: Peter the Great. Perhaps farther."

Brenthoven rubbed his chin. "I wasn't aware of that."

"There is much that America does not know about Russia," the ambassador said. "And there is much that Russia does not know about America. Even with the Cold War behind us, our countries do not understand each other."

He shook his head. "We thought we understood you as adversaries, but we were deluding ourselves. Now we attempt to understand you as allies, and we are still … what is the word? *Baffled*? We are still *baffled* by you."

Brenthoven nodded. "Both of our governments have mastered the art of misunderstanding," he said. "But Mr. Ambassador, this is one case in which we can *not* afford misunderstanding."

"You are quite correct," the Russian Ambassador said.

"I'm glad we're in agreement," Brenthoven said. "Are you in a position to discuss the level of U.S. involvement? Or is that a matter better arranged by our respective presidents?"

Ambassador Kolesnik held up a finger. "Again we misunderstand each other. I agreed that our countries must make every effort to avoid miscommunication during this crisis. I did not agree to American involvement in my country's internal affairs. My instructions from my government are quite specific. This matter will be handled by the Russian military, under the command of the Russian government."

"Mr. Ambassador, the nuclear missiles aboard that submarine have more than enough range to reach the United States. With all due respect, sir, that's exactly what they were *designed* to do. Unless you have some method of guaranteeing that they will not be launched against American cities, I don't see *how* we can sit back and treat this situation as an internal Russian issue."

"You can treat it as an internal issue because that's exactly what it *is*: an internal issue," the ambassador said. "As to a guarantee that your country will not be targeted, I think we can make such a promise."

The answer took Brenthoven by surprise. "Pardon me, sir … Are you saying that there is some sort of foolproof technical safeguard that prevents the missiles from being fired?"

The ambassador brushed a speck of lint from the left sleeve of his suit jacket. "As with your own missile submarines, there are certain mechanical and electronic safeguards in place, but their effectiveness depends upon the loyalty of the crew. If the crew of K-506 is disloyal, as their actions so far seem to indicate, we cannot rely on those safeguards. With the cooperation of the First Officer, the Missile Officer, and most—or *all*—of the crew, the captain of that submarine can launch those missiles whenever he wishes."

Brenthoven frowned. "What you're saying is …"

"I'm saying we must assume that K-506 *can* launch its missiles."

"Mr. Ambassador, now I'm *really* confused," Brenthoven said. "How does this guarantee that the United States will not be targeted by that submarine's missiles?"

"K-506 is running southwest, toward the southern tip of the Kamchatka peninsula," the ambassador said. "Senior naval officers in our Ministry of Defense are confident that the submarine will attempt to pass through the Kuril island chain and into the Sea of Okhotsk, where it will hide under the Siberian ice pack."

"And how does this help us?"

The ambassador held up his right hand and tugged at the cuff of his shirt sleeve with the fingers of his left hand. "Because we have, as you say, an ace up our sleeve." He dropped his hands into his lap. "The attack submarine *Kuzbass* is patrolling the Kuril island chain. At this very moment, orders are going out from our Pacific Fleet headquarters. *Kuzbass* will intercept and destroy K-506 at the entrance to the Sea of Okhotsk."

Brenthoven rubbed the back of his neck. "Mr. Ambassador, that sounds like a good strategy to me, but what if K-506 manages to slip past your attack submarine? We have a renegade nuclear missile submarine on our hands, with enough firepower to jumpstart Armageddon. Do you have a backup plan, in case *Kuzbass* doesn't get the job done?"

"Of course," the ambassador said. "If K-506 makes it into the Sea of Okhotsk, which our Ministry of Defense assures me will not happen, our naval units will trap him under the ice pack. They will keep K-506 safely contained under the ice until our attack submarines can hunt him down and sink him."

"What if the submarine breaks through the ice layer and surfaces? American submarines break through the ice pack all the time. If K-506 surfaces through the ice, how will you stop it from launching its missiles?"

The ambassador shook his head. "K-506 is a Project 667 BDR class submarine. We call this type of submarine the *Kal'mar* class. Your NATO designation is *Delta III*. This class of submarine was not constructed with the hull reinforcements required to punch through ice." He shrugged. "If they *try*, the ice slices into their hull and they sink like your *Titanic*. The crew drowns, or freezes to death in minutes. They do *not* launch missiles."

The *Titanic* had been a British ship, not American, but this didn't seem to be a good time to point that out. Brenthoven sighed. "I hope you are right, Mr. Ambassador. But I don't believe my president will share your confidence. Unless I'm very much mistaken, he is going to insist on U.S. military involvement."

"My instructions from my government are quite specific," the ambassador said again. "This is an internal Russian matter; and it will be handled by the Russian military, without help or interference from outside forces."

"President Chandler will not be pleased," Brenthoven said.

Kolesnik smiled. "No one will be pleased. This is the nature of Russian politics."

"I'll relay your intentions to my president," Brenthoven said. "He will want to discuss the matter with *your* president."

The Russian ambassador's smile vanished. "I'm certain that he will. And President Turgenev will look forward to his call. But the outcome will be the same. There will be no U.S. involvement in this matter."

CHAPTER 17

USS TOWERS (DDG-103)
NORTHERN PACIFIC OCEAN (SOUTH OF THE ALEUTIAN ISLANDS)
THURSDAY; 28 FEBRUARY
1120 hours (11:20 AM)
TIME ZONE -10 'WHISKEY'

Captain Bowie opened the watertight door and led the way out onto the starboard side main deck. The two civilians, Ann Roark and Sheldon Miggs, followed him out into the morning sunlight, stamping their feet and adjusting their coats as their breath steamed in the chilly Alaskan air.

Bowie suppressed a smile. It wasn't really all that cold out here. The temperature was less than a degree below freezing, but the sudden transition from the warm interior of the ship made the air seem colder than it really was. The psychological effect was further magnified by the light coating of frost on the Kevlar life rails and most of the topside surfaces.

Bowie rapidly scanned the horizon and then the sky, automatically checking for other vessels, navigational hazards, aircraft, and weather features that could endanger his ship. The sky was a vivid cobalt blue, marred only by a handful of wispy cirrus clouds above the jet stream. The sea within his arc of vision was clear of visible threats. He turned his eyes back to the civilians.

The two could have hardly been less alike. Sheldon Miggs was a plump little dumpling of a man, with a bad comb-over and bright, lively eyes that signaled a keen wit and playful spirit. He was quick to laugh, even quicker to smile, and seemed genuinely fascinated by Bowie's ship and crew.

By contrast, Ann Roark was slim, dark haired, and pretty in a severe sort of way. From what Bowie had seen, the woman rarely smiled, and—unlike her co-worker—she didn't seem much impressed by the ship, the crew, or the Navy in general. Oh, she was civil enough. Her conversation was never less than polite, but it was never *more* than polite either. And there was always something in her expression that hinted at a kernel of detached contempt.

Not for the first time, Bowie felt a fleeting urge to ask Ms. Roark what it was about him, his ship, or his people that she found so distasteful. He let the urge pass. She was entitled to her own opinions, however unflattering they might be to Bowie or to his chosen profession. All that really mattered was her performance, and *that* had been superb.

Bowie still couldn't believe that she'd managed to pull off the rescue of the *Nereus*. But she *had* pulled it off, despite his doubts. The woman was nearly as odd as her robot, but she was damned good at her job, no question about it. And as far as Bowie was concerned, that earned her a bit of slack.

Miggs clapped his gloved hands together several times and looked around. The grin on his face was positively child-like. He was excited by the prospect of exploring the ship with the commanding officer as tour guide.

Roark was just as plainly disinterested. Bowie had half-expected her to decline his invitation, but her desire to maintain the appearance of courtesy had apparently overridden her disinterest. She probably saw this as a necessary customer relations function, to be endured rather than enjoyed. Keep the Navy guys happy so they'll keep signing the R&D checks.

"Every time I see this ship, it's a different color," Miggs said. "Is that a stealth feature?"

Bowie nodded. "It is." He used the fingers of this left glove to brush away a small patch of frost on the bulkhead next to the watertight door. The surface under the frost was not the traditional haze gray color of U.S. Navy ships, but a dusty blue-gray. "We call this PCMS," he said. "It's short for Passive Countermeasure System." He nodded toward Miggs. "Poke it with your finger."

Miggs did so. "It's springy. Like rubber."

"There's some rubber in it," Bowie said. "But mostly it's made up of polymerized carbon fiber, which makes it absorbent to radar."

"So this is like that stuff they use to make the stealth bombers?" Miggs thumped the springy material with the tip of his index finger. "What do they call that? RAM? Radar Absorbent Material?"

"RAM is the Air Force version," Bowie said. "We call the Navy implementation PCMS. It's the same basic idea, but we have to use different technology."

Roark looked at the bulkhead but didn't touch it. "Why is that? Was there something wrong with the Air Force way of doing things?"

"Not at all," Bowie said. "But a B-2 bomber weighs about a hundred and sixty tons, and it's constructed mostly from advanced composites, with low radar signatures." He patted the bulkhead. "A Flight Three *Arleigh*

Burke Class destroyer displaces nearly ten *thousand* tons, and it's built mostly from steel, which has a very *high* radar signature. Put simply, the Navy faces different technical challenges than the Air Force, so we have to take a different technological approach."

He smiled. "But we're not above stealing good ideas from the Zoomies." He waved a hand toward the superstructure of his ship. "Take a look at her topside design and tell me the first thing that pops into your head."

"It looks a little ..." Miggs paused, as if unsure how to phrase what was on his mind. "... *strange*. Sort of ... squashed, and oddly shaped."

"That's as good a way to put it as any," Bowie said. He looked up at the low pyramid shapes of the destroyer's minimized superstructure and the steep rake of her short mast. "There are no right-angles in the topside design. No perfectly vertical surfaces, and damned few perfectly horizontal surfaces, apart from the decks. It's called an advanced-geometry design. Every angle is calculated to minimize radar reflections. We got the idea from our buddies in the Air Force, and I believe we even cribbed some of their math for calculating the angles."

Miggs poked the springy PCMS tile again. "How well does it work?"

"Well, the exact numbers are classified," Bowie said. "But the ballpark figures are releasable to the public. *Towers* is 529 feet long, 66½ feet wide, and her radar cross section is just a hair larger than your average fiberglass motorboat."

Miggs looked impressed. "They can do all that with some tricky angles and these rubber tiles?"

"Not entirely," Bowie said. "Those are just the most obvious changes. If you'll notice, the life lines are made from Kevlar. Until a few years ago, life lines were made from braided steel cable, which has a much higher radar signature than Kevlar." He used the toe of one boot to point toward an oval seam in the deck. "You may also notice that the deck fittings are all retractable. Every chock, padeye, and cleat on the ship can fold down into a form-fitting recess below the deck, and lock out of sight. That shaves a little more off our radar cross section. It all adds up."

"You mean it all *subtracts*," Ann Roark said.

"Right," Bowie said. "That's what I should have said. It all *subtracts*. It all goes to make us stealthier."

"So why do these tiles change color?" Miggs asked.

"That's a different feature of the PCMS," Bowie said. "Ordinary PCMS tiles are just gray. But our PCMS tiles are impregnated with a special pigment that changes color in response to shifts in lighting. Under bright sunlight, it turns about the shade you're seeing now, which is supposed to be nearly ideal for blending into the haze boundary between sea and sky. When the lighting starts to fall off, the pigment turns darker. It gets nearly black when the ship is in total darkness."

Miggs raised his eyebrows. "Wicked."

"We call it *phototropic camouflage*," Bowie said, "and it does make us a little harder to spot visually and with optically-based sensors. But—popular myth to the contrary—it does *not* make us invisible."

Ann Roark flipped up the collar on her coat, and burrowed her hands into her pockets. She looked out to sea without speaking.

"Let's head forward," Bowie said. "We can look at the gun and the forward missile launcher. Along the way, I'll show you what we do to mask our infrared signature."

He turned toward the starboard break, but before he had taken two steps, the watertight door behind him opened and Lieutenant (junior grade) Patrick Cooper stepped out.

Lieutenant (junior grade) Cooper came to attention and saluted. "Captain, the XO sends his compliments, and requests your presence in your at-sea cabin. You have classified Flash message traffic, sir. Immediate execute orders."

Bowie frowned. Immediate execute? That didn't make any sense. *Towers* wasn't on the emergency surge list. The ship wasn't even technically qualified for deployment yet.

He nodded. "Thanks, Pat." He turned to the civilians. "I'm afraid I'm going to have to leave you for a few minutes. Duty calls. But Lieutenant (junior grade) Cooper will be glad to take over as your tour guide until I return."

Cooper's eyebrows went up. He obviously hadn't expected to get roped into tour-guide duty.

Bowie winked at the two civilians. "Pat's a smart guy, and he's just about ready to transfer to Naval Postgraduate School, so be sure to ask him plenty of difficult questions."

Miggs smiled and returned the wink. Roark did not.

⚓ ⚓ ⚓

Three minutes later, Bowie was sitting at the little stainless steel fold-down desk in his at-sea cabin, staring at a hardcopy radio message.

```
//SSSSSSSSSS//
//SECRET//
//FLASH//FLASH//FLASH//
//272042Z FEB//

FM     COMPACFLEET//
TO     COMTHIRDFLEET//
       USS TOWERS//
       USS ALBERT D. KAPLAN//

INFO   COMSEVENTHFLT//
       CTF ONE TWO//

SUBJ/SURVEILLANCE TASKING/IMMEDIATE EXECUTE//

REF/A/RMG/ONI/270812Z FEB//

NARR/REF A IS OFFICE OF NAVAL INTELLIGENCE ASSESSMENT OF LIVE-
FIRE HOSTILITIES ON KAMCHATKAN PENINSULA 27FEB//
```

1. (UNCL) AS OUTLINED IN REF A, LARGE-SCALE ARMED CONFLICT BROKE
OUT IN AND AROUND THE KAMCHATKAN CAPITAL CITY OF PETROPAVLOVSK
AT APPROXIMATELY 0600Z 27FEB. INITIAL INDICATIONS SUGGEST THAT
FIGHTING IS MILITARY IN NATURE, AS OPPOSED TO INSURGENT. ONI
ASSESSMENT OF SCALE INDICATES MAJOR COMBAT OPERATIONS, CENTERED
IN THE AREA OF RUSSIAN NAVAL FACILITY AT RYBACHIY.

2. (SECR) U.S. INTELLIGENCE AGENCIES IN RECEIPT OF UNCORROBORATED
REPORTS THAT UNIDENTIFIED ASIAN COMBAT TROOPS, POSSIBLY CHINESE, ARE
PRESENT IN LARGE NUMBERS IN PETROPAVLOVSK. SAID TROOPS REPORTED TO
BE HEAVILY INVOLVED IN COMBAT OPERATIONS. THESE REPORTS ARE
UNCONFIRMED AT THIS TIME. U.S. INTELLIGENCE AGENCIES UNABLE TO
ASSESS LEVEL OF ASIAN AND/OR CHINESE MILITARY INVOLVEMENT, IF ANY.

3. (SECR) AT LEAST ONE (1) DELTA III CLASS BALLISTIC MISSILE
SUBMARINE IS BELIEVED TO HAVE DEPLOYED DURING OR SLIGHTLY PRIOR TO
ONSET OF HOSTILITIES. ONI HAS TENTATIVELY IDENTIFIED DELTA III SSBN
AS HULL NUMBER K-506, THE ZELENOGRAD. THIS IDENTIFICATION
CORROBORATED BY RUSSIAN DIPLOMATIC SOURCES. REF A REFERS.

4. (SECR) INITIAL ASSESSMENT OF DELTA III MOVEMENT SUGGESTS THAT
SSBN IS TRANSITING TO SEA OF OKHOTSK, WHERE IT MAY ATTEMPT TO
HIDE UNDER ICE PACK. REF A REFERS.

5. (SECR) RUSSIAN GOVERNMENT REPORTS AKULA CLASS SUBMARINE
KUZBASS PATROLLING IN VICINITY OF KURIL ISLANDS. KUZBASS HAS
ORDERS TO INTERCEPT AND DESTROY K-506 AT OR NEAR ENTRANCE TO SEA
OF OKHOTSK. REF A REFERS.

6. (SECR) DELTA III SUBMARINE BELIEVE TO BE ARMED WITH SIXTEEN
(16) SS-N-18 MISSILES, EACH CARRYING THREE (3) NUCLEAR WARHEADS
IN MIRV CONFIGURATION. RUSSIAN AND U.S. GOVERNMENTS UNABLE TO
CONFIRM THAT DELTA III HAS OVERRIDDEN SAFEGUARDS TO PERMIT
INDEPENDENT LAUNCH. ALL PARTIES, U.S. AND RUSSIAN, AGREE THAT
WORST CASE SCENARIO MUST BE ASSUMED. REF A REFERS.

7. (SECR) ONI AND NATIONAL RECONNAISSANCE OFFICE HAVE
INDICATIONS THAT RUSSIAN MILITARY IS RAMPING UP TO AN ADVANCED

STATE OF COMBAT READINESS. HUMINT SOURCES CONFIRM THAT RUSSIAN
NUCLEAR FORCES HAVE BEEN ORDERED TO INCREASED ALERT STATUS.
APPROXIMATELY FIFTY-PERCENT (50%) OF THE RUSSIAN PACIFIC FLEET
IS PUTTING OUT TO SEA.

8. (SECR) RUSSIAN GOVERNMENT HAS FORMALLY DECLINED OFFERS OF
U.S. MILITARY ASSISTANCE. RUSSIAN DIPLOMATIC SOURCES INSIST
THAT COMBAT OPERATIONS IN KAMCHATKA AND UNAUTHORIZED DEPLOYMENT
OF DELTA III NUCLEAR MISSILE SUBMARINE ARE INTERNAL RUSSIAN
MATTERS. AS SS-N-18 MISSILES HAVE THE RANGE AND CAPABILITY TO
STRIKE NUMEROUS U.S. TARGETS WITH NUCLEAR WARHEADS, SENIOR U.S.
LEADERS ARE NOT INCLINED TO TREAT THIS AS AN INTERNAL RUSSIAN
PROBLEM.

9. (SECR) USS TOWERS AND USS ALBERT D. KAPLAN ARE DIRECTED TO
DETACH FROM CURRENT DUTIES AND DEPART THEIR RESPECTIVE OPERATING
AREAS UPON RECEIPT OF THIS MESSAGE. PROCEED AT MAXIMUM
AVAILABLE SPEED TO INTERNATIONAL WATERS IN VICINITY OF SOUTHERN
KAMCHATKA PENINSULA FOR COVERT SURVEILLANCE OF DEVELOPING
EVENTS. AS MENTIONED ABOVE, RUSSIAN GOVERNMENT HAS DECLINED
U.S. MILITARY ASSISTANCE, AND PRESENCE OF U.S. WARSHIPS MAY BE
TREATED AS PROVOCATION. IN VIEW OF THIS, BOTH UNITS ARE
DIRECTED TO OPERATE WITH MAXIMUM STEALTH, AND TO AVOID DETECTION
BY RUSSIAN MILITARY FORCES. DO NOT CROSS INTO RUSSIAN
TERRITORIAL WATERS.

10. (SECR) ADDITIONAL ORDERS AND AMPLIFYING INTELLIGENCE
INFORMATION TO FOLLOW.

11. (UNCL) THIS IS A TRICKY ASSIGNMENT, BUT I KNOW YOU'RE UP TO
THE JOB. GOOD LUCK. ADMIRAL DAVIS SENDS.

//272042Z FEB//
//FLASH//FLASH//FLASH//
737465616C7468626F6F6B732E636F6D
//SECRET//
//SSSSSSSSSS//

Bowie read the message through twice before looking up at his
executive officer, Lieutenant Commander Nicolas Bishop. "What do you
think, Nick?"

The XO grimaced. "You know I'm a can-do kind of guy, Captain. But
we are *not* ready for this. Not even close. The crew is only about half-
way through the training cycle, about forty-percent of our missile cells are
empty, and we don't even have a helicopter embarked yet."

Captain Bowie nodded. "I'm not too worried about the helo," he said.
"We probably couldn't use it anyway. Our orders are to make like the
Invisible Man, and while SH-60s might be good helos, they're not exactly
stealthy."

"We're going to have to borrow a helo from somewhere, sir," the XO said. "In the short term, at least. These are immediate execute orders. We don't have time to pull into port, and we've got to get our civilian guests off the ship before we head into harm's way."

"Good point," Bowie said. He sighed. "I agree with your assessment, Nick. We're *not* ready for this. But it doesn't look like we're going to have much of a choice." He scanned the message again. "I'll contact the bridge and order the Officer of the Deck to steam due-west to get us moving in the right direction until the Navigator has a chance to lay out a new nav-track. Have Ops get on the satellite phone and arrange a helo for the civilians, and then pass the word to have all officers gather in the wardroom for briefing and tactical planning."

He dropped the message on his desk. "We should try to tune into a satellite news feed. CNN may not exactly be a reliable intelligence source, but if things are really heating up in Kamchatka, they probably know about it by now. I've got a feeling we're about to stick our head in the lion's mouth. If we don't want to get it bitten off at the neck, we're going to need all the smarts we can get."

CHAPTER 18

U.S. NAVAL HOSPITAL
YOKOSUKA, JAPAN
FRIDAY; 01 MARCH
0901 hours (9:01 AM)
TIME ZONE +9 'INDIA'

Lieutenant Eric Hogan, MD, United States Navy, yawned and rubbed the back of his neck as he ambled down the corridor toward the nurse's station. He needed a cup of coffee, but first he wanted to order some more labs on Seaman Landry, the young Sailor with the heart arrhythmia. The patient was lean and muscular, an obvious gym-hound, so the arrhythmias were probably just premature ventricular contractions, triggered by an electrolyte imbalance, or too much exercise.

But the patient's skin showed signs of pigmentation loading. That might mean nothing, but it could be a subtle symptom of hemochromatosis. They'd better pull some more blood and run the genetic differentiation tests, just to be on the safe side. The kid was probably tired of being poked with needles, but the only other way to rule out hemochromatosis would be a liver biopsy, and the seaman would like that a lot less.

Hogan made a left at the nurse's station, and walked the thirty or so feet to his office. He'd punch the new test orders into the computer, and then he could slip down to the break room for that coffee. And maybe a sweet roll, if the stuff in the vending machine didn't look too wilted.

He swung the door open to find two people waiting in his office: Captain Krantz, the commanding officer of the hospital, and a stranger wearing a dark gray civilian suit.

The captain nodded. "Good morning, Dr. Hogan. Come in, please. And close the door."

Hogan hesitated for a fraction of a second. He'd been stationed at Naval Hospital Yokosuka for the better part of two years, and the commanding officer had *never* come down to his office before. What was going on here? He supposed he was about to find out.

It was not a large office. Hogan had to squeeze past the civilian to reach a standing spot near his bookcase.

He nodded to his superior. "Good morning, Captain. What can I do for you, sir?"

Captain Krantz crossed his arms in front of his chest and leaned a hip against Hogan's desk. His words and tone of voice were cordial, but his posture and body language were overtly defensive. The captain was *not* a happy camper.

"Dr. Hogan, this is Agent Ross, from the Defense Intelligence Agency. He and his partner, Agent DuBrul, have just arrived on this morning's MEDEVAC flight from the Philippines. They were escorting the MEDEVAC patient, whom—I'm led to understand—is a foreign citizen under the protection of the U.S. State Department."

Hogan nodded, still not seeing what any of this had to do with him, or what the captain and this agent were doing in his office.

The man identified as Agent Ross was almost professionally nondescript. He was of about average height and weight, and his medium brown hair was cut in a style (or perhaps *anti*-style) typical of middle class office workers. Even his face was unremarkable. He had the sort of features that your eyes could glide over without settling. You could see the man, and then instantly forget him.

Only his eyes stood out. They were a quite ordinary shade of blue-green, but there was a concentration of focus in the agent's gaze that was nearly feral in quality.

Hogan was struck by the sudden and oblique certainty that this oddly-intense man remembered every person he had ever seen, and every word that had ever been spoken within his range of hearing. That almost certainly couldn't be true; the human mind didn't operate that way, but the impression stuck with Hogan anyway.

"The patient's real name is Oleg Yurievich Grigoriev," Ross said. The agent's voice was flat and atonal, an acoustic match for his undistinguished appearance.

"That information is classified," he continued. "The patient will be registered in this facility under the cover name of *Dmitry Hugo*. You will refer to him only by his cover name, and no member of the hospital staff is to be given any information regarding his identity, his medical condition, or his treatment regimen without direct authorization from Agent DuBrul or myself."

Hogan looked at his commanding officer. "Sir, I don't understand what's going on here. We're a U.S. military facility. We're prohibited from treating foreign civilians, and we're not trained or equipped to do cloak and dagger work. In any event, my patient load is already over max allowance. I ..."

The captain interrupted. "Dr. Hogan, your other patients will be handed off to other doctors. I'll take some of them myself, if I have to. As of this moment, you are relieved of all other duties for the duration of this case. Mr. Grigoriev ... excuse me, Mr. *Hugo* ... is your *only* patient. He will remain your sole priority until he leaves this hospital."

"Captain, I can't just ..."

"That's an order, Lieutenant."

"But, sir ..."

"*Lieutenant!*" It was a command.

Hogan nodded once. "Aye-aye, sir."

The captain's voice softened. "I don't like this any more than you do, doctor. But my orders come directly from Vice Admiral Gibson, the Surgeon General of the Navy. Those orders have been countersigned by Commander Naval Forces Japan, and Commander Pacific Fleet. I've been ordered to give these agents extreme latitude in the treatment of this patient, and to comply with any and *all* security protocols they require. That includes enforced secrecy and armed guards, if required."

He glanced at the agent, and then back to Hogan. "The patient, Mr. *Hugo*, is suffering from multiple gunshot wounds. His condition is critical, but stable, and I've been directed to assign my most experienced gunshot doctor to his case. You did three tours treating combat casualties in Iraq, so that would be *you*, Dr. Hogan. Do you have any questions?"

Hogan suppressed a huff of incredulity. He had about four thousand questions. In all likelihood, most of them would never be answered. He decided to try an easy one.

"What will I do for staff, Captain?"

"You can hand-select a team of nurses and corpsmen. Get your list to the XO, and we'll pull them out of the duty rotation and put them at your fulltime disposal."

"Try to select people who can keep their mouths shut," Agent Ross said. "Keep your team as small as possible. Use whoever you need to get the job done, but don't pad the roster. The fewer people we involve, the easier it will be to keep this low-key. And make damned sure they understand that they talk about this to *no one*. I don't want to lock up any of your people for talking out of school, but I will if I have to."

"You can't arrest people for talking," Hogan said.

Ross showed him a grim little smile with no amusement in it. "Wrong answer. This is a matter of the utmost national security. A leak could endanger the lives of literally *millions* of American citizens. If one of your people talks and I find out about it, I'll shoot him for treason myself, and take my chances with a Federal judge."

Hogan threw a questioning look at his commanding officer. Was this clown for real?

"I don't think we need to resort to threats," Captain Krantz said.

Ross straightened the lapels of his suit jacket. "I just want to make sure everyone understands how serious this is. We all have to be on the same wavelength here."

"This is crazy," Hogan said. "I'm a doctor, not a spook, or an operative, or whatever you call it."

"A doctor is all we want you to be," Ross said. "Leave the spook stuff to us."

Hogan said nothing.

"I can't tell you very much," Agent Ross said. "You don't have the clearance, or the need to know. But I'll tell you what I can, so that you'll have some idea of why these precautions are necessary. Does that sound reasonable?"

"I guess so," Hogan said.

"Mr. *Hugo*," Ross said, placing emphasis on the cover name, "was—until recently—the go-between in a deal between two foreign powers. I can't give you details, but the deal involves the transfer and possible employment of weapons of mass destruction. I'm talking the *big* stuff; not piddly crap like Anthrax or chemical warfare."

Hogan and his commanding officer watched Agent Ross without speaking.

"Six days ago," Ross said, "one or both of the foreign powers in question decided that Mr. Hugo's services were no longer required. They left him in an alley in Manila, with a half-dozen 5.8mm assault rifle bullets as a parting gift. They think he's dead, and we've gone to considerable effort to encourage that belief. If they find out that he is *not* dead—if, for instance, they should discover that their former associate is recovering in a U.S. military hospital in Japan—they're going to want to come back and finish the job. Because Mr. Hugo knows things that they cannot allow us to discover. And Mr. Hugo has already indicated that he's willing to share that information with us, in exchange for political asylum."

Agent Ross raised his eyebrows. "The guys who tried to murder Mr. Hugo are not nice people, Dr. Hogan. We don't want those people visiting your hospital. We don't want them going after you, or your staff, or your collective families. Because—if this slips—they *will* come after you, doctor. And they prefer to operate with leverage, so they'll probably go after your families first. Do you understand?"

Hogan nodded. His mouth suddenly felt too dry to speak.

"Excellent," said Agent Ross. "Your captain has kindly consented to loan us a private room on the fourth deck. I believe you usually reserve them for Flag Officers and government VIPs. Agent DuBrul and the MEDEVAC crew are getting Mr. Hugo settled into the room now, and setting up basic equipment with the help of the fourth deck staff."

"We know the fourth deck personnel are going to ask some questions," Captain Krantz said. "So Agents Ross and DuBrul have supplied us with a ready-made cover story. We're hoping that it will keep questions to a minimum."

Ross nodded. "Hospital personnel will be informed that Mr. Hugo is a mid-echelon diplomat, attached to the office of the assistant secretary of state for Eastern European Affairs. Further questions will not be encouraged. If people get too nosey, we'll drop hints that Mr. Hugo was injured by Chechen separatists during a diplomatic mission in the Caucasus mountains. We'll also let it be known that the incident is under investigation, and that anyone who pokes his nose into an ongoing Federal inquiry will find himself answering some very unpleasant questions."

Hogan nodded mutely.

"Either Agent DuBrul or I will be within eye contact of your patient at all times," Ross said. "Security will be supplemented around-the-clock, by an armed Marine guard. The Marines have been briefed. They will not interfere with your duties. Make sure your people don't interfere with *theirs*."

He held out a green cardboard folder. "Here's the patient's medical file. It covers his treatment following the shooting. In addition to the paper file, the folder contains digital copies of all x-rays, pre-op and post-op photos, lab results, MRIs, what have you. We need to talk to this patient, doctor. We need to ask him a lot of questions, and he has to be conscious enough and healthy enough to answer. That's your job."

Hogan accepted the folder without opening it.

"You can look that over, and start making your list of personnel," Ross said. He glanced at his watch. "Let's meet in Mr. Hugo's room in an hour."

"Agent Ross?" Hogan's voice was nearly a croak. "What if your cover story doesn't keep the lid on?"

Ross shrugged. "Then the guys who shot your patient are going to come knocking. And a lot of innocent people are going to get hurt."

CHAPTER 19

WHITE HOUSE
PRESIDENTIAL EMERGENCY OPERATIONS CENTER
WASHINGTON, DC
FRIDAY; 01 MARCH
9:24 PM EST

President Chandler nodded toward the television screen. "Run it again, Greg."

National Security Advisor Gregory Brenthoven pointed the remote control toward the oversized television and punched a button.

White House Chief of Staff Veronica Doyle, Secretary of Defense Rebecca Kilpatrick, and the Chairman of the Joint Chiefs of Staff—Army General Horace Gilmore—sat in silence as the video disc chapter-skipped to the beginning and the recorded news feed began again.

The screen filled with an establishing shot of Sergiei Mikhailovich Zhukov, framed against the giant statue of Lenin in the park at Ploshad Lenina. A light snow was falling, adding to the thick blanket covering the ground. A pair of uniformed soldiers stood behind the newly self-proclaimed President of Kamchatka, *Nikonova* assault rifles held at port arms, their breathing marked by plumes of vapor.

The ticker at the bottom of the screen flared with the CNN logo and a graphic depicting a map of the Russian Federation with the Kamchatka peninsula broken off like a piece from a jigsaw puzzle. A snippet of the Russian national anthem played as the words *'Crisis in Russia'* scrolled below the graphics.

The camera zoomed in for a close-up until Zhukov filled the screen. Dressed in a double-breasted greatcoat of dark wool and a black Ushanka hat, he looked like an old Soviet hardliner, which indeed he was.

Zhukov stared into the camera and began speaking in Russian. The voice of the CNN interpreter cut in a few seconds later with the English translation.

"I speak now to the people of the *Rodina*—the great land of Russia, who is mother to us all. You have learned by now of the events unfolding in this small corner of our great nation. Perhaps you have heard our struggle described as an uprising, or an insurgency." He shook his head. "Those are the wrong words. Those are the words of weak-willed fools who would have you believe that what happens here is the act of a handful of delinquents and miscreants." His heavy eyebrows came down like hammers. "No! This is not an uprising. This is not a riot among criminals. It is a *revolution*. It is a spark to ignite the flame that will illuminate the world!"

Zhukov turned his head to the left and then to the right. "Look around you, people of Russia. Look at what we have become. Look at how far the great Russian empire has fallen. A few short years ago, we were the greatest country this earth had ever seen. And now we are the largest third-world nation in history."

His voice climbed to a shout, nearly eclipsing the voice of the CNN translator. "Where has our greatness gone? Where has our power gone? Where has our honor gone? And the will of the great Russian people? I will *tell* you where they have gone! They have been *stolen* from us. They have been leached away from us by treachery and fraud."

Zhukov lowered his voice. "The West could not defeat the Soviet Union with tanks, and missiles, and soldiers. Our might was too great. Our courage was like iron. So they defeated us with lies, and with lust for material objects. They were afraid to face the naked power of the Soviet military, so they attacked our national ideals instead. They whispered their capitalist perversions into our ears until our minds were clouded. They eroded our internal values, made us lust after designer jeans and cellular telephones until we lost all touch with our moral center."

His eyebrows drew even tighter. "And it worked. We stumbled blindly into their velvet-lined trap and we were destroyed."

"Look at us," he said again. "Look at the Rodina, the great land of Russia, the invincible Soviet empire. We are nothing. We are *less* than nothing. We have traded our national identity, our strength, and our self-respect for microwave ovens and video games. We made a whore's bargain with the enemies of our country, and now we lay in the gutter, violated and bleeding, wondering how we could have fallen so far."

He pointed a thick index finger toward the camera. "It stops *here*! It stops *now*! Like Vladimir Ilyich before me, I *DECLARE* THE REVOLUTION! I have raised the sword and drawn the blood of the true Russia's enemies. There will be more blood, I am certain. But no price is too high for reclaiming Russia's rightful place in the world."

"What has happened here is only the first step," he said. "I proclaim the independence of Kamchatka. As of this moment, Kamchatka is a sovereign country, entitled to the recognition and rights enjoyed by all nations. And I will make this new nation the cornerstone of the reborn Russia."

Zhukov's features softened. "My fellow Russians, I do not raise my fist against you. We are brothers and sisters, children of the Motherland. Together we are the rightful inheritors of the Russian dream, and together we will seize that dream and return our nation to its former greatness. I invite you, all true people of Russia, to join me in taking back that which is rightfully ours."

His voice changed pitch, became lower and harder. "To the false government in Moscow, I say this … You cannot stop what has begun here. You are not the leaders of this nation, no matter what titles and honors you have conferred upon yourselves. You are parasites and fools. You have betrayed the very people you were sworn to protect. You have brought Russia to her knees. Now I order you to stand aside as the true patriots of this country lift their beloved mother to her feet."

Zhukov lifted his right hand and clenched it into a fist. "If you attempt to interfere, the will of the Russian people will rise up to crush you. And I, Sergiei Mikhailovich, will be the instrument of their anger."

He slowly lowered his fist. "You have read your reports by now. You know what I have at my disposal. But what you do not know—what you *cannot* know—is that my resolve is stronger than you can imagine. If you test me, I will do that which you fear above all things. I will use the weapons at my disposal."

His eyebrows came down until his eyes were nearly slits. "I do not bluff, and I will not negotiate. The revolution is *now*, and it is utterly unstoppable. Your choice is simple. Step aside, or die."

The camera held on Zhukov's face for a few seconds as the English interpretation wound down, then the scene cut to the CNN studio where a grim-faced news anchor began the inevitable follow-up commentary.

The national security advisor thumbed the remote again, and the screen froze. "That's about it, Mr. President. The rest of the news cycle amounts to speculation and tail-chasing."

President Chandler closed his eyes and rubbed his temples with the heels of his hands. He opened his eyes and let out a deep breath. "Somebody please tell me that this lunatic is bluffing."

The secretary of defense nodded. "He may very well *be* bluffing, sir. The Russian Ministry of Defense says he's full of hot air, at least with regard to his thinly-veiled threats about going nuclear. Our satellite imagery confirms that Zhukov's rebels were only able to put one ballistic missile submarine to sea. The other two ballistic missile subs are still tied to the pier at Rybachiy naval station, possibly because he couldn't find enough nutcases among the Russian sailors to crew more than one submarine. But whatever the reason, all of Zhukov's eggs are in one basket. If the Russians can take out that one missile sub, Mr. Zhukov's nuclear threat evaporates."

The White House chief of staff leaned back in her chair. "Madame Secretary, how sure are we that the Russians *can* knock out that missile sub?"

"The Russians are pretty confident," the secretary of defense said. "Their attack submarine, the *Kuzbass*, is in an excellent position to intercept and destroy Zhukov's ballistic missile sub before it reaches the Sea of Okhotsk."

The president made a steeple of his fingers. "So we're waiting for *one* Russian submarine to destroy *another* Russian submarine? Do we have a fallback plan?"

"We don't think we're going to need one," General Gilmore said. "Mr. President, the *Kuzbass* is an *Akula* class attack sub. Fast, quiet, and very *very* good at hunting other submarines. The missile sub, the *Zelenograd*, is an older Delta III class boat. Her missiles are deadly against land-based targets, but the Chief of Naval Operations assures me that she won't last ten seconds in a shooting match with an *Akula*."

Gregory Brenthoven smiled, *"His* missiles."

The General frowned. "Pardon me, sir?"

"Russian ships and submarines are male," Brenthoven said. "But never mind that. I didn't mean to interrupt. Please continue, General."

The general scratched his chin. "That's about it, sir. The *Kuzbass* will sink the missile sub. If that doesn't work, the Russian Navy chases the missile sub under the ice pack, where they can hunt it down and kill it at their leisure. I guess that's our fallback plan: let the Russian Navy trap the missile sub if they can't kill it outright."

Veronica Doyle glanced at her palmtop computer. "And we're absolutely certain that this submarine can't launch missiles through the ice?"

Brenthoven nodded. "The Delta III has no ice penetration capability. Once that submarine is under the ice, it won't be able to launch."

"There could be millions of lives at stake here," the president said. "I'm not comfortable with any plan that amounts to chasing the snake into a corner and tossing a blanket over it. And I'm not particularly crazy about leaving it up to the Russians to do the work."

"Understood, sir." the secretary of defense said. "But our options are fairly limited at the moment. Moscow has made it unmistakably clear that

U.S. involvement is *not* welcome. Their diplomatic language is only about two notches short of outright threats. If we insert ourselves into what they regard as an internal situation, we may find that *both* sides are ready to shoot us in the head."

"What you're basically telling me," the president said, "is that we sit on our hands and hope nobody decides to push the button?"

"We're not happy about it either, sir," General Gilmore said. "The Navy has ordered a pair of stealth destroyers into the area to keep an eye on things, and the Air Force and National Reconnaissance Office are getting us all the satellite coverage we need. We'd like to get one of our own subs up there, but—with Russia trying to kill Zhukov's sub, and Zhukov's insurgents trying to kill Russian subs—that could easily blow the lid off the powder keg. Both sides in this conflict are ready to shoot first and ask questions later. Any direct involvement on our part is likely to provoke the kind of response we don't even want to *think* about."

"Which brings us back to sitting on our hands," the president said.

The door opened and a young Marine lieutenant walked in, carrying a red and white striped folder. He went directly to General Gilmore, the Chairman of the Joint Chiefs, and spoke softly to the general as he handed over the folder.

General Gilmore opened the folder and read the short document it contained. After a few seconds, he laid it on the table in front of him. "Mr. President, we've just received word from the Russian Ministry of Defense. The *Kuzbass* has been destroyed."

The president's eyebrows shot up. "*What?* How did an aging missile submarine manage to get the drop on an *Akula* class hunter-killer?"

"It wasn't the missile sub," General Gilmore said. "Apparently the *Kuzbass* was destroyed three days ago, during a scheduled training exercise with a TU-142 anti-submarine warfare aircraft based out of Yelizovo. The exercise was scheduled as a non-firing event, but early assessments suggest that the TU-142 dropped one or more torpedoes on the *Kuzbass*." He looked down at the folder. "The timing of the exercise appears to correspond to an unidentified explosion recorded by our Navy's acoustic surveillance arrays in the region."

The White House chief of staff cocked her head to one side. "The Russians are just *now* finding out that one of their submarines was destroyed three days ago?"

The general nodded. "I'm not intimately familiar with the communication cycles for Russian submarines, but I know that *our* subs like to communicate as little as possible. They have to surface or come to periscope depth to raise an antenna above the water, and that makes them vulnerable. It makes them easier to detect acoustically, and their electronic transmissions can give away their position. Since their mission and their survival depend on remaining undetected, they communicate as little as possible."

"There are technologies for letting a submerged submarine know that it needs to come shallow for communication," the national security advisor said. "We call our methods *bell-ringers*. I don't know what the Russians call theirs."

"Neither do I," the general said. "But the Russians have been trying to communicate with the *Kuzbass* since Wednesday morning, with no joy."

The president frowned. "This anti-submarine warfare aircraft that attacked *Kuzbass*, where was it from?"

"It was based out of Yelizovo, Mr. President," General Gilmore said.

"And this Yelizovo is on Kamchatka?"

The general nodded. "Yes, Mr. President."

The president looked up at the television. The CNN news anchor was still frozen in mid-syllable. The words "Crisis in Russia" jittered slightly at the bottom of the screen, an artifact of the DVD player's pause feature. "Anybody here think the timing of the attack on *Kuzbass* was a coincidence?"

No one spoke.

"This dovetails too neatly with the onset of hostilities in Petropavlovsk," President Chandler said. "Zhukov planned the attack on *Kuzbass*, and he set it up in advance. He needed to ensure that his missile submarine had a clear path into the Sea of Okhotsk."

The secretary of defense pinched her lower lip. "The Russians are going to bottle that sub up. It'll be trapped under the ice, and it won't be able to launch its missiles."

The president shook his head slowly, his eyes still locked on the motionless image of the television newscaster. "Zhukov is thinking farther ahead than we are. He's *planning* farther ahead. He's got it all laid out. He already knows how he's going to launch those missiles, ice or no ice."

The president sat up and looked at the secretary of defense. "Zhukov's not bluffing. He can launch. He's *planning* to launch. Count on it."

CHAPTER 20

USS TOWERS (DDG-103)
NORTHERN PACIFIC OCEAN
SATURDAY; 02 MARCH
1835 hours (6:35 PM)
TIME ZONE +11 'LIMA'

Ann Roark took a sip of her coffee and made a face. "Ugh! How do the Navy guys drink this crap?"

Sheldon Miggs finished pouring his own cup from the wardroom coffee urn, and carried it carefully to the chair next to Ann's. "Are you kidding? This is good Navy java." He made a face of mock machismo. "It'll put hair on your chest, Sailor!"

Ann treated him to her best *you-are-a-complete-idiot* glare. "In case you haven't noticed, I'm not a Sailor. And unlike certain middle aged wanna-bes, I don't have any desire to *be* a Sailor." She glanced down at her chest. "Nor do I want hair sprouting from my cleavage. That's a waxing experience I don't even want to *think* about."

She lifted one eyebrow and stared pointedly at Sheldon's receding hairline. "But if this stuff really grows hair, you should think about rubbing some on your head."

Sheldon grinned. "Forty-thousand comedians out of work, and I have to get paired up with *Donna* Rickles."

Ann took another sip of the acrid coffee and swallowed with another grimace. "Who?"

Sheldon sighed. "Never mind, little princess. I'll explain when you're older."

Ann rubbed her nose with her middle finger, making certain that Sheldon could see that she was flipping him a covert *bird*.

After a few seconds, she let her hand drop and picked up her coffee cup, trying to decide whether or not to risk a third sip. Maybe if she downed two or three quick swallows, her taste buds would be too stunned to object. "So what's the latest from Captain Bligh? Any word on when we're getting off this floating madhouse?"

Sheldon took a big swallow of coffee. "His name is Captain *Bowie*. And they're trying to arrange rendezvous with a replenishment ship so they can do an underway refueling. We'll do a helo transfer to the replenishment ship, and then hopscotch from one ship to another until we get within helicopter range of Japan. They hop us over to one of the Japanese islands, and we catch a flight back to the States."

Ann snorted. "We were practically *in* the States thirty hours ago. These boneheads should have dropped us off in Alaska before heading out for parts unknown."

"The ship has immediate orders," Sheldon said. "The captain can't tell me *what* they've been ordered to do, but he did make it clear that it's time critical—whatever it is. They didn't have time to pull into port."

"That's not our problem," Ann said. "It's *their* problem. And it doesn't give them license to drag us off to who-knows-where. We're not members of the Secret Navy Club, and they can't just take us wherever they want without our consent. That's kidnapping."

"It's not kidnapping," Sheldon said. "And we already gave our consent, when we signed the releases to come onboard the ship in the first place. Somewhere in all that paperwork was a paragraph to the effect that this is a warship, and it's subject to no-notice changes of mission. There was also a line in there pointing out that the needs of the Navy come first, and the ship can't guarantee the time and date of our return." He sighed. "You signed it, Ann, and so did I. It's a standard clause. Every civilian tech-rep signs the same thing."

"And that gives them the right to treat us like cargo?"

"They're *not* treating us like cargo. We've got good accommodations, they're feeding us the same food that their senior officers eat, and we're getting paid overtime and sea-bonuses for every extra day we have to spend on the ship. So get your fur down and try to enjoy the trip. We're riding a stealth destroyer on a high-speed run to a secret location. How much cooler does it get than that?"

Ann took another swallow of the horrid Navy coffee. "You may be enjoying yourself, Sheldon, but I'm not. I came here to demonstrate the Mouse prototype; I didn't sign on for secret missions. Why didn't they get a helicopter to pick us up when we were still close to Alaska?" She deliberately avoided the stupid Navy-speak abbreviation. The word was *helicopter*, not *helo*. And Mouse was a *robot*, not an *unmanned underwater vehicle*. Who did these clowns think they were kidding, anyway?

"They tried to get us a helo," Sheldon said. "But the flight deck on a destroyer is only rated for certain types of aircraft. Most civilian helicopters aren't configured for landing on a small-decked ship. And there aren't exactly a ton of Navy-configured helos in the Aleutian Island chain. The Ops Officer couldn't get the right kind of aircraft lined up before we were out of flight range."

Ann set her coffee cup on the table with a thump. "You believe everything the uniforms tell you, don't you? Why are you always making excuses for them? They screwed up. Why can't you just admit that?"

Sheldon set his own cup down gently. "Why do you hate them so much?"

Ann rolled her eyes. "Now we're doing dialogue from *A Few Good Men*? This is the part where I'm supposed to ask why you *like* them so much? Well, newsflash, Sheldon—I *don't* hate them. I can't say I *like* them very much, but that's not the same thing. And it isn't even really *them* I dislike. As military guys go, Navy people are probably less offensive than most. But they make their living killing people, Sheldon. Did you ever stop to think about that? Worse than that, they *signed up* to kill people. They didn't get drafted or forced into the job. It was a career decision for them. You chose customer relations; I chose electronics and robotics; and they selected *war* as their chosen profession."

Ann picked up her coffee cup, but didn't drink from it. Couldn't Sheldon see it? At some point in their lives, every one of these military-drones made a conscious decision to make war for a living. They stood in line, took written tests, endured humiliating physical examinations under the guise of health care, and willingly submitted to training designed to program their minds for wholesale slaughter in the name of *truth*, *justice*, and *the American way*.

Sheldon shook his head. "It's not like that, Ann. These guys aren't itching for a fight. If you watched some of their training exercises, you'd know that. I've seen them at work for years, and you'd be amazed at how far they'll go to prevent a fight. Their entire mindset is built around rules of engagement and safeguards to prevent escalation. Given the opportunity, they'll do their very best to avoid pulling the trigger."

"Don't tell *me* about the military," Ann said. "I was an Army brat, Sheldon. I grew up around people like this. I know what they're like. They practice for war. They *train* for war, and they *think* about war, and they *prepare* for war. If you think about it, that's a pretty sick thing to do for a living."

"You don't get it," Sheldon said. "Firefighters prepare for fires every day. They train to fight fires, and they think about fighting fires, and they practice fighting fires all the time. But that's just so they'll be ready when the need arises. It doesn't mean they *hope* your house is going to burn down. Being ready to fight fires is not the same as wanting to do it."

Ann stood up. "No, Sheldon, *you* don't get it. Firefighters don't *cause* destruction; they stop it." She pointed to a trio of paintings on the far wall: a young officer in an old-fashioned white uniform, flanked by paintings of two warships. "These guys blow stuff up. Buildings. Homes. People. These guys don't put the fires out. They *start* the fires. That's what they do."

She turned and stalked out of the wardroom, letting the door slam behind her.

CHAPTER 21

The first wave of the attack came from the south, a flight of five TU-160 bombers, cutting through the night sky 13,000 meters above the dark surface of the Pacific ocean. Code-named "Blackjack" by NATO, the dart-shaped supersonic jet aircraft were equipped with variable-geometry wings that made them capable of covert low-altitude flight profiles. But there was no need for deceptive maneuvers tonight. The launch point for their weapons was well outside the detection range of any radars or sensors based on the Kamchatka peninsula.

The mission plan called for the bombers to approach at altitude, make their attacks, and retreat at altitude—all without concern for stealth. And the Russian pilots followed their orders precisely.

The only hitch in the plan was minor, and easily corrected. The bombers caught a tailwind on the north-bound leg of the mission, and they reached the designated launch coordinates three minutes ahead of schedule. In accordance with the strike plan, the aircraft turned left and circled once before re-converging on the launch point three minutes later.

At exactly 0920 Zulu (10:20 PM local time), the bombers launched their weapons. Twenty Kh-555 cruise missiles, four from each of the bombers, dropped away from the planes and fell several hundred meters before their engines fired.

In unison, twenty pairs of stubby wings extended and snapped into place, and twenty Soyuz R95-300 turbojets flared to life, smearing translucent streaks of blue flame against the night sky.

Immediately after the transition to powered flight, one of the missiles experienced an engine flameout. Robbed of its power, the weapon tumbled out of the sky, to disintegrate upon impact with the ocean below.

Each of the remaining missiles automatically initiated a satellite uplink, to check its geographic location against the constellation of Russian

GLONASS positioning satellites in orbit 19,000 kilometers above the earth. Satisfied that their respective positions were within acceptable mission parameters, each missile dove to its programmed cruise altitude just 100 meters above the waves.

By the time the missiles reached their first navigational waypoint, the bombers had already turned west toward home. For the crews of the TU-160s, the mission was over. For the nineteen cruise missiles streaking toward Kamchatka, the mission was just beginning.

⚓ ⚓ ⚓

Russian Naval Formation:

The second wave of the attack came from a trio of Russian *Sovremenny* Class Destroyers steaming in a single column formation a dozen kilometers off the eastern coast of Kamchatka. All three ships—the *Osmotritel'nyy*, the *Boyevoy*, and the *Burny*—had seen hard duty during the Cold War, but not one of them had ever fired a shot under conditions of actual combat.

The strike plan had called for a fourth ship, but the *Bezboyaznenny* had suffered a crippling electrical fire during the transit, and had been forced to limp ignominiously back into port with the help of oceangoing tugs. Given the condition of the Russian surface navy and the high-speed transit from Vladivostok, most of the Russian Sailors considered it something of a minor miracle that three of the four ships had made the journey intact.

Standing on the bridge of the *Osmotritel'nyy*, Kapitan, Second Rank Igor Volkov stared through the port side bridge windows of his ship. As the senior naval officer in the formation, he was in command. In accordance with his orders, all three warships were running black—their radars and radios silent, all external lights extinguished. Out on the horizon, the Kamchatkan coastline was a smudge of shadow against the darkened waves.

The ships moved slowly, barely maintaining steerageway, partly to prevent the formation of visible propeller wakes, and partly to ensure that they would be within range of their targets when Volkov gave the order to commence fire.

In addition to missiles and torpedoes, each of the warships was armed with two AK-130 naval gun systems: one mounted near the bow, and the other near the stern. Designed and built during the Cold War, the AK-130s each carried a pair of liquid-cooled 130 mm cannon barrels on triaxially-stabilized gun mounts. Roughly equivalent in speed and firepower to the 5-inch naval artillery of the United States Navy, the AK-130 was one of the most powerful gun systems in the modern world.

The guns were already locked onto their respective target coordinates, elevation drive motors moaning quietly as the fire control computers kept the long steel cannon barrels stabilized against the rolling motion of the ships. Like the ships themselves, the guns had been designed and built during the Cold War, by Soviet engineers and technicians who had no doubt assumed that their handiwork would someday be used to kill Americans. But the guns were not aimed at Americans. They were aimed at Russian buildings, in a Russian city. And when the guns spoke in anger for the very first time, their rain of death would fall on Russian citizens.

Volkov continued to stare out the bridge windows at the darkened coast of Kamchatka. A lifetime spent defending his country, and it all came down to this. He had been ordered to kill his own people.

He knew it had to be done. The insurrection had to be stopped in its tracks or many more people would die. Maybe even the entire world, if that mad idiot Zhukov managed to make good on his nuclear threats. But understanding the necessity did not make Volkov feel much better about killing his own countrymen.

Some of Zhukov's words had the ring of truth to them. Russia *did* have problems. *Big* problems. And some of those problems were undoubtedly the result of his country's blind leap into an economic and political model that the Russian people did not understand. But the solution to Russia's problems was not conquest. The Rodina could not regain her footing by holding a gun to the world's head.

The clock clicked over to 2300 (1000 Zulu). Volkov lifted the handset of the radio telephone and held the receiver to his ear. He took a breath and broke the long-held radio silence. "All ships, this is Formation Command. Commence firing."

The night was shattered by man-made thunder as six gun barrels spat fire and steel into the darkness. An instant later, the secondary barrels for all six gun mounts fired as the double-barreled weapons fell into reciprocating cycles of load and shoot.

Volkov lowered the radio telephone handset to its cradle just as explosions began erupting along the coastline. He had no way of knowing that some of those explosions came from a flight of nineteen cruise missiles whose arrival had been timed to coincide with the naval bombardment from his ships. He felt every fireball that mushroomed in the darkness, and he mentally took responsibility for every one. They seared themselves into his brain, and he imagined that he could hear the screams of the injured and dying, transmitted to him across the impossible distance on the carrier wave of his own guilt.

He wondered if there might not be a special corner of Hell reserved for warriors who murdered their own people. And in the gloom of the unlit bridge, Volkov began to pray.

CHAPTER 22

Consciousness came slowly to Oleg Grigoriev, and its return was not at all welcome. He decided not to try opening his eyes yet.

He was inhumanly tired, and he felt as though every millimeter of his body had been beaten with an iron pipe. The worst of the pain was held at a distance by the drugs given to him by the American doctors. He could sense the ugly mass of it, waiting for him on the other side of the protective haze of narcotics. If the doctors relaxed their vigil, it would come for him again.

He tried to raise his right hand, the one that was free from those damnable tubes and needles. A few centimeters above the mattress, his muscles failed and his hand fell back to the green hospital sheet. He was as weak as a child. No ... Weaker. A child could stand. Grigoriev could not even lift his own arm.

What had happened to the tough old Russian bear? Had a few Chinese bullets really brought a battle-hardened Red Army soldier so low? Perhaps they had.

All he could do for now was rest and wait for his body to mend. His strength would begin to return as his wounds were healed. Or would it?

His brain was muddled by the drugs, perhaps too clouded to take accurate stock of his body. The pain wasn't getting better; he was sure about that. He didn't seem to be getting stronger. His body was so feeble that he could only remain awake for a few moments at a time. Was he actually improving? It didn't feel that way.

For the first time, he wondered if he might be dying. The Americans had not said so. But their government wanted the information in Grigoriev's brain. They needed his cooperation. If he was dying, they might not tell him.

Or perhaps they would. The Americans were confusing. Their values and priorities were so odd. The doctors, nurses, and orderlies in this place wore military uniforms and insignia, but nearly all of them seemed to put medical duties ahead of military obligations. They were healers first, and warriors second. Or maybe, not at all.

It was puzzling. Did it make these people less dangerous as adversaries? Or more dangerous? He didn't know. And Zhukov, the bastard who had thrown Grigoriev to that pack of Chinese wolves in Manila, probably didn't know either.

Grigoriev opened his eyes. That small act took far more effort than it should have. The room was a smear of blurred shapes.

He blinked once, and concentrated on dragging the shapes into focus.

One of the American agents, the tall one, spotted Grigoriev's open eyes and crossed to the bed in two or three long strides.

They watched him closely, these Americans. Not so much the medical people. They monitored his breathing and heartbeat, the dressings on his wounds, and the collection of machines wired to Grigoriev's body like a telephone switchboard. The others, the ones in the dark suits, were never more than a meter or two away from Grigoriev's bed. They even watched him when he was sleeping; he was sure of it.

The men in suits would be CIA. Or perhaps FBI. It didn't matter. For Grigoriev's purposes, one would work as well as the other.

He took a breath and steeled himself to speak. "Bring paper ..." His voice was a whispering rasp.

The man in the suit stepped closer. "I'm Agent DuBrul ..."

"Bring paper," Grigoriev whispered again. The words hurt his throat, and he nearly ran out of air on the last syllable. He breathed heavily for a few seconds, gathering strength before continuing.

The American agent reached into his pocket and pulled out a notebook. "I have paper."

"Write this ..." Grigoriev rasped.

"I'm ready," the agent said. He stood with pen poised above the notebook.

"Five ... eight ..." Grigoriev paused to catch his breath. "... two ... nine ..." He paused again. "One ... five ... five."

He was fighting for breath now. His blood was roaring in his ears, and he could feel the wound in his chest pulsing in time to the pounding of heartbeat. One of the medical machines close to his bed began bleating rhythmically.

The door flew open, and a doctor came straight to his bed.

"Two ..." Grigoriev croaked. "... Zero ..."

"That's enough," the doctor said. He leaned over Grigoriev. "Just relax, sir. Don't try to talk."

The agent looked at his notebook and read back the numbers. "Five-eight-two-nine-one-five-five-two-zero. Is that correct? What does that mean?"

"I said that's *enough*!" the doctor snapped.

The pain came out of nowhere, squeezing Grigoriev's heart like a fist. His vision was narrowing. "Tell ..." The room was a tunnel now, the doctor and the agent at the far end of a lengthening tube of darkness. "Tell ... your ... president."

The bleating of the machine became a continuous squeal, and the hospital room disappeared.

CHAPTER 23

Standing at the mouth of the cave, Sergiei Mikhailovich Zhukov looked down the snowy side of Koryaksky mountain toward Petropavlovsk, the capital city of his new nation. The missile attacks and naval bombardment had ceased—for the moment at least—and thick columns of smoke were rising from at least a dozen places in his city, to mingle with the slate gray clouds blowing in from Siberia.

Zhukov could not hear the sirens from this distance, but he was certain that they were in full-cry as emergency crews rushed to contain fires and rescue the injured. The distance also insulated him from the cries of the wounded and the dying. That was probably for the best. He could not allow his human instinct for compassion to influence his thoughts and actions. He must follow the example set by Lenin, and accept the fact that blood, and pain, and death were part of the cost of revolution.

Later, when the struggle was won and Russia had regained her rightful position as a world power, the people who died here would be properly honored. He would see to that. The history books would record this as the *Siege of Petropavlovsk*, and he would have the names of those who lost their lives here engraved on every monument in the new Russia. But those were thoughts for the future. If he was going to bring that future about, he needed to concentrate on the present.

He looked again at the columns of smoke. As he had expected, the majority of the damage appeared to be concentrated on the naval station at Rybachiy, and the Oblast government buildings at Ploshad Lenina. Those doddering old fools in Moscow were reacting exactly as he had predicted. By attacking the seat of his government and his largest military base, they hoped to cut off the head of his revolution and break its back in a single

121

stroke. It obviously hadn't occurred to them that he would not sit still and wait for their axe to fall.

The attacks had been brief, but surprisingly ferocious: an astonishing amount of firepower brought to bear in a very short period of time. The Ministry of Defense had taken a page from America's book, and tried their own version of the infamous *Shock and Awe* tactic. But Zhukov had studied American tactics as well. More importantly, he had studied the tactics of America's enemies. One of the best lessons had come from the mountains of Afghanistan ... *Your enemy cannot destroy what he cannot find.*

Kamchatka was one of the most volcanic regions on the globe. Koryaksky, Avachinsky, and Kozelsky, the three dormant volcanic mountains closest to Petropavlovsk, were riddled with lava caves, and Zhukov had equipment, supplies, and men hidden in most of them. If the mighty United States military could not root Taliban fighters out of the mountains and caves of Afghanistan, the crumbling Russian army would have no better luck trying to pry Zhukov's own forces out of the caverns and volcanoes of Kamchatka.

Not that they wouldn't try, once they discovered that their clumsy attempt at a decapitation attack had failed. But he had no intention of letting things go that far.

Weapons were engines of power. The more terrible a weapon was, the greater its power. Lenin had understood that. So had Stalin and Khrushchev. But Brezhnev, with his love for expensive clothes and cars from America and Western Europe, had not understood. And the imbeciles who had stumbled along so blindly in Brezhnev's footsteps had shown even less understanding of the simple logic of power.

The door to the command post opened behind him, and Zhukov turned to see one of his lieutenants walk between the pair of Chinese soldiers who guarded the entrance to the facility. The lieutenant strode briskly toward his new president, sparing not even a glance for the Chinese guards, as though even the act of looking at them was beneath him.

Zhukov understood the lieutenant's feelings. Apart from the fact that Asians were ethnically classified as *chernyee*, or *black*, to the burgeoning groundswell of racism in Russia, these chernyee were mercenaries. They had come here to fight, not because they supported the reestablishment of communism in Russia, but because their politburo—the Central Committee of the People's Republic of China—was willing to trade the lives of forty thousand combat troops for access to crucial nuclear missile technology.

Their black uniforms had been stripped of labels and insignia; they carried no identification or personal effects, and the serial numbers had been removed from their weapons. They had even been delivered by civilian automobile transport ships, with no traceable connection to the Chinese government. Their political masters in Beijing were taking every precaution to allow themselves maximum deniability if Zhukov's plans for revolution went astray.

Of course, the Chinese soldiers had been told none of this. They had been told only that they were part of a covert combat action that was crucial to the defense of their country. They had all received bonuses equal to three years worth of pay, with the promise of a matching bonus upon successful completion of the mission. That, plus the rigid discipline of the Chinese military, was enough to ensure their functional loyalty for the moment at least.

Zhukov had no illusions that the chernyee bastards would stay bought, but he wouldn't need them for very long. They were not the core of his revolution. They were merely the torch needed to light the fire.

The lieutenant halted, came to attention, and saluted. "Comrade President, there is news."

Zhukov returned the salute and accepted a small bundle of papers from the lieutenant's gloved left hand. "Thank you, Comrade Lieutenant." He glanced down at the papers. "Give me a summary."

The lieutenant dropped his salute, but remained at attention. "Comrade President, your staff is downloading press statements from *Pravda*, *Izvestia*, and several western news sources. They are all carrying essentially the same story. Moscow has issued a formal statement that the revolution has been put down. They claim to have wiped out our command and control infrastructure, and they are speculating that most of our senior officers and officials were killed by their cruise missile attacks. They confirm the destruction of your offices at Ploshad Lenina, and your private residence. You are listed as missing and presumed dead, Comrade President."

Zhukov smiled and thumped himself on the chest. "I must admit that I feel pretty good for a walking corpse."

The lieutenant returned his smile. "Yes, sir! The papers also report that the threat of nuclear action has passed, and that the *Zelenograd* is trapped under the ice pack, where it will be located and destroyed shortly."

Zhukov felt his smile widen a fraction. This was the news he had been waiting for. He nodded toward the man. "Thank you, Comrade Lieutenant. You may return to your duties."

The lieutenant saluted, did an about-face, and marched past the Chinese guards and into the command post.

When the door had closed behind the man, Zhukov looked down at the printouts from the newspaper websites. He'd read them later. For now, it was enough to feel them in his hand. Once again, Moscow was reacting as he had predicted.

He turned his eyes to the pillars of smoke rising from the city below him. He would let the story percolate through the various news medias for another couple of hours, to give most of the supposed experts an opportunity to weigh in on the swift destruction of his revolution. Then he would give the order for the next phase of the operation, and reveal to the world that so-called Russian government was populated by liars and fools.

CHAPTER 24

ICE PACK — NORTHERN SEA OF OKHOTSK
LATITUDE 58.29N / LONGITUDE 155.20E
SUNDAY; 03 MARCH
1001 hours (10:01 AM)
TIME ZONE +11 'LIMA'

The timing was precise. All six charges detonated at the same instant, and a circular stretch of the ice pack exploded into an expanding cloud of water vapor and ice fragments. When the rumble of the blast had faded to silence and the last of the scattered ejecta had fallen back to surface of the ice pack, a large opening—about thirty meters in diameter—remained in the ice. Between the displacement effect of the shockwave and the heat of the expanding gases, the hole was nearly clear of debris, leaving a sizeable circle of the Sea of Okhotsk open to the frigid Siberian sky.

Left alone, the newly-formed pocket of open sea would have begun to skin-over with new ice almost immediately. But it was not to be left alone, because the detonation of the shaped charges was only the tiniest precursor of the energies about to be channeled through this particular section of frozen ocean.

The water near the center of the opening began to foam, and the surrounding ice began to vibrate. An enormous bubble broke the surface of the water, followed a millisecond later by the blunt-nosed cylindrical shape of a Russian R-29R nuclear missile.

Still riding the supercavitating gas bubble of its submerged launch system, the 35-ton missile had barely cleared the surface of the water when the liquid-fueled rocket engines of its first stage ignited. Nitrogen tetroxide merged with unsymmetrical dimethylhydrazine to feed the missile's fiery exhaust. With a roar like an insanely-massive blowtorch, the weapon leapt toward the sky on a silver-white column of smoke and flame.

Accelerating rapidly, it was moving at 5 kilometers a second—roughly four times the speed of a high-powered rifle bullet—when it blew through the thin layer of cirrostratus clouds in the upper troposphere and shot into the stratosphere. Three seconds later and still accelerating, the first stage burned out and the missile passed through 25,000 meters, where the deepening blue of the sky gave way to the blackness of space.

The engines of the second stage fired, blasting the upper third of the missile up and away from the burned out and empty hulk of the first stage. Relieved of its burden, the missile gained still more speed, climbing away on its own pillar of flame while the remains of the discarded first stage fell back to earth like a man-made meteor of scorched aluminum-magnesium alloy.

The second stage burned out at an altitude of 200 kilometers, triggering timed electrical pulses to a ring of small explosive charges in the mating collar that joined the second stage of the missile to the warhead bus. The explosives detonated instantly, fracturing the aerodynamic collar along carefully-engineered structural stress points. The inertia imparted by the small explosion was enough to separate the warhead bus from the expended second stage.

Referred to by missile engineers as *mechanical separation*, this final severance of the payload from its launch vehicle marked the end of the *boost* phase of the trajectory, and the beginning of the *ascent* phase. Moving at 7 kilometers per second, the bluntly-conical warhead bus no longer needed rocket engines to complete its journey. From this point forward, the earth's gravitational pull and the physics of ballistic flight would do all the work.

The trajectory of the weapon began to flatten now, nosing over into a curving arc toward the east, and that mass of land known to humans as *North America*.

⚓ ⚓ ⚓

21ST Space Operations Center (Sunnyvale, California):

Technical Sergeant Diane Claxton watched the screen of her SAWS console and inhaled softly through clenched teeth. This couldn't be right. This just *couldn't* be right. Ignoring the pulsing red alert icon at the top of her display screen, she tapped a rapid series of commands into her console and called up an off-axis view from another early warning satellite. The second bird—another U.S. Air Force *Eagle Eye* series surveillance satellite—was at the extreme edge of its operational footprint, so the images it produced were grainy and poorly-focused. Despite the lack of optical clarity, the feed from the second satellite confirmed the findings of the first.

Technical Sergeant Claxton adjusted her communications headset so that the microphone hung a few inches in front of her mouth. She keyed the mike. "Senior Watch Officer, this is Station Five. Eagle Eye is tracking a ballistic missile launch alert in sector green, grid reference twenty-eight alpha. The launch point appears to be south of Siberia and west of Kamchatka. Looks like the Sea of Okhotsk." She tapped in another sequence of keystrokes. "I have off-axis confirmation from a second Eagle Eye bird. Missile trajectory is east, toward California."

A voice crackled in the sergeant's left ear. "This is the Senior Watch Officer; I copy ballistic missile launch alert in sector green, grid reference twenty-eight alpha. Cross-check with PAVE PAWS for radar confirmation."

PAVE PAWS, short for Precision Acquisition Vehicle Entry Phased Array Warning System, was a long-range land-based radar network operated by the U.S. Air Force's Space Command. Its primary mission was to detect and track ballistic missiles that might pose a threat to U.S. territory.

It took less than a minute for the PAVE PAWS radar installation at Beale Air Force Base, California to corroborate the inbound missile. By that time, the installation at Clear Air Force Station, Alaska had locked on and was also tracking the missile. Both radars confirmed the findings of the Eagle Eye satellites: an unannounced missile launch, with a ballistic trajectory toward the United States.

The Senior Watch Officer lifted the handset of a blue telephone. The phone had no buttons or dial; it was a direct connection to North American Aerospace Defense Command in Cheyenne Mountain, Colorado. The Senior Watch Officer swallowed and then spoke the words he had trained for many times, but never expected to say. "This is Tripwire Command. I have emergency flash traffic for CINCNORAD... Code word *PINNACLE*."

⚓ ⚓ ⚓

White House, Presidential Emergency Operations Center (Washington, DC):

President Chandler was glad he was sitting, because his knees were so weak that he wasn't sure he could stand. He glanced around the room at the military and civilian personnel who staffed the PEOC. To outward appearances, they were going about the details of their respective jobs as if nothing out of the ordinary was happening. People studied video screens, worked at computer stations, spoke quietly into telephones and communications handsets, wrote on clipboards, and exchanged printouts and folders with the same intense but subdued efficiency they showed on any other day. How did they do that? How could they calmly go about their business when a nuclear missile was screaming toward the United States at twenty-five times the speed of sound?

Was it their training, or some unnatural level of personal discipline? Was it possible that it was all a front? Could they all be faking it, putting on the outward signs of professional detachment when they were really quaking in their boots?

This last idea made sense to him, because that's exactly what *he* was doing at the moment. On the outside, he was the leader of the most powerful nation on earth, thoughtful, decisive, and utterly unruffled by the emergency unfolding around them. On the inside, he was one step short of peeing in his pants. He wanted to run around the room, shrieking at the top of his lungs—not that his shaky knees were up to such an energetic task at the moment.

He jerked his gaze to the wall-sized geographic display screen. The image looked so harmless, just a thin red line curving from the Sea of Okhotsk to a point somewhere above the middle of the Pacific Ocean. As he watched, the arc disappeared from the screen for a fraction of a second, and then reappeared—redrawn slightly longer as the missile came closer to the West Coast of his country.

For all of its graphic simplicity, that curving red line represented destruction and death on a scale almost beyond the scope of imagination. In all of history, only two nuclear weapons had been used against human targets. Between them, the bombs codenamed '*Fat Man*' and '*Little Boy*' had devastated the Japanese cities of Hiroshima and Nagasaki, killing over 150,000 people. Another half million people had died from nuclear radiation over the following five years. The combined yield of those first two atomic bombs had been 36 kilotons: the destructive equivalent of 36,000 tons of conventional explosives.

The missile hurtling through the black reaches of near-earth space carried *three* warheads, each with a destructive yield of 200 kilotons. Combined, the destructive power of those warheads was more than fifteen times greater than the two most terrible weapons ever turned by man onto his fellow men.

A door opened at the rear of the room and the president glanced over his shoulder to see National Security Advisor Gregory Brenthoven walk into the operations center, followed by a young Marine lieutenant. The lieutenant made a beeline toward the Deputy Watch Officer, and the national security advisor pulled out a chair and seated himself at the briefing table.

The president turned back to the geographic display. The curving red line on the screen flashed again, and grew longer. The unfinished end of the arc continued to edge its way eastward, toward the coast of California.

The carnage at Nagasaki and Hiroshima had been so dire that the leaders of the most powerful nations in the world had, for the first time in history, shied away from using one of the weapons in their collective arsenals. Nuclear bombs and missiles had been built, tested in remote areas, and stockpiled against some unthinkable future. But they'd never again been used against human beings. Not until now...

The president felt a shudder coming on, and he clamped down on his muscles to suppress it. The Commander in Chief of the United States military could *not* get the shakes during a crisis.

It wasn't a personal fear thing. At least he could comfort himself with that knowledge. He'd been in life-threatening situations before, and he'd never reacted this way. He didn't want to die, but he wasn't terrified by the idea. He knew that it was in him to sacrifice his life, if the circumstances demanded.

This wasn't about self-preservation, or the safety of his family. That missile couldn't get anywhere *near* Washington. From its estimated launch position in the Sea of Okhotsk, the R-29R missile could hit any American city west of Denver. That put Washington, DC about 1,500 miles outside the target zone.

Personal safety wasn't the issue here. The *real* danger was in what that missile could trigger.

On the table in front of him lay a heavy ten-ring binder, with anodized aluminum covers and color-coded pages. Its official title was the _Single Integrated Operational Plan_, or _SIOP_. It was the strategic blueprint for nuclear war—America's plan for employing the ultimate Weapons of Mass Destruction.

The binder was open to *Section Orange*, the pages the color of children's aspirin. Bold block letters at the top of every page identified this section as "**RETALIATORY NUCLEAR STRIKE OPTIONS**."

But the president wasn't looking at the SIOP. His eyes remained fixed on the geographic display. That harmless looking line of red pixels on the video screen could turn out to be the opening stroke of Armageddon. He might be looking at the first shot of the last war mankind would ever fight. The one Einstein had spoken of as the end of the human species.

The president took a breath and exhaled sharply. "Talk to me, general. Give me the latest."

General Horace Gilmore, Chairman of the Joint Chiefs of Staff, looked up from a red and white striped folder of computer hardcopy. He paused for a second, as though marshalling his thoughts.

"Sir, we're getting the last of the readiness confirmations now. We are at DEFCON 1: full offensive and defensive nuclear readiness. All active missile squadrons are at full alert, and all Minuteman III silos are at launch-standby. The Navy has issued pre-launch warnings to all deployed Trident ballistic missile subs. The Air Force is scrambling B-2 bombers from Whiteman Air Force Base, and B-52s from Minot, and Barksdale."

The president held up a hand. "Wait a second … We're *already* launching bombers?"

The general nodded. "Yes, sir. It's standard operating procedure."

The president frowned. "*Strategic* bombers? Carrying *nuclear* weapons?"

General Gilmore nodded again. "Affirmative, Mr. President. Standard precautionary deployment." He glanced down at the computer printouts in the red and white striped folder. "The Vice President and the Secretary of Defense are in route to…"

The president cut him off. "Hold it. Just stop right there. I have *not* authorized the deployment of nuclear weapons. Who in the hell is launching bombers with nuclear payloads?"

Gregory Brenthoven cleared his throat. "Ah … Mr. President, that's a standard response. As soon as we confirmed the presence of an inbound nuclear missile, the Commander in Chief, North American Aerospace Defense Command declared an Air Defense Emergency. Precautionary deployment is within the scope of his authority, but that's as far as he can go without presidential authorization. He can put bombers in the air, but he can't order them to attack. Only *you* can do that, sir."

"That's correct, sir," the general said. He pointed to the open binder on the briefing table. "It's all spelled out in the Single Integrated Operational Plan. CINCNORAD is just ensuring that our strategic bomber wings don't get caught on the ground when that missile's warheads start hitting their targets."

The president paused for a second, and loosened his necktie. "I interrupted your briefing, General. Please continue."

The general glanced down at the striped folder. "Vice President Wainright and the Secretary of Defense are in route to the Alternate National Military Command and Control Center at Site Romeo. Per your orders, Homeland Security is issuing civil defense warnings to all cities and towns west of Burlington, Colorado. After we know the impact zones for the warheads, Homeland Security will coordinate with FEMA and the

National Weather Service to calculate fallout footprints. Then they'll issue radiation warnings in the affected areas and initiate quarantine protocols if necessary."

President Chandler nodded, partly in response to what the general had *not* said. When news of the incoming warheads began to take hold, there would be panic in the western states—assuming that it hadn't started already. The civil defense warning would advise people to stay off the roads and take shelter indoors, in their own homes where possible. But how many people would actually follow the guidelines? And how many would run to their cars and bolt for the nearest highway out of town?

The interstates would be jammed, and a lot of people were going to get hurt in the mad rush to get away from the cities, even in areas far removed from the actual target sites. There would be looting, rioting, and crimes of opportunity.

The loss of life due to ill-conceived panic reactions would probably exceed the casualty counts from the bombs, wherever they happened to strike. That made for a compelling argument against warning the civilian populace of an impending attack.

But the citizenry *had* to trust its leaders in times of crisis. If the Russian warheads fell on civilian targets without warning, the country would come apart at the seams the instant the public realized that the government had known the truth and chosen to hide it. After that, no amount of good intent would be able to stop the slide into chaos.

The problem was complicated by the fact that they didn't yet know where the warheads were going to fall. If they could narrow down the list of potential targets, they could confine the emergency warnings to only the areas that were likely to be hit. That would presumably reduce the scope of the panic, which should help limit the resulting injuries. Fewer people stampeding away from target zones should translate into fewer traffic accidents, fewer heart attacks, fewer suicides ... fewer instances of all the myriad ways that frightened humans could find to hurt themselves.

But that was part of the terrible beauty of the MIRV design. The warheads would not be locked into their final trajectories until just minutes before they re-entered the atmosphere. By then, it would be too late to warn anyone.

Despite the predictable consequences, there was no real choice. The people *had* to be told, even if the act of warning them sent some of them to their deaths.

On the geographic display, the curving red line flashed again and grew longer.

A Marine captain walked to General Gilmore's side, stopped, and spoke softly.

The general nodded, and turned to the president. "Sir, the hotline is up. We've got it patched through to your secure telephone, and President Turgenev is on the line."

The president reached for the phone. "Thank you."

In movies, the famed hotline between Washington and Moscow is usually depicted as a futuristic-looking red telephone, often decorated with flickering lights and strange mechanical reinforcements intended to convey the impression that the phone is somehow armored or bombproof. In at least one popular action film, the handset of the famous red phone was locked to the cradle by a formidable-looking steel clamp that could only be released by a key worn on a chain around the neck of the president.

But the Secure Terminal Equipment phone sitting on the briefing table looked like any other black multi-line telephone—the kind you might find on a desk in any office building. Only the narrow horizontal slot in the front of the base suggested that the STE phone might be something out of the ordinary.

The Marine captain leaned across the table and inserted a *Fortezza-Hyper* series encryption card into the slot. The phone beeped once softly, and the word 'SECURE' appeared in the rectangular LCD call display.

The young officer slid the phone across the table top until it rested directly in front of the president. "Ready, sir."

President Chandler lifted the handset.

His Russian counterpart, President Anatoliy Petrovitch Turgenev, spoke almost immediately.

"Mr. President ... *Frank* ... Are you on the line?"

The Russian president's voice sounded hollow and metallic, a side-effect of digital compression, and the encryption/decryption process that scrambled and unscrambled the signal. His English was accented, but very fluent.

"Yes, Anatoliy," the president said. "I'm on the line."

"It's a pleasure to hear your voice," the Russian leader said. "I only wish we were speaking under better circumstances."

"So do I," the president said. "So do I."

"This attack is not the work of my country," Turgenev said. "Zhukov is a maniac. He is operating without the support, or the consent of my Government. You must believe that, Frank."

"I *do* believe it," the president said. "I'm well aware of your efforts to put down Mr. Zhukov's coup. But those efforts have failed, and the situation is now beyond your control. Frankly, Anatoliy, it may have gone beyond *anyone's* control."

There was a pause before the Russian president spoke again. "Frank ... Mr. President, I know that this crisis requires your full concentration, and I don't want to delay you or distract you. But I must ask for your assurance that the United States will not retaliate with nuclear weapons."

President Chandler felt his grip on the telephone receiver tighten. "Pardon me?"

"The government of the Russian Federation would like your personal guarantee that the United States will not attack targets in Russian territory with nuclear weapons."

It was President Chandler's turn to pause.

"I'm, sorry," he said slowly, "I do not believe I can make that guarantee."

There was silence on the other end of the line. On the big display screen, the red arc grew longer as the Russian missile continued its trajectory toward California.

After several seconds, the Russian leader spoke again. "Mr. President, if we cannot reach some agreement, this situation can easily get out of hand."

"My country is under nuclear attack," the president said. "The situation has *already* gotten out of hand."

"I am attempting to prevent an escalation," Turgenev said softly.

"I understand that," the president said. "And the United States has no intention of escalating this conflict, if that can be prevented. We're preparing to intercept the warheads now. If we're successful, and there are no further attacks, your government and mine can consider how to proceed. But if nuclear warheads fall on American soil, the United States *will* retaliate in kind."

"I see," the Russian president said. "May I at least ask that you confine your counterstrikes to targets in Kamchatka?"

"Of course," President Chandler said. "Our retaliation will be directed against the rogue element who launched this attack, not against your country. Will that be satisfactory?"

"I don't know, sir," the Russian president said. "I will convey your message to my government. Let us hope for the best."

"Yes," said the president. "Let's do that."

He replaced the telephone receiver gently in its cradle, and looked up at Chairman of the Joint Chiefs. "Give me a status update, General. Where are we with this?"

General Gilmore checked the latest printouts in his striped folder. "Mr. President, our ground-based Midcourse Defenses at Fort Greely and Vandenberg are preparing to launch EKVs," he said. "We're going to try to intercept the incoming missile over the Pacific."

From earlier briefings, the president knew that an *EKV* was an *Exoatmospheric Kill Vehicle*: a ground-launched missile designed to intercept a ballistic warhead in flight, and destroy it before it could reenter the atmosphere.

"Understood," he said. "What are our chances of successfully intercepting the warheads in space?"

General Gilmore adjusted his black-rimmed glasses. "Frankly, Mr. President, the odds are not great. Our Ballistic Missile Defense System is still only partially operational. Some of the significant technologies are either still under development, or not fully tested. The system has demonstrated fairly good results against single-warhead test missiles that closely simulate the type likely to be employed by Iran or North Korea. But multiple warheads ... *MIRVs* are a different matter. They're significantly more difficult to intercept."

"Because it's harder to hit *three* targets than it is to hit *one*?"

"Not three targets, sir," the general said. "*Seven.*"

The national security advisor frowned. "Seven? I thought this missile only carried *three* warheads."

"That's correct," said General Gilmore. "But the R-29 was designed to deliver up to seven warheads. When the *START* agreement was ratified, the Russians reduced the payload to three warheads, to comply with the terms of the treaty. They replaced the other four with decoys that mimic the size, shape, weight, and movement of the real thing. They even copied the thermal signature and tumble pattern. We can tell the decoys from the real ones in a laboratory, but there's no way to spot the difference while they're falling out of the sky at mach twenty-five. Only three of the reentry vehicles from that missile are going to be real nukes, but we have no way of knowing *which* three."

"So we have to go after all seven," Brenthoven said.

"Unfortunately," the general said. "We can either shoot them all down before they reach their targets, or wait until they hit the ends of their trajectories and see which ones don't detonate."

President Chandler shook his head. "And we waste just as much energy taking out the decoys as we do killing the real warheads?"

The general nodded. "Yes, sir. That's pretty much the whole idea behind MIRV technology ... to complicate the hell out of the problem of intercepting ballistic missiles."

The president smiled weakly. "Sounds like the Russians have done a pretty good job of that."

"That's not the half of it, sir. The R-29R was engineered by the Soviet Union at the height of their Cold War paranoia. It may be a few years old, but it's a tricky son-of-a-bitch."

The general's eyes narrowed a fraction. "The warhead section, or what the engineers call the *bus*, has a four-chamber liquid fuel rocket engine. Every time it launches a warhead or a decoy, it maneuvers before it launches the next one. Moving at multi-mach speed, even a relatively small amount of vertical or horizontal displacement can create a significant amount of lateral vector, sending each warhead or decoy on a different trajectory—toward a different target. And to just to make things *really* confusing, the R-29R spits out plenty of anti-radar chaff to confuse our sensors and interceptor missiles."

"You make it sound impossible," the president said.

"It's not impossible, sir," the general said. "But the odds are *not* in our favor. Since we can only bring a relatively small number of EKVs to bear, there's a strong possibility that one of the warheads will slip past our interceptors. If we're really unlucky, they might *all* get through."

The president swallowed. "Understood. What's our fallback plan if any of the warheads evade our EKVs?"

"Then it's the Navy's turn at bat, sir," General Gilmore said. "The Aegis cruiser, USS *Shiloh*, is operating off the California coast. The ship has the Ballistic Missile Defense upgrades to its SM-3 missile systems. If the EKVs fail, the ship will attempt to intercept the warheads in the late stages of the midcourse phase, shortly before the warheads reenter the atmosphere."

"And how do our chances look with *that*?" the president asked.

The general shook his head. "It's a coin toss, sir. The Navy's systems have had even less testing than the land-based systems. The CNO seems to think pretty well of them, but it's difficult to know if that's a dispassionate evaluation, or just pride of ownership."

The president drummed his fingers on the mahogany tabletop. "And if the Navy's missiles can't get all the warheads, what then?"

"That depends on where the individual warheads are targeted, sir," the general said. "When the reentry vehicles go into the terminal phase of their trajectories, one or more of them might pass within range of a Patriot III battery. If so, the Army will get a crack at shooting them down. The good news is that the Patriot III missile system is the most thoroughly developed and tested component of our Ballistic Missile Defense System. It's had a good operational track record against short-to-medium range tactical missiles in the Middle East. The bad news is that we haven't got nearly enough coverage. There aren't enough Patriot batteries deployed in the western states to cover half the cities or military bases. If some of the incoming nukes are targeted on unprotected areas, they're going to get a free ride to the target."

The general's voice didn't change, and his tone carried no trace of derision. But he undoubtedly knew that his Commander in Chief had cut spending for additional Patriot batteries from the last two annual defense budgets.

At the time, the decision had seemed both right and obvious. It had looked like an easy opportunity to fulfill the public trust and reduce some of the strain on the wallet of the American taxpayer. After all, nobody was crazy enough to launch a nuclear missile at the United States.

President Chandler glanced up at the slender red line on the geographic display. It flashed and grew longer.

Against all conceivable reason, somebody had been that crazy after all.

⚓ ⚓ ⚓

R-29R:

The warhead bus reached apogee at an altitude of 1,200 kilometers. As the weapon rode through the high point of its trajectory, its onboard computer took optical sightings of three different stars and calculated the elevation angle of each, as referenced to an imaginary line from the center of the warhead bus to the center of the earth. The time of the sightings and the results of the calculations were compared to celestial navigation tables stored in the computer's memory to determine the precise position and orientation of the warhead bus. That position was, in-turn, compared to the position calculated by the weapon's inertial navigation system. The results were well within optimal parameters, and the onboard computer concluded that a corrective engine burn would not be required prior to warhead deployment.

The bus began its curving descent toward the earth, gaining additional speed as it nosed over and plunged back down into the steepening well of gravity.

30th Space Wing, Vandenberg Air Force Base (Santa Barbara County, California):

With a low-pitched groan of shielded hydraulics, the armored hatch cover slid to one side, revealing the octagonal opening to an underground missile silo set deep in the reinforced concrete. Fifty yards away, the hatch cover of another silo slid open at the same time, and fifty yards beyond that, a third silo cover duplicated the motion of the first two.

A gush of smoke spewed forth from each open silo, followed a fraction of a second later by the cacophonous roar of three Lockheed Martin booster rockets. In unison, the trio of interceptor missiles shot toward the clear blue California sky, each trailing a wake of flaming exhaust gases. Hydraulic motors groaned again, and the silo hatches began to slide back into position.

About 2,300 miles to the northwest, at the Army missile complex at Fort Greely, Alaska, four more interceptor missiles blasted into the sky. Before the missile silos were fully closed, all seven missiles were climbing toward space at 3.9 miles per second.

R-29R:

Six hundred kilometers above the Pacific Ocean, the computer in the missile's warhead bus transmitted simultaneous trigger pulses to five electronic relays. Each relay was wired to an electromagnetic latching mechanism and a small, shaped explosive charge. The electromagnetic latches snapped open, releasing the conical shroud that housed the nuclear warheads. A millisecond later, the tiny explosive charges fired, splitting the shroud into five sections, and propelling them out and away, opening the interior of the bus to the vacuum of near-earth space.

The removal of the larger cone revealed seven smaller cones, the narrow ends of which were pointed into the line of flight, toward their ever-nearing targets. Each of the seven cones was a reentry vehicle, wrapped in a carbon fiber heat shield impregnated with phenolic resin. Four of the reentry vehicles were decoys. The other three were Soviet-built 200 kiloton nuclear weapons. To all external appearances, the decoys and the real warheads were identical.

At a precisely-timed instant, another relay tripped, and another tiny explosive charge fired. The first of the reentry vehicles was shoved away from the bus, its nose pointed downward in the direction of the trajectory that it would follow into the atmosphere and then to its target.

As soon as the deployed reentry vehicle was clear, the computer in the warhead bus fired two of its four liquid fueled rocket engines for six-tenths of a second. The short burn was enough to displace the bus slightly to the north, placing it in perfect alignment for the deployment of the second reentry vehicle.

Over the next ninety-eight seconds, the process was repeated and then repeated again, until all seven reentry vehicles had been deployed. When the last warhead was on its way, the bus performed a final burn of its rocket engines, aligning itself for its own terminal trajectory into the earth's atmosphere. Four hundred kilometers below, the planet rushed up to meet it.

CHAPTER 25

At 3:23 p.m. Pacific Standard Time on the 2nd of March, the Emergency Alert System transmitted warnings of inbound nuclear weapons to all areas of the United States within the target footprint of the Russian R-29R missile. The alert area encompassed most of California, the lower 75 percent of Nevada and Utah, the upper half of Arizona, the northwest corner of New Mexico, the western half of Colorado along a curving line, and a sliver of the southwest corner of Wyoming.

Every AM, FM, and satellite radio station within those states suddenly found its scheduled broadcast preempted by a raucous two-tone attention signal, followed by the baritone voice of a Federal spokesman, warning of the possible approach of multiple nuclear warheads. "Seek shelter immediately," the strange voice advised. "Get off the roads as quickly and safely as you can. Do not attempt to evacuate. You are safest inside a building. Stay away from windows if possible, and avoid looking toward the sky until the all-clear signal is given. Parents are advised to account for all children immediately, and move them to the nearest available shelter."

The voice continued to offer warnings and instructions.

The signal went out over television simultaneously, taking control of every cable network, every broadcast facility, and every satellite television provider in the target states. The two-tone attention signal was the same, and the voice of the Federal spokesman came out of the speakers of every operational television in the affected areas, regardless of what channel they happened to be tuned to.

The face of a human announcer might have been reassuring to the more panic-prone viewers, but every television screen showed the emblem of the Emergency Alert System: the letters E-A-S in bright red capitals against a radially-divided blue silhouette map of the United States.

139

The words of the spokesman scrolled across the bottom of the screen as subtitles, the text alternating between English and Spanish.

Although not required to by law, streaming internet radio stations picked up the alert signal and ran it as a live feed. Several major cellular telephone providers—also operating on a volunteer basis—sent text messages to every phone number in their client rosters, advising customers to get off the streets, take shelter, and locate a television or radio for further instructions.

Many of the inhabitants of the affected areas followed the advice provided by the Emergency Alert System. They rounded up their children and sought shelter in their homes, as far away from windows as they could manage. But a lot of people—too many—decided that the only real safety lay in getting as far away from cities and military bases as possible. They ran to their cars and raced for the nearest roads out of town.

⚓ ⚓ ⚓

EKV:

Three hundred kilometers above the earth, Exoatmospheric Kill Vehicle #6 shifted into terminal guidance phase. Somewhere far below, the Lockheed Martin rocket that had boosted the kill vehicle into sub-orbital space was now tumbling back into the upper reaches of the atmosphere.

The EKV could not see its target. In point of fact, it had no awareness of the target's existence. It knew nothing of lethal aim-point guidance, convergent trajectories, or even that it was hurtling toward its own destruction at more than 25,000 kilometers per hour. The EKV's sole attention was focused on the beam of digital telemetry streaming up from the antennas at Vandenberg Air Force Base. It monitored the beam continuously, and reacted instantly to the maneuvering commands imbedded in the digital signal—firing pitch, roll, and yaw thrusters on command—making minute corrections to its own motion vectors to match the predicted position of a Russian warhead that it could never see.

The EKV carried no explosive. It was a hit-to-kill weapon, designed to destroy its target with the kinetic energy created by its tremendous speed, in much the same way that speed and inertia could transform the simple lead pellet of a rifle bullet into a lethally destructive projectile.

The timing was flawless. The microsecond clock in the kill vehicle's digital brain clicked down to zero at the precise instant that the EKV reached its designated coordinates in space. The kill vehicle and the target warhead slammed into each other at a combined closure rate of more than

50,000 kilometers per hour. The resultant explosion was like the flare of a tiny sun, as the tremendous force of the impact was converted instantly to several hundred megajoules of raw heat.

EKV #6 and its unseen target were no more.

⚓ ⚓ ⚓

U.S. Strategic Command (STRATCOM), Offutt Air Force Base, Nebraska:

Seen from the tracking screens of the Command and Control, Battle Management, and Communications Control Center of the United States Strategic Command, the destruction of EKV #6 and its target was considerably less dramatic. There were no brilliant flares or explosions, just a soft computer bleep, followed by three brief messages in the alert window:

► **TELEMETRY LOST, EKV #6**

► **TRACK NOT CONTINUED, BALLISTIC TARGET "FOXTROT"**

► **SUCCESSFUL INTERCEPT PROBABILITY = 97.4%**

Air Force Major Lionel Humphrey read the lines of text and let out a shaky breath. It was working ... It actually seemed to be working ...

"Yeah!," one of the console operators exclaimed. "Oh yeah! I think it's gonna ..."

"Shut up!," Lionel snapped. His voice was overloud in the quiet of the control room. "Don't jinx it," he said in a softer tone. "Just shut the hell up ... and let it happen."

⚓ ⚓ ⚓

Interstate 8 (San Diego, California):

The unofficial and un-recommended evacuation of San Diego began within minutes of the first emergency alert bulletin. The word tore through the city like wildfire. San Diego was a prime military target: the aircraft carriers at North Island ... the amphibious warfare base on Coronado ... the warships at 32nd Street Naval Station ... the submarine base at Point Loma. Any enemy who wanted to cripple the U.S. would nuke San Diego with the very first barrage of missiles.

It seemed like good logic. And in the pressure cooker of a city succumbing to terror, the idea morphed from educated guess to solid fact in the space of mere minutes. Suddenly, the word was everywhere … San Diego was a confirmed target. The only way to survive was to get out of the city *NOW*! People jumped in their cars and ran for the freeways like lemmings.

The first casualties were from a pileup on Interstate 8, near the Grossmont Boulevard exit—the inevitable product of too many vehicles moving too quickly through too small an area.

Near the middle of the pack and rolling at eighty miles an hour, the driver of a white Ford pickup misjudged his following distance and slammed into the rear of a green Toyota minivan. With a crunch of buckling steel and collapsing plastic, the minivan careened to the left, smashing into the right front fender of a silver BMW Z8 convertible and slewing the sports car sideways into the side of a fourth vehicle.

Startled by the unexpected impact, and by the split-second shock of his driver-side airbag ballooning instantly into his face, the BMW driver snatched his foot away from the accelerator pedal, and stomped on the brakes. It was an utterly natural reaction. Given the same set of circumstances, a lot of drivers would have done precisely what he did. But it was exactly the wrong thing to do.

With that simple act of reflex, a multi-car fender-bender was transformed into a chain-reaction, propagating backward through the speeding lines of traffic as cars, trucks, motorcycles, and buses crashed blindly into the wall of suddenly stationary vehicles to their immediate front. And amidst the rending of metal and the shattering of glass, drivers and passengers were crushed and broken right along with their vehicles.

The Russian warheads had not even penetrated the atmosphere, and already American citizens were beginning to die.

⚓ ⚓ ⚓

Alaska Regional Hospital, Anchorage, Alaska:

Charlie Sweigart tapped gently on the door to Gabriella's room, and then opened it enough to stick his head in. "Hello?"

There was no answer. Gabriella was sleeping.

Charlie shuffled into her room, his hospital slippers making soft shushing noises as they slid across the tiled floor. He wheeled his IV rack in behind himself, taking care that his IV tubes didn't catch on anything as he quietly closed the door. He probably didn't need the IV anymore. He was over the hump now, and well on the road to recovery, but the doctors kept reminding him that advanced hypothermia was nothing to play around with.

He felt okay now, or at least well enough to finish his recovery at home. Of course, there might not be any home left to go to. His apartment was in San Diego, and if the news reports were accurate, California was coming unglued. Even if the missiles were shot down, or turned out to be a hoax or something, his two-bedroom loft in Mission Hills might not survive the panic that was ripping through his city.

There was nothing he could do about that now. The missiles would strike, or they wouldn't. His little home would be preserved, or it would be destroyed. Ten minutes from now, the lid might come off the pot completely, and the superpowers could all start lobbing nukes at each other. Planet Earth might finally get its Third World War, but nothing Charlie could do from this hospital would make the slightest bit of difference. He could do nothing but wait, and Gabriella's room seemed like a good place to do that.

He turned and looked at her. The sight nearly stole his breath away.

The tall ocean scientist was curled on her side, blue hospital sheets bunched and tangled around her long-limbed body, golden hair fanning across the pillow and spilling over the curve of her cheek. For a half-second, Charlie thought about brushing the hair from her cheek so that he could see her face more clearly. But he didn't want to wake her, and he wasn't at all certain that his touch would be welcome.

Gabriella had said things to him in those last few minutes of consciousness aboard the *Nereus*. Charlie knew that her words might have been nothing more than a delirious symptom of her advancing hypothermia, or even a wishful hallucination from his own cold-addled mind. He didn't care. He wanted to believe in them anyway. And he didn't want to break the fragile spell of his hopes by waking her.

He wanted Gabriella's words to be real, and he wanted her to mean them. But he couldn't control that, any more than he could control the warheads hurtling toward his country. So he stood and watched the gentle rhythm of her breathing. And his heart was so full that he almost didn't care if the world came to an end.

U.S. Strategic Command (STRATCOM), Offutt Air Force Base, Nebraska:

With another computer bleep, another trio of messages appeared in the alert window of the STRATCOM tracking screens:

►   **TELEMETRY LOST, EKV #4**

►   **TRACK NOT CONTINUED, BALLISTIC TARGET "DELTA"**

►   **SUCCESSFUL INTERCEPT PROBABILITY = 97.4%**

To his right, Major Lionel could hear a man's voice whispering, "Thank you, Jesus. Thank you, Jesus. Thank you, Jesus."

Lionel, who hadn't felt the slightest desire to pray since he'd outgrown bedtime prayers at the age of nine, suddenly wondered if this might not be a good time to start again.

⚓ ⚓ ⚓

Highland Shipping and Commercial Freight (Provo, Utah):

Randall Dixon kicked open the door to the shipping office. The flimsy interior door gave way easily under the sole of his size-11 work boot. Particle board fractured and the simulated wood grain laminate split into several pieces as the broken door swung around on its hinges to bounce off the wall adjoining the doorway.

He hefted the ball-peen hammer he'd grabbed from the cab of his Freightliner. He caught a blur of movement out of the corner of his left eye as a little turd of a man dove for cover behind one of the desks. Dixon grinned. "Knock-knock, asshole."

Silence, and then a quiet scuffling sound as that weasel Gillespie tried to burrow his worthless ass further out of sight.

Dixon took aim at a desk lamp and swung with the hammer. The lamp disintegrated in a shower of electrical sparks and broken glass.

"Eleven violations," he growled. The hammer came down again, pulverizing an acrylic paperweight full of tiny starfish. The blow sent several pieces of paper fluttering to the floor.

"Eleven violations," Dixon said again. "You wrote me up for every piddly-ass rule you could think of, didn't you, you useless sack of shit?" To punctuate the last word, he brought the hammer down again. A coffee cup was jolted off the edge of the desk. It lay on its side, draining dark liquid into the coarse gray weave of the industrial carpet.

"It ain't enough for you to get me kicked off the long-hauls where a man can earn a living wage," Dixon said. "You gotta go after my ticket, don't you? I break my hump for this company for eight years, and that's how you're gonna repay me—by jerking my license to drive a rig."

The only answer was a series of muffled beeps. Gillespie was trying to use his cellular phone to call for help.

Dixon raised the hammer and held it cocked. The next time he swung, it would be to bash in the little pencil-pusher's brains. "Calling the cops, ass-wipe?" He laughed. "Won't do you no good. You ain't heard? Russian missiles headed right for us. In about five minutes, we all gonna be dead. Our ashes are gonna be glowin' in the dark like one of them science fiction movies."

He flexed his grip on the wooden shaft of the hammer and began edging around the end of the desk, moving quietly so Gillespie wouldn't be expecting him.

"You're going *first*, you little shit," he said. He spoke more softly now, hoping that Gillespie wouldn't be able to tell that he was moving closer.

"If I'm gonna be dead in five minutes," he said, "I want the pleasure of killing you my*self*!"

On the last syllable, he lunged around the end of the desk and leapt toward Gillespie. The little man squealed in terror and threw his hands up to protect his face.

Dixon brought the hammer down with every ounce of anger in his soul. He felt one of Gillespie's wrists break as the blunt steel head of the heavy tool blurred through its arc without slowing. With a crack like the snap of a bullwhip, the hammer collided with Gillespie's skull.

The first whack probably killed the bastard, but Dixon hit him six or eight more times just to be sure the job was done properly. Then he dropped the hammer on the floor and went outside to smoke a cigarette and wait for the end of the world.

⚓ ⚓ ⚓

U.S. Strategic Command (STRATCOM), Offutt Air Force Base, Nebraska:

The computer emitted its now-familiar bleep, and three more lines of text appeared in the alert window:

► **TELEMETRY LOST, EKV #7**

► **TRACK NOT CONTINUED, BALLISTIC TARGET "GOLF"**

► **SUCCESSFUL INTERCEPT PROBABILITY = 75.1%**

Lionel scanned the last line. *Seventy-five percent?* Not a lot of safety margin there, but a kill was a kill. They'd managed to knock out three of the inbound warhead shapes so far. It was impossible to know how many of the destroyed targets had been decoys and how many had been real warheads.

Maybe they'd gotten all three of the warheads already, and the remaining four were all decoys. Then again, maybe all three successful intercepts had been decoys, and all three of the real warheads were still out there. The only way to be certain was to destroy them *all*.

The tracking computer bleeped again, and new lines of text appeared on the screen:

► **TELEMETRY CONTINUED PAST INTERCEPT POINT, EKV #2**

► **TRACK CONTINUED PAST INTERCEPT POINT, BALLISTIC TARGET "BRAVO"**

► **SUCCESSFUL INTERCEPT PROBABILITY = 00.0%**

The words hit Lionel like a punch in the stomach. Zero percent? Telemetry continued past Intercept Point? *ZERO percent?*

"Oh shit!" one of the console operators said. "We missed one of them. One of the warheads got past us."

"Calm down," Lionel said. His voice contained a calmness that he did not feel. "Maybe it wasn't a real warhead. Maybe it was one of the decoys."

Please, just let it be the one, he thought. Let us get the rest of them. Let us knock the rest of them out of the sky. Please.

But the next alert message announced the failure of EKV #5, followed closely by the failures of EKV #3, and EKV #1.

Of the seven inbound warhead shapes, the ground-based interceptor missiles had managed to kill only three. Four of the targets had gotten past them.

Lionel could see them in his mind's eye: four darkly conical shapes, streaking through the blackness of space, bending their trajectories downward. Toward his country. Toward the very people who depended upon Lionel to protect them.

How many of those shapes were nuclear bombs? One of them? None? Three? There was no way of knowing, but the warheads would shortly be passing into the reentry phase of their trajectories. Within the next few minutes, the question would answer itself.

Lionel stared at the screen, and the alert messages announcing the failed intercepts. It was up to the Navy, now. He hoped they were up to the challenge.

Like many of his fellow Air Force types, Lionel didn't think much of the swab jockeys. They had too much mouth, too much money, and not enough of the Right Stuff. But he'd give a year's pay to see them show up the Air Force right now. If they could knock down all four of the remaining targets, he'd plant a big sloppy kiss on the first Navy type he met. Male or female, eighteen years old or eighty, seaman or admiral. Lionel didn't care. He just wanted them to finish the job. Nothing else mattered. Nothing.

⚓ ⚓ ⚓

Vista Del Rio Assisted Living Community (Long Beach, California):

Harvey Calloway muted the audio on the little bedroom television and hobbled over toward the window. With the sound turned off, he could hear the noise from outside more clearly. Down in the street, car horns were blaring and people were shouting. Harvey heard a pop in the distance that might have been a gunshot, but he couldn't tell. He was in his nineties and even with his hearing aid turned all the way up, his hearing was pretty bad.

The window was only seven or eight feet away, but it took him a minute or so to cover the distance. The arthritis in his hips and knees made his steps short and difficult, the soles of his slippers scuffing painfully across the carpet in the shuffling walk that his great granddaughter called 'choo-choo feet.' He hated having to walk like that, but at least he could still make it around on his own. A lot of guys his age couldn't get out of bed. Hell, come to think of it, most guys his age were already dead.

He was grateful to still be walking, arthritis and all. But he missed the bouncy swagger of his youth. Harvey had been something else in those days. Nothing but balls, good looks, and a big toothy grin. And man had he cut a figure in his uniform.

Harvey had been a U.S. Navy fighter pilot during the big one. In '42, he'd flown F4F Wildcats against the Vichy French over North Africa. And later he'd gone eyeball-to-eyeball with the Japanese at places like Tarawa, Leyte Gulf, and Okinawa. He'd even bagged himself a couple of Zeroes at the Great Marianas Turkey Shoot. He'd been flying the F6F by then.

The Hellcat ... Now there, by Lord, had been an aircraft. Fueled and armed, she had weighed in at more than 15,000 pounds, but she'd danced on the breeze like a ballerina. And she'd given old *'Snake Eyes'* Harvey Calloway and his squadron mates absolute dominance of the skies over the Pacific.

He craned his neck and looked through the window at the California sky. They'd beaten the Vichy Frogs, the Krauts, and the Nips. Everyone said they'd beaten the commies too, but Harvey had never really bought that. Everybody with a lick of sense knew the Russkis were bent on world domination. And suddenly they just throw down their guns and give up the fight, without firing a shot? Other people might believe that crap, but Harvey knew better. It had all been a trick, to get America to relax and drop her guard. The commies had been lying quiet and waiting for their moment to strike. And now it had come. Now the sneaky bastards were launching their A-bombs at America.

The guy on television was telling everybody to stay in their homes. Don't panic. Don't try to run. Harvey shifted his eyes to the traffic jam in the street below his window. It wouldn't be too hard to follow the television guy's advice. Even if he could still drive, there wasn't a prayer of getting out of here before the bombs started to fall.

Of their own accord, Harvey's eyes pointed themselves toward the drawer of the nightstand beside his bed. There, behind pill bottles, handkerchiefs, and paperback novels, was an old companion: a Navy-issue .45 that had followed him home at the end of the war. He wasn't supposed to have a gun here; it was against about a dozen of the rules for Vista Del Rio tenants. Harvey had smuggled it in wrapped up in a sweater, because he couldn't make the staff understand that he needed it for protection.

"We have a security system here," the Placement Manager had told him. *"We have alarms on the doors and windows, and a roving security patrol. You don't need to worry about burglars, Mr. Calloway. I promise you—you'll be safe here."*

But the .45 wasn't for burglars. It was for a different kind of protection. Harvey had promised himself a long time ago that he'd use it the very first day that he couldn't get to the toilet by himself. A man shouldn't have to go through life with hoses shoved into his orifices, and plastic bags of slop hanging from the side of his bed. *That* was something worth protecting yourself from.

Harvey blinked and looked out the window again. Those commie A-bombs should be falling any minute now ...

USS *Shiloh* (CG-67):

Two armored hatches snapped open on the cruiser's forward missile deck, revealing the weatherproof fly-through covers that capped the upper ends of two vertical launch missile cells. At the same instant, another pair of hatches snapped open on the ship's aft missile deck.

Some fraction of a millisecond later, all four of the fly-through covers were blasted into fragments as two pairs of SM-3 missiles rocketed out of their vertical launch cells and roared into the afternoon sky on bright columns of fire.

In the darkened confines of the ship's Combat Information Center, the Weapons Control Officer keyed the microphone of his communications headset and spoke into the tactical communications net. "TAO—Weapons Control. Four birds away, no apparent casualties. Targeted one-each on the four ballistic inbounds." The rumble of the departing missiles was still faintly audible as he spoke.

The Tactical Action Officer's reply came over the net a second later. "TAO, aye. Is there enough time to prep a second flight of birds in case we miss on some of the intercepts?"

The Weapons Control Officer keyed his mike again. "TAO—Weapons Control. That's a negative. The inbounds are moving at about 14,000 miles an hour. We get one crack at this, sir. By the time we get off a second flight of birds, the inbounds will be outside of our missile engagement envelope."

The reply was several seconds in coming. "TAO, aye. Let's hope we don't miss the first time."

SM-3 Missiles:

At about the time the Tactical Action Officer was releasing his mike button, the four missiles were shedding their first stage boosters, and igniting the Dual Thrust Rocket Motors of their second stage engines.

The missiles gained speed and altitude quickly, ejecting their second stage boosters as they were climbing out of the upper stratosphere and into the lower reaches of near-earth space. Three of the SM-3 missiles performed this transition perfectly. The fourth missile did not.

A pre-stressed retaining pin in the mating collar between stages failed to shear under the calculated strain of stage separation. The mating collar did not separate, and the second stage booster did not drop away as it had been designed to do.

The missile's computer was programmed to detect many types of technical casualties, but this simple mechanical failure had not been anticipated by the weapon's designers. Unable to sense that the second stage booster was still attached, the missile's computer transmitted the ignition command to the third stage rocket motor on schedule. The jet of hot expanding exhaust gasses, which should have poured harmlessly into the near vacuum of space, were channeled into the small chamber between the second and third stage motors. Unable to contain the expanding pressure wave, the airframe exploded, spewing streaks of shrapnel and fire into the void of the upper stratosphere.

⚓ ⚓ ⚓

USS *Shiloh* (CG-67):

The Weapons Control Officer read the flashing warning message on his screen, and keyed his microphone. "TAO—Weapons Control. I'm showing a pre-intercept failure on Bird #4."

"Weapons Control—TAO. I copy your pre-intercept failure on Bird #4. What happened?"

The Weapons Control Officer scanned his readouts for a clue to the cause of the failure. After a few seconds, he keyed his mike again. "TAO—Weapons Control. I have no idea what went wrong, sir. Bird #4 just dropped off the scope."

"TAO, aye. How long until we find out how our other birds are doing?"

"TAO—Weapons Control. It should be any time now."

"Weapons Control—TAO. Is there no chance at all that we can get another bird up there to replace #4?

The Weapons Control Officer looked at the converging vectors on his display screen. "TAO—Weapons Control. No chance, sir."

He released the mike button. "No chance at all."

⚓ ⚓ ⚓

SM-3 Missile #2:

Thirty seconds before impact, the Kinetic Warhead separated from the third stage booster. Unlike the EKVs of the ground-based interceptors, the Mark-142 Kinetic Warhead was equipped with onboard sensors. It detected the target immediately, and used a brief series of pulses from its maneuvering thrusters to improve its angle of approach to the intercept point.

As with the EKVs, the KW's arrival at the intercept point had to be timed to coincide with the arrival of its target. A millisecond too soon, and the KW would pass through the intercept coordinates ahead of its quarry. A millisecond too late, and the target would blow through the intercept coordinates before the KW arrived. In either case, the Russian warhead would slip past the KW and the intercept attempt would fail. The timing had to be nearly perfect.

It was.

The Soviet-built R-29R reentry vehicle arrived at the calculated intercept point at the exact same instant as the Kinetic Warhead. Several million Newton-meters of additive linear force were spontaneously translated to thermal energy. With a blindingly bright flash that no human eye would ever see, SM-3 missile #2 obliterated its target.

⚓ ⚓ ⚓

USS *Shiloh* (CG-67):

The Weapons Control Officer watched his screen. "TAO—Weapons Control. Splash one!"

Before the Tactical Action Officer could acknowledge the report, the Weapons Control Officer keyed his mike again. "TAO—Weapons Control. Splash two! And splash three! I say again, three hits—three kills."

A cheer went up in Combat Information Center, and somebody shouted, "Nice shooting, Ensign. Kick ass and take names!"

The Weapons Control Officer nodded absently. He wanted to shout and cheer with the rest of them, but they couldn't see what he could see.

On the tactical display in front of him, the speed vector for the last Russian warhead continued to track across the screen. In a few brief seconds, it disappeared as the hurtling weapon passed out of the *Shiloh's* engagement envelope.

It was gone, and he couldn't do anything to stop it.

R-29R:

The Russian missile's last remaining reentry vehicle dropped into the ever-thickening atmosphere of the planet below. Its cone shape and internal weight distribution made the device tail-heavy, giving it a nose-up attitude that oriented the widely rounded base into the axis of fall. The reentry vehicle effectively "backed" into the atmosphere, capitalizing on the principles of blunt body gas flow to carry away much of the fiery heat of reentry. The remaining heat load, though still nearly twice the melting temperature of steel, was absorbed and ablated by the vehicle's pyrolytic graphite heat shield, which charred, sublimed, and then burned away in fractional layers.

The design of the heat shield was not Soviet technology, but the product of military espionage. Early in the Cold War, Soviet intelligence agents had copied the blunt body reentry shape from the work of American aeronautical engineers H. Julian Allen and Alfred J. Eggers Jr., and the ablative layering technique from America's Mercury space program. And now that American technology was screaming back toward the nation of its birth at several times the speed of sound.

The heat shedding was critical to the vehicle's mission, because—a few centimeters on the other side of the superheated skin—delicate circuits and mechanisms were at work. The conical device streaking toward the earth was not a decoy. It was a 200 kiloton KBS-34 series nuclear warhead, and it was in the process of arming itself for detonation.

White House, Presidential Emergency Operations Center (Washington, DC):

The red arc on the wall-sized geographic display screen was almost complete now. As President Chandler watched, it flashed and grew a fraction longer.

The firing envelopes of the Army's Patriot III missile batteries appeared on the screen as green circles. The circles were large; the Patriot system had a good effective range, but there weren't enough of them to provide adequate coverage. And none of the Patriot batteries intersected the final flight path of the Russian warhead.

As General Gilmore had predicted, the bomb was getting a free ride on the final leg to its target.

⚓ ⚓ ⚓

Warhead:

The sequence started slowly, but built in speed as the reaction began to escalate. When the reentry vehicle fell past 50,000 meters, a relay clicked open, channeling electrical power into a ring of high-voltage capacitors that encircled the core of the weapon. With a whine like angry mosquitoes, the capacitors began to charge.

At 10,000 meters, another timed relay clicked open. Near the narrow end of the cone, a pair of electrical solenoids rammed their actuator rods downward, forcing pistons into either end of a pressurized cylinder of tritium gas. The pressure within the cylinder exceeded the failure point of a foil membrane that isolated the cylinder from a connected manifold of stainless steel capillary tubes. The foil membrane ruptured, and the pressurized tritium was forced through the manifold, into the steel tubes, and through them into the spherical void between the primary and secondary stages of the bomb.

At 3,000 meters, the ring of capacitors fired, dumping their stored electrical power into a precisely-constructed network of wires. The length of each wire was known to within a nanometer, and its electrical resistance had been calculated to nine decimal places. The attention to engineering precision paid off. The signals shooting through those wires reached their respective destinations with nearly perfect synchronicity.

Ninety-six electrical initiators fired at the same instant, detonating ninety-six trapezoidal blocks of high explosives surrounding a spherical shell of radioactive plutonium 239. The charges were carefully shaped to focus their destructive force inward, toward the center of the plutonium sphere. It was not an explosion, but an implosion.

Faced with more than a million atmospheres of external pressure, the spherical plutonium shell collapsed inward, toward the envelope of tritium gas and the secondary stage of the bomb. The plutonium, already much denser than lead, was further compressed by the converging shock wave of the implosion.

Tortured beyond the boundaries of elemental stability, the plutonium shifted from its natural process of gradual radioactive decay, to an accelerated state of induced fission. The nuclei of many of the plutonium atoms were crushed or split by the extraordinary mechanical force of the compression wave. The shattered nuclei emitted heat, photons, X radiation, gamma rays, and neutrons. The neutrons were flung out to strike adjacent atoms like randomly fired bullets, shattering previously undamaged plutonium atoms and releasing larger quantities of heat, light, radiation, and still more neutrons.

Through a process known as *doubling*, the chain reaction escalated. Fifty damaged atoms became a hundred. Then one hundred became two hundred, and two hundred became four hundred. In the space of a few nanoseconds, the chain reaction grew a million times more powerful than the implosion that had triggered it.

Heat, radiation, and mechanical force erupted outward in a thunderous explosion of atomic energy.

But it didn't stop there. The mechanical force and radiation of the primary stage attacked the secondary core of depleted uranium at the heart of the bomb. Tritium atoms merged with uranium atoms, and the expanding fission reaction was magnified by nuclear fusion.

The fireball and shock wave grew, and everything they touched was obliterated. Every living creature within their hideous circle of effect was instantly incinerated.

And the telltale mushroom cloud, not seen in battle since the annihilation of Nagasaki, climbed toward the blue California sky.

CHAPTER 26

NARITA INTERNATIONAL AIRPORT
CHIBA PREFECTURE, JAPAN
SUNDAY; 03 MARCH
0904 hours (9:04 AM)
TIME ZONE +9 'INDIA'

Ann Roark elbowed Sheldon Miggs in the ribs. "*Ask* somebody, damn it!"

Ann's eyes were glued to one of the courtesy televisions mounted high up the side of a support column in the airport departure lounge. The television was showing the feed from a Japanese news program. The images on the screen alternated between studio shots of a Japanese anchorman who looked like Ryuichi Sakamoto, and still images and video clips from some kind of breaking news story centered in California. At least it seemed to be California, as a green silhouette map of the state appeared periodically in the graphics window next to the anchorman.

The screen cut from a quick establishing shot of the White House, to archival footage of a nuclear explosion—complete with trademark mushroom cloud, to an overhead helicopter shot of a major traffic pileup on an unidentified freeway, to what looked like rioting and general pandemonium in the streets, and back to the nuclear mushroom cloud.

Something had happened. Something *huge*. But what *was* it?

The voiceovers and the on-screen text were all in Japanese, which Ann could not read or speak a word of. She glanced around at the groups of Asian travelers clustered around every visible television. Most of them stood in what appeared to be stunned silence, while a few spoke to their fellows in intense whispers.

The news feed cut back to the Ryuichi Sakamoto lookalike for a few seconds. Then it switched to a still shot of the U.S. Pentagon, jumped to footage of ambulances and paramedics helping injured people, dissolved to a still shot of a city skyline that might have been San Diego, and then returned to the nuclear explosion.

Ann looked over at Sheldon, whose attention was focused entirely on trying to get his cell phone to work.

Ann sighed. "Will you let that damned thing alone? You're about three thousand miles outside of your cellular provider's coverage area. You're not going to get a signal in freaking Japan. Okay?"

Sheldon shook his head. "I upgraded my service plan to include Japan and South Korea. I've *got* a signal. That's not the problem." He punched several buttons and put the phone to his ear. "I need to check on my Mom and my dogs, okay?"

Ann looked back to the television screen. The Japanese news station was running a feed from CNN now. A blonde anchorwoman stood in the foreground, speaking into one of those stupidly oversized network microphones. In the distant background, the Pentagon was visible. Ann listened carefully to catch the anchorwoman's words, but the local station was running the Japanese translation in place of the original English voice track.

A graphic window appeared beside the American news correspondent. A computer animatic of a fiery mushroom cloud blossomed above the CNN logo. The words, "NUCLEAR ATTACK" appeared over the animated image in a red diagonal banner.

Sheldon closed his cell phone with an audible thump. "Damn it. I can't get through. The phone lines on the West Coast must be overloaded with traffic. Whatever the emergency is, it must be ..."

He glanced up at the television screen in time to catch the end of the NUCLEAR ATTACK animation. "Nuclear attack? Where? I mean, who got hit?"

Ann shot him a look. "That's what I've been trying to get you to find out. Now ... Will you please freaking *ask* somebody?"

Sheldon shoved the cell phone into his travel bag. "You've got a mouth. Why haven't *you* asked somebody?"

Ann rewarded him with another dirty look. "I don't speak Japanese."

Sheldon raised an eyebrow. "What am I? Secret Ninja Boy? I don't speak Japanese either."

He looked around. "Besides, at least two-thirds of these people speak English. I guarantee it."

Ann stared at him without speaking. He knew why she hadn't asked. She couldn't deal with members of her own culture. Fifty percent of Sheldon's job was talking to people so that she didn't have to.

Sheldon groaned theatrically. "Okay. I'll go ask somebody."

He climbed out of his seat and stumped across the room to the closest cluster of locals.

Ann watched him as he struck up a conversation with a thirtyish Japanese couple. They were total strangers, but Sheldon smiled at them almost immediately. His hands flitted about like birds as he talked. His face was alive with interest.

How did he *do* that? She knew the smile and the interest were genuine. He could walk up to complete strangers in a foreign airport and make an immediate connection. How in the hell did he do that?

Sheldon turned toward Ann. He pointed in her direction, then to himself, and finally to the news story on the television screen. He spoke. The couple responded, and Sheldon spoke some more.

The Japanese man glanced back at Ann, nodded a couple of times, and began using the finger of one hand to trace and retrace something against the palm of his other hand. A curve? It looked like he was drawing and redrawing a curve with his fingertip. Then, he used the fingertip to point to a spot in mid-air, about six inches to the left of his open palm. He poked that spot several times with his fingertip, as though punctuating a sentence with multiple periods.

Sheldon nodded, bowed slightly to the man and to his wife, and walked back toward Ann.

As she watched him approach, Ann was struck by the notion that Sheldon came from an entirely different planet. Or maybe *she* did. Sheldon seemed to fit, after all. He could talk to the corporate suits, the computer geeks, the gung-ho military types, and total strangers—all with apparently equal facility. He could find a way to fit in just about anywhere, even in countries where he didn't speak the language. Ann, on the other hand, only seemed to relate to machines. Maybe *she* was from another planet. If so, she was ready to go home to Planet Z-X-55, or wherever she came from.

Sheldon dropped heavily into the seat next to her. "It was a nuclear attack," he said.

Ann sat up. "What? Where ..."

Sheldon held up a hand. "Slow down. It's okay. Some whack-job revolutionary in Siberia launched a bunch of nuclear warheads at the West Coast. Our military shot them down. All but one, anyway. That one hit about a hundred miles west of San Diego. Blew up a big piece of water. Probably killed a few million fish."

"Wait a minute," Ann said. "You're telling me they *missed*? Somebody tried to nuke the West Coast, and they freaking *missed*?"

"Looks like it," Sheldon said. "The one that got through missed, anyway." He tugged at his lower lip. "Or maybe our guys knocked it off course. They hit all the rest of the warheads. Maybe they hit that one too, but it wasn't destroyed. Just knocked off course, so it landed in the ocean instead of San Diego."

He grinned at Ann. "Pretty good shooting, huh? The media's constantly telling us that Ballistic Missile Defense is a waste of our tax dollars. But it looks like it did the job."

Ann looked up at the television screen. The Japanese news program was showing the ambulances again. Injured and bloodied people being tended to by paramedics. Blue and red police lights flashing. Broken windows, and people running.

She nodded toward the television. "What's all this, then? If the military knocked out all the bombs, what happened to all these people? How did so many people get hurt?"

Sheldon's momentary grin vanished. "Panic. When the missile warnings went out, a lot of people just lost their minds. They all thought they were about to be blown to kingdom come. They freaked out, ran for the hills, barricaded their doors. All the crazy things that people do when they think they're about to be killed."

His eyes darted to the Japanese couple he'd spoken to a few minutes earlier. "That gentleman over there told me that some kids in Alameda torched a whole strip mall. The cops didn't get there in time to stop the fire, but they did manage to nab some of the firebugs. Turns out that the ringleader convinced his buddies that some kinds of missiles are attracted to heat sources. I guess they thought the fire would lure the bombs away from their neighborhood."

Sheldon shook his head. "People get crazy when they're really scared. They hurt each other. They hurt themselves."

"The government should have known this would happen," Ann said. "They shouldn't have sent out the warnings. They knew people would lose their minds. This is their fault."

Sheldon exhaled loudly. "Come on, Ann. You're going to think the worst of them no matter *what* they do. You know you are. That's how your brain is wired."

He unzipped his travel bag and began fishing through the contents with his hand. "If the government had kept this quiet, you'd be screaming for blood right now. You'd be sitting next to me, talking about the *conspiracy of silence* and *the people's right to know*. You'd be telling me that the people should have been warned."

Sheldon pulled out his cell phone and flipped it open. "No offense, Ann, but you get a lot of mileage out of not liking people. You know that, don't you?"

Before Ann could answer, he punched a string of numbers and hoisted the phone to his ear.

Ann started to slip in a comeback, but she stopped herself. What was the point? The best she could hope for would be to piss off Sheldon, the one person who seemed to be able to put up with her.

She let her eyes wander around the terminal. People were still gathered around the televisions, staring up at the curved glass screens for a glimpse of the chaos on the other side of the ocean.

Her eyes lit on a huge electronic monitor showing arrivals and departures in Japanese and English. She let her gaze slide down the list of departing flights, pretending for a second that one of them might list an outbound flight to Planet Z-X-55. She was ready to get off this planet.

With a flicker of shifting letters and numbers, the information on the monitor was updated. Times and gate numbers reshuffled themselves as various airlines adjusted their schedules.

Every flight to the United States was now listed as 'Canceled.'

CHAPTER 27

WHITE HOUSE
PRESIDENTIAL EMERGENCY OPERATIONS CENTER
WASHINGTON, DC
SATURDAY; 02 MARCH
7:17 PM EST

The national security advisor cleared his throat. "Ah ... Mr. President?"

The president didn't answer. The Single Integrated Operational Plan lay untouched on the briefing table in front of him. The thick binder was still open to Section Orange: "**RETALIATORY NUCLEAR STRIKE OPTIONS**."

Of all the documents Frank Chandler had been shown, trained on, or briefed about, this was the one he'd least expected to ever need. He understood its purpose. He knew that it had been created specifically for the kind of situation they were in now, but he'd never really believed that this moment would arrive.

And yet ... somehow ... it had come.

Gregory Brenthoven cleared his throat again. "Mr. President, we *have* to respond."

The president raised a hand for silence. He couldn't seem to think properly.

His eyes drifted down to the SIOP. The open section of the document was divided into numbered subheadings:

6.2-A **Counterforce Responses**

6.2-B **Countervalue Responses**

6.2-C **Punitive Responses**

Counterforce referred to the targeting of missile silos and military sites, to destroy the enemy's ability to make war. *Countervalue* meant attacks

160

against cities and the killing of the general civilian populace, to break the enemy's national will.   And *punitive* responses were designed as punishment: in essence, "spanking" an enemy nation with nuclear weapons.

The terms were so sterile, so scrubbed of emotional cues, that they invited the reader to ignore their grisly implications.   There was no hint that selecting any of the proffered choices might condemn millions of human beings to death.

The president absently grasped the tab marked **6.2-C**, and flipped the binder open to the section on "**Punitive Responses**."   Again he encountered three subdivisions:

6.2-C.1   Punitive Responses (Disproportionate)

6.2-C.2   Punitive Responses (Proportionate)

6.2-C.3   Punitive Responses (Minimal)

He selected the third tab, and thumbed the pages to "**Punitive Responses (Minimal)**."   He read the opening paragraphs.

The decision matrices described in this subsection contain non-conventional response options calculated to demonstrate strategic restraint while signaling the willingness to employ nuclear weapons. They are designed to minimize human casualties within the target zone, and limit damage to the physical infrastructure of the target nation.

Where possible, any strike option selected under this subsection should be preceded by and followed by diplomatic overtures to the government of the target nation.   The content of such overtures should include language that discourages further aggression against the United States and/or U.S. allies, by implying or overtly declaring a willingness to escalate to a more robust nuclear response.   For suggested language and further information, see the U.S. Department of State Recommendations outlined in Annex-D.

Again, the words were almost mind-numbingly banal.   If this had been a routine government document, the president might have chalked up the monotonous writing to the self-importance of the bureaucratic mindset. But such cumbersome sentence construction and oblique word-choice probably had not occurred by accident.

In the nineteen-eighties, a political satirist had referred to the SIOP as '*The Cookbook for Ending the World*.' That little slice of dark humor hadn't gone over well in the corridors of military power, but—with all social and political niceties stripped away—that's exactly what the SIOP was. It was the instruction manual for ultimate genocide. Every paragraph in the fat metal binder was monstrous, in both intent and in consequence. Every neatly-numbered option lead to incalculable human atrocity.

The military officers and government officials responsible for wordsmithing the plan had understood that. And they had known that some president might one day have to sit where Francis Benjamin Chandler was sitting right now, and issue orders that would kill massive numbers of people.

So they had buried the ugly truths behind tediously flat phrases, perhaps in the hopes of granting their president a sufficient amount of emotional distance to make decisions that no human being is equipped to make.

If that had really been their intent, it had worked, at least in part. President Chandler found that the semiotically-neutral language of nuclear warfare made it possible for him to consider courses of action that would have been unthinkable if they had been couched in more accurate terms. If he'd been required to utter words like *slaughter*, *massacre*, or *incinerate*, he could not have forced them out of his mouth.

The drafters of the Single Integrated Operational Plan had foreseen that particular hurdle, and they'd built a corrective mechanism directly into the document. Each nuclear strike option had been assigned a so-called *brevity code*, consisting of a single word paired with a numeral. By referring to an attack plan or a target list by its brevity code, the president and the National Command Authority could discuss options and give orders, while avoiding the kinds of words that trigger mental shutdown and emotional overload.

The brevity code for attacking suspected nuclear weapons facilities in Iran was *Typhoon Three*. The code for hitting every power plant and electrical distribution facility in North Korea was *Castle Eight*. The code for total destruction of every city in China was *Zebra Two*. And the brevity code for unrestricted thermonuclear war—the end of the world—was *Angel Seven*.

It was the supreme euphemism: the extermination of all human life, concealed behind a hopeful-sounding word and a randomly-selected numeral.

The president slammed the heavy binder shut with a great deal more force than he'd intended.

Angel Seven.

The code phrase stuck in his brain. Einstein had named it *World War III*. The bible called it *Armageddon*. The Vikings had known it as *Raganarøkr*, the *Twilight of the Gods*. But the Single Integrated Operational Plan called it *Angel Seven*.

He shoved the binder away from him. The answer, if there was one, was not hidden in the pages of the Cookbook for Ending the World.

He rubbed his eyes, took a breath, and looked up at the Chairman of the Joint Chiefs. "General Gilmore, keep us at DEFCON 1. Have STRATCOM and NMCC prepare a list of prioritized recommendations. Make sure your personal recommendations are on the top of the stack."

He turned to his national security advisor. "Of course you're right, Greg. We *have* to respond. We cannot spend the rest of our lives squatting in bunkers and waiting for Zhukov to drop the other shoe. I want a full strategy meeting in the Sit Room in two hours. Defense, Security, and State."

He pointed at the geographic display screen, where the red arc of the Russian weapon still burned. "Whatever we do, our number one priority must be to destroy that missile submarine. We got lucky the first time. Zhukov only fired one missile. We threw everything we had at it, but we still didn't get all the warheads. What happens if Zhukov launches *ten* missiles?"

The president stood up and pushed his chair back from the table. "We've got a maniac out there with a nuclear arsenal, and he's already shown that he's not afraid to use it. This is not going to end until *we* end it."

He lowered his voice. "Or until that crazy bastard ends it for us."

CHAPTER 28

Sergiei Mikhailovich Zhukov, president of the newly-independent nation of Kamchatka and future premiere of the soon-to-be-restored Soviet Empire, rifled through the sheaf of news reports that his staff had downloaded from the Internet. The American press was so helpful—freely spreading information that Zhukov's enemies should be keeping to themselves.

He flipped a page and smiled at a printed news photograph of smashed shop windows and battered-looking looters in handcuffs. There was pandemonium in the western states, especially California. The freeways were jammed. Businesses were in turmoil. Petrol stations were extorting ten dollars a gallon for gasoline, and bottled water and canned food were rapidly vanishing into the pockets of a burgeoning black market. Police and emergency services were being overwhelmed by a population that was rushing to escape the next barrage of nuclear warheads.

The missile launch had occurred less than three hours ago, and already opponents of the American president were criticizing their leader's handling of the crisis. The bolder of them were calling for Chandler's resignation, with a small but vocal minority demanding impeachment. One of the man's more famous detractors had publicly announced that it was time for the Farm Boy President to go back to the farm. The media carried every second of the escalating controversy, and splashed it across newspapers, television screens, and Internet websites.

Such were the benefits of their so-called *free press*. The American news industry was not the voice of the common people as that country's founding fathers had intended. It had become a self-important money-hungry conglomerate, peddling the worst sort of sensationalist garbage to the unknowing masses. And the people didn't realize that things should be

164

any different, because this filth-slinging gossip machine was all they'd ever seen.

Zhukov dropped the stack of reports on his desk. For all its shortcomings, the American media was becoming his best ally in this fight, exactly as he had planned.

Lenin had once written that one man with a gun can control 100 men without one. Well, the gun was in the hands of Sergiei Mikhailovich Zhukov now. And he was depending on the American news industry to tell the world exactly how lethal that gun was, and—more importantly—where it was pointed.

CHAPTER 29

WHITE HOUSE SITUATION ROOM
WASHINGTON, DC
SATURDAY; 02 MARCH
9:45 PM EST

White House Chief of Staff Veronica Doyle, took her seat to the left of the president's chair. She leaned close to her boss. "Sir, I think we're ready to begin."

The president nodded toward the Chief of Naval Operations. "Admiral, you're up."

Admiral Robert Casey, slid back his chair and got to his feet, straightening his immaculate navy blue uniform jacket as he stood. He gave a respectful nod toward his Commander in Chief. "Thank you, Mr. President."

The CNO swept his eyes over the mix of civilians and military personnel seated around the long mahogany table. To the president's right, sat Chairman of the Joint Chiefs of Staff, Army General Horace Gilmore, and Secretary of Homeland Security Becka Solomon. To the president's left, were White House Chief of Staff Veronica Doyle, and National Security Advisor Gregory Brenthoven. On the admiral's side of the table were Secretary of Defense Rebecca Kilpatrick, Secretary of State Elizabeth Whelkin, and Vice President Dalton Wainright.

The admiral picked up a small remote control and slid his thumb across a dial. The lights in the Situation Room dimmed, and a large projection screen slid out of the ceiling at the far end of the conference table. He pressed a button and a map appeared on the screen. The majority of the image was taken up by a large body of water, roughly rectangular in shape. The water was surrounded by landmasses to the north and west, by a dagger-shaped peninsula to the east, and by a narrow chain of islands to the south.

A black dot appeared on the eastern edge of the peninsula, near the southern tip of the dagger shape. A label below the dot identified it as *Petropavlosk-Kamchatkskiy*.

"Approximately four days ago, armed hostilities broke out in Petropavlosk, the capital city of Kamchatka. Our intelligence sources determined that the conflict was the opening stroke of a military revolution, led by Sergiei Mikhailovich Zhukov, the Governor of Kamchatka. Subsequent statements by Governor Zhukov confirm that he is attempting to break away from the Russian Federation, and establish Kamchatka as an independent and sovereign nation. Governor Zhukov has declared himself president of what he claims is now the *country* of Kamchatka. He has made it clear that he views this act as the first step toward reconstituting the Union of Soviet Socialist Republics, and the re-conquest of the former Soviet satellite countries."

The admiral continued. "During the early stages of the fighting, a Delta III class nuclear ballistic missile submarine got underway from Rybachiy naval station, outside of Petropavlosk."

The admiral keyed his remote, and a black and white photograph of a submarine appeared in a pop-up window on the left side of the screen. "We identified it as *this* submarine—the *Zelenograd*, hull number K-506—built by the Soviet Navy during the Cold War, and later maintained in service under the navy of the Russian Federation. Our identification has been confirmed by the Russian Ambassador."

The admiral pressed another button, and the remote in his hand projected a laser pointer, which he directed toward the screen.

"The submarine rounded the southern tip of the Kamchatka peninsula, and transited through the Kuril island chain into the Sea of Okhotsk, the large body of water shown on this map. The Sea of Okhotsk is to the immediate south of Siberia, and it shares the extreme cold of the Siberian winter."

The CNO clicked the remote again, and the map on the screen was replaced by an aerial photograph of a rugged icescape. "At this time of year, the northern eighty percent of the Sea of Okhotsk is completely iced over, and the ice pack is heavy. It's possible that Governor Zhukov timed his coup with this in mind. The Sea of Okhotsk is to the immediate west of the Kamchatkan peninsula, allowing Zhukov to hide his missile submarine under the Siberian ice pack, and still effectively keep it in his backyard."

The admiral looked at the faces around the table. "The Delta III class submarine carries sixteen nuclear missiles, each of which is armed with three 200 kiloton warheads. That's about three times the firepower needed to destroy every city in the western United States. So the deployment of submarine K-506 constitutes an imminent threat to our national security, as the events of the last few hours have proven."

The CNO returned to his chair and nodded toward the national security advisor. "Before I continue, I'd like to ask Mr. Brenthoven to give us a short synopsis of the diplomatic situation."

Brenthoven stood up. "Thank you, Admiral." He straightened his tie. "I met with Ambassador Kolesnik shortly after the missile submarine put out to sea. On the instructions of President Chandler, I proposed that the United States and the Russian Federation share diplomatic and military resources in dealing with the problem. But our overtures toward a joint solution were rejected."

Brenthoven glanced down at his notes. "The government of the Russian Federation insisted that the coup in Kamchatka and the deployment of the K-506 were internal Russian matters. Speaking through his ambassador, President Turgenev declined all offers of diplomatic assistance, and he specifically refused to allow American military participation."

"I pointed out that the striking range and firepower of the R-29R missiles put the entire western United States in danger of nuclear attack. Ambassador Kolesnik assured me that there was no danger to the U.S. He reminded me that Delta III class submarines, which they refer to as the *Kal'mar* class, do not have ice penetration capability. They weren't built with the proper hull configuration, or the right kind of structural reinforcements needed to punch through ice. He assured me that if that submarine tried to break through the ice, its hull would be sliced open and it would sink like the *Titanic*. He promised me that the Russian Navy would keep the K-506 trapped under the ice pack, where it could not fire its missiles, and they would destroy the sub long before it posed a threat."

Brenthoven nodded toward the admiral and sat down. "As we all know, that's not exactly how things worked out."

Admiral Casey stood up again and pressed a button on his remote. The photo of the ice pack was replaced by the map. A red circle appeared, near the northeast corner of the Sea of Okhotsk. A label next to it displayed the latitude and longitude: 58.29N / 155.20E.

"Three and a half hours ago," the admiral said, "the submarine in question launched an R-29R series nuclear missile from this approximate position. The launch was detected by a U.S. Air Force *Eagle Eye* surveillance satellite. The launch and missile trajectory were confirmed by PAVE PAWS radar installations at Beale Air Force Base, California, and Clear Air Force Station, Alaska."

"The R-29R missile is a *MIRV*, which is to say that it carries multiple warheads that can be directed at geographically-separated targets. The missile variant we're up against carries three nuclear warheads, and four decoy warheads that simulate the radar, infrared, and flight characteristics of the real warheads in every respect. It's impossible to tell the real warheads from the decoys until they hit their targets, so we had to attempt intercepts on all seven warheads."

He clicked the remote, and a map of the Pacific ocean appeared, with Siberia and Kamchatka near the left edge, and the western United States near the right edge. A curved red line stretched from the left side of the map to the right, climbing from its start point west of Kamchatka to an apex near the top of the map, and then curving back down to a point in the ocean, just west of the California coast line. At irregular intervals along the curve, thinner red lines arched out, each at a different angle, but all pointed in the general direction of the American coast. Clusters of blue lines sprouted from locations in Alaska and California. At various places on the map, each blue line intersected with a red line. In some cases, the red and blue lines terminated at the point of intersection. In other places, the colored arcs simply crossed, each continuing on its way, past the spot where intersection should have occurred.

"Seven ground-based interceptor missiles were launched from the western U.S.," the admiral said. "Three from Vandenberg Air Force, and four from the Army missile complex at Fort Greely. Between them, the ground-based interceptors knocked out three of the inbound warheads."

Four gray lines appeared on the screen, sprouting from what appeared to be the open water of the eastern Pacific. Three of these new lines converged with red lines and terminated them. The fourth gray line ended abruptly, well short of intersection with the remaining red line. The last red arc continued uninterrupted to a spot in the ocean near the California coast.

"The cruiser, USS *Shiloh*, launched two pairs of sea-based interceptor missiles against the remaining warheads, destroying three out of four. The fourth warhead, as you know, impacted in the ocean and detonated about a hundred miles west of San Diego. Based on satellite imagery and seismic readings, we estimate the yield at approximately 200 kilotons. Just about exactly what we would expect to see out of an R-29R warhead."

He keyed the remote again. On the screen, six dashed red lines appeared, each attached to one of the interrupted arcs that represented an intercepted missile. All six of the dashed lines curved down to points in the ocean, at varying distances from the California coast.

"This is a projection of the unfinished trajectories of the six warheads that were intercepted. Based on their position and movement vectors at the moment of intercept, these are the calculated impact points for each warhead if we had not managed to knock them down. You'll note that all seven warheads, including the six we intercepted and the one we missed, would have fallen in the ocean. In other words, we don't think that any of the warheads were aimed at targets on U.S. soil."

He paused a second, to let the impact of that statement to sink in. "The analysts at the Office of Naval Intelligence offered three possible interpretations of this information. I present them in no particular order. First, the missile might have suffered a mechanical failure that threw the warheads far enough off course to miss their respective targets. Second, the crew of K-506 may lack the expertise to successfully program the P-29R missile guidance package. And third, it's possible that Governor Zhukov, despite his heavy-handed threats, lacks the will to attack American targets with nuclear weapons. Each of these three theories had supporters at ONI and in the Pentagon. Many of the people looking at this problem felt that one of the three was likely to be the answer. That is, until we discovered *this* ..."

Once again, the admiral keyed the remote. Three red circles appeared on the screen. Two of them were centered on projected impact zones for warheads that had been shot down. The third was centered on the impact zone for the warhead that had slipped by the interceptors to detonate west of San Diego. The three circles formed a nearly perfect diagonal line, with two of the circles grouped close to each other at the southeast end, and the third by itself at the northwest end.

"These impact points were from warheads 1, 5 and 6, numbered for the order in which they were deployed by the missile. As you can tell, #6 got past our interceptors. Numbers 1 and 5 were shot down."

The admiral laid his remote on the table. "The impact points for the remaining warheads were randomly distributed. But 1, 5, and 6 formed a pattern. We now believe that 1, 5, and 6 were the live nuclear warheads, and the randomly distributed impacts—2, 3, 4, and 7—were the decoys."

Secretary of State Whelkin rubbed her left earlobe. "I assume there's a significance to this pattern, Admiral?"

Admiral Casey returned to his seat. "Yes, Madam Secretary. We believe there is. One of the analysts at ONI did a bit of measuring. It turns out that the first warhead was targeted exactly 300 miles west of San Francisco. The second was aimed exactly 200 miles west of Los Angeles. And the third—the one that got past us—detonated exactly 100 miles west of San Diego. Three hundred miles, two hundred miles, and one hundred miles. In that order."

"It's a countdown," General Gilmore said. "Three—two—one. After that, comes *zero*."

Admiral Casey nodded. "Or *ground* zero, which is the traditional name for the center point of a nuclear attack."

The president frowned. "You think Zhukov was sending us a message? With nuclear weapons?"

"That's a distinct possibility, Mr. President," the admiral said. "Governor Zhukov may have been communicating with us in a way that transcends all threats and saber-rattling. We think he was telling us that this was our freebie. This was our one and only warning shot. Three-two-one-zero. Every impact point calibrated to the position of a major city. The next time he shoots, it won't be offset into the water. It will be right on top of the targets. Ground zero. And he's going after major centers of population."

The White House chief of staff pulled out her palmtop computer and started punching buttons. After a few seconds, she looked up. "Six and a half million people," she said.

The president raised an eyebrow. "What's that?"

"I just pulled the census projections for San Francisco, Los Angeles, and San Diego," Doyle said. "Sir, if those three warheads had hit their targets, they would have killed about six and a half million people."

"I see," said the president. He looked at the Chief of Naval Operations. "I think you're right, Admiral. Mr. Zhukov is sending us a message. He's telling us that the gloves are off, and next time, he kills *millions*."

Becka Solomon sat back in her chair. "Mr. President, if we're reading this correctly, we're going to have to evacuate the entire western United States."

"I'm not even sure that's possible," the vice president said. "We couldn't get a million people 200 miles up the road from New Orleans before Hurricane Katrina hit. How are we going to move seventy million people across half the country?"

"I don't know," Solomon said. "But Zhukov has got forty-five nuclear warheads left, and he's communicated quite clearly that he's not afraid to use them. We've got way too many population centers within reach of those missiles. Los Angeles, San Diego, Portland, Cheyenne, Seattle, Las Vegas, Denver, Phoenix, Albuquerque, Sacramento, Salt Lake City, Reno, Great Falls, Spokane … Zhukov could wipe out every city and major town west of the Texas panhandle, and still have a few warheads left over for a rainy day."

"We cannot evacuate the western United States," the president said. "It would take us years to prepare for a move that big, and I'm not sure this country would survive the effort. The economy would be devastated—maybe completely destroyed. There are no resources to transport that many refugees, much less house them or feed them. And how would we provide medical care and emergency services for eighty million displaced people?"

He shook his head. "A lot of frightened people are trying to run east, and we can't do anything about that. I'm not going to call out the troops and try to force people to stay in the target zone. If they want to run, we have to let them run. That by itself is going to damage this country in ways I don't want to think about. But we cannot undertake the job of moving eighty million people. We're not even going to try."

He looked at the CNO. "The only way to stop this, is to kill that submarine. How do we do that, Admiral?"

"Mr. President," the admiral said. "We're obviously going to have to project military force into the Sea of Okhotsk. We'll have to go in there after the submarine. And that's going to be a bit of a problem."

"Why is that?"

"Geography, sir. The Sea of Okhotsk is landlocked on three sides by Russian territory. Siberia is to the north; Russia is to the west; and Kamchatka is to the east. Governor Zhukov may claim otherwise, but Kamchatka *still* happens to be Russian territory. The only entrances to the Sea of Okhotsk are to the south, through the Kuril island chain, which—as you may have guessed—is Russian territory as well. Which means that all of the land surrounding the Sea of Okhotsk is owned by the Russian Federation. To their way of thinking, that makes the whole sea their national property. The United States and the international community don't happen to agree, but that's how the Russians see it. As far as they're concerned, that's their back yard. They're not going to want us in there."

"I don't understand," the Vice President said. "If we can't go into the Sea of Okhotsk, how are we going to get the sub?"

The Secretary of Defense smiled. "The admiral didn't say we can't go in there, Mr. Vice President. He said the Russians aren't going to like it. And he's right. They won't like it. But they can't stop it. According to international law, the Russian Federation doesn't own that water. They like to *think* they do, but the law, the United Nations, and the international community say otherwise. We do not acknowledge the Russian claim of ownership."

Vice President Wainright scratched the lobe of his right ear. "Why is that? If the Russians own all the land surrounding the water, doesn't that mean they own the water too?"

The CNO shook his head. "No, sir. International law says that a country's national waters extend twelve nautical miles from the coastline. You've heard of the twelve mile limit? That's what the term refers to. If you go thirteen miles off shore, you're in international waters. Luckily, there are several passages through the Kuril islands that are more than twenty-four nautical miles wide. Our units can transit through the straits without passing within the twelve-mile limit of any of the islands. We can get into and out of the Sea of Okhotsk without crossing into lawfully-recognized Russian waters."

Secretary of State Whelkin held up her hand. "I understand that international law backs our right to enter this body of water, Admiral. But are the Russians going to sit still if we send a military force into what they clearly regard as their private sea?"

"They're definitely not going to be happy about it, Madam Secretary," the admiral said. "But we send Navy ships and aircraft into the Sea of Okhotsk periodically, despite the protests of the Russian government. They're called *freedom of navigation exercises*, and the U.S. has been doing it since the beginning of the Cold War, when the Soviet Union tried to claim ownership of the Sea of Okhotsk. We do it to demonstrate our right of free passage and to remind the Russian government that the United States does not acknowledge their claim of ownership. So we know the Russians aren't going to like it, but they're somewhat accustomed to seeing our warships and aircraft in there."

"Isn't this a bad time to be provoking the Russians?" the White House chief of staff asked. "We know from the intelligence assessments that the Russian government is already about to blow its top. And they're cranked up to maximum nuclear readiness levels, just like we are. Is it smart to poke a stick into the hornet's nest?"

"One of *their* political leaders has just launched three of *their* nuclear missiles toward *our* coast line," Secretary of Defense Kilpatrick said. Her voice was low, but as hard as steel. "As far as I'm concerned, they should be worried about provoking *us*."

"Unless we're prepared to stay at DEFCON 1 until the spring thaw, we don't really have a choice," Gregory Brenthoven said. "That's a nuclear-powered submarine. A Delta III can remain submerged for months at a time, and the ice pack in the Sea of Okhotsk gives it excellent concealment and protection. The commander of the K-506 has maneuvered his boat into a superb tactical position. He'd have to be stupid to come out of there, and he is *not* stupid. If we want to kill that submarine, we're going to have to go in there after it.

"How do we do that?" the president asked. "What are our options?"

"We can't send ships in there at this time of year," Admiral Casey said. "The ice will cut them to ribbons."

The admiral's eyes went back to the large display screen. "Where the hell is global warming when we need it?"

No one laughed.

"What about aircraft?" the Vice President asked.

"We can over-fly with aircraft," the admiral said. "But they can't really do much. Airborne sensors can't see through the ice pack, and air-launched torpedoes and depth charges will just hit the ice face and break up. They're not designed to punch through ice."

"That submarine has figured out how to shoot through the ice," General Gilmore said. "How are *they* doing it?"

"That's the big question, General," the CNO said. "Our engineers are certain that the Delta III does not have ice penetration capability. The differences in design and construction are so major that it would take a couple of years in a shipyard dry dock to modify a Delta III for ice penetration. We track the maintenance and deployment of foreign missile submarines very carefully. If K-506 had been in the yards for a major hull rebuild, we'd know about it."

"Could the missiles just punch through?" the Secretary of Homeland Security asked. "Like a bullet?"

The Secretary of Defense shook her head. "I don't think so. Those missiles are fast, but they're also delicate machines. It would be like a Lear jet slamming into a brick wall at several hundred miles an hour. It would knock a hole in the wall, but the Lear would be hamburger afterward." She shook her head again. "Any missile that hits the ice is *not* going to fly afterwards."

The national security advisor sighed. "Which brings us back around to the original question," he said. "How is Zhukov's submarine shooting through the ice?"

"We don't know yet," the Chief of Naval Operations said. "All we can do is speculate."

"Fair enough," the president said. "Speculate."

The admiral nodded. "Sir, our best guess is that they've got explosive charges pre-positioned at various locations around the ice pack. When they need to launch, they sail to a spot at a safe distance from the nearest prepared position, and trigger the explosives. As soon as the spray and debris settle, they've got a nice big hole in the ice. They pop off a missile through the hole, and get out of the area before anybody comes looking for them."

He shrugged. "It's only a guess, Mr. President. But if the charges are the right size and they're properly placed, we think there's a good chance that it would work. We don't know if that's what they're actually doing, but it's one way they *might* be doing it."

"Could they be torpedoing the ice?" Vice President Wainright asked. "Then they wouldn't have to limit themselves to a few pre-positioned locations. They could make a hole anywhere they wanted."

"I don't think so, sir," said the CNO. "A torpedo explosion is fairly concentrated. It does a lot of damage in a relatively small area. It would take a lot of torpedoes to make a big enough hole to shoot through. If our guess is correct, they're using multiple explosives packages spread out over a comparatively large area. The demolitions experts over at Spec Warfare think it would take about five or six shaped charges, drilled into the ice in a big circle, and all wired to a central detonator. The detonator would be connected to some type of external receiver that the submarine can trigger from remote."

"How many of these prepared spots do you think they've got?" the president asked.

"We have no idea, sir," the admiral said. "But everything that's happened so far indicates that Mr. Zhukov has been planning this for a long time. He's had months to line up his assets, while nobody was watching. He might have three or four shooting spots prepared. Or a dozen. If we knew how many, and where they were, it would make catching that sub a lot easier. But we don't know. At the moment, we're not even sure if our theory is correct. They may be using an entirely different method to shoot through the ice. Something we haven't thought of."

"We're not going to solve the mystery right now," the president said. "But we still need a plan for getting to that submarine."

"Sir," the admiral said. "We really only have one option. For the reasons we've already discussed, we can't send ships or aircraft. We're going to have to go after K-506 with another submarine. That would have been my first choice anyway. The best way to kill a submarine is with another submarine."

He checked his briefing notes. "USS *Tucson* is operating near Japan. I can have her through the Kuril Islands and into the Sea of Okhotsk in about six hours. I can get the *Seawolf* up there in about 12 hours, and the *Bremerton* about three or four hours after that. I'd like to have one of the other *Seawolf* class boats, but the *Connecticut* and the *Jimmy Carter* are both too far out of position. So we have to make do with one *Seawolf* class and two *Los Angeles* class boats. I don't see that as a problem, though. The *Los Angeles* class are top-notch boats. Born hunters. They'll get the job done."

"Are three submarines going to be enough?" the president asked. "The Sea of Okhotsk looks like a big piece of water."

"It is, sir," the admiral said. "It's over 600,000 square miles. Roughly two and a half times the size of Texas. But we're fairly confident that the K-506 will keep to the eastern half of the sea. Governor Zhukov isn't going to want his ace in the hole to get too close to Mother Russia. He doesn't want to risk losing it. Also, the farther west that submarine moves, the more U.S. targets he puts out of missile range. If he wants to keep his strike options open, he can't stray too far west. I think three attack subs are about right to search the eastern end of the sea. Any more, and they'll start getting in each other's way."

The president nodded. "What's your fall-back plan?"

"We're going to try to figure out how Zhukov is communicating with his submarine. If we can interrupt his channel of communication, we can keep him from sending launch orders to the sub. That won't necessarily help us kill the K-506, but it should prevent any more nuclear strikes while we track it down."

"So you have to zero-in on their radio frequency, and break their encryption?" Secretary Solomon asked.

The admiral shook his head. "No, Madam Secretary. Ordinary radio waves only penetrate a few feet into water. A submerged submarine can't transmit or receive radio unless it extends an antenna above the surface, or floats what we call a *trailing wire*. Neither one of those options works under ice. To transmit through water and ice, you have to use extremely low frequencies, with long enough wavelengths to penetrate. Our navy uses this method, and so do the Russians. We call our system *ELF*. They call their system *Zevs*. We use slightly different frequencies and transmission technologies, but the basic idea is the same. But Zhukov can't access the Zevs system. There's only one transmitter station, and it's located near *Murmansk*. The Russian navy controls it, so there's no chance that Zhukov is using it."

The Secretary of State rested her elbows on the table. "Could he have built his own transmitter station? For Zevs, or ELF?"

'No, Madam Secretary," the admiral said. "The facilities are enormous, and far too expensive. The entire economy of Kamchatka for twenty years wouldn't cover the cost. In any case, the antenna feed lines have to be about thirty miles long. You can't hide a construction project that large. Not in the Congo, not in the arctic, not in the Sahara. Not even in Kamchatka. We don't know what method they're using, but do know that it's not Zevs or ELF."

"ONI is looking at this right now," he said. "So are DARPA, and the Applied Physics Laboratory at Johns Hopkins. There's got to be an answer. We'll find it." He faced the national security advisor. "With your permission, Mr. Brenthoven, I'd like to put the National Security Agency and the National Reconnaissance Office on the problem as well. Those guys spend all their time peeking over fences and listening at keyholes. They might have some ideas about how Zhukov is talking to his sub."

Gregory Brenthoven nodded. "I'll put them on it."

The president looked around the table. "We deploy the *Tucson*, *Seawolf*, and *Bremerton* into the Sea of Okhotsk to locate and destroy the K-506. We simultaneously investigate Zhukov's method of communicating with his missile submarine. Does anyone have any objections to the plan, or any refinements to add?"

No one spoke.

The president pushed back his chair and stood up. "Go with it, Admiral. And keep me informed at every step."

He paused, and was about to speak again when the door opened and a Secret Service agent walked in, escorting White House Communications Director Roger Chu.

The man crossed quickly to the head of the table. He was visibly trembling. "Please forgive the interruption, Mr. President, but there's a breaking story on CNN that you need to see immediately, sir." His eyes darted to the screen and then instantly back to the president. "My assistant is burning the clip onto disk right now. It should be here in a couple of minutes."

"Thank you, Roger," the president said. "While we're waiting for the video, why don't you give us the short version?"

Chu swallowed. "Yes, sir." He looked around the table and saw that every face was turned in his direction. His voice wavered. "Mr. President, Governor Zhukov has just made another public statement to the media. Actually, it was a demand—issued to the United States, the Russian Federation, and Japan. He wants every submarine in our collective military inventories on the surface in the next three hours. He says he has agents in numerous countries, monitoring commercial imaging satellites. He says he knows exactly how many submarines we have at our disposal, and he wants every one of them out in the open, where he can see it. Attack subs, missile subs, all of them. Then he wants us to put them all in port, and keep them there. But first we have to bring them all to the surface, where he can see them."

"That's crazy," the Secretary of Defense snapped. "Mr. President, we can't do that."

"The deadline is 6:00 AM, Greenwich Mean Time," Roger Chu said. The man was close to tears. "Governor Zhukov says if a single submarine from *any* of our nations is not clearly visible on the surface, he'll launch nuclear weapons against …" Chu looked down at a piece of paper in his hand. It was shaking so badly that he had trouble reading the list he had copied there. "Moscow, Vladivostok, Saint Petersburg, Tokyo, Osaka, Yokohama, Los Angeles, Seattle, and Denver."

Chu lowered the paper, still clutched in his trembling hand. "Mr. President … Governor Zhukov said something about a *surprise package*, sir. He said he would also hit three cities that are *not* on the list. But he didn't say which country those three cities were in."

The room was utterly silent.

Roger Chu emitted a sound that might have been a sob.

"Mr. President, we can't do that," the Secretary of Defense said again. "I'm not just talking about our national policy against negotiating with terrorists, sir. I'm talking about strategic defense. Our attack subs would be bad enough, but we *can't* reveal the locations of our missile submarines. The second we put those missile boats on the surface, our national security goes up in smoke. Our deterrence will be gone. Our second strike capability will be gone. We *have* to keep our missile submarines hidden. Otherwise, we can't protect this country."

The president looked at his Director of Communications. The normally rock-solid man was on the verge of breaking down.

"Does anyone see any alternatives?" the president said. "Any ideas at all, I don't care *how* crazy."

Gregory Brenthoven exhaled sharply. "We … My God, I can't believe I'm saying this … We launch a pre-emptive nuclear strike against Kamchatka. We wipe out Zhukov before he can issue launch orders to his submarine."

"That's not going to work," the Chief of Naval Operations said. "The Kamchatka peninsula is about 140,000 square miles. That's nearly the size of California, and we don't have any idea where—in all of that territory—Zhukov might be hiding. How do we know we can even *hit* him? And what happens if we *don't* hit him?"

"I agree," the president said. "If we launch nuclear strikes against Kamchatka and we *don't* kill Zhukov, he's going to incinerate every city and town west of the Rocky Mountains."

"Then we hit it *all*," Brenthoven said. "We turn the entire peninsula into a fucking parking lot."

The Secretary of State shook her head. "No, Greg. They're right. We don't know what instructions Zhukov has given to the captain of his missile submarine. Maybe the guy's got orders to nuke *everything* if he loses communication with Zhukov. We can't take that chance. If we can't take the submarine out of the equation, we can't shoot at Zhukov."

"Well, shit!" the president said. "Shit, shit, shit, and double-shit. What do we do now?"

"I hate to say this," the CNO said. "But we're going to have to put our subs on the surface."

"We cannot knuckle under to a fucking madman," Secretary of Defense Kilpatrick said. "We can't do it. We just *can't*."

"We don't have a choice," the president said. "I'm not going to sacrifice six million American lives to protect our national prestige. If we have to kiss this guy's ass, then we get on our knees and pucker up. Right up until the moment that we stick a knife in his heart."

He turned his eyes to the Chief of Naval Operations. "Put the submarines on the surface Bob. All of them. Do it now."

He shifted his gaze to his secretary of state. "Liz, we need to open immediate diplomatic dialogues with Japan and Russia. Make sure they intend to comply with Zhukov's deadline. Hopefully, they're smart enough to realize that this nutcase is not bluffing. If they balk, tell them we're working on a plan to neutralize the threat, and that we'll share it with them as soon as we nail down the details. In the meantime, they need to get their submarines on the surface so that Zhukov doesn't start launching nuclear missiles."

The president lowered himself into his chair. "We're back to square one," he said. "We've got to figure out how to destroy the K-506 without submarines."

He slammed his fist on the table. "And then we're going to go and kill the maniac who started this nightmare."

CHAPTER 30

ICBM: A COLD WAR SAILOR'S MUSINGS ON THE ULTIMATE WEAPONS OF MASS DESTRUCTION

(Reprinted by permission of the author, Retired Master Chief Sonar Technician David M. Hardy, USN)

At the close of the Second World War, German rocket engineers under the direction of Wernher von Braun were engaged in developing the A9/A10: a powerful two-stage missile capable of reaching across the Atlantic Ocean to attack New York and other American cities. The A9/A10 development effort was part of a larger program called *Project Amerika*, which was dedicated to the creation of specialized bombers, rockets, and other weapons, to be used in Germany's eventual conquest of the United States.

If it had ever been completed, the A9/A10 would have been the first Intercontinental Ballistic Missile in history. Instead, it became the theoretical model from which later ICBMs would be built.

The program came to a halt in 1945 with the surrender of the German military, but Wernher von Braun and a number of his fellow scientists were quietly whisked away to America, where they became the core of the rocket and missile research programs for the U.S. military.

Having foreseen the collapse of the Nazi regime, von Braun's team had managed to conceal and protect many of their blueprints and research papers. In some cases, the recovered technical documents were nearly as useful as the scientists themselves.

This was certainly true for the Soviet Union. Because Soviet agents in post-war Germany did not immediately recognize the potential value of Hitler's rocket scientists, the Soviets acted too slowly to capitalize on this brief opportunity. Consequently, when Soviet rocket designer Sergei Korolev began constructing his nation's missile program, he had captured German blueprints to work from, but almost no German technical expertise to help him decipher them. To paraphrase a prominent military

180

historian: *The United States had already snatched up all the good German engineers.*

But—Germans or no-Germans—the race was on. Although they had been allies in the fight against the Nazis, the United States and the Soviet Union had very different plans for reconstructing the world in the aftermath of the war. The relationship between the two nations had been strained even when they'd been in formal alliance. With the dissolution of the alliance, mutual suspicion deepened into outright hostility. Even as World War II was ending, the Cold War was beginning.

As a result of military and industrial buildup, economic capacity, and postwar positioning, the Soviet Union and the United States emerged as the so-called *superpowers*. The rivalry between them was intense from the outset, but it was also one-sided. America had the atomic bomb. Soviet Russia did not.

Then, in August of 1949, the Soviet Union detonated its own atomic bomb at Semipalatinsk, Kazakhstan. The US intelligence community would later learn that the Russian weapon had been an almost direct copy of the American 'Fat Man' bomb dropped on Nagasaki. In point of fact, the Russian atomic bomb was more a product of espionage than research. But the source of the information paled beside a single inescapable fact ... The Soviet Union now had nuclear weapons.

The balance of power no longer leaned in America's favor. It had become a true balance, with the growing might of the US on one side, offset by the growing might of the USSR on the other.

In 1952, America briefly regained a significant technological edge with the first successful test of a nuclear fusion weapon: the infamous *hydrogen bomb*. This development brought another quantum leap in destructive potential. Previous *fission*-type nuclear weapons had yielded explosive forces in the kiloton range, equal to the destructive power of several thousand tons of TNT. *Fusion*-type or hydrogen weapons offered explosive yields in the megaton range, equal to the destructive power of several million tons of TNT. The deadliest weapon in history had just become, quite literally, a thousand times more destructive.

This new capability gave the United States a tremendous strategic advantage, but the shelf-life of that advantage was very short. In 1953, the Soviet Union tested its own fusion weapon, the *Sloika* ("Layer Cake"). Once again, the US and USSR had rough military parity, and the nuclear balance of power had been reestablished.

The superpowers differed on virtually everything, from political ideologies, to economic models, to human rights, to the very future of mankind. The Soviets believed that the Communist ideal was destined to spread to every nation on earth. Fearing that very thing, the US began building military and political alliances in Western Europe, Southeast Asia, and the Middle East. The intent was to 'contain' the threat of communism, and to guard against Soviet military aggression.

This philosophy led to the signing of the *Treaty of Brussels* in 1948, and a year later, to the formation of the *North Atlantic Treaty Organization*, or NATO.

The Soviet Union interpreted these alliances as a direct strategic threat, and responded in 1955 by forming the *Warsaw Treaty of Friendship, Cooperation and Mutual Assistance* (better known to history as the 'Warsaw Pact'). Essentially a military alliance of socialist states in Eastern and Central Europe, the Warsaw Pact was intended to counterbalance the threat posed by NATO.

Sides had been chosen. The battle lines had been drawn for an entirely new kind of war.

Until the 1940s, even the most lethal of weapons had been limited in their capacity for destruction. As horrific as the machineries of warfare had become, their deadliness had never been absolute. Even the bloodiest battles tended to leave survivors on both sides—among the victors and among the vanquished. No matter how high the death toll rose, it was never high enough to completely eradicate the population of the defeated nation.

The destruction of Hiroshima and Nagasaki changed that. With the advent of nuclear warfare, it became possible (at least theoretically) for one country to utterly annihilate the inhabitants of another country.

In hindsight it seems incredible, but the nuclear warhead became both the symbol of absolute national power, and the ultimate tool of military force projection. In their ceaseless contest for strategic dominance, the United States and the Soviet Union poured enormous amounts of funding and effort into building, testing, and stockpiling new and more powerful nuclear weapons.

As the nuclear arsenals of the superpowers grew, the technology of weapons delivery platforms advanced to keep pace. Propeller driven bombers gave way to jet bombers, and then to supersonic jets.

By the mid 1950s, the jet bombers of America's Strategic Air Command were operating in a state of around-the-clock readiness, continually prepared to obliterate every city and military target in Soviet Russia. The Soviets held their own bombers in a similar state of readiness, poised to rain nuclear death on the United States with equal efficiency.

The total extermination of a nation's inhabitants was no longer an abstract theory. The assembled firepower of either of the nuclear superpowers was now sufficient to virtually guarantee the annihilation of populations on a national scale.

For the first time in history, two adversarial nations had become so powerful that they did not dare take their disagreements to the field of battle. Any direct military contact between the superpowers might lead to an exchange of nuclear weapons, and any nuclear combat—no matter how small in scale—could lead to a cycle of retaliation and counter-retaliation, until a small conflict escalated into a full-scale nuclear war. Neither nation could hope to survive an unrestricted nuclear attack, and a growing body of scientific research suggested that a major nuclear war might well destroy all life on planet earth.

In the context of nuclear warfare, traditional concepts of victory and defeat lost all meaning. No one could win a war in which there were no survivors. Victory and defeat were replaced by a doctrine known as *mutually assured destruction*, which is often referred to by the somewhat-appropriate acronym: *MAD*.

The threat of mutual destruction kept the NATO alliance and the Warsaw Pact from battling each other directly, so the superpowers sought and found indirect methods of combat. They fought small wars by proxy, taking opposite sides in battles between third-party countries as a substitute for the direct military confrontation that neither side dared to risk. They competed for supremacy in industrial capacity, scientific achievement, technological advancement, space exploration, and even cultural development. The competition for military dominance was more intense than ever.

Advances in jet bomber technology had given each side the ability to reach and destroy the cities of its adversary within hours. But the dawning of the space age made that timeline seem almost ludicrously slow. Each side wanted—and felt that it needed—a vehicle that could deliver nuclear attacks against its national enemies within minutes.

The solution had already been addressed, at least in principle, by the Nazi A9/A10 missile program. Hitler's unfinished ocean-spanning missile incorporated liquid fueled engines for supersonic flight speeds, multiple rocket stages for altitude and flight range, and enough payload capacity to carry a nuclear warhead.

Under the technical guidance of expatriated German engineers, the United States undertook several separate programs to build Intercontinental Ballistic Missiles. In part, the division of effort was a reflection of the rivalries between the different branches of the US military, but notes and documents from the 1950s suggest that President

Eisenhower may have seen value in taking several different approaches to solving such a difficult technical problem.

The Army Ballistic Missile Agency, and the recently-formed US Air Force, concentrated on land-based missile designs. By contrast, the US Navy plan was to launch nuclear ballistic missiles from submerged submarines. Navy leaders reasoned that land-based launch facilities could be located and bombed. Submarines, on the other hand, could move freely and stealthily around the world, remaining hidden from America's enemies, and launching nuclear strikes from unexpected locations.

Despite the advantage of multiple programs and the benefit of German engineering expertise, the United States did not win the race to launch the first Intercontinental Ballistic Missile. The Russians reached that milestone first, launching the R-7 *Semyorka* missile in August of 1957. The first successful launch of an American Intercontinental Ballistic Missile, the *Atlas-A*, took place four months later, in December of the same year.

This emerging class of nuclear super-weapons was initially referred to by the abbreviation 'IBM,' short for Intercontinental Ballistic Missile. This caused some confusion, because the International Business Machine company was already popularly identified by those same three letters. To avoid further misunderstanding, the US military revised the missile abbreviation to include the letter 'c' from the word 'Intercontinental.' The new weapons were re-designated as ICBMs.

The superpowers continued to build newer and more advanced ICBMs. Hardened concrete missile silos were carved into the mountains, fields, and prairies of Russia and the United States. The American Atlas ICBMs were joined by *Titan I* missiles, *Titan II* missiles, *Minuteman I*, *Minuteman II*, and *Minuteman III* missiles, and the *MX Peacekeeper* missile series. The Soviets followed the R-7 ICBMs with the *R-9* series missiles, the *R-16* series, *R-24*, *R-29*, *R-36*, and their successors.

The US Navy's planned fleet of nuclear ballistic missile submarines became a reality with the active deployment of the submarine-launched *Polaris* series missiles, and then the *Poseidon* series, and then the *Trident* series. The Soviets designed and deployed their own nuclear ballistic missile submarines, each generation with increasingly lethal nuclear weapons aboard.

The nuclear superpowers had finally obtained the Holy Grail of modern warfare: the ability to completely exterminate an enemy nation in mere minutes. By way of ultimate consequence—whether intended or unintended—each of the major adversaries now had the power to destroy the entire human race.

The last war and ultimate destruction of mankind, was just the push of a button away.   The world found itself hovering on the brink of Armageddon.

CHAPTER 31

White House Chief of Staff Veronica Doyle rummaged in the top drawer of her desk until she found the slim plastic form of a television remote control. She pointed the remote toward a small high-definition screen tucked into a bookshelf to the right of her desk.

The screen flared to life, and Doyle caught the last twenty seconds of a commercial about medical insurance. She fiddled with the remote, bringing the volume up to an audible level just in time to hear the insurance firm's duck mascot blurt the name of the company in a brassy nasal twang that could easily be mistaken for a quack.

Doyle smiled, briefly. That silly duck always made her want to laugh, which—she understood quite well—was the entire point of the advertising campaign.

The famously-trademarked quack faded into silence, to be instantly replaced by the opening musical fanfare of an equally-famous news debate program.

The *Crosstalk* logo appeared: a pair of animated three dimensional arrows—one red, the other blue—rushing toward each other from opposite sides of the screen. They collided in the center with an explosion of silver light, which dissolved quickly to an establishing shot of a television news studio. The camera held this angle long enough for the viewing audience to register the elegantly high-tech trappings of the studio set, and its three-sided interview table. Then the camera zoomed in for a close-up of the show's celebrated moderator.

The moderator smiled, revealing a set of perfect white teeth below piercing blue eyes. "Good evening," he said, "and welcome to Crosstalk. I'm your host, Darren Cartwright."

The camera panned right, revealing the show's first guest, a lean and hawkish looking man in his late thirties, a flawlessly-tailored black business suit stretched over his angular frame. "With us tonight, we have John Gohar of the National Center for Strategic Analysis, and Republican Senator Richard Blair, ranking member of the Senate Armed Services Committee."

The camera panned left, centering on the show's other guest, a fiftyish man in slightly rumpled tweed jacket. The senator nodded toward the camera, with the tiniest suggestion of a wink. His maroon necktie was loose, and it was obvious that the top button of his shirt wasn't fastened. The message of his wardrobe was reinforced by his thoughtful but relaxed facial expression, and the easy set of his shoulders.

Veronica Doyle smiled. Dick Blair had long been a bitter opponent of the Chandler administration, but the old scoundrel was good; she had to give him that. He was the very image of a seasoned elder statesman: purposeful, intelligent, informed, consummately professional, and—above all—clearly undaunted by the challenges of national leadership.

The camera cut back to the moderator of the show. With the opening pleasantries out of the way, Cartwright traded his introductory smile for a more serious expression. On a wall-sized video screen behind his head, the Crosstalk logo gave way to an aerial shot from a helicopter, loitering above the entrance to a harbor. Superimposed lettering identified the scene as San Diego, California.

In the foreground, the black shape of a submarine was silhouetted against rolling waves, its wake a line of white foam across blue water. In the middle distance, two more submarines could be seen making their way toward the breakwater.

The screen shuffled through a series of similar scenes: submarines tied to piers or returning to various harbors, sometimes accompanied by Navy tug boats, sometimes not. With each changing scene came an identifying caption … Kings Bay, Georgia; New London, Connecticut; Bangor, Washington; Norfolk, Virginia; Pearl Harbor, Hawaii …

The screen finally settled on a view looking out across empty ocean waves, with no submarines in sight. The subtext of the video was clear; *our nation has no submarines at sea.*

The moderator looked into the camera. "We are witnessing an event that is literally without precedent. For the first time since the creation of America's nuclear submarine force, every submarine in our country's arsenal has been ordered to return to port."

He turned toward the guest on his right. "Mr. Gohar, you're first in the hot seat tonight. How does the recall of our submarines affect national military strategy? And, more to the point, does this move leave our country open to attack?"

Gohar frowned slightly. "Those are deceptively simple questions, Darren. I can't really give useful answers without putting your questions into some kind of meaningful context. For all practical purposes…"

Senator Blair cut him off. "Thirty seconds into the program, and you're already starting with the doubletalk!" he snapped. "President Chandler has handed over control of our nuclear submarines to a proven enemy of the United States. Not *one* of our submarines. Not *some* of our submarines. *All* of them!"

He gestured toward the video screen, the gently rolling waves devoid of any manmade object. "How much context do we need to understand that?"

The moderator raised a hand. "Please, Senator… You'll get your chance to respond."

Gohar cut a quick sideways glance toward the senator. "As I was saying…" He paused, as though waiting for another interruption. "For all practical purposes, we already *have* been attacked. We've had a nuclear detonation within a hundred miles of a major U.S. city, and—if we hadn't managed to intercept them—we would have had two more detonations within a few hundred miles of the west coast."

Gohar looked directly into the camera. "We're dealing with a madman here. He has an entire arsenal of nuclear warheads at his disposal, and he's already proven that he's not afraid to use them against the United States."

"Of *course* Zhukov is not afraid," the senator said. "We've got a president who goes belly-up at the first sign of a threat. Why in the hell should *anybody* be afraid to attack us?"

"Excuse me," the moderator said. "I'd like to get back to my original question."

Gohar ignored him. "Six and a half million," he said. "That's how many people would be dead if those three warheads had reached their targets."

He glared across the table toward his opponent. "I realize that they're not your constituents, Senator Blair, but surely we don't have to risk the incineration of six and a half million Americans to uphold your sense of national dignity."

Sitting at her desk, Veronica Doyle cracked another smile. *Ouch! Let's see how fast old Dick backs away from that one…*

"I'm not talking about dignity," the senator growled. "I'm talking about national security. Strategic deterrence. National policy. Do any of these words ring a bell?"

Veronica Doyle picked up the remote and turned off the television. The show was just warming up, but she'd heard all she needed to hear.

A lot of people around the beltway were already treating Richard Blair as the presumptive Republican nominee for the next presidential election. He was clearly positioning himself for the nomination. One thing was certain; the crafty old bastard had identified the theme of his campaign.

CHAPTER 32

Bowie woke into darkness, his heart still pounding in his chest as the dream grudgingly released its grip on his mind. He lay in the bunk of his at-sea cabin, tangled in his sheets, his throat burning with remembered adrenaline.

He blinked away tears and concentrated on slowing his breathing while his brain sorted through the jumbled logic of the nightmare, separating dream images and memories of the past, from the realities of the present. The urgency of the dream began to give way, the memories gradually fading from his conscious thoughts.

This was *not* the Siraji minefield. There was no torpedo clawing its way up the wake of his wounded ship. Those events belonged to the past. They were gone and done with, no matter how many times they came back to haunt his sleep.

The parade of corpses was fading as well. Bowie was lying in his bunk alone. He was not standing in Combat Information Center, and he was not surrounded by the broken and bloody ghosts of the Sailors who had died under his command.

He stared toward the darkened ceiling, and didn't reach for his wristwatch. He didn't want to know what time it was. Not yet. He didn't want to know how much sleep he'd had, or rather, how *little*.

He thought about trying to go back to sleep.

Maybe tonight would be different. Maybe this time, the dream wouldn't come again. Maybe he would sleep, with no dreams at all. He jerked the sheets away from his legs. And maybe the Tooth Fairy would leave a quarter under his pillow.

The dream didn't come often. Sometimes it left him alone for days at a time, and once he'd gone three weeks without a single troubled night. But sooner or later, it always came back. *Always.*

If he let himself fall asleep now, he'd be back in the minefield, standing shoulder to shoulder with Clint Brody, and Alex Sherman, and Julie Schramm, and all the rest of them—with their torn and burnt flesh, and their mangled limbs.

They wouldn't question him, or accuse him. They hadn't done it in life, and they didn't do it in the dream. They just stood there, mangled and lifeless, reminding Bowie of the terrible price that each of them had paid for following his orders.

Damn.

He might has well get up. He wasn't going to get any more sleep tonight.

Bowie sat up on his bunk. He was reaching for his coveralls when the phone rang. He fumbled for it in the dark, locating it by touch, and unlatching the receiver from the cradle.

He held the phone to his ear. "Captain speaking."

The voice of his Executive Officer came over the line. "Captain, this is the XO. I apologize for disturbing your sleep, but we've got Flash message traffic, sir. Immediate execute."

Bowie yawned. "Thanks, Nick. I'll meet you in the wardroom in a couple of minutes."

He yawned again. "You've seen the message. Is this something we're going to need to wake up the Department Heads for?"

"I think so, sir," the XO said.

"Alright," Bowie said. "Roust them out, and head them up to the wardroom. I'll be up there in two shakes."

He hung up the phone. Immediate execute? That could only be one thing.

The XO hadn't given him any details, because the ship's regular internal telephones were non-secure. He'd find out in a minute, when he read the message. But it *had* to be the submarine. Bowie couldn't think of anything else that would justify Flash message traffic with Immediate execute orders.

He stood up and began pulling on his coveralls. The *Towers* was getting orders to go after the Russian missile sub. That had to be it.

They were going to go kill the submarine. He whistled through his teeth. Nothing like a little taste of déjà vu to get the morning started off right.

CHAPTER 33

NEW KOBOSHI HOTEL
CHIBA PREFECTURE, JAPAN
MONDAY; 04 MARCH
0326 hours (3:26 AM)
TIME ZONE +9 'INDIA'

Someone was knocking on the door.

Ann Roark grunted and rolled over, pulling a pillow over her head.

The knocking continued, this time accompanied by a voice. "Ann ... Get up."

It was Sheldon.

Ann opened one eye. The miniscule Japanese hotel room was still dark, the only illumination coming from the green digits of the clock radio and the red LED on the ceiling smoke detector. The muted glow of streetlights against the backs of the curtains made the window a rectangle of lesser darkness.

Ann tried to focus on the clock, but her vision was too blurry to resolve the digits into anything meaningful.

Sheldon knocked again. "Wake up, Princess Leia. It's time to go save the galaxy ... *Again.*"

Ann reluctantly peeled back the covers and half-stumbled out of bed, shuffling in the general direction of the door. She located a doorknob, twisted it, and found herself gazing blearily into the dark confines of the hotel room's tiny closet. She shoved it closed, located the correct door, and opened it.

The light from the hallway nearly blinded her. She shielded her eyes with a hand that felt like lead, and squinted toward her intruder. Sheldon stood in the doorway, silhouetted against the brightness like a Blake painting of an angel radiating heavenly glory.

Ann turned away from this vision of ersatz splendor, and reached through the open door of the bathroom to flip on the vanity lights.

"Get in, and shut the door," she said. "That hallway light is killing me."

She shuffled back into the room, hearing Sheldon close the door behind himself. She flopped face down onto the bed like a rag doll.

She clamped her eyes tightly closed, and then forced herself to open them again. "Did you get through to Powder and Booty?"

Powder was Sheldon's three year-old cocker spaniel, a shaggy buff-colored powder-puff of a dog, with a lolling tongue and a golden disposition. 'Booty' was Ann's name for Buddy, the eight month-old Yorkshire Terrier-Chihuahua mix that Sheldon had gotten as a companion to Powder. Ann had taken to calling the smaller dog *Booty*, because he seemed to take savage glee in leaping up to nip unwary people on the rump. The scruffy little rat was, quite literally, a pain in the butt.

"I got a call through to my mom," Sheldon said. "She's scared half out of her wits, but otherwise she's doing okay. I'm glad she lives up in the hills, because she tells me that Oceanside is coming unglued."

He sighed. "Powder and Buddy are doing fine, by the way."

Talking about Booty made Ann gradually realize that her own booty was currently on display. She was dressed in her bed clothes: an old *Phantom of the Opera* tee-shirt and faded green panties. Her butt was pointed straight at the ceiling.

With a nearly-convulsive jerk, she rolled over, adjusting her tee-shirt to cover her panties. Had Sheldon peeked at her ass when her back was turned? He'd almost certainly *wanted* to. Between Stairmaster and Pilate's, her butt was in pretty good shape, and she knew that Sheldon was healthy and hetero. He probably hadn't looked, though. Sheldon had an annoying habit of doing the right thing, even when nobody was watching.

She tugged the shirt down a little lower, trying to make sure her panties were safely out of view. "What time is it?"

Sheldon checked his watch. "Almost three-thirty."

"In the morning? Three-thirty *AM*?"

"I'm pretty *sure* it's AM," Sheldon said. "It's still dark outside. But this is Japan, and the rules may be different here. Maybe the sun doesn't come up on any particular schedule."

Ann yawned. "Why …" Her question was interrupted by a second yawn. "… are you waking me up at three-thirty in the freaking morning, Sheldon?"

"You need to get packed," Sheldon said. "The Navy wants us back."

Ann yawned a third time. "The Navy wants us back *where*?"

"Back on the ship," Sheldon said. "USS *Towers*. I got a call from corporate about twenty minutes ago. The Navy wants us to do some more work with Mouse. Apparently, Captain Bowie asked for us by name.

They're sending a van to drive us to the Air Force Base at Yakota. We
catch a helo flight from there."

Ann forced her eyes wide enough to stare at Sheldon. He was still
standing near the door, illuminated by the bathroom vanity lights. "*I'm* the
tech, she said. Why did corporate call *you*?"

Sheldon grinned. "They called us both. But you turn your cell phone
off at night. I leave mine on. I imagine you've got a voicemail on your
phone right now."

Ann rubbed her eyes, and rotated her head to loosen her neck muscles.
"What kind of work does the Navy expect us to do?"

"I don't know," Sheldon said. "I talked to Rick Kramer from Norton
corporate liaison. He couldn't give details over the phone. Evidently it's
all pretty hush-hush. But Rick *did* say that it's going to be dangerous. We
have to sign liability waivers and security agreements."

Ann shook her head. "I'm not at the Navy's beck and call. They can't
order me to go anywhere. And they certainly can't order me to
intentionally put myself in danger."

"Nobody's ordering us," Sheldon said. "The Navy's *asking* for us.
They need our help with something."

He shrugged. "I'm going. There aren't any flights to the States
anyway. Might as well go do some work and earn some hazard pay. It
beats sitting around a hotel room the size of a shoebox, watching Japanese
game shows."

"I'm not going," Ann said. "The Navy can kiss off."

"Okay," Sheldon said. "I'll tell Rick, and they'll send somebody else."

"They can't do that," Ann snapped. "Mouse is *my* baby. I did half the
fabrication, and I wrote most of the code. Nobody knows that robot like I
do."

"I understand that," Sheldon said. "But Mouse doesn't belong to you,
Ann. It's a very expensive prototype that happens to be the property of
Norton Deep Water Systems. And Norton has an extremely lucrative
contract to build a few *hundred* Mouse units for the United States Navy.
Ann, you know that corporate isn't going to piss off their *numero-uno*
customer. If the Navy wants a Mouse technician, Norton's going to send
them one. If it's not you, it'll be somebody else. But it's going to happen.
You know that."

He turned back toward the door. "I'll call Rick, and tell him to get
another tech out here."

Ann sighed. "Alright! I'll go, damn it! Just get out of here so I can
pack and get dressed."

Sheldon checked his watch again. "The van will be here in about forty minutes. Why don't we meet in the downstairs coffee shop in half an hour?"

"Okay," Ann said. "Have some caffeine ready when I get down there. Otherwise, I may have to kill you."

"Will do." He reached for the doorknob.

"Sheldon?"

He paused. "Yeah?"

"Did you look at my butt when my back was turned?"

"Ah … no. I thought about it, but it didn't seem polite."

Ann threw a pillow at him. "You're too freaking nice for your own good. Now, get the hell out of my room and let me get dressed."

Sheldon laughed. "Meet you downstairs."

⚓ ⚓ ⚓

Thirty minutes later, Ann walked through the front door of the coffee shop. The lighted plastic sign by the entrance identified the shop as *Hero Coffee Star*. The accompanying logo included a bright red Art Deco coffee pot, rendered in the style of a 1950s Flash Gordon rocket ship.

The interior décor of the coffee shop followed the retro-science fiction theme. The walls were airbrushed with cartoon murals of alien lunarscapes, dotted with improbable-looking domed cities in which the buildings all resembled old-school jukeboxes.

Sheldon was seated at a small round table that had been silk-screened to look like the planet Saturn. As promised, he had a cup of coffee waiting on the table in front of Ann's chair.

He was looking the other way as she approached, and humming a strange little tune—bouncy, but with an odd rhythm.

Ann sat down and started doctoring the coffee with sugar and powdered creamer. "Do you really have to make that much noise this early in the morning?"

"It's stuck in my head," Sheldon said. "From a Japanese commercial."

He hummed the tune again, and used his spoon to gently tap out the notes against the rim of his coffee cup. The musical clink of the metal on porcelain seemed to goad him into song. "Kitty paws," he sang. "Like Santa *Claus*, but kitty *paws*…"

Ann snorted, and had to grab a napkin to keep from spewing coffee. "Kitty paws? What were they advertising?"

Sheldon took his own swallow of coffee. "Have you ever watched Japanese commercials?"

"No."

"You can never tell what they're advertising," Sheldon said. "At least *I* can't. They don't make any sense to me, but a lot of them are pretty funny."

"I don't care what language it's in," Ann said. "How can you watch a commercial and not know what they're advertising?"

"The language isn't the problem," Sheldon said. "It's the cultural subtext. The Japanese contextual cues are totally alien to me. They go right over my head."

Ann snorted again. "That's the dumbest thing I've ever heard." She set down her coffee cup. "I don't claim to understand people, but I *always* know when somebody's trying to sell me something. Describe this commercial to me, and I'll tell you what they're selling."

Sheldon leaned back in his seat. "Okay … Let's see … It starts out with a view of the earth, seen from outer space. The camera zooms in closer, until you see the Japanese islands, from great altitude and through cloud cover. Then the camera drops through the clouds, and you're looking down on a major city—Tokyo, maybe. It zooms in even closer, past the tops of the buildings, and then down to a beautiful little Japanese tea garden, sandwiched between two enormous glass skyscrapers. In the middle of the tea garden is a black European sports sedan. Something really sharp looking. Maybe a Saab. I don't remember. And draped across the hood of the sports sedan is a tall dark haired woman, European or American, with legs that go on forever. She's wearing a strapless black evening gown, slit way up the thigh to show plenty of leg, a pair of black stiletto heals, and a little headband with black Cat Woman ears attached. The narrator is talking a mile-a-minute in Japanese, while an off-camera choir of little Japanese girls sing the jingle in English. "Kitty paws … Like Santa *Claus*, but kitty *paws* …""

Sheldon sat up, and took another sip of coffee. "Then the camera pulls in tight on the tall woman's face. She does sort of a sexy-pouty thing with her lips, raises an eyebrow, and says, *"the excitement has arrived …"*

Sheldon looked at Ann. "So, what do you think they're selling? Japanese tea gardens? European sports cars? Evening wear and sexy shoes? For all I know, they were selling those little Cat Woman ears."

Ann glared at him. "You just made that whole thing up. Nobody would shoot a commercial like that."

"I *didn't* make it up," Sheldon said. "That's what I'm trying to tell you. Japanese commercials are *all* like that. They don't make sense to anybody who wasn't born into the culture."

He set down his coffee cup. "When we get back to the States, I'll find that commercial on the Internet, and download it for you. I'm really not joking." He laughed, and started singing again. "Kitty paws ... Like Santa *Claus* ..."

He chopped off in mid-note. His cell phone was ringing. He flipped it open and held it to his ear. "Sheldon Miggs."

He listened for a second. "Thanks. We'll be right out."

Sheldon closed his phone, and took a final gulp of coffee. "Grab your bags. The excitement has arrived. In this particular case, the excitement takes the form of a U.S. Air Force van, with a government-issue driver."

He pushed back his chair and stood up. "How about it, Cat Woman? Ready to go rescue mankind from certain destruction?"

CHAPTER 34

ICE PACK — EASTERN SEA OF OKHOTSK
LATITUDE 55.18N / LONGITUDE 154.17E
MONDAY; 04 MARCH
0614 hours (6:14 AM)
TIME ZONE +11 'LIMA'

The titanium cylinder hung suspended in the water 100 meters below the ice, at the end of a Kevlar-jacketed cable. The cylinder was anodized in a flat gray color, the precise shade of which had been calculated by marine biologists to resemble neither food, nor predator. The protective Kevlar cable jacket had been molded in the exact same color, for the same reason.

The sea creatures inhabiting the strange twilight world beneath the ice pack were ravenously hungry, and the more predatory species guarded their territories with jealousy. Although the Kevlar and titanium were tough enough to resist easy damage, it was important that they not invite attacks by any fish or mammal that might mistake them for an enemy, or for an easy meal.

This last was particularly critical, because the titanium cylinder was an acoustic transducer. It transmitted and received audio signals underwater, and those signals were modulated to closely simulate the noises produced by the shrimp-like krill that lived under the ice pack in teaming schools.

When it was broadcasting, the transducer made the same frying bacon hiss produced by swarms of krill as they fed on ice-algae and phytoplankton. Because the krill themselves were a major source of nutrition for many of the fish and sea creatures living in the water beneath the ice pack, that meant that the transducer's signals sounded like food. And—the durability of titanium and Kevlar aside—a piece of equipment that *sounds* like food, should not *look* like food as well. The carefully non-food coloring of the cable and transducer had been selected with this in mind.

Apart from the obvious drawbacks inherent in making sounds like an easy meal, the feeding noise of the krill was nearly perfect for masking a

198

digital audio signal.   The crackling hiss was rich with white noise, a jumble of high and low frequencies into which binary information could be encoded with ease.

The advantages of this were twofold. It would be nearly impossible for an outside listener to decode the digital messages without the proper encryption/decryption algorithm.   But more importantly, the sound of feeding krill occurred naturally in the waters under the ice pack. If an acoustic surveillance sensor happened to intercept a transmission, the sound would be classified as typical ambient noise made by local sea life. No sensor operator or acoustic analyst in the world would recognize it as a manmade communications signal. For all practical purposes, that made the system invisible to anyone who did not already know of its existence.

The encryption/decryption algorithm at the heart of this covert transponder system had been programmed by a pair of graduate students from the Massachusetts Institute of Technology. Perhaps one or both of the students had eventually grown to suspect that their enigmatic employer did not really represent an eco-friendly alternative energy firm, as he had claimed. Perhaps the young programmers had also guessed that the true purpose of the software had nothing to do with bio-density surveys. But any misgivings the two students might have felt were now moot. Both men had been killed within hours of delivering the final version of their software.

Detectives from the Cambridge Police Department were investigating both deaths, but had failed to turn up evidence of a connection between the cases. One of the students had slipped in a hotel shower and cracked his skull.   The other had been killed by a hit-and-run driver.   The circumstances of the cases were quite different, and both deaths appeared to be accidental. Even so, the police found it exceedingly suspicious that two students from the same department at MIT had died on the same afternoon.

At various points in the investigation, the homicide detectives considered and discarded a long list of possible suspects, including friends of the victims, fellow students, known enemies, relatives, girlfriends, possible romantic rivals, and several smalltime drug dealers known to ply their wares near the MIT campus.

The drug angle was a stretch. Neither of the victims were known users, and the toxicology screens from their autopsies showed no traces of any controlled substances. The dealers had been added to the list when the detectives realized that they'd run out of suspects. With two college-age men dead under suspicious circumstances, it was possible that drugs were somehow involved, and no one seemed to have any alternative leads.

But the suspicions of the police—whatever they might have been—did not involve trained assassins from the Chinese military, nor covert under-ice communications systems, nor hijacked Russian nuclear submarines. Which meant that the Cambridge police had no chance of actually figuring out who had murdered their two students, or why.

⚓   ⚓   ⚓

A little over 4,600 nautical miles northwest of Cambridge, Massachusetts, the motive for the MIT murders was gliding quietly through the frigid waters beneath the Siberian ice pack. Submarine K-506 had been built as part of the Soviet Union's Project 667BDR construction program: the *Kal'mar* class—what the NATO countries called the *Delta III* class.

Although the submarine was more than three decades old, and much noisier than current generations of missile subs, it was still quiet enough to escape detection at low speeds. So it moved slowly and deliberately, creeping through the dark waters under the ice at less than four kilometers per hour—just enough speed to keep water moving across the rudders and stern planes, for steering and depth control.

At a range of one kilometer from the designated coordinates, the submarine's *Burya* underwater communications system began transmitting an acoustic signal into the water. The signal sounded nothing like an ordinary Burya transmission. The equipment had been modified to broadcast and receive only the crackling and hissing signal that so closely mimicked the feeding noises of the under ice krill.

The signal was received by the cylindrical titanium transducer. Thin wafers of piezoelectric crystal within the transducer resonated in time with the vibrations of the sound waves. The tiny stresses created by these vibrations caused the crystal wafers to alternately contract and expand. The fluctuations were nearly microscopic in scale, but each deformation of the piezoelectric crystals generated a minute pulse of electricity.

The technology had been invented for quartz movement wristwatches, but it worked equally well in this application. Each electrical pulse was channeled into a transistor, where it was amplified for better examination. The amplified pulses were then routed to a binary discriminator circuit, where they were converted to digital ones, or digital zeroes, depending upon their strength and polarity.

The stream of digital pulses from the discriminator circuit passed through a splitter bus, and then a short length of ribbon cable, to reach a microprocessor configured as a binary parser.

The parser stripped out ambient ocean sounds and the masking junk information that had been woven into the acoustic signal to disguise it as random biological noise. The output of the parser was a complete and coherent digital message, rendered in perfectly-legible binary code.

The digital message shot up the fiber-optic wires at the core of the Kevlar cable, and followed the cable through the thick ice layer, to another microprocessor, sheltered in an insulated protective housing under a few centimeters of concealing ice and snow.

The second microprocessor examined the contents of the digital signal, to determine whether or not it contained a *destruct* command. If a destruct command had been present, the microprocessor was programmed to detonate an array of shaped explosive charges drilled into the ice in a circular perimeter.

No destruct signal was present, and the explosives were not triggered.

The microprocessor reverted to its secondary program, encrypting the digital signal to protect its contents. When the encryption process was complete, the computer immediate re-encrypted the signal, using an entirely different code scheme. The double-encrypted block of digital code was uploaded to the outgoing message queue of a satellite phone within the same insulated enclosure.

On command, the phone dialed a pre-programmed telephone number, accessing a commercial communications satellite network. When the connection protocols were synchronized, the hidden telephone unit transmitted its waiting message to a ComStar IV series satellite in standard commercial orbit.

The satellite phone account was legitimate, one of many commercial accounts opened for this specific purpose. The registered account owner was a dummy corporation in Spain, again one of many established solely for this operation. But the bills were paid on time, and the account had never been flagged for suspected misconduct.

Other than an automated notation to charge the call against the user's account, no human or machine in the telecommunications industry paid any attention whatsoever to the call. It was a routine commercial transaction. The message from K-506 joined the flow of ordinary daily phone traffic, and no one was any the wiser.

When the call was completed, the satellite phone kept the connection open, and transmitted the access code for its voicemail box. There was one waiting message, which the satellite phone downloaded, before terminating the call.

The incoming message was double encrypted in the same manner that the outgoing message had been. It was routed from the phone's message queue to the adjoining microprocessor, which unraveled both layers of encryption, before shooting it back down the Kevlar cable toward the hanging titanium cylinder.

The process continued in reverse, and ended when the transducer injected a stream of white noise into the water, 100 meters below the ice. The transmission sounded a great deal like the ordinary noises of feeding krill, and not at all like tactical instructions to a nuclear missile submarine.

A kilometer away the K-506 received its updated orders. With slow but deliberate speed, the submarine turned and began to move north.

CHAPTER 35

National Security Advisor Gregory Brenthoven walked into the empty room. The high-backed leather chairs were all pushed against the long mahogany table. The air was still, and quiet.

Brenthoven closed the door, and stood alone on the heavy wine-colored carpet.

Something was tugging at his mind, a tiny prickle at the fringes of his subconscious. He couldn't put a finger on it, but knew that he had missed something. Some little detail that had slipped past his conscious mind without making an impression. He didn't know what it was, but he had a feeling that it was something important.

He walked the length of the table, stopping behind the chair where he usually sat. At the far end of the room, the projection screen was retracted into its recess in the ceiling. The remote control lay in the middle of the table.

Without knowing why, Brenthoven picked up the remote, and pressed the button that raised and lowered the screen. Electric motors whispered, and the screen descended, hanging at the end of the table like a blank tableau.

He pulled his chair out from the table and sat down, his eyes studying the empty display screen. Something in his mind stirred. He almost had something, flickering just out of sight at the edge of his memory.

What was it? Something he had watched on this screen, maybe?

He pressed another button, calling the hidden projector to life. The default image appeared on the screen: the presidential seal, set against a blue background.

Another series of buttons called up a menu of available presentation files. Admiral Casey's Sea of Okhotsk brief was at the top of the *recent files* list. Again without knowing why he did so, Brenthoven called up the CNO's briefing package.

He paged through the images slowly, studying each in turn. The map of the Sea of Okhotsk. The circle representing the launch point. The photograph of the Russian submarine. The map of the Pacific. The curving lines of the incoming warheads. The converging arcs of the interceptor missiles.

He reached the end of the presentation. Nothing

With a sigh, he dropped the remote on the table. The clatter of plastic against wood seemed to echo in the quiet of the empty room.

He'd been hoping that one of the images might jar something in his memory. But nothing was coming to him.

He leaned back in the chair and rubbed his eyes. Nothing. Damn it.

He'd go back to his office. Maybe it would come to him if he stopped thinking about it so much.

Or maybe there was no '*it.*' Maybe the '*it*' was nothing more than wishful thinking. Maybe he wanted so badly to find an answer, that his brain was conjuring phantoms.

He didn't know. He reached for the remote, and pointed the device toward the screen to shut off the projector.

On the screen, the map of the Sea of Okhotsk was showing. In the northeastern corner was the red circle that represented the submarine's launch position. The adjoining label showed the latitude and longitude of the circle: 58.29N / 155.20E.

Brenthoven's finger reached toward the power button. It paused, hovering above the button. He studied the numbers ... 58.29N / 155.20E.

Why did they seem familiar? Because he'd seen them during the admiral's brief?

No, that wasn't it. Now that he thought about it, they'd seemed familiar *then* too. He'd seen that same sequence of digits somewhere else, in a different context.

He read them aloud. "Five ... eight ... two ... nine ... one ... five ... five ... two ... zero ..."

Damn it! Where had he seen them before? He almost had it now ...

The answer hit him, and he sat up straight in the chair. He reached into the breast pocket of his jacket for his little leather-bound notebook. His fingers fumbled it, and he nearly dropped it.

He rifled through the pages until he found his notes from a recent intelligence brief. There it *was*. The same sequence of numbers. Five—eight—two—nine—one—five—five— two—zero.

The unidentified numbers that the Russian courier, Oleg Grigoriev, had given to the DIA agents from his hospital bed in Japan. And that had been the day *before* Zhukov's submarine had launched the first missile.

Grigoriev had given them the position for the first missile launch, *before* the launch had occurred. He'd known ahead of time. He might very well know the *rest* of the planned launch positions as well.

Up to this point, that bastard, Zhukov, had been five steps ahead of them at every turn. If Grigoriev knew the rest of the launch points, they could get ahead of Zhukov for the first time. They could finally move from defense to offense. They could end this thing.

Brenthoven pulled out his cell phone and speed-dialed the White House chief of staff. The instant she picked up the phone, Brenthoven said, "I don't care what he's doing. I need to speak to the president. *Now.*"

CHAPTER 36

USS TOWERS (DDG-103)
WESTERN PACIFIC OCEAN
MONDAY; 04 MARCH
2218 hours (10:18 PM)
TIME ZONE +11 'LIMA'

Ann Roark stumbled climbing the aluminum stairs to the USS *Towers* wardroom. She would have fallen if Sheldon hadn't grabbed the sleeve of her jacket and steadied her.

The young Sailor who had led them here from the flight deck looked back down from the head of the stairs. "These ladders are sort of steep, Ma'am. You've got to watch your footing."

Ann rolled her eyes. Like she needed a teenager to tell her how to walk. And they weren't *ladders*; they were *stairs*. Any idiot could see that. Why did the Navy have to use a different word for everything? Why couldn't they say *floors*, and *walls*, instead of *decks*, and *bulkheads*? It was like they went out of their way to make things as complicated as possible.

Ann started climbing again. She was so tired that she had trouble lifting her feet enough to make it up the steep incline of the stairs. And the rolling of the ship wasn't doing anything to steady her.

Even Sheldon, Mr. Perpetual Happy-face, was showing signs of wear and tear. He didn't look quite as bad as Ann felt, but the fatigue was visible in his face. They'd been travelling for fifteen or sixteen hours since Narita. First the van ride to the Air Force base, and then three helicopter flights, with stops to refuel the aircraft on two ships along the way. They'd probably crossed a couple of time zones in there somewhere, but Ann's brain was too tired to do the math.

Her ears still felt numb from a very long day spent listening to the shriek of poorly-insulated aircraft engines. Little creature comforts, like soundproofing, were evidently not a priority to the U.S. military.

It was after ten o'clock, and the lighting in the ship's hallways had been dimmed from bright white, to soft red. In Navy lingo, it was after *Taps*. Couldn't they just call it *lights out*, like everybody else on the planet?

They reached the top of the stairs, and Sailor Boy led them through a short passageway toward a door that Ann recognized as the entrance to the ship's wardroom.

She stopped, and lowered her bags to the floor. "Wait a second," she said. "Can't you take us to our staterooms first? I'd like to drop off my bags."

What she *really* wanted was to get a few hours of sleep. Her brain felt like it was stuffed full of cotton. Did the Navy boneheads really think they could drag her out of bed at three in the morning, jerk her all over the Pacific for sixteen hours, and then put her straight to work?

The young Sailor smiled. "Just leave your bags here in the passageway. I'll take them down to your staterooms. The captain wants to see you right away, Ma'am."

The kid's tone of voice pushed Ann's annoyance up another notch. She resisted the temptation to parrot his words right back in his face. *'The captain wants to see you right away, Ma'am.'*

The kid was probably only nineteen years old—twenty at the outside—and the Navy already had him mentally conditioned. He honestly could not conceive of someone not giving the exalted *'captain'* exactly what he wanted.

Automatic obedience was dangerous. Couldn't these people see that? Couldn't they see what it could lead to? Ann wondered what Sailor Boy would say, if she told him that his almighty captain could go to hell.

Sheldon lowered his bags to the floor and nudged Ann gently with his elbow. "Come on, let's go save the world."

Ann didn't budge.

Sheldon cocked his head and showed Ann his most elaborately pitiful puppy-dog face. "Am I going to have to sing the 'Kitty Paw' song?"

Against her will, Ann felt herself smile a little. "Alright, asshole," she said. She nodded toward the young Sailor. "Let's go, Popeye. The excitement has arrived."

The Sailor knocked on the wardroom door, and opened it, but didn't enter. He stepped to one side, holding the door for Ann and Sheldon.

Sheldon muttered a *thank you* as he stepped past the Sailor. Ann followed Sheldon into the wardroom without comment.

Captain Bowie stood when they entered the room. He smiled, and motioned for them to sit.

"Welcome aboard *Towers*," he said. "It's good to have you back."

He nodded, and a young Sailor in a blue smock jacket and white paper hat stepped forward to place cups of steaming coffee in front of the only two empty chairs at the table.

By the looks of it, nearly every officer on the ship was present. At least Ann thought they were all officers. She had never bothered to learn to distinguish military rank insignias, but they all wore khaki uniforms.

Ann took the chair on the right. She skipped the preliminaries, and reached straight for the sugar and cream.

Sheldon returned the captain's smile as he settled into the chair to Ann's left. "Thank you for inviting us back, Captain. We're glad to be here."

Ann raised her eyebrows, but didn't comment. They hadn't been *invited*. They'd been freaking *summoned*. And she was, most assuredly, *not* glad to be here.

She sipped at her coffee, and was mildly surprised to find that it wasn't horrible. Not as good as coffee in the real world, but better than the acrid glop they usually served aboard ship. No doubt the improvement had something to do with the presence of the captain. When the big boss was in the house, the cooks probably put in a little extra effort.

Ann took a larger swallow. Well, maybe not *too* much extra effort.

Captain Bowie took his seat and pulled his own coffee cup across the table toward himself. "I realize that we got you up before the roosters," he said. "And I know you've been in the air most of the day. I'm sure you're both exhausted, so we'll try to keep this as short as possible."

"Thank you, sir," Sheldon said.

"We'll sketch out the basic tactical situation tonight," the captain said. "Then we can sleep on it, and get into the details tomorrow morning."

Sheldon fought off a yawn. "Works for me."

The captain faced one of his people, a redheaded woman with a rounded face that seemed out of proportion to her trim build. "Chief McPherson, can you get us started?"

Chief McPherson stood up. "Aye-aye, sir."

She laid a navigational chart on the table top, and unrolled it, weighting the corners with coffee mugs so that the curled paper didn't roll itself back into a tube. A series of lines and symbols had been drawn on the chart using colored pencils. "Before we jump into the tactical situation," she said, "how covert is your Mouse unit's underwater transponder system?"

Ann shrugged. "We don't really know yet."

"What do you mean?" the chief asked.

"The Navy contract requires Mouse to be capable of covert operations," Ann said. "So the transmissions from his acoustic modems are designed to mimic natural ocean sounds. Wave action, biologics, stuff like that. In theory, his communications should be really difficult to detect or identify."

"How difficult?" Chief McPherson asked.

"We're still in the development process," Ann said. "The system has only been tested against a handful of underwater sensors. We won't have hard data until the detection vulnerability surveys are complete, and they're not scheduled to start until the end of the year."

Captain Bowie spoke up. "So you *think* it's covert, but you're not certain?"

"That's right," Ann said. "I can't give you a better answer until we finish the testing."

The captain rubbed his chin. "I don't think we can risk an unknown that large. The plan we have in mind depends on keeping your Mouse unit hidden from the submarine."

Ann shifted in her chair. "What submarine?"

The chief turned her eyes toward Ann, and then to Sheldon. "How much do you know about what's been going on in Kamchatka?"

"A little bit," Sheldon said. "We caught some of it from the TV news in Japan, but that was in Japanese. Our hotel rooms had CNN on cable, so we got some follow-up in English. We know that there's been some kind of military revolution in one of the Russian territories. And the rebels launched several nuclear missiles toward California, but they were intercepted. We know there's pandemonium on the West Coast, and all of the flights are canceled." He raised his hands and dropped them. "I guess that's about it."

The chief nodded. "Actually, it was only one missile," she said. "But it was armed with three nuclear warheads."

"CNN is claiming *seven* warheads," Ann said.

"There were seven *reentry vehicles*," Chief McPherson said. "Three of them were nuclear warheads. The other four were decoys, designed to tie up our resources, and force us to expend interceptor missiles."

She pointed to a small symbol on the chart, a red downward-pointing arrow enclosed in a red circle. "The missile was launched from a nuclear submarine at this position, in the northeastern Sea of Okhotsk, about thirty-seven hours ago. The sub in question is hull number K-506, a Delta III class, built in the nineteen-seventies. It carries sixteen ballistic missiles, each of which is armed with three nuclear warheads and four decoys. It's already fired one missile, so it's still got fifteen missiles left in the launch tubes. *That's* the submarine we're talking about: the one that launched nukes at the West Coast."

"And we can't take a chance on spooking it," the captain said. "If we use your acoustic communications system and the sub intercepts one of your signals, it's going to kick up to flank speed and run like hell. It'll hide so far up under the ice that we'll never get close to it."

"I agree, sir," Chief McPherson said. "We may just have to settle for cueing. Send the Mouse unit under the ice to do the job in full auto mode, with no external comms. If it finds anything, it comes back out, drives to the surface, and calls us on low-power UHF."

"That's detectable too," one of the officers pointed out.

"True," the chief said. "But only at short range line-of-sight, and not by the sub. The UHF signal might get intercepted by an aircraft, but a submerged submarine will never pick it up. It's not a perfect solution, but it's probably the best we can do."

"You're probably right," the captain said. "Can anyone suggest an alternative?"

No one spoke up.

"Alright," he said. "We go with the UHF, and stay away from underwater comms. If Mouse gets a hit, it comes to the surface and calls us on low-power UHF."

He looked at Chief McPherson. "Continue, please."

The chief leaned over the chart and the red symbol with her fingertip. "This is '*datum*.' It's the last known position of the submarine."

She waved a hand in a big loop over the chart. "The maximum submerged speed of a Delta III is about 25 knots. If the sub is running pedal-to-the-metal, it could be 900 nautical miles from datum by now. In other words, it could be anywhere in the Sea of Okhotsk."

Sheldon craned his neck to get a better view of the chart. "Why are you assuming that the sub is going to stay in the Sea of ..." He paused. "How do you pronounce it again?"

The chief smiled. "The Sea of *Okhotsk*. We call it the Sea of *O*, for short."

"Thanks," Sheldon said. "So why are you assuming that the submarine is going to keep to the Sea of O? If it can run 900 miles in 36 hours, it could be through those islands and out into the Pacific right now."

"We don't think he's going to come out," Captain Bowie said. "As long as that sub skipper stays in there, he's got the tactical advantage."

"How so?" Sheldon asked.

"The Sea of Okhotsk is covered by the Siberian ice pack," said Chief McPherson. "Ships can only get into the very southern end of the sea, because of the ice. As long as it stays in there, the sub can hide under the ice, where it's protected. If he comes out into the open ocean, we're going to eat his lunch, and he knows it."

Ann set her coffee cup on the table. "Where do *we* fit into this? I assume you dragged us out here for a reason."

"That submarine still has forty-five nuclear weapons on board," Captain Bowie said. "We've been assigned to engage it before it launches another nuclear attack. Unfortunately, our options are extremely limited. Guns and missiles are no good against a submerged target, and we can't use ASROC missiles because of the ice cover. That leaves torpedoes."

"Okay," Ann said. "I'm still not seeing the connection. We don't know anything about missiles, or torpedoes, or any of that stuff."

"Our Mk-54 torpedoes weren't designed for under-ice operations," Chief McPherson said. "We're concerned that acoustic reflections under the ice could prevent the torpedoes from finding their target. Specifically, we're worried that the Mk-54's active sonar will lock on to the ice keels that protrude from the underside of the ice pack, and attack *them* instead of the submarine."

"I hope you don't think *we* can answer that question," Ann said.

"Not at all," the chief said. "At the moment, no one can answer it. I've spent about three hours on the satellite phone with the torpedo engineers at Raytheon. They designed the Mk-54, and *they* don't know the answer either. They'll have to conduct extensive field tests to be certain, but they ran some quick and dirty computer simulations for me, and the results don't look good. Our torpedoes will probably *not* be able to locate the submarine in the under-ice environment."

"That's where your Mouse unit comes in," the captain said. "We need it to go after the submarine under the ice pack."

Ann was tired, and her weariness made her a little slower on the uptake than usual. So it took a few seconds for the meanings of the captain's words to sink in.

She frowned, almost certain that she'd misunderstood him. "You're saying you want to use Mouse ... as a *weapon?*"

Captain Bowie shook his head. "Not exactly. What we need ..."

Ann held up a hand. "Mouse isn't configured for combat. He wasn't designed to fight."

"We know that," Bowie said. "We don't expect the Mouse unit to attack the submarine. That wouldn't work. Your machine can't carry a heavy enough explosive charge to guarantee a kill."

"So what *do* you have in mind for Mouse?" Sheldon asked.

Bowie crooked a finger toward Chief McPherson, who laid an odd-looking device on the table top.

It was shaped roughly like a double-decker hamburger—round, with a domed top and a slightly concave bottom. It appeared to be constructed of metal and plastic. Several circuits and mechanical fixtures had been strapped to the outside using the red waterproof adhesive cloth that the Navy called *ordinance tape*.

"This is the acoustic transducer from a Mark-63 expendable mobile target," the chief said. "The 63s are training tools. We toss them in the water, and let our Sonar Operators track them for practice. But in this case, we're only going to use the acoustic section, so we pulled that part out and modified it."

She pointed to the hodge-podge of add-on circuits. "It's not pretty, but we've got it configured to respond to a coded external pulse. If we ping this thing with the right frequency, it kicks into beacon mode, and begins transmitting a loud acoustic signal that our torpedoes can track."

"I'm totally lost," Ann said. "Where does Mouse figure into this?"

Bowie spoke up. "The beacon has a magnetic base. We want Mouse to locate the submarine, and attach the beacon to its hull. Then, we need Mouse to come back out from under the ice and report back to us, so we know that the beacon is in place."

"Okay," Ann said slowly. "Then what?"

"Then Mouse keeps an eye on the sub for us," the captain said, "and lets us know if it comes within weapons range of the ship. When the sub gets close enough, we trigger the beacon so our torpedoes can lock on."

"You want Mouse to be the finger man," Ann said. "He doesn't do the killing; he just points the finger, and you guys take care of the dirty work."

"Well," the captain said. "I suppose …"

"Just a second!" Ann's voice came out much louder than she'd intended. Her words seemed to reverberate in the suddenly-quiet wardroom. "How many people are on that submarine?" she asked. Her voice was softer now.

"We don't know exactly," Chief McPherson said. "The crew compliment of a Delta III is 130, but we're not sure if the sub got underway with full manning. Fighting had already broken out in Petropavlosk when the K-506 put out to sea, so they may not have a complete crew."

"But it's around 130 men?" Ann asked.

The chief nodded. "That's about right."

"What are their names?"

The question seemed to puzzle everyone in the room.

Captain Bowie studied Ann, a slight frown on his blandly handsome face. "I'm sorry, I don't think I understand."

"The men on the submarine," Ann said. "What are their names?"

No one spoke. Every pair of eyes in the wardroom stared at her.

"You tell me that there are 130 people on that submarine," Ann said. "And you want me to help you kill them."

She locked eyes with the captain. "I've never killed anyone in my life," she said. She snapped her fingers. "Now, just like *that*, I'm supposed to help you murder 130 people I've never even met?"

She slumped back in her chair, letting her weight sag onto the base of her spine. "If I'm going to see the faces of more than a hundred strangers in my dreams every night for the rest of my life, I want to know their freaking names. I don't think that's too much to ask."

The silence held for nearly ten seconds, before Sheldon broke it. "Ann, we should at least listen ..."

"No!" Ann snapped. She looked around the table, meeting each pair of eyes in-turn. "I'm through listening."

"Mouse does not kill people," she said. "*I* do not kill people. Not today. Not tomorrow. Not *ever*."

She stood up. "If that's what you brought us here to do, you've wasted your money and my time."

Before anyone could respond, she walked out the door.

CHAPTER 37

The stocky old Russian lay in the hospital bed, the slow rise and fall of his chest the only movement in his body. The heart monitor mounted to the wall near his bed beeped in a soft continuous rhythm.

Agent Ross watched the unconscious man for several long seconds before turning back to Dr. Hogan. "How much longer is he going to be like this?"

Hogan glanced at the heart monitor, and then down at the medical chart in his hand. "There's no way to know," he said.

"Doctor, that's not good enough," Ross said. "We've got a madman holding three countries hostage with nuclear weapons. And some of those weapons are pointed right here, toward Japan."

Ross exhaled through his nostrils. "This is a good sized naval base. Chances are, we're standing at ground-zero for one of those nukes."

He looked back toward the unconscious form of Oleg Grigoriev. "I've got to find out what that man knows. I need to know how much longer he's going to be out."

"I can't tell you that," Dr. Hogan said. "Because I don't *know*." He sighed. "The patient suffered a major pulmonary embolism, secondary to the gunshot wound in his chest. He coded on us, and we nearly lost him. Your partner was here when it happened. Ask *him*."

"Agent DuBrul has given me his report," Ross said. "But he's not a doctor. He can't tell me when the patient will be ready to talk again."

"Neither can I," Hogan said. "That's what I've been trying to explain to you, Agent Ross. I *know* how important it is that you talk to this man. But I don't know when he's going to be conscious again. His vitals are fairly steady at the moment, but he's not in good shape. We could lose him at any second."

Hogan studied the patient. His voice was solemn. "This patient could open his eyes ten minutes from now, or ten days from now. Or he may never open them again. Even if he does, there's no guarantee that he'll be coherent. A pulmonary embolism restricts blood flow to the brain. The patient may have significant mental deterioration. There's no way to know until he comes around."

"*If* he comes around," Ross said

Dr. Hogan nodded. "Yeah," he said. "*If.*"

CHAPTER 38

USS TOWERS (DDG-103)
WESTERN PACIFIC OCEAN
TUESDAY; 05 MARCH
0609 hours (6:09 AM)
TIME ZONE +11 'LIMA'

When Ann opened the door to her stateroom, she found Sheldon standing in the hallway, leaning against the wall, or the bulkhead, or whatever the damned thing was called.

She shot him a quizzical look. "Are you waiting for me?"

Sheldon nodded. "Come on. I'll buy you breakfast."

"How long have you been standing there?"

"A while," Sheldon said.

"Why didn't you knock?"

He shrugged. "I figured you needed your sleep. Anyway, it's not like I've got anything to do today."

He gave Ann a patented Sheldon smile. "You want some breakfast, or not?"

Ann looked one way down the hall, and then the other. "Lead the way. I can never find anything in this metal maze."

"Follow me, Madam," Sheldon said. "One guaranteed five-star military breakfast coming up."

Ann followed. "Right. I'll settle for not getting food poisoning."

As usual, Ann was totally lost. Every door, valve, and electrical junction box was stamped or stenciled with a number. She knew the numbers were all part of some kind of coordinate system for locating equipment, and for finding your way around the maze. But she didn't like ships enough to invest the effort required to learn the numbering scheme. So she was stuck with trying to recognize landmarks in a world where everything had the same utilitarian blandness about it.

She spotted the door to the wardroom, and was surprised when Sheldon walked past it without stopping. "I think you just missed our exit," she said.

216

Sheldon started down one of the steep metal staircases. "I thought we'd go down to the crew's mess, and eat with the enlisted personnel this morning."

"Why? Have our wardroom privileges been revoked?"

"Not as far as I know," Sheldon said. "But the Combat Systems Officer told me they're holding a tactical planning meeting in the wardroom this morning. And we've sort of cut ourselves out of the tactical loop."

"You mean *I* cut us out of the loop," Ann said.

Sheldon stopped at the foot of the stairs and turned back toward Ann. "We're a team," he said. "It doesn't matter who threw the penalty flag. We're both out of the game. So I figure we should stay clear of the wardroom until they're finished with the planning meeting."

"What do you think they'll do?" Ann asked.

Sheldon started walking again. "I'm sure they'll try to helo us out of here as soon as possible," he said over his shoulder.

"That's not what I meant," Ann said. "I mean what will they do without Mouse? What's their Plan-*B*?"

"I don't think they've got a Plan-B," Sheldon said. "Unless I'm mistaken, Mouse was something like their Plan-*Z*. I think they exhausted every tactical option they could come up with before they ever *considered* something as crazy as Mouse."

He stopped again, and turned to face Ann. "Mouse is prototype technology," he said. "It's full of bugs, and it's undependable. They know that. And you and I, Princess Leia, are civilians. That makes us unpredictable, and difficult to manage. They can't order us around. In other words, we're undependable too. And they know *that*."

Sheldon tilted his head forward and looked out of the tops of his eyes. "Do you really think these Navy guys would be calling on undependable civilians with undependable equipment if they had another option?"

Ann didn't answer.

Sheldon continued walking. Ann followed. About fifty feet later, they came to a long line of Sailors, all dressed in blue utility uniforms.

"I believe this is what they call the *chow line*," Sheldon said. He sniffed the air theatrically. "Mmm … Smell that? That's good Navy chow."

Ann wrinkled her nose. "Yuck!"

She sighed. "You think I'm wrong, don't you?"

"It's a matter of taste," Sheldon said. "Shipboard food isn't for everybody."

"Not about that," Ann said. "About Mouse. You think I'm wrong for not helping them, don't you?"

"What I think doesn't matter," Sheldon said. "You're the only person you have to look at in the mirror. And I can certainly understand your position. You didn't sign on to kill people. Not even indirectly."

"No," Ann said. "I didn't."

Sheldon said nothing.

The line moved ahead a little, and Sheldon lifted two thick plastic cafeteria trays off of a spring-loaded metal rack. He passed one to Ann.

"You'd help them, wouldn't you?" Ann asked.

The line moved another pace forward, and Sheldon pulled two sets of knives, forks, and spoons out of round metal holders.

"Yeah. I *would* help them," he said. He sorted out a set of utensils and passed it to Ann.

She accepted the small bundle of flatware. The metal was warm, and still a little damp. The utensils were obviously fresh from the dishwasher.

"Why?" she asked. "I know you, Sheldon. You haven't got a violent bone in your body. Why on earth would you participate in the killing of 130 human beings?"

Sheldon started to say something, and then checked himself. "Let's talk about this later. This is not a good conversation to have, just before we eat."

"*Now*," Ann said. "Answer my question."

Sheldon exhaled sharply. "Did you ever study First Aid?" he asked. "Do you know what a tourniquet is?"

Ann nodded.

"I was a Boy Scout when I was a kid," Sheldon said. "I had merit badges like you wouldn't believe. I *loved* it. I was on my way to Eagle Scout. And one summer, I took my little brother camping on Dutch Island, in the Wilmington River. I was fifteen that year, and Charley was thirteen. We had to get there by boat. And man, it was the stuff of pure adventure.

"Imagine it," he said. "Two boys on an island by themselves. It was *Huckleberry Finn* and *Treasure Island*, all rolled into one. And on the third day of the camping trip—it was supposed to be the last day—the hatchet bounced off a knot when Charley was chopping firewood. The blade hit his left wrist, and it cut him *bad*."

The chow line had moved forward, but Sheldon made no attempt to follow it. He put his tray back on the rack, and returned his utensils to their holders. Then he turned toward Ann. "I couldn't stop the bleeding," he said. "I tried direct pressure, and pressure points, and all of the First

Aid tricks in the Boy Scout handbook. But nothing would stop the bleeding."

Sheldon swallowed, and looked away from Ann. "And all I could think of was a tourniquet."

Someone tapped Ann on the shoulder and she turned to see a line of Sailors bunching up behind them. She tugged Sheldon to the side, and waved for the Sailors to go around.

Sheldon's voice was hoarse now. "I remembered my scout training," he said. "They told us to *never* use a tourniquet unless there was no other choice. Don't use one unless it's a choice between the tourniquet and death. Because the limb begins to die the second you tighten down the tourniquet. It shuts off the blood flow to the wound, but it shuts off the blood flow to the entire limb as well. Most of the time, after a tourniquet has been used, the doctors have to amputate the arm or the leg."

Sheldon wiped at one of his eyes. "My little brother is bleeding all over the pine needles," he said. "And I can't stop it. Nothing is working. It's coming out like a fountain, and I cannot stop it. And I know, if I put a tourniquet on Charley's arm, the doctors are going to have to amputate. They're going to take the arm off."

Sheldon looked at Ann. "Charley's thirteen years old, and they're going to have to take his arm off. But there's nothing else I can do. My belt is too thick to work, but I've got boots on, with heavy laces. I double one of them up, tie it off just below Charley's elbow, and I slide a little piece of tree branch in for tension. And I twist that stick, tightening the tourniquet. And I twist it again. In my heart, I know with every turn of that stick, that I'm killing Charley's arm. But I twist, and I twist again, until the bleeding stops. And then I carry Charley to the boat, and I head for the docks at Tidewater."

Ann returned her tray to the rack, and her eating utensils to the round holders.

"Come on," she said. She turned away from the waiting line of Sailors and started walking.

Ann had no idea where she was going, but Sheldon followed her through the maze of passageways. She came to a staircase and climbed. After a few wrong turns, she found a watertight door that led outside. Sheldon followed her out into the frosty pre-dawn air.

The wind hit them immediately, and it was far colder than Ann was expecting. The sun was a feeble glow below the slate gray horizon, and the sky was still dark enough for the stars to stand out clearly.

Ann's teeth began to chatter, and her eyes started to water. She wondered if the cold-blasted tears would freeze on her skin.

They'd only stay out here for a minute or two, but Sheldon needed the change of scenery to reset his mental clock. They'd be okay for a couple of minutes. At least Ann hoped they would.

She looked at the dark and motionless form that was Sheldon. She couldn't see his eyes, but his body posture suggested that he was looking toward the dusky blur of the horizon.

Ann hesitated. She wanted to ask a question, but she was not at all sure she was ready to hear the answer. She braced herself for the worst, and took a breath. The cold air bit at her lungs. "What happened to Charley?"

"They saved his life," Sheldon said softly. "He lost his left arm, but the doctors saved his life."

"No," Ann said. "*You* saved his life."

"Yeah," Sheldon said. "I guess."

His face was still pointed toward the horizon. "You asked why I would help the Navy guys destroy the submarine," he said. "*That's* why. Because sometimes there aren't any good choices. Sometimes you have to choose between something *bad*, and something *worse*."

He shivered, and looked down toward the darkly rolling waves. "There are 130 people on that submarine," he said. "And I don't want to hurt *any* of them. But there are *millions* of people in Washington, and Oregon, and California, and Colorado ..."

He turned toward Ann. "I'm a liaison and logistics guy," he said. "Not a technician, or an operator. I can't make Mouse do his stuff. That's your end of the business. So this all comes down to *you*. If you help the Navy destroy that sub, you'll have 130 deaths on your conscience. I'm not going to lie to you, Ann. You probably *will* have nightmares. Hell, I'm just the hand-shaker and the pencil-pusher, and *I'll* probably have nightmares. But if you do nothing to stop that sub, and it launches more nukes at the United States ..." His voice trailed off.

"I wonder, Ann," he said quietly, "How many nightmares will we get, if we let a million people die?"

CHAPTER 39

"Okay," Captain Bowie said. "Let's go around the table again. There's a solution to this, people. We just haven't found it yet."

He looked to his left. "XO?"

The Executive Officer of *Towers*, Lieutenant Commander Bishop, took a deep breath. "ONI thinks the bad guys have pre-staged explosives at various positions around the ice pack. Maybe there's some way to detect them. If we can get some helos to over-fly the ice, they might be able to pick up infrared sources, or MAD signatures from the hardware attached to the explosives."

"That's a good thought," Captain Bowie said. "We'll borrow a couple of helos from Seventh Fleet to try it out." He looked to the XO's left. "Chief?"

Chief Sonar Technician Theresa McPherson pursed her lips. "I'm not getting any brainstorms, Captain. All I can think of is the obvious. We slip north, under cover of darkness, and get as close to the ice pack as we dare. We deploy the towed array, and run slow search patterns along the southern edge of the ice. About an hour before sunrise, we pull the tail in, and head south before we get caught with our fingers in the cookie jar." She shrugged. "If we search three or four nights in row, we might get lucky and catch the sub down near the southern end of the ice."

"That sub is going to be in creep mode," the XO said. "Slow and quiet. You think you'll be able to detect him?"

"It'll take a lot of luck, sir," the Chief said. "In these latitudes at this time of year, we've got about 14 hours of darkness every night. Over a few nights, that adds up to a lot of search time. If one of the Russian sailors does something careless, like leaning a broom handle against a

221

pipe, it might create a sound-short. If we get lucky, that will put some vibration in the water where our tail can pick it up."

"That sounds pretty iffy," Captain Bowie said.

Chief McPherson nodded. "It's *extremely* iffy, sir. I don't think my lucky rabbit foot is going to be big enough to handle it. I just can't think of anything else to do."

The Anti-Submarine Warfare Officer, Lieutenant (junior grade) Patrick Cooper, cleared his throat. "Uh … Captain? Is there any way we could try using that Mouse unit *without* the help of the civilian technician? We've got a lot of smart people on this ship, including some pretty savvy computer geeks. Maybe one of them can figure how to program the Mouse unit to do what we want."

The captain shook his head. "It's tempting, Pat. And I've thought about it, believe me. But we can't afford to get this wrong. We may only get one shot at that submarine. If we screw it up because we don't know how to program that damned robot properly, we may miss our only opportunity to end this."

"Then you need somebody who isn't going to screw it up," a woman's voice said.

The words came from the entrance to the wardroom. The assembled officers and chiefs turned to see the civilian technician, Ann Roark, holding open the wardroom door. Standing in the passageway behind her was the other civilian, Sheldon Miggs.

The Roark woman nodded toward the captain. "Permission to come aboard your wardroom, or whatever. Sorry, I forgot to knock. I'm not exactly up on the finer points of military etiquette."

Captain Bowie nodded. "Please, come in, both of you. Have a seat."

The civilians entered the room and found chairs.

"Thank you, Captain," Sheldon Miggs said.

Ann Roark leaned back in her chair. "I apologize for last night, Captain. I'm not a fighter, as you've probably figured out. And I have serious trouble with the idea of killing people."

Her fingers drummed nervously on the table top. "But we're here to help. Whatever you need Mouse to do, we'll try to help you do it."

Captain Bowie studied her for several seconds. "We're going to try to destroy the K-506," he said. "And that means killing over a hundred people. Are you sure you can handle that?"

Ann Roark swallowed heavily, but nodded. "I'm not going to pretend that I'm okay with killing the crew of that submarine. But I understand that it has to be done. And I can shelve my personal issues and *do* it. I guess it comes down to the choice between something *bad*, and something *worse*."

"It does indeed," Captain Bowie said. "That's precisely what it comes down to."

Chief McPherson raised her eyebrows. "If you don't mind my asking," she said. "What exactly changed your mind?"

Ann Roark looked at her coworker, Sheldon Miggs. "Something I read in the Boy Scout Handbook," she said.

CHAPTER 40

National Security Advisor Gregory Brenthoven looked up at the knock on his door. "Enter."

The door opened, and Cheryl White from the National Reconnaissance Office walked in, carrying a brown leather briefcase. "Good morning, Greg. Can I bother you for a minute?"

Brenthoven motioned her to the chair on the other side of his desk. "Morning, Cheryl. What have you got?"

White sat down, and extracted a yellow folder from the briefcase. The edges of the folder were bordered with black diagonal stripes. She laid the folder on the desk top, and opened it to reveal a thin stack of photographs.

"Remember when you asked NRO to look for signs of Zhukov's submarine communications system?"

Brenthoven nodded. "Of course."

"We haven't found hide nor hair of it," White said. "Not yet, anyway. But what we *did* find was pretty interesting."

She pointed to the top photo on the stack. "These were shot by Forager 715, one of the Air Force's Oracle III surveillance satellites, as it passed over southeastern Russia on the twenty-sixth of February. The satellite's primary surveillance mission was a nuclear reactor facility in Iran, so Forager was on the outbound leg of its orbit when these photos were taken. The altitude was about 500 kilometers and increasing, which is outside of the optimal range window for the satellite's cameras. The clarity isn't great, but the shots are readable."

Brenthoven looked at the satellite photo. A pair of blurred oblongs were visible against a dark background of ocean. "These are ships?"

White nodded, and moved a different photo to the top of the stack. "This is the same shot, enlarged and digitally enhanced."

224

In this photo, the two oblongs were clearly ships, with blocky white superstructures running most of the length of each vessel.

"The SAWS operator assigned to Forager 715 ran these enhancements," White said. "His name is Technical Sergeant George Kaulana. He processed this image through silhouette recognition, and correctly identified both of these ships as car carriers. Specifically, they're the Motor Vessel *Shunfeng*, and the Motor Vessel *Jifeng*. They're 20,000-ton Roll-on/Roll-off vessels, or what we call *Ro-Ro*'s. Both built by HuangHai Shipyard in China."

"I'm with you so far," Brenthoven said, "but I don't have any idea where you're going with this."

White shuffled another picture to the top of the stack. The oblong smudges of the ships were much smaller, and the large gray form of a dagger-shaped landmass dominated the upper part of the image. "Both ships were on a scheduled run from China to Mexico," White said. "According to the voyage plans filed by the owners of record, the ships were supposed to deliver 4,000 Chinese economy cars from Zhuhai to Veracruz. But both ships made an unscheduled course deviation. They turned north, out of the shipping lanes, and pulled in to Petropavlosk, Kamchatka instead."

Brenthoven tapped a pencil against the top of his desk. "Hmmm ..."

"*Hmmm* is an understatement," White said. "Four thousand import cars don't show up on time, and the Mexican importer doesn't demand an inquiry, and he doesn't file a complaint. Two merchant ships, worth several hundred million dollars apiece, sail off into Never-never land, and nobody files a piracy report, or sends out a presumed-lost bulletin. Not so much as an insurance claim. And nobody, and I *do* mean *nobody*, is asking where those 4,000 cars went. Not the exporter who shipped them. Not the importer who was supposed to receive them. Not the car manufacturer, who's suddenly out two entire shiploads of shiny new product. Nobody."

Brenthoven paused, giving these strange fragments of information a few seconds to assemble themselves in his brain.

"We looked up the Mexican importer," White said. "And he never heard of this shipment. So we tried calling the Chinese exporter. Their company reps won't return our phone calls."

She straightened the stack of photos, and slid them back into the yellow and black folder. "There weren't any cars, Greg. That was a smokescreen. Those 4,000 Chinese economy cars never existed. Those ships were carrying something else."

Brenthoven nodded. "Our intel sources have been saying from the get-go that Kamchatka is crawling with Asian shock troops. I've been pulling my hair out trying to figure out how Zhukov managed to smuggle them in."

He tossed the pencil on the desk. "I think you just solved *that* little mystery."

CHAPTER 41

On those rare occasions when he ventured out into the streets of Lynnwood, Jason Hulette looked like exactly what he was: a gangly and plain-featured seventeen year-old boy from a middle class family. Jason was an ordinary kid—or in his own eyes—perhaps something *less* than ordinary. The real world seemed to regard him as somewhat unsatisfactory, and the feeling was decidedly mutual.

As unremarkable as he might have been in real life, when immersed in his realm of-choice, Jason was an entirely different creature. Within the boundless datascape of the Internet, he was a virtual demigod—known, respected, and even feared under the hacker alias '*Apocalypse-for-you*,' which he spelled as *Ap0kA1yp$e4U*, in his own personal brand of the geek proto-language known as *Leet*.

Jason sometimes shortened his alias to *Ap0k*, in open homage to his favorite Keanu Reeves movie. The web was not a second life for him. It was the world: the only one that mattered. The physical universe outside of his parent's front door was a shabby and disappointing substitute.

Jason/Ap0k was the leader and founding member of a loosely organized coven of Seattle hackers who called themselves the *d34d kR0w k0n$p1r4$y* (Dead Crow Conspiracy). Although he fervently denied it, Ap0k had cribbed the name idea from the famous Texas-based hacker gang, the Cult of the Dead Cow. Original creation was not one of his personal strengths. His best ideas were always adaptations of concepts invented by other people.

The plan he put into action on the fourth of March was no exception. Ap0k didn't create any of the ideas or technologies involved. He just strung the elements together in a new and interesting way.

With the near-miss nuclear attack now slightly more than forty-eight hours in the past, some of the frenzy was dying down in the western states. The east-west roadways were still flooded with cars as the unscheduled

migration surged eastward, but most of the remaining people in the
threatened states were starting to quiet down. The world had not ended.
The attack had not been repeated, and the U.S. military had managed to
knock out most of the missiles, or bombs, or whatever. Perhaps flaming
death was not going to fall out of the sky after all.

As life in the Western United States began to settle into a shaky
equilibrium, two thoughts occurred to Ap0k. First: Seattle, which was an
armpit of a city in his opinion, had not received its fair share of blind
panic. And second: the attack itself had not harmed a single person, or
damaged a single house, or flattened a single convenience store.

There was plenty of destruction; that was for sure. Car crashes,
burning buildings, injuries, and even deaths. But those effects hadn't
come from the nuclear bombs. They'd been caused by the spur-of-the-
moment craziness that comes with uncontrolled hysteria.

It slowly dawned on Ap0k that the damage had been a strictly social
phenomenon, caused by the rapid spread of information. Or more
correctly, the rapid spread of *mis*information, as the bombs had all been
aimed toward the ocean. The mobs of people who had freaked out and
started trashing things had never been in any immediate danger. The
threat had not been real. But it had *looked* real, and it had *sounded* real.
And that had been enough.

To Ap0k, this revelation suggested all sorts of possibilities. Because
the rapid spread of misinformation happened to be one of the things that he
and his fellow dead crows did best.

On the afternoon of March the 4th, Ap0k and the Dead Crow
Conspiracy hacked into the Emergency Alert System computer network
for the Greater Seattle area. The plan was to trigger the Emergency Alert
System, and seize control of every radio and television station within Area
Codes 360, 206, 253, and 425. Then, when they had a million or so
viewers and listeners glued to their televisions and radios, the dead crows
would inject their own fake broadcast into the network.

They'd recorded the audio track in a walk-in closet, draped with
blankets to muffle outside noises. They'd copied the timing and format of
an actual emergency announcement, and modulated Ap0k's voice to sound
like the baritone of the real EAS announcer. They'd even screen-grabbed
a copy of the Emergency Alert System television banner.

With the recording playing over the background of EAS banner, the
announcement looked and sounded just like the real thing. Ap0k was sure
that the radio and television audiences wouldn't be able to tell that the
broadcast was fake. He was right.

The dead crows were extremely proud of their handiwork. They were already congratulating themselves for having dreamed up the hoax of the century. Their little scam would go down in history, like the *War of the Worlds* radio broadcast panic of 1938. People would run screaming, and piss their pants, and overload the 911 switchboards, and drive their cars into telephone poles. The Dead Crow Conspiracy would become the stuff of hacker legend.

At 3:55 PM, Ap0k transmitted the *go* signal to his hacker buddies. The assault on the EAS server farm began simultaneously, from nineteen manned sites around Seattle, and over a thousand *zombie* machines, recruited for the task by a Trojan horse software application that hijacked control of infected PCs without the knowledge or consent of the computer owners.

Under the combined onslaught, the firewall and anti-virus engines protecting the servers crumbled in less than a minute.

At 3:56 PM, the bogus emergency announcement created by the dead crows went out over the Emergency Alert System throughout the Greater Seattle area. The message was seen and heard through every operating radio and television in the network footprint. Nearly a million and a half Seattle area residents were informed that *ten* nuclear warheads were screaming toward their fair city, and that all military attempts to intercept the missiles had failed.

There were no such warheads, of course. They existed only in the fevered   imaginations of Ap0k and his dead crow buddies. But the residents of Seattle had no way of knowing that. They had no reason to suspect that the warning was anything but genuine.

The recorded voice of the fake EAS announcer went on to inform the million-plus victims of his hoax that the bombs would arrive in twenty minutes. Seattle would be completely obliterated. Everyone who wanted to live should evacuate the city immediately, or perish in radioactive fire.

The seventeen year-old boy who styled himself as Ap0kAlyp$e4U had promised his buddies that the d34d kR0w k0n$p1r4$y would be remembered by history. And so they were.

Jason Wesley Hulette and ten of his accomplices and co-conspirators were arrested and tried for domestic terrorism and treason. They were collectively charged with over forty-thousand counts of manslaughter, more than a million cases of assault with intent to wound, and three-quarters of a trillion dollars in property damage.

The remaining eight members of the dead crows were identified, but none were brought to trial. They had been killed in the panic that burned the city of Seattle to the ground.

CHAPTER 42

Sheldon leaned over Ann's left shoulder. "How's it coming?"

Ann stopped typing, her fingers frozen in midair above the keyboard of her laptop. "Sheldon, if you ask me that question one more time, I'm going to duct tape your mouth shut."

"I just want to help," Sheldon said.

"Go away," Ann said. "Stop asking me questions. That will help a *lot*."

"You're absolutely sure that there's nothing I can do?"

Ann leaned back and crossed her arms. "Am I *absolutely* sure? *Absolutely*?"

She pretended to study the matter for several seconds and then shrugged in apparent contrition. "I guess I'm not totally-positively-*absolutely* sure. I suppose ... if you *really* feel the need to contribute ... I should let you get in here and try to do your part."

She held a fingertip against her lower lip. "Let's see ... This an entirely new mission profile for Mouse. He's got to perform some specialized functions that aren't built into his core program, so you should probably start by dumping the mission package I created for the submersible rescue, and purging the robot's scratch memory and persistent memory. When that's finished, upload a clean copy of the core program from the master disc packs, and sort through the mission library for the modules that most closely match the functions Mouse is going to need. Then, append those files to his core program, and modify any parameters that need adjustment. Don't forget to load the program mods for covert search, and under ice operations, and don't forget to disable his acoustic communications module. You'll also need to load the bottom contour database for the operating area, the navigation data, and the environmental package, including currents, known navigation hazards, projected salinity profiles, and thermal structures of the water column. And when you're done, run an end-to-end, and a loop-back test, and debug to check for errors."

She smiled with exaggerated sweetness. "If you're going to take care of all that, I'll go grab a cup of coffee and a Danish."

"I get the picture," Sheldon said. "I don't know how to do any of the stuff you need to accomplish."

Ann gasped in mock surprise. "You don't?"

Her fingers starting pecking away at the laptop again. "Then will you *please* stop interrupting me, so that *I* can do it?"

"Yeah," Sheldon said. "I'm sorry."

Ann stopped typing again. "I'm jerking your chain, Sheldon. I've already done all that junk. I just need to run one last program integrity test, to check for disagrees and resource conflicts, and then I'm done here."

She tapped a key and leaned back. "There. That should take that about ten minutes to cycle. When it's finished, as long as there aren't any errors, our buddy Mouse should be ready to go play in the water."

She checked her watch. "That's pretty good timing. The Navy boys tell me that the sun will be setting in about fifteen minutes. Since we're doing all this sneaking stealth business under cover of darkness, that works out just about perfectly."

Ann stood up and stretched to get the kinks out of her back. "Come on, Cowboy. If you absolutely must help, you can lead me through this metal labyrinth to the wardroom. I really *do* want some coffee and a Danish."

⚓ ⚓ ⚓

An hour later, Sheldon and Ann stood with a bunch of Sailor types on the boat deck, bundled up in heavy foul weather coats, and stomping their feet to keep warm. The sun was down now, and the moon wouldn't rise for several hours yet. The darkness was broken only by the stars and the dim glow of amber-lensed deck lamps, cranked down to minimal intensity.

Mouse hung beneath the boat davit, a dark silhouette dangling at the end of the lifting cable for the destroyer's Rigid-Hulled Inflatable Boats.

That particular bit of engineering had been Ann's idea. At her suggestion, the robot's lifting hardware had been made compatible with the single-point boat davits used aboard Navy warships. Any ship that carried RHIBs could launch and recover a Mouse unit without installing special equipment. From the Navy's perspective, that made Mouse cheaper to buy and easier to integrate into the fleet, which—by extension—made it more likely that the Lords of Navy Procurement would decide to purchase lots of Mouse-series underwater robots from Norton Deep Water Systems.

As far as the company was concerned, the Navy procurement contract was the whole point of the Mouse project. Ann's priorities were quite different, but they still came back to the bottom line. The Navy was Norton's best customer. If the Navy didn't buy underwater robots, then Norton would have no reason to build them. And if Norton didn't build underwater robots, then Ann would have to either abandon her chosen profession, or go to work for Big Oil. And that was *not* going to happen.

Ann might not care for the military yahoos, but at least they thought they were doing the right thing. They were well-intentioned, if misguided. Those planet-killing bastards in the oil industry ... they were a whole different breed of bad news. There were no good intentions in them at all: just mindless greed, with no thought to long-term consequence.

Ann looked up at the shadowy form of the disk-shaped robot hanging from the end of the boat davit. Norton had provided the funding, and the engineers, and the facilities, but Ann had breathed life into the strange little machine. Mouse was the culmination of her very best ideas, and the product of the hardest work she had ever done.

She exhaled sharply, the freezing Siberian air turning her breath to vapor in front of her face. She had poured her soul into this project. No way would she do that for the oil companies. Never.

Ann felt a jarring thump through the soles of her feet, followed by a prolonged scraping noise and a groaning of metal that she felt more than heard. The ship seemed to shudder until the groaning died away.

She looked at the nearest Sailor. "What the hell was *that*?"

"Probably a growler," the man said.

"A *what*?"

"A growler," the Sailor said. "A chunk of sea ice. Smaller than an iceberg, or a bergy bit. Maybe the size of a refrigerator."

"There are chunks of ice out here the size of refrigerators?" Ann asked. "And they're not freaking icebergs?"

"That's right," the man said.

Ann couldn't see his face properly in the darkness, but the Sailor had an older voice. He was probably one of the senior petty officers, or maybe a chief.

"We're transiting through the Kuril islands," he said. "Passing into the Sea of Okhotsk, which is mostly covered by ice. The plan is to skirt the southern edge of the ice pack. As long as we don't get too close to the pack edge, we'll mostly run into grease ice. That's usually just slush—not fully frozen. We'll get some growlers too, about like the one we just rubbed up against. If we're lucky, we won't run into any bergy bits."

"What are those?" Sheldon asked.

"Baby icebergs," the Sailor said. "Maybe the size of a house. Not big enough to qualify as real icebergs. You don't get real bergs in the Sea of O."

Ann's mouth felt suddenly dry. She nodded, though the man probably couldn't see her in the darkness. "No icebergs," she said. "That's good to know. At least we don't have to worry about sinking."

The man laughed, but there didn't seem to be a lot of humor in it. "I didn't *say* that." He stomped on the deck, the sound of his boot audible in the darkness. "Our hull is steel," he said. "But it's only a little more than a half-inch thick. A decent sized bergy bit will go through us like a can opener."

"Please tell me you're joking," Sheldon said.

"I wish I was. Even a good sized growler could do a number on us, if we hit it the wrong way."

"What about that killer radar?" Ann asked. "No sparrow shall fall, and all that crap. You can see the ice with that, right?"

"We're in EMCON," the man said. "Stealth mode. The SPY radar could probably see most of the ice, but it would give away our position. We're running without it."

"So how do we avoid hitting one of those baby icebergs?" Sheldon asked.

"We've got lookouts posted," the Navy man said. "They're watching the water in front of the ship. If they see anything off the bow, they tell the bridge and we turn to avoid it. We should be okay."

"Correct me if I'm wrong," Ann said. 'But didn't the *Titanic* have lookouts posted too? That particular method of ice avoidance didn't work out too well for those guys, as I recall."

"You've got a point there," the Navy man said. "But we have two advantages over the *Titanic*. Our watertight integrity systems and damage control technology are about a century more advanced."

"Fine," Ann said. "What's the other advantage?"

The man laughed again. "We *know* we're not unsinkable," he said. "So we're a lot more careful."

"That's comforting," Ann said. "Now, we just…"

"Just a sec," the man said. "I'm getting a call from the bridge."

He paused for a couple of seconds, and then said, "Boat deck, aye!"

He snapped his fingers. "Peters! Shut off the deck lights. Everybody! Lights off—*now*!"

The amber lamps went off abruptly, plunging the deck into total darkness.

The Sailor spoke again. "Bridge—Boat deck, all lights are out. We are dark."

"What's going on?" Sheldon asked softly.

"Jets," the Navy man said. "CIC can't get a lock on the Bogies without lighting off our radar, but our Electronic Warfare guys are tracking emissions from at least four Zaslon S-800's."

"What does that mean?" Ann asked.

"It means there are at least four MiG-31 fighter jets out there, probably flying the edge of the ice pack to check for uninvited party guests."

"Like *us*," Sheldon said.

"Yeah," the man said softly. "Like us. So we're running quiet and dark, and generally hoping that they don't detect us. There's a good chance that they won't. We're pretty damned stealthy when we shut down all the toys."

Ann stared up into the night sky, trying vainly to spot something moving against the backdrop of stars. "What happens if they find us?" she asked.

"Depends on who they belong to," the Sailor said. "If they're out of mainland Russia, they'll more than likely just report our position back to their base. That will stir up some shit, because the Russians don't like us up here, but it'll be mostly be political. We probably won't get shot at."

"What if they're *not* from mainland Russia?" Sheldon asked.

"Then they're out of the Yelizovo air base on Kamchatka," the man said. "Which means that they belong to our pal, Mr. Zhukov. If it's *those* guys, they'll shoot us between the eyes about ten seconds after they find out we're here."

"This is insane," Ann said. "We're dodging icebergs in the dark, and playing hide and seek with freaking fighter jets. What are we going to do for an encore? Juggle chainsaws?"

The Sailor chuckled. "You know what they say. It's not just a job. It's an adventure."

"I'm not joking," Ann snapped. "What the hell are we doing here? We're practically asking to get killed."

"This is what we *do*," the man said. "This is our job. We're kind of like Secret Service agents. We step in front of the bullet, so that our country doesn't have to."

"That's crap," Ann said. "That whole military-ethos/warrior-Zen thing is nothing but a load of self-aggrandizing macho bullshit."

"It's not bullshit, ma'am," the Sailor said. "We've got a trigger-happy lunatic threatening to incinerate the Western United States. If he manages to unleash ten percent of the firepower at his command, he'll kill more people than every war in history combined. Our job is to stop him any way we can. Even with our lives."

The man sighed. "We don't want to die, Ms. Roark. We want to go home to our families. We want to drink beer, and watch football on television, and barbecue hotdogs, and play catch in the back yard with our kids. But we *will* step into the path of the bullet, if that's what it takes to stop the bad guys. Like I said—it's what we do."

Ann was about to reply, when the man spoke again. "Just a sec. The bridge is talking to me."

After a few seconds, he said, "Bridge—Boat deck, resume operations, aye."

He cleared his throat. "The Bogies have passed us by," he said. "Peters, get the lights back on."

The amber lamps came back to life. They seemed almost painfully bright after the long minutes of total darkness.

"Alright," the Sailor said. "The bridge says we're in position. Let's get *R2D2* in the water, and see if he can find a submarine."

CHAPTER 43

"Ya zamyors..."

The old man's voice was barely more than a whisper, but it snapped Agent DuBrul instantly back to alertness. His head came up and his body posture stiffened. The chair had lulled him into drowsiness. He stood up and took a quick step to the side of the hospital bed.

Swaddled in the green hospital sheets, Oleg Grigoriev looked like a poor job of embalming. His eyes were sunken, and his once swarthy skin was thin and papery. The iron-hard Soviet Sergeant had all but disappeared now, leaving in his place this dwindling husk of his former self.

The old man's face had become a mirror. Gazing into its unsettling depths, David DuBrul saw the reflection of his own mortality. For the first time, he could truly imagine his own death. And for the first time, he knew in his heart that it was not an intellectual abstraction. It was a real thing. A true thing.

At some point in the future—whether an hour from now, or fifty years from now—he would draw his very last breath. When he released that final purchase of air, his life would flow out with it, expelled from its frail human vessel to mingle with the atoms of the universe. And David DuBrul would cease to exist.

He hoped that it wouldn't be like this, that he wouldn't die like this poor old Russian—failing by slow and painful inches in an unfamiliar bed, in a building full of strangers.

"Ya zamyors," Grigoriev whispered again.

DuBrul nodded. "You're cold?" He took a folded blanket from a side table, and spread it over the patient.

"Is that better?" He spoke in English. His Russian was fluent, but he knew that Grigoriev's English was at least as good. And he did not want to speak to this man in his mother language.

From a standpoint of spy craft, the decision was not a good one. According to the book, if you had the language skills, you followed the subject into whatever dialect he was most comfortable using. It was easier that way to establish trust, which made your subject more likely to speak freely. Also, the need for mental translation made most people select their words carefully when speaking in a foreign tongue. Within the easy flow of their primary language, they tended to blurt out things might never be revealed under the more deliberate syntax of another tongue.

DuBrul didn't care. He wanted the information in this man's head. He needed it. But he would not speak in the language of the old man's friends and loved ones in order to draw it out. He would not smile, and pretend to be a friend. The old man deserved better than that.

Grigoriev blinked several times, and struggled visibly to focus his eyes. "U vas est' karta?"

DuBrul reached for a folder on a bedside table. "Yes," he said. "I have a map."

The DIA agents had hoped that this moment might come, and they'd prepared for it with a map of Kamchatka and the Sea of Okhotsk mounted to a sheet of foam core poster board. It weighed only a few ounces, but was stiff enough for easy manipulation by weakened fingers.

DuBrul held the map over the bed, within easy reach of the patient. The lines of latitude and longitude were clearly marked, and the place names had oversized labels, Russian above English.

The old man raised a shaky hand, and pointed one trembling finger toward a spot on the map, in the northeastern quadrant of the Sea of Okhotsk. DuBrul recognized the location from which K-506 had launched the first missile attack. He drew a small circle on the map using a felt tipped pen.

"Zdes'," Grigoriev whispered. "Here. Zashishennaja pozicija."

Agent DuBrul recognized the term. Zashishennaja pozicija translated loosely into 'protected position.' It was the Russian equivalent of the word defilade: a position fortified against attack by geographic barriers. Hills, ravines, that sort of thing.

DuBrul repeated the words. "Zashishennaja pozicija. I think I understand. These are the coordinates the submarine can shoot from, is that right? These are the places where explosives have been set to blow holes in the ice pack?"

"Da," the old man whispered. "Strelyat. To shoot from ..."

"How many zashishennaja pozicija are there?" DuBrul asked. "How many places can K-506 shoot through the ice?"

The old man's hand dropped back to the sheets. He closed his eyes and breathed heavily for nearly a minute. At last, his eyelids fluttered open again. "Pyat," he hissed.

DuBrul nodded again. Five.

Grigoriev lifted his finger to the chart again. His hand shook so badly that it took a few seconds to settle down. "Zdes'," he breathed.

DuBrul circled the spot on the map.

Grigoriev's palsied finger moved a few inches and touched the map again. "Zdes'."

DuBrul marked the new spot with another circle. Again the finger moved, and DuBrul drew a fourth circle.

A shudder passed through the old man's body and his hand fell away from the chart. The heart monitor mounted to the wall near his bed began beeping rapidly. The cardiac trace on the screen blinked from green to red.

DuBrul turned away from the patient. "Doctor?"

He raised his voice. "Doctor? Get in here!"

The door flew open, and Dr. Hogan covered the distance to the bed in two quick strides. He glanced at the monitor, and then looked over his shoulder. "Get a crash cart in here, now!"

Another shudder wracked Oleg Grigoriev's body. His eyes seemed to roll back in their sockets, and a ribbon of foamy saliva rolled from the corner of his mouth.

A nurse and a pair of Hospital Corpsmen rushed in, pushing a cart full of medical equipment.

DuBrul backed away, to give them room to work, but the patient's eyes suddenly locked on his face. "Here," the old man croaked. "Come ... here ..."

Agent DuBrul edged past the nurse to the side of the bed. "I'm here."

The nurse started to object, but Dr. Hogan shook his head.

Grigoriev wheezed. "Karta ..."

"Right here," DuBrul said. He held up the map.

Grigoriev's finger rose with agonizing slowness. It brushed a spot near the southern end of the sea. "Zashishennaja ... ," he muttered. "... pozicijaaaa ..."

A final spasm contorted the man's body, and then he lay still. The heart monitor emitted a continuous whine.

DuBrul marked the last spot, and backed away from the bed. He stood with the map clutched in his hand, watching the medical team work feverishly over their patient. He made no move to interfere, but he could see that they were wasting their time. The tough old Sergeant was gone.

Long minutes later, as the frantic resuscitation attempts began to wind down, DuBrul looked at the map. His five hastily-drawn circles marked the places that Grigoriev had indicated. The locations from which K-506 could detonate pre-positioned explosives, and blow shooting holes in the ice cover.

The northeastern position had already been used; DuBrul was sure of that, leaving four spots from which the submarine could shower its targets with nuclear weapons.

The circles he had scrawled were inexact. He knew that. The old Russian had been too weak and too shaky to indicate the positions with precision. And if—by some miracle—he had managed to identify precisely the correct points, the area enclosed by each circle would still encompass many square miles of ice.

DuBrul and Ross had understood in advance that using the map would yield imprecise results. But after the Russian's previous collapse, it had seemed unlikely that Grigoriev would recover enough strength to pass detailed verbal information, like map coordinates. So they had agreed on a setup that would permit the patient to communicate by pointing.

Instead of precise navigational coordinates, they had approximate locations, with built-in margins of error. Not exactly ideal, but—outside of James Bond movies—intelligence information was rarely absolute.

With a few jabs of his finger, Grigoriev had reduced the search area from over a half a million square miles, to a few hundred square miles. The area of uncertainty had just shrunk by a factor of two thousand, or maybe even three thousand. As far as DuBrul was concerned, that was pretty damned good work. It was a lot better than they usually managed.

He tucked the map under his arm and walked to the door, signaling to the Marine guard to follow him. The medical team had abandoned their attempt to revive the patient. They were taking last minute readings and making final chart entries—following the procedures required to certify the time of death.

Agent DuBrul paused to look back at Oleg Grigoriev one last time. "Spaciba," he said softly. "Thank you, old warrior. Go with God."

CHAPTER 44

President Chandler leaned against the railing of the Truman Balcony, and looked across the south lawn to the crowd of protesters gathered on the Ellipse. The District of Columbia was experiencing its last hard cold snap of the year. The temperature was hovering just above freezing, and there were two inches of snow on the ground. But the protesters didn't care. Their shoes had trampled the Ellipse so thoroughly that the snow had been churned into muddy brown slush.

The Secret Service was now estimating the head count at thirty-thousand, and the mob was still growing. Or—more correctly—the *mobs* were still growing. There were several groups down there. The *Peace-At-All-Costs* lobby was rubbing shoulders with the *Nuke-the-Bastards-Now* gang, and the fundamentalist *This-is-the-Wrath-of-God* faction was marching beside the *America-Must-Rule-the-World-for-its-Own-Good* cult.

Those weren't the real names of the organizations represented here, of course, but their platforms were nearly all that silly, and that simplistic. Most of them couldn't find Kamchatka on a map, and probably fewer than one out of twenty could spell the name of the country that had suddenly inflamed their passions. But they all knew exactly where the president had gone wrong in managing this crisis, and they all knew exactly how to fix it.

The answer is simple—*lay down our arms and live in peace with other nations.* The answer is simple—*blow those sons-of-bitches to kingdom come.* The answer is simple—*outlaw all foreign trade and shut off all foreign aid. Let the commies and the ragheads try to get along without American dollars.* The answer is simple—*fill in the blank here ...*

Except that the answers were all different, and *none* of them were simple. The protesters down on the Ellipse disagreed with each other

240

about nearly everything, but they were united on one point. They all wanted Francis Benjamin Chandler to get the hell out of the White House, and make room for the kind of leader who could save the nation in its moment of peril. Of course, depending on which group you talked to, the next person in the Oval Office should either be a Democrat, a Republican, a Libertarian, an unaligned independent, or a pair of Wiccan Siamese Twins with the secret communications frequency of the alien mother ship.

The president snorted, and the exhalation turned to steam in the cold morning air.

"Uh, Mr. President?" The voice belonged to National Security Advisor Gregory Brenthoven.

The president turned to see the man standing at the open door leading to the yellow room.

He beckoned with his fingers. "Come on out, Greg. I'm just having a look at the newest members of the Frank Chandler Fan Club."

Brenthoven stepped out onto the balcony and closed the door. He looked out at the roiling crowd on the Ellipse. "What do you think they want, sir?"

"That's easy," the president said. "They want world peace, unrestricted warfare, a global economy, utter severance of all foreign trading agreements, open borders, and strict isolationism."

Brenthoven grinned. "So it's business as usual, sir?"

The president raised his hands and let them drop. "Pretty much."

He sighed. "What have you got, Greg?"

Brenthoven walked over to the railing. "The Russian courier, Oleg Grigoriev, is dead, sir. Medical complications from the gunshot wounds."

The president nodded gravely, and looked back out toward the growing mob of his detractors. "That puts me in a bit of an emotional conflict," he said. "On the one hand, a man has lost his life. As a human being, my first thought should focus on the tragedy of that loss. But I'm also the Commander-in-Chief of a nation under siege. And I have to confess that I'm more concerned about losing a possible source of critical intelligence. Because some of the secrets that Mr. Grigoriev took to the grave could drastically affect the future of this country, and the world."

"I understand, sir," the national security advisor said. "But he didn't take quite everything to the grave."

The president turned and met Brenthoven's eyes.

"Mr. Grigoriev confirmed the CNO's theory that the submarine is shooting from prepared positions, where explosives have been planted in the ice cover. There were five positions. Governor Zhukov apparently called them ..." Brenthoven paused, reading the unfamiliar words from his notebook. "... *zashishennaja pozicija*."

He sounded the words out clumsily. "That appears to be the Russian term for a protected position, or a hidden place to shoot from."

"I see," the president said. "And did Mr. Grigoriev happen to provide us with the coordinates of any of these protected positions?"

"He gave us approximate locations, Mr. President," Brenthoven said. "One of them corresponded pretty closely with the first position that the submarine launched from. If the other four are in the same ballpark, accuracy-wise, we've got the remaining launch positions narrowed down fairly well."

The president frowned. "Why didn't he just feed us the latitudes and longitudes? That's what he did the first time, right?"

"He was too weak, sir," Brenthoven said. "The DIA agent in the hospital room reported that Mr. Grigoriev literally used his dying breath to pass this information to us."

"It's pretty tough to complain about *that*," the president said. He paused for nearly a minute. "Are we getting this information to our Navy ships?"

The national security advisor nodded. "COMPACFLEET is sending the message out now, sir. And the Chairman of the Joint Chiefs is putting together a tactical proposal for your consideration."

"What's he got in mind?"

"I haven't seen the details yet, sir," Brenthoven said. "But the general plan is to send Explosive Ordnance Disposal teams onto the ice pack to locate and disarm Zhukov's explosives. If the submarine can't blow holes in the ice, it can't launch missiles."

"That could give us the opening we need to finish this," the president said. "If that sub can't launch, Zhukov's nuclear threat goes down the drain."

The national security advisor nodded. "That's the idea, Mr. President."

"The upside is obvious," the president said. "What's the downside?"

"Our positional information is only approximate, sir. The EOD teams are probably going to have trouble finding the explosives. And they'll be exposed out on the ice. The longer they have to work out there, the greater the chance that they'll be discovered by Zhukov's people."

The president frowned at this thought. "If Zhukov catches us trying to pull his fangs, he's going to want to punish us."

"Do you think he'll launch another attack, sir?"

The president sighed. "I don't know, Greg. He's certainly crazy enough."

"Maybe our EOD people can get the job done without getting caught."

"Maybe," the president said. "We're due for a bit of luck."

"Yes, sir," the national security advisor said.

Neither man made the obvious comment. So far, every lucky break they'd gotten had arrived too late to do any good.

CHAPTER 45

USS TOWERS (DDG-103)
WESTERN PACIFIC OCEAN
WEDNESDAY; 06 MARCH
0603 hours (6:03 AM)
TIME ZONE +11 'LIMA'

Ann watched the screen of her laptop computer, waiting for the small green icon that would appear when Mouse reported his position.

The robot was operating autonomously, following his mission program without human supervision or input. Because communications signals might reveal his presence to the enemy submarine's acoustic sensors, he was not sending any updates back to the *Towers*. He would not report in until his mission was complete and he was clear of the ice pack, either because he had located the target submarine, or because the allotted search period had expired and he had transited to the rendezvous coordinates.

Ann glanced at the digital time readout in the lower right hand corner of her computer screen. Mouse's search program wasn't scheduled to end for another ten minutes yet, so she really didn't expect to see anything yet.

There was no need to hover over the computer, but she couldn't tear herself away. Every time she walked away from it for thirty seconds, she found herself drawn back to the little screen by an irresistible force. She felt like an overprotective mother, hanging around the bus stop a half hour before the school bus was due to bring her child home.

Ann had reason to be nervous. There were plenty of things that could go wrong. Mouse was designed to navigate safely beneath ice cover, but he'd never been under the ice for this long before. Until now, it had only been for a couple of hours at a time, for testing purposes. The conditions had been controlled then, with divers waiting to go after the robot if anything went wrong. There were no controls here. There were no divers, and there was no backup plan.

Also, several of the program modules Mouse was using now had never been put through their paces before. Ann was confident that the software code was pretty stable, but bugs were still cropping up now and then.

There was no telling what the robot might do if his software crashed while he was deep under the ice. He could ram himself into an ice keel, or take a wild excursion out of the operating area, to wind up in parts unknown when the power in his battery cells ran down.

The robot might already be lying in pieces on the bottom of the sea, destroyed by an unrecognized technical defect, or some flaw in his program code. The mission could have failed ten minutes after it had started, and Ann wouldn't find out until the robot failed to report at the end of its search patterns.

Someone leaned over Ann's left shoulder. "Has the prodigal robot returned?" It was the red headed Sonar Chief. Her name was Mc-something-or-other.

Ann shook her head. "Not yet. He's not due to report in for another few minutes."

The other woman tilted her head. "The way your eyes are welded to that computer screen, I figured that he must be overdue."

Ann felt the corners of her mouth come up just a little—that strange half-smile thing she always found herself doing when strangers tried to engage her in polite conversation. "No," she said. "Mouse isn't late. I'm just a little … nervous."

"I can understand that," the chief said. "But don't let it worry you if your robot comes home empty-handed the first few times. Anti-Submarine Warfare is slow. The search part is, anyway. After you find the target, things can heat up pretty damned fast. But until then, it's mostly a waiting game."

Ann nodded. "Thanks."

"My sonar gang is back in TACTASS, pulling in the towed array," the Navy woman said. "We didn't get anything either." She shrugged. "I didn't really think we would. Even the old Delta boats can be pretty quiet when they're running slow and dark. But it was worth a shot. We could still get lucky. Maybe we'll catch a sniff tomorrow night. Or maybe your Mouse unit will."

"I hope so," Ann said.

The Navy woman extended her hand. "Theresa McPherson. Around the CPO Mess, they call me *Teri*, or *Mac*. Everybody else just calls me *Chief*."

Ann shook the woman's hand. "Ann Roark," she said. "Or just Ann. I don't have any idea what they call me around the CPO Mess. And I probably don't want to know."

Chief McPherson laughed and started to say something, but she was interrupted by a short burst of static from an overhead speaker box, followed instantly by a man's voice.

"TAO—EW, I'm tracking four I-band emitters, bearing zero-three-seven. Zaslon S-800 series phased array radars. Looks like MiG-31s. Probably two flights of two."

A half-second later, a woman's voice came out of the speaker in response. "EW—TAO, four I-band emitters bearing zero-three-seven, aye. Which way are the Bogies tracking?"

"EW—TAO, Bogies have very slight left bearing drift with rapidly-increasing signal strength. The CPA is going to be right over the top of us, ma'am."

From the forward end of Combat Information Center, Ann heard a woman say, "Damn it!"

The words didn't come through the speaker. The woman hadn't spoken them over the communications net.

Ann turned to the chief. "What was all that about?"

"The Electronic Warfare techs are reporting to the Tactical Action Officer that Russian aircraft are coming our way. From the radar transmissions, the planes appear to be MiG-31 fighter jets. If they don't change course in the next couple of minutes, they're going to fly right over us."

"Will they see us?"

Chief McPherson shrugged. "Don't know. Our stealth technology is good. We're not easy to detect on radar, and the phototropic camouflage makes it hard to spot us visually. But the moon is up, and it's three-quarters full. If one of those pilots looks the wrong way, he might catch our silhouette in the moonlight."

"That's the best stealth technology you could get for my tax dollars?"

Chief McPherson smiled. "You didn't pay enough taxes to buy a Star Trek cloaking device, Ann. We're sneaky as hell, but we're not invisible. If somebody looks right at us, he's going to see us."

The female voice came over the speaker again. "EW—TAO, give me a recommended course for minimized radar cross-section, and stand by to launch chaff. Break. Weapons Control—TAO, have Aegis and CIWS ready to come on line at a second's notice if those Bogies start shooting. Break. RCO—TAO, get SPY ready to transmit on zero-notice. If the situation goes hot, we'll need to get radar information to fire control immediately."

As the individual stations began acknowledging their orders, a male voice came over a different set of speakers. "Commanding Officer, your presence is requested in Combat Information Center."

Ann could feel the tension level in the darkened room go up dramatically. Men and women at electronic consoles around the compartment began pushing buttons and speaking into headsets in low voices.

She heard the clang of an opening door, and a voice called out, "the captain's in CIC."

Captain Bowie strode into the room, making a bee-line for a woman seated in a chair at the focus of three large tactical display screens. The captain and the woman went into a hushed conference immediately.

Ann nodded toward the woman. "Who's she?"

"That's Lieutenant Augustine. She's the Tactical Action Officer. She's in charge of fighting the ship."

"Is that her regular job?"

"She's the Operations Department Head," Chief McPherson said. "TAO is a watch station. It rotates with the watch turnover. OPS has got the bubble now, because she's the best TAO we've got, and the captain figured things might get hairy."

Ann regarded the female officer without speaking.

Chief McPherson cocked an eyebrow. "What? You didn't think the gals just came along to clean the ashtrays, did you?"

A voice broke over the speaker. "TAO—EW, I've got multiple X-band seekers, centered on bearing zero-three-five. We've got Vipers, ma'am. I count three ... make that four. I say again, EW has four inbound missiles, bearing zero-three-five!"

The woman's voice came back instantly. "TAO, aye! Launch chaff, now! Break. All Stations—TAO, we have inbound Vipers! I say again, we have missiles inbound! RCO, go active on SPY. Break. Weapons Control—TAO, shift to Aegis ready-auto. Set CIWS to auto-engage."

Ann's stomach contracted into a knot. "They're shooting at us?"

"Yeah," Chief McPherson said. "We've got missiles coming towards us, and our radar's not up yet."

She gave Ann's shoulder a quick squeeze. "I've got to get to my station. Put on your seatbelt and keep your head down. And hang on to that laptop if you don't want to lose it. The ride is about to get bumpy."

She wheeled around, and trotted away before Ann could respond.

Ann heard a quick succession of muffled thumps. "TAO—EW, launching chaff. Six away."

The reports kept coming through the overhead speaker. "TAO—RCO. SPY is active. Transmitting data to fire control."

"TAO—Weapons Control. Aegis is at ready-auto. CIWS is set to auto-engage."

Ann fumbled at the sides of the chair until she located the seat belt. She belted herself in, and then grabbed her laptop computer, hugging the black plastic rectangle to her chest like a sheet of armor plate.

Mouse would be coming to the end of his run, now. The robot might already be out from under the ice pack, bobbing on the surface, waiting for retrieval. Ann knew without asking that no one would care.

"TAO—EW, inbound Vipers are showing staggered monopulse radar signatures. I think we're looking at AS-23 *Kronos* missiles, ma'am. Recommend we avoid jamming. Some of the Kronos variants have home-on-jam capability."

The Tactical Action Officer's voice came back a second later. "EW—TAO, my memory might be failing me, but I don't think the MiG-31 can carry the AS-23 missile."

"TAO—EW. I don't know what they can carry, ma'am. I'm just telling you what's on my slick."

Ann listened to the chatter and wondered what in the hell they were talking about.

Without warning, the ship gave a violent series of tremors, accompanied by a sequence of tumultuous rumbles that seemed to shake the teeth in Ann's head. She cried out, but her voice was nearly swallowed up in the cacophony of sound.

In the ear-ringing silence that followed, another report came over the speaker. "TAO—Weapons Control. Twelve birds away, no apparent casualties. Targeted two each on the inbound Vipers, and one each on the Bogies."

The giant display screens at the far end of the room flickered with cryptic symbols. Their meaning was as foreign to Ann as the unintelligible reports tumbling out of the speakers, but she knew enough to realize that her future was being spelled out in that intricate dance of shapes and lines.

Somewhere out there in the darkness of the pre-dawn Siberian morning, engines of death were screaming towards each other at fantastic speeds. And it came to Ann that guided missiles were complex and intricate machines. They were robots, like her Mouse, but a thousand times faster and more single-minded of purpose. Mouse could do many things. But these robots could only destroy.

The realization that she might be minutes—or even *seconds*—away from death, crashed over Ann like a freezing wave. She was suddenly glad that she didn't have a job to do, because her muscles were locked in place. She couldn't swallow. She couldn't breathe.

She wanted to leap out of the chair and run away from this craziness. But where would she go? Even if her paralyzed body would agree to take instructions from her brain, which she very much doubted, there was nowhere to go. Nowhere but a freezing and alien ocean, and this ship—which had suddenly become a target.

On the big screens, a cluster of blue symbols rushed toward a cluster of red symbols. With a quick series of flashes, about half of the red and blue symbols vanished from the screen.

"TAO—Air, splash two Vipers."

Another voice followed without pause. "Weapons Control concurs. The remaining two Vipers are now inside our minimum missile range. We cannot reengage with missiles."

As Ann watched, one of the red symbols veered to the side and disappeared.

"TAO—EW, splash Viper number three. One taker on chaff!"

Ann wasn't quite sure what the exchange of words meant, but it seemed that three of the incoming missiles had been destroyed. One of the red symbols tracked toward the center of the screen without pausing.

Two more red symbols flashed and vanished. "TAO—Air, splash two Bogies."

The remaining red image kept coming.

Ann began to tremble. She didn't know how to read the catalog of symbols sprayed across the screens. She didn't know the color codes, or the significance of the shapes, or the meanings of the blocks of letters and numbers that followed close on each symbol like the tail on a kite. She knew none of these things. But something in her instinctively knew that when the inverted red V shape reached the middle of the screen, she would die.

Another red symbol flashed and disappeared. "TAO—Air, splash Bogie number three. Bogie four is bugging out."

"TAO, aye."

The red inverted V continued without pausing. It had nearly reached the center of the screen, and no one seemed to be doing anything about it.

Ann clamped her mouth shut, willing herself not to scream when the moment came.

A throaty metallic rumble split the air, like the roar of an unmuffled lawnmower engine. The sound was followed by the muted boom of an explosion. Not far away, but not on the ship either.

There was perhaps three seconds of near silence, broken only by the hum of electronic cooling fans, and then a cheer went up around Combat Information Center. Some unseen person shouted, "Go CIWS!" followed by a wolf whistle.

The overhead speaker crackled again. "TAO—Weapons Control. Splash Viper number four."

Ann took a breath for the first time in nearly a minute. The cool air felt strangely unfamiliar as it rushed into her lungs. She felt her muscles begin to relax.

She wasn't dead.

She gradually became conscious of the laptop computer still clutched against her ribs. She unfolded her arms and opened the computer. Her movements were jerky, as her muscles were still flushed with unneeded adrenaline. That must be why she was feeling slightly giddy.

She smiled weakly to herself, and looked at her computer. Mouse's friendly green triangle symbol stared back at her from the screen. Her child had reached the bus stop safely. He was ready for his mother to take him home for milk and cookies.

Ann was fine. She was alive. Mouse was fine. And now they'd pick him up and bring him home for cookies.

Ann giggled at the thought. Her laughter was shrill, and oddly modulated. It dragged on long after real humor would have failed, but she couldn't seem to make herself stop.

People were beginning to stare at her now, but her mind had become a disconnected jumble of missiles, and cookies, and exploding airplanes, and milk-drinking robots. Out there somewhere in the pre-dawn darkness, the mangled bodies of the jet pilots would be sinking through the waves … settling to the bottom of the sea.

The laughter died as suddenly as if someone had flipped a switch. Ann felt slightly dizzy. She took a deep breath to clear her head. She let it out slowly, deciding as she did so that it seemed to be working; her thoughts were becoming a little less manic.

And then she vomited all over the floor of Combat Information Center.

CHAPTER 46

Sergiei Mikhailovich Zhukov hurled the clipboard toward the lieutenant who had just handed it to him, not ten seconds earlier. The clipboard sailed past the young officer's head, missing his left cheek by less than a centimeter. It was a tribute to the man's training that he neither ducked nor flinched.

"They did *what?*" Zhukov screamed.

The officer continued to stand at attention. "Comrade President, they have shot down three of our fighter planes. MiG-31s, flying out of Yelizovo. The fourth plane was fired upon, but not damaged. It escaped and returned to base."

"Who?" Zhukov yelled. "Who fired upon my planes?"

"We do not know, Comrade President," the lieutenant said. "The planes were patrolling the southern edge of the ice pack, in accordance with your standing defense plan, sir. They encountered a surface vessel of some kind, operating without lights and without radar near the ice. The vessel was within the exclusion area, and it was not one of ours, so the planes attacked it with missiles, per your orders."

Zhukov nodded curtly. "And?"

"A missile battle ensued, Comrade President. Three of our planes were shot down. The pilot of the fourth plane believes that the unidentified vessel may have been a missile boat. He reports that the radar signature was much too small for a major combatant ship. The pilot is unable to identify the country of origin."

"I see," Zhukov said. His voice was deathly quiet now. "And where is this pilot?"

"In his quarters at Yelizovo air station," the lieutenant said. "Having a vodka, I imagine. His comrades were killed in front of his eyes. I understand that he is quite shaken."

"I'm sure he is," Zhukov said. He ran a hand through his hair and cleared his throat. "Send a message to the commander of the air station at Yelizovo. I want the pilot taken out in the snow and shot, within the hour."

The lieutenant cocked his head "Sir?"

"We are facing the enemies who brought down the Soviet Empire," Zhukov said. "We cannot defeat them with incompetence and cowardice. The fool should have pressed the attack, not run away like a frightened child."

He glared into the lieutenant's eyes. "Have the pilot shot. Do it *now*."

The young lieutenant swallowed and snapped out a salute. "Right away, Comrade President." He made an abrupt about-face, and marched from the room.

CHAPTER 47

USS TOWERS (DDG-103)
WESTERN PACIFIC OCEAN
WEDNESDAY; 06 MARCH
1929 hours (7:29 PM)
TIME ZONE +11 'LIMA'

"More coffee, ma'am?" The wardroom mess attendant held out a silver pot and tipped it slightly forward, indicating that he was ready to pour. It was the young Sailor who had escorted Ann and Sheldon from the flight deck to the wardroom on their return to the ship.

Ann looked at her watch and shook her head. It was time, maybe a couple of minutes past time. The Navy guys would already be out there on the boat deck, standing around in the cold and the dark, wondering what was keeping that crazy civilian woman.

Ann knew the answer to that question, but she didn't want to admit it. Not even to herself. She was afraid.

The ship had been sailing north at high speed since an hour before sundown. Now they were back up near the ice pack again, not far from the area where they'd been attacked at the end of Mouse's last run. Those fighter jets—or others like them—were still out there somewhere, and now they were alerted to the presence of U.S. warships in the area. Last time, the planes had stumbled across the ship by blind chance. This time, they would know exactly what they were looking for. They would be waiting.

Ann discovered that she was waiting too. Her ears were waiting for the distant growl of jet engines and the shuddering roar of launching missiles. Her muscles were waiting—preparing themselves to re-experience the paralysis that had been her body's fear response to the aircraft attack. Her stomach was waiting to void itself of the breakfast and coffee that she'd foolishly allowed herself to consume. And her soul was waiting for that liminal moment—the critical threshold at which her fellow voyagers would either kill, or be killed, or both.

She looked at her watch again. She was definitely late, now. It was time to go out there and do her job. She decided to stand up and get it over with, but was surprised to find herself still sitting in the wardroom chair. Her body seemed to be on strike.

She frowned, and grabbed the arms of her chair, ready to push herself to a standing position. And found herself still seated.

She was still puzzling over this when the young Sailor spoke.

He set the coffee pot on the table. "Ma'am, can I ask you a question?"

Ann nodded.

"Are you…" the Sailor halted in mid-question. He swallowed, and spoke again. "How did you end up working on robots?"

Ann had almost no skill for reading people, but she knew instantly that this was not what the kid really wanted to ask. He had changed his mind at the last second, shied away from his real question—whatever that was.

She decided to answer him anyway.

"When I was about ten years old, I saw this movie called '*Silent Running*.' Have you ever seen it?"

"I don't think so," the Sailor said. "Is that one of those old submarine flicks? Like '*The Enemy Below*,' or something like that?"

"No," Ann said. "It's science fiction. It's about the future, when the Earth is so polluted that the atmosphere can't support trees or plants any more."

The mess attendant waited for her to continue.

"There are these giant spaceships in orbit," Ann said. "They carry all that's left of the world's forests in these enormous geodesic domes. And on one of those ships is this guy named Freeman Lowell. He's sort of a botanist and ecologist. He takes care of the forests."

Ann stopped. Why was she doing this? She didn't talk about her private life to *anyone*. Why was she spilling her guts to this kid? Was she looking for an excuse to stall, because she was too freaking scared to go do her job?

"Lowell doesn't get along with the other people on his ship," she said. "The others all care about different things than he does. He doesn't think the same way they do, or value the same things. He doesn't really understand other people, and he doesn't like them very much."

The Sailor was staring now, but Ann forged ahead.

"Lowell likes the trees, and the bushes," she said. "Because he understands them. He also likes the robots that take care of the ship, for the same reason. He appreciates the clean logic of their thinking. They make sense to him. He doesn't have to be witty, or charming, and he doesn't have to try to fit in. The plants and the machines accept him for who he is. They don't ask him to be anything else."

"I've watched that movie about a thousand times," Ann said. "The robots weren't real; they were human actors in little robot costumes. But they *looked* real. And I knew from the first second I saw them that I wanted to work with robots."

She shrugged. "I guess I'm cut from the same cloth as Freeman Lowell. Machines make sense to me. Robots make sense. It's people I can't figure out."

The Sailor gave her a judicious nod. "Robotics is a big field," he said. "What made you decide to specialize in the *underwater* stuff?"

Again, Ann felt certain that this wasn't the question the kid really wanted to ask.

"Three-quarters of this planet is water," she said. "If I'm going to do anything worth doing, the ocean seems like a good place to start."

The mess attendant paused for several seconds, as if unsure about how to phrase whatever was on his mind. He cleared his throat. "Ma'am, are you ... scared?"

Ann felt the heat rise to her face. *"What?"*

"Scared," the Sailor said. "You know ... *afraid?"*

Ann wanted to slap the little bastard. Was *that* was this was about? Popeye the Sailor Man getting her to open up, so he could laugh in her freaking face?

His Sailor buddies must have been talking up a storm, all about the crazy civilian woman who had yakked all over Combat Information Center. They'd probably laughed their asses off about that.

But the kid wasn't smiling, and there was nothing critical in his voice.

"I'm scared," he said quietly. "I've been to the head twice, and I still feel like I'm going to piss my pants."

The kid paused, and Ann realized that he wasn't jerking her around. He really was scared. Maybe even as frightened as she was.

"I told my Senior Chief," he said. "I figured there's no point in hiding it if I'm not tough enough for combat. You know what Senior Chief said?"

Ann shook her head. "What did he say?"

"He told me *everybody* is scared shitless in combat. Everybody except maybe crazy people, and complete idiots. He told me that's natural. Fear is an instinctive reaction to danger. Somebody's trying to kill you, you're gonna get scared. Senior Chief says you have to learn to work through the fear—get past it, so you can do your job, even if you're scared half to death."

The Sailor picked up the coffee pot and used a white dish towel to wipe the spot where it had been. "You think that's true, ma'am? You think it's okay to be scared, as long as you do your job?"

"I don't know," Ann said. "I'm probably not the best person to ask. I mean, it *sounds* true. Maybe it *is* true."

"Are you scared?" the Sailor asked again.

"I'm terrified," Ann said.

The kid turned away and carried the silver pot back to the coffee maker. "Me too," he said. "It's not so bad right now. I'm on mess attendant duties. I clean, I serve meals, and I clean some more. There aren't exactly lives hanging on my every action. If I screw up, the coffee gets cold, or breakfast is late. Nobody dies."

He shook his head. "But this is only temporary duty for me. When I go back to my division, I'll be a Fire Control Technician again. If I get scared *then*, I mean *really* scared—too scared to do my job—people are going to get killed. You know what I mean?"

Ann nodded. That was a lot of weight to hang on the shoulders of a nineteen-year-old kid. Hell, that was a lot of weight to hang on *her* shoulders. But it was true for the frightened young Sailor, and it was true for Ann.

What was it that Sheldon had said? "How many nightmares will we get, if we let a million people die?"

It all came back to that again—Ann's fears and her doubts, weighed against the lives of countless human beings. Or more precisely, Ann's personal safety weighed against the safety of thousands, or even millions, of people. Put in those terms, it wasn't a very difficult decision to make.

Ann glanced at her watch. She was late, but not *that* late. The boat crew would still be up there, waiting to lower Mouse into the water for the next phase of his search.

Ann stood up; the spell that had bound her to the chair was broken. "Can you help me find the boat deck?" she asked. "I have to go do my job now."

CHAPTER 48

The beefy Sailor who called himself Boats stared down over the side of the ship at the robot circling slowly in the dark ocean swells. The big man shook his head sadly. "If you can't get your machine to sit still, ma'am, I don't see how we're gonna be able to get a line on the damned thing."

Ann followed the Navy man's gaze. Sunrise was still two hours away, and the waves looked like liquid obsidian under the cold illumination of a three-quarter moon. But Mouse's brightly-colored hull provided enough contrast to be faintly visible in the moonlight.

Ann burrowed her hands more deeply into the pockets of her foul weather coat. Even with the gloves on, her fingers were freezing in the raw subarctic air. She didn't even want to *think* about how cold the water was.

"Mouse's emergency maintenance subroutine has been triggered," she said. "When he gets damaged, he's programmed to return to his launching coordinates, drive to the surface, and circle until he's picked up for repairs."

"How did he get damaged?" Boats asked.

"I have no idea," Ann said. "Maybe he collided with something, or one of his seals started leaking. He might have developed an electrical problem: a short, or a blown component. I won't be able to tell until we get him out of the water, and I can download his error logs."

"You can't stop him?" one of the Sailors asked.

Ann didn't see which one of the Navy men had spoken, but it wasn't Boats. The voice was younger: one of the other members of the boat deck crew.

"I can't control him from remote," Ann said. "Not when he's in emergency maintenance mode."

257

She shuddered, dreading the very thought of what she was about to say next. "I'm going to have to go into the water, and shut him off by hand."

Boats exhaled explosively. "No ma'am! Not a chance! You are *not* going in the water."

The Sailor's tone made the hair on the back of Ann's neck bristle. "That's not your decision," she snapped. "That's *my* robot down there, and I don't work for you."

"No ma'am," Boats said. "You don't work for me. But this is my boat deck, and I'm not letting you go in the water unless the captain orders me to."

Ann made an effort to keep her voice from rising. "I've got a wetsuit and swim gear," she said. "I'm an excellent swimmer, and I've done this before. More than once."

"I'm sure that's true, ma'am," the big Sailor said. "But this ain't Southern California. The water temperature here is low enough to kill you in fifteen or twenty minutes. You'll be unconscious in half that time. You don't have the equipment or the training to work in water this cold."

"That's ridiculous," Ann said. "I won't be down there more than a couple of minutes."

Boats shook his head. "You won't be down there at all, ma'am. Not while *I'm* running the boat deck."

Ann snorted. "How are you planning to stop me? Tie me up, and throw me in the brig?"

"This is a destroyer," the Sailor said. "We don't have a brig. But we will use physical force, if that's what it takes to keep you out of the water."

Ann looked down at the dim form of Mouse, still driving in wide clockwise circles. "We've got to shut him down, or we'll never get the lifting cable on him."

"You're right about that," Boats said. "We're going to have to put a swimmer in the water."

Ann frowned. "You just said…"

Boats cut her off. "*Our* swimmer. He's got the cold water gear, and he's got the training."

"Wait just a second," Ann said.

"We don't have time to argue about this," Boats said. "The ship is gonna turn south in about a half hour, so we won't be too close to the ice when the sun comes up. If you want your Mouse gadget to be aboard when we get out of here, we'd better get a move on."

Before Ann could respond, Boats pointed to one of the shadowy Sailor shapes huddled on the boat deck. "Peters, go get yourself suited up. I'm calling the Bridge for authorization. As soon as I get the thumbs-up, you're going over the side."

"Really?" the other Sailor muttered. "That's just fucking fabulous."

"What was that?" Boats growled. "I don't believe I heard you."

Peters coughed, and spoke more clearly. "Aye-aye, Boats."

Boats nodded. "That's what I *thought* you said. Now, get your butt in gear; we're running out of darkness."

⚓ ⚓ ⚓

Ten or fifteen minutes later, as she listened over a set of headphones to the teeth-chattering grunts and mumbled curses of the Navy swimmer, Ann discovered—to her secret disgust—that she was glad Peters had gone into the water in her place. She could actually *hear* the bone-numbing cold in the young Sailor's voice.

Peters had only been in the water a couple of minutes, and his speech was already thick, and slurred.

Ann, who had never been much colder than she was right now—standing on the boat deck, could not even imagine what it must be like down there. Just the sound of the man's increasing discomfort was beginning to make her own muscles contract and cramp. The frigid water was leaching the life out of him, and Ann was listening to it happen.

"Almost ... got ... it ...," Peters murmured thickly. "Almost ..."

The sound of a ragged exhalation came through the headphones. "Fuck! Missed ... I ... fucking ... missed ... it..."

Ann stood at the lifelines, looking down toward the water. The eastern sky was beginning to lighten now, and she could see the swimmer's orange wetsuit, bobbing near the yellow form of the robot. The suit was thick, and supposedly designed for cold water dives, but it didn't sound like it was doing Peters a lot of good.

That was probably a false impression, she knew. Without his protective suit, the Sailor might already be unconscious by now, or dead.

She watched Peters thrash in the water as he made another lunge for the cover plate on the robot's dorsal access port. The trio of propulsion pods on the machine's stern were still pushing it forward, relentlessly powering through another in a series of continuous clockwise circles.

The retaining latches on the cover plate were mounted flush with the curve of the hull, to minimize hydrodynamic drag. To release them, Peters had to depress each one, and turn it ninety degrees.

Ann knew from experience that this was not an easy task, even in relatively comfortable water temperatures. Mouse was streamlined, wet, and very slippery. The robot pitched and rolled with the waves, and the continuous thrust from the propulsion pods had the effect of constantly scooting the rounded machine away from you.

Peters had three of the latches released. He had only one more to go, but it didn't look or sound like he was up to finishing the job.

The Sailor wasn't talking at all now. His breathing had become an irregular rhythm of strangled groans.

Ann looked up at Boats. The sky in the East was still growing brighter, and the big Sailor was becoming easier to see by the minute.

"That's enough," she said. "Peters can't do it. We've got to pull him out of the water."

"Yeah," Boats said solemnly. "I was just thinking the same thing."

He nodded to the two Sailors holding the swimmer's tending line. "Standby to heave around."

A muffled exclamation came over the headphones. The words, if they *were* actually words, were totally incomprehensible. But the tone of voice carried an unmistakable note of triumph.

Ann turned back toward the water, her eyes scanning rapidly until they located Peters and Mouse. The access cover on the robot's spine was open, and Mouse was no longer circling. Peters had released the final latch, and hit the emergency kill switch.

"Good job," Ann said quietly. She looked up at Boats. "Let's lower the hook, and get them *both* up on deck."

⚓ ⚓ ⚓

Ann sat in her stateroom an hour later, drinking crappy Navy coffee and uploading Mouse's error logs to her laptop. Mouse was safely strapped to the boat deck, and the ship was headed south at high speed, trying to distance itself from unfriendly territory before the sun was too far above the horizon.

The swimmer, Peters, had been half-led/half-carried toward some place called *sickbay*. Ann wasn't quite sure what that meant, but it sounded Navy enough to arouse her instinctive skepticism.

Then again, maybe the sickbay thing wasn't as iffy as it sounded. Sheldon probably knew all about it. She'd ask him later. Right now, she needed to figure out what had gone wrong with her baby.

A soft bleep informed her that the upload was complete. She wiggled her fingers to limber them up, and reached for the computer keys.

The situational response algorithms in Mouse's core program were written in *ARIX*, Norton's proprietary programming language. Like many adaptive computer languages, ARIX had a built-in parser for translating error codes into an easily-understood English-based syntax.

Ann didn't need the parser. She was perfectly comfortable reading the codes in their native hexadecimal.

She located the most recent time index, the last error recorded before the robot had been powered down. The hexadecimal code read, "46 41 55 4C 54 30 30," which translated as, *FAULT 00*.

That wasn't exactly a surprise. FAULT 00 indicated a critical error that Mouse couldn't identify. It was a catch-all error designation, common for complex machines in the prototype stages. That particular fault would appear less and less often, as Mouse's self-diagnostic capabilities were redesigned and improved over time.

The previous time index showed the same hex code, as did the time index before that, and the one before that, and the one before *that* ...

Ann scrolled through several screens of recorded time indexes, seeing hex code 46 41 55 4C 54 30 30 repeated again, and again, and again. The fault—whatever it was—had obviously occurred several hours earlier. She had to work backwards through a few thousand repetitive error codes to locate the triggering event.

After paging through a seemingly endless number of screens, all completely identical except for the time indexes, Ann finally spotted what she was looking for. The triggering event had occurred almost exactly five and a half hours into Mouse's search mission.

Prior to the occurrence of the fault, every time index read, "54 52 41 4E 53 49 54." That was the hex code for *TRANSIT*. Mouse had been operating in normal search/transit mode, carrying out his search plan without errors or problems.

At the five and a half hour mark, the instant before the error had been triggered, the hex code had changed to 43 4F 4E 54 41 43 54, for a single processing cycle, followed by hex code 4D 49 53 53 49 4F 4E.

Ann's heart froze as she stared at the screen. The two strings of characters seemed to stand out more brightly than anything else in the jumble of letters and numerals on the laptop display.

Ann swallowed, and closed her eyes, trying to change those two error codes by force of will. She must have looked at the screen wrong. Her eyes were getting tired. Because those codes couldn't be right. They *couldn't* be.

She opened her eyes. The codes were still there, staring at her out of the laptop screen like a pair of accusing eyes.

Ann tried not to think about what they meant, but her brain performed the translation automatically. The first code translated as *CONTACT*. The second translated as *MISSION*.

She slammed the lid of the laptop closed. Damn it. Damn it, damn it, *damn* it!

Mouse had done his job. He had found the submarine. And then, when the robot had attempted to shift from transit mode into mission mode, he'd run into the same software glitch that Ann had been wrestling with for weeks. Right in the middle of the mode shift, his software had faulted and then triggered his emergency maintenance subroutine.

He'd been close enough to complete the mission, and instead, he'd turned away and returned to his launching coordinates.

How had that happened? Ann had written a software patch, to bypass that very problem. What had gone wrong? Why hadn't it worked?

She opened the lid of the laptop, backed out of the error logs, and loaded the program modules she had written to prepare Mouse for this mission.

It took her only a few seconds to find the address in the program where the patch should have been installed. It wasn't there.

Oh god! How had that happened? Had she forgotten to install the patch? She couldn't have. There was just no way.

But she *had* forgotten. She'd been so cocky, so sure that she had done everything perfectly. And she had somehow forgotten a critical step. Maybe even *the* critical step.

This whole mess with the missile submarine could have been over by now, if she'd done her job. But she'd forgotten.

Or *had* she? What if it hadn't been an accident? Or rather, what if she'd *wanted* to forget? Was that possible?

She didn't like these Navy people. That wasn't exactly a secret. And she didn't want to be party to killing the crew of that submarine. That wasn't a secret either.

Maybe she had made some subconscious decision to screw this up. She didn't think so. It didn't feel that way. But how would she know? How could she be sure?

What if this had been their one chance to get the sub? And she had screwed it up.

She closed the laptop again. What the hell was she going to do now?

CHAPTER 49

The U.S. Marine Corps CH-53D helicopter was flying low—the pilot hugging the ice, trying to blend his aircraft into the ground clutter to minimize detection by hostile radar.

Aft of the cockpit, Gunnery Sergeant Thomas Armstrong and the three other Marines assigned to his EOD response element occupied only a small corner of the helicopter's 30-foot-long cargo/troop compartment. The team's detection gear and disruption equipment took up more room than the team itself, but the big compartment was still nearly as empty as the icy terrain they were flying above.

Gunny Armstrong looked over his team. Hicks and Travers were sleeping. Staff Sergeant Myers was peering out through one of the starboard windows. They were good Marines, all three of them. They were trained, and motivated, and damned good at their jobs. Gunny was proud to have them under his command.

He turned to look out of his own window. "This ain't gonna work," he said. He spoke at a normal volume, and his voice was lost against the howl of the helicopter's turbines and the chop of the rotors. He was talking to himself, anyway. No one was *supposed* to hear. "This ain't gonna work," he said again. "It ain't gonna work … It ain't gonna work … It ain't gonna fucking work."

He tugged the folds of his neck gator into a more comfortable position, and hauled the zipper of his ECWCS parka up another few notches. The parka, like the rest of Gunny's Marine Corps issue survival gear, was part of the 2nd generation Extended Cold Weather Clothing System. And— like all the other ECWCS gear—it was patterned in the leafy greens, browns, and tans of the woodland camouflage scheme. There was supposed to be a white outer garment, for operations in snowy environments, but the Supply Sergeant had checked the wrong block on the requisition form, and they'd gotten a shipment of meat thermometers or something stupid like that.

So much for that camouflage shit. In their pretty green suits, Gunny and his fellow EOD techs were going to stand out against the ice and snow like a bulldozer in a bathtub. If anybody came looking for them, they'd be screwed. Of course, there was a good chance that they were screwed anyway.

Through the scratched Plexiglas window, the ice below was nearly a blur, sliding under the belly of the aircraft at 190 miles per hour. This entire mission was a blur. The whole thing had been thrown together at the last minute, with almost no preparation. And that was a good way to get Marines killed.

The plan called for the chopper to insert the team, and then turn south and head for the open sea, where it could refuel with one of the destroyers operating over the horizon. According to intel, the Op-Area was crawling with MiGs, and the CH-53 had a radar cross-section the size of a barn. Moving the aircraft to a standoff position made good tactical sense, but Gunny Armstrong didn't like the idea of having his Marines stranded on the ice.

If the mission went sour, their options for rapid emergency evac were basically zero. Not that the ancient 53 was much of an evac platform anyway. The damned thing was older than Gunny's father. It leaked, and rattled, and shook so hard that it wobbled your teeth. If this job was really as important as battalion was making it out to be, why hadn't somebody called up one of the V-22s instead of this flying relic?

His only satisfaction lay in the knowledge that Master Sergeant Pike and Response Element One weren't riding any better. They were at the western end of the Op-Area, flying in a CH-53 just as rickety as this old piece of crap, toward the Alfa and Bravo sites.

Gunny's people, Response Element Two, had been assigned to the Charlie and Delta sites, at the eastern end of the Op-Area. Element One and Element Two had both been directed to work from north-to-south, disarming the northern sites first, and then moving down to handle the southern sites. The longer the disarming efforts dragged on, the more risk there was of being spotted by hostile forces.

In theory, by getting the most distant sites out of the way first, the teams would put themselves closer to evac if anything went wrong in the second half of the mission. It wasn't much of a theory in Gunny's book, since the risk of getting caught wouldn't be any greater in the second half of the operation than it was in the first half. But that was the sort of half-bright thinking that the rear echelon types were famous for.

Nobody was calling this a suicide mission, but that's what it was starting to smell like. His team of Explosive Ordnance Disposal techs had been assigned to locate and disarm multiple pre-positioned explosives packages of unknown size, strength, and configuration. They had no idea of what these packages might look like, no idea of how sensitive they might be to intrusion or tampering, and only rough estimates of their locations. To put the icing on the cake, they'd be working in near-arctic conditions, under a sky dominated by hostile air cover.

If *that* wasn't brilliant tactical planning, Gunny didn't know what was. He grunted. Some genius back at G3 needed to have his ass kicked for dreaming up a goat rodeo like this. If they got out of this alive, Gunny might just have to go look up the idiot in question, and kick down the door to his fucking office.

The idea made the Marine grin—a cold and feral expression, with no trace of humor in it. He was nearly ready for the purge now. Nearly annoyed enough, and worried enough, and frustrated enough for the final piece of his emotional preparation.

The *purge* had been Colonel Ziegler's term, back when Gunny Armstrong had been a punk Pfc. with the 11th MEU in Iraq.

"You don't start a patrol when you've got to take a dump," Colonel Z had said. "You hit the head *before* you hit the trail. You get all the shit out of your body, so it doesn't slow you down."

"Well you've got to do the same thing for your *brain*," the colonel had said. "You can't go into combat with a bunch of unnecessary shit clogging up your brain. You've got to offload it. You've got to *purge* it. You've got to call up all of your doubts and angers ahead of time. Think about it. Stew over it. Get *mad* about it. And then *get rid of it*. Let it go, just like taking a dump. So when the time comes to be a Marine, you've got nothing else on your mind but being a Marine."

As far as Gunny Armstrong was concerned, it had been good advice. It had gotten him through three tours in the sandbox. He figured it would probably see him through this mess as well.

He was mad now, and scared, and all the things a Marine cannot afford to be when he's in the field. He could feel the knot of emotions building inside him, rising through his bones like the shriek of the chopper's turbines. He wondered for a second if he should sneak something in there about his ex-wife, just to really push things over the top.

But he didn't need it. He felt the internal safety valve in his chest lift, venting his rage and his fear, and he made no move to stop it. He slammed a fist into his sternum, to make sure that the imaginary tank of feelings emptied itself entirely. "Ooh-rah!" he said to himself. "Ooh-fucking-rah!"

The ritual did its job. He felt the calm descend over him. He was ready. He was focused. The only thoughts in his mind were of the mission, and his Marines. Everything else was insignificant bullshit.

The copilot's voice crackled in the left ear of his headset. "Two minutes, Gunny."

Gunny Armstrong felt for the talk button and keyed his mike. "Two minutes, aye. Thanks for the ride, Lieutenant."

He looked out the window at jagged terrain of the ice pack. It was time to go kick some ass. Time to go be Marines.

CHAPTER 50

USS TOWERS (DDG-103)
WESTERN PACIFIC OCEAN
THURSDAY; 07 MARCH
0821 hours (8:21 AM)
TIME ZONE +11 'LIMA'

Captain Bowie leaned back in his chair, and set his coffee cup on the wardroom table. "Let me get this straight," he said. "Your Mouse unit decided on its own to abandon the search, and return to the position where we launched it?"

Ann Roark nodded. She didn't like the way this conversation was starting out.

"That's right," she said. "According to Mouse's internal error logs, he operated without problems for the first five and a half hours of the run. Then an event that occurred during the run triggered a spontaneous mission abort."

"Do you have any idea what that event was? What triggered this spontaneous mission abort?"

Ann took a breath and nodded. "I know what caused it. But it's a little bit complicated."

The Navy man lifted his coffee cup and took a swallow. "I've got a few minutes. See if you can spell it out for me."

Ann sighed loudly, and then instantly regretted it. She was a civilian, and technically free to say whatever she wanted, but she knew that senior military people didn't react well to signs of reticence or dissatisfaction.

Her father had been a major in the Army, until a roadside bomb outside of Ramadi had turned his up-armored HMMV into a few thousand pounds of Swiss cheese. Major Dad had been big on discipline and outward displays of respect. He'd been quick to decode Ann's body language for any hint of dissent or defiance. He'd interpreted every huff, every roll of the eyes, and every hunched shoulder as a sign of rebellion: a challenge to his authority.

There wasn't a lot of reason to believe that this Navy captain would be any different. With that single pronounced sigh, she had telegraphed her frustration in a language that the military mind could only interpret in one way. She might as well have told him to fuck off. God, she hated dealing with these people. They made her crazy.

Ann nearly sighed again, but she caught herself, realizing that it would only rebroadcast her frustration. She shifted mental gears, and tried to think of a way to phrase the problem with Mouse.

"*Search mode* is not much different than *transit mode*," she said finally. "As it moves through the water, the robot is using its onboard sensors to scan for the submarine, but it's essentially following a programmed series of navigational waypoints. We set the waypoints ahead of time, when we plan the search pattern. I upload the coordinates of each waypoint to the robot prior to launch, and Mouse travels from one waypoint to the next, like following a trail of breadcrumbs."

The captain nodded for her to continue.

"As long as Mouse was searching for the submarine," Ann said, "he was essentially operating in directed transit mode."

"I've got that," Captain Bowie said. "So what happened?"

Ann paused. He *really* wasn't going to like this part. "Mouse found the submarine," she said. "About five and a half hours into the search."

She spoke quickly now, trying to get across the rest of her message before Bowie's brain had a chance to process the first part.

"That's what triggered the problem," she said. "When he found the sub, Mouse shifted from *directed transit mode* to *autonomous mission mode*, so he could carry out the next phase of the operation and plant the beacon on the hull of the submarine. And during the mode shift, something glitched in his operating program. I haven't had a chance to look at it in detail yet, but I think it was that same program error we were getting a couple of weeks ago, when we were running tests … before we rescued that submersible."

"You wrote a software patch for that, didn't you?" Bowie asked.

"Yeah," Ann said. "A workaround. It didn't fix the bug in the program code. It just bypassed the problem, and allowed Mouse to keep working if the error showed up."

"So what went wrong?" Captain Bowie asked. "Was this some unforeseen permutation of the error? Something your software patch couldn't handle?"

Ann hesitated before answering. It would be easy to lie here, attribute the problem to untraceable software glitches. Mouse was a prototype, and they *knew* he had bugs. If she blamed the problem on unreliable software, she'd probably never get caught.

She decided to stick with the truth. It might bring her some grief, but she wouldn't have any trouble looking at herself in the mirror.

"I screwed up," she said. "There was nothing wrong with the patch. I just forgot to re-upload it."

"I thought it was already installed," Bowie said. "You uploaded it weeks ago, when you were getting the Mouse unit ready to search for the *Nereus*."

"It *was* installed," Ann said. "But the program parameters needed for this mission were different from the ones we used for the submersible. I decided that our best chance of success would be to get a clean load. Dump the old operating program, and reload from scratch. That gave me a clean slate to work with when I was modifying the operating program for this mission."

Bowie looked at her without speaking.

Ann plunged on. "I had about a hundred things to do to prepare Mouse to go after this submarine. I had to modify a *lot* of code to give him the functions he needs to get the job done. And I didn't remember to reinstall the patch. I just ... *forgot*."

"You forgot?"

"Yes," Ann said. "I forgot. I don't know how. I thought I had everything covered, but I was trying to cram two days worth of programming into a few hours. And I missed something. I forgot the patch. I ... forgot."

"So your Mouse unit found the damned submarine, and—instead of planting the beacon and alerting us to the sub's position—your robot ran back to its launch position and drove around in circles?"

Ann nodded. "Yes."

It was the first time she'd heard one of the Navy people use the dreaded *R-word* to describe Mouse. But given the nature of the conversation, there wasn't much pleasure in the tiny victory.

Bowie glanced at the wardroom clock. "We could have engaged the submarine seven hours ago. We could have brought this whole tragic mess to an end."

"I know that," Ann said. "I'm sorry. It wasn't intentional. It was an oversight. An accident."

Bowie drummed his fingertips lightly on the table top. "Are you sure about that?"

His tone of voice took Ann by surprise.

"What do you mean?"

"Are you certain it was an accident?" Bowie asked. "You've made it plain since the minute you came aboard. You don't like me; you don't like this ship; and you don't like the Navy."

Ann started to respond, but he kept talking.

"I don't know what you've got against us, and I frankly don't care. Your opinions are your business. You don't *have* to like us. You don't even have to *pretend* to like us. It doesn't matter to me, as long as you don't actively antagonize my crew, or let your personal views interfere with the job. But now it looks like they *are* interfering with the job, Ms. Roark. They're interfering with the mission of my ship. We had an opportunity to finish this, but I think you might be more interested in jerking our chain than in getting the job done."

He set his coffee cup down a little too hard. "Between the United States, Russia, and Japan, there are literally hundreds of millions of human beings living under the threat of nuclear extinction because of that submarine. We could have stopped it. We could have ended it seven hours ago. When you're going over your list of reasons to hate the Navy, add that to your list of things to think about."

"Wait just a freaking second," Ann snapped. "You think I did this on *purpose*?"

Bowie lowered his voice. "I don't know. *Did* you?"

"It was an *accident*," Ann said. "A stupid freaking accident. I forgot. I made a mistake."

"The mistake was *mine*," Bowie said. "I underestimated your contempt for my crew, and the mission of this ship. I misjudged your desire to see us fail."

He pushed his chair back from the table, and walked to the door. He reached for the doorknob.

"You're so full of shit," Ann said. "Do you know that?"

Bowie spoke over his shoulder. His words were quietly icy. "We're finished with your services," he said. "I'm calling for a helicopter to pick you and Mr. Miggs up as soon as possible. I don't want you on my ship any more."

Ann felt a lump rising in her throat. This man—this idiot—wouldn't even listen to her.

"You're so full of shit," she said again. Her voice was shaky now. "What happened to that song and dance you were giving me when we were trying to rescue the *Nereus*? Do you remember? All that crap about how I didn't sign on for any of this, and you know that Mouse is only a prototype and he isn't ready for the job, but he's your best hope. Does any of that ring a bell? You said no one would blame us if the mission went wrong. Remember *that*?"

She felt a hot tear roll down her cheek. "Well guess what, Mr. Captain, sir? Mouse is *still* a freaking prototype, and he's *still* not ready for this job. But I'm not trying to blame this on the robot. I could have done that, and you wouldn't have known any better. Instead, I told you the truth. I screwed up. In case you haven't noticed, *you're* not the one who failed here. *I* am. And I'm not trying to cover it up. I told you the truth because I want the chance to fix it. I want to make it right. I just need another chance." The last word came out as a sob.

Captain Bowie stood without speaking for several seconds. Then he released the doorknob and turned around. "I *did* say those things," he said. "And I told you no one would blame you if the mission went south."

He walked back toward the table. "Maybe I *am* full of shit," he said. "At least on the current point of discussion."

"You *are*," Ann sniffed.

Bowie smiled ruefully. "I'm willing to stipulate that, for the moment. But I'll have to ask you not to voice that particular sentiment in front of my crew."

He sat back down in his chair. "Where do we go from here?"

Ann wiped her eyes with the back of her hand. "We try again," she said. "I upload the patch to Mouse's program code, and—as soon as the sun goes down—we put him back in the water and start over."

"Do you really think that's going to work?" Bowie asked.

"Mouse found your damned submarine before," Ann said. "He can find it again."

CHAPTER 51

3RD EXPLOSIVE ORDNANCE DISPOSAL COMPANY
ICE PACK — SOUTHERN SEA OF OKHOTSK
THURSDAY; 07 MARCH
1113 hours (11:13 AM)
TIME ZONE +11 'LIMA'

Gunnery Sergeant Armstrong crouched behind an ice hommock about forty yards from the device, and watched through binoculars as Staff Sergeant Myers and Corporal Hicks backed away from the explosive charge buried at the 8 o'clock position. Gunny wasn't looking at Myers or Hicks, who were both easily visible without the binoculars. He was examining the ice around their feet, looking for any sign of booby traps that might have been missed during the initial recon.

Myers and Hicks moved slowly and cautiously, taking care not to disturb the twisted pair of wires that connected the shaped-charge to the initiator, about fifty feet away. Myers was scanning the snowy terrain with a Föerster Mark-26, moving in as straight a line as the rugged surface of the ice pack would permit. Hicks was his observer and assistant, providing a second set of eyes and hands as they were needed.

The Mk-26 was a fluxgate magnetic gradiometer; it could locate hidden metal objects by detecting the fluctuations they caused in the earth's magnetic field. Myers and Hicks were nearly finished with the magnetic sweep. They'd already done the visual sweep, the infrared sweep, and sampled the air down-wind of the device using a hand-held Fido detector to sniff for vapors and residue: the telltale molecular traces given off by explosive chemicals.

This was the last step of the secondary reconnaissance. Gunny Armstrong had performed the initial recon himself, with Sergeant Travers covering observe and assist. He was confident that he had the configuration of the device thoroughly sussed out.

Myers was performing the entire recon again, to be certain that Gunny hadn't missed anything on the first pass. Gunny didn't expect him to find anything new, but the procedures laid out by the 60 Series EOD manuals were clear: two separate reconnaissance sweeps, conducted by two pairs of qualified Explosive Ordnance Disposal technicians. There were exceptions to the rule, in time-urgent operations, or when there weren't enough techs available. But Gunny's team had the personnel and the time. They were going to do it by the book.

The device itself was relatively straightforward. Six shaped-charges were spaced evenly around the perimeter of a large circle, maybe a hundred feet in diameter, all wired to an initiator package in the middle of the circle.

Gunny and Myers had both scanned the initiator using an RTR-4 real-time x-ray unit. The package appeared to consist of two modules of electronic circuits, housed in an insulated enclosure about the size of a shoebox. There were no indications of explosive charges in or near the enclosure.

A Kevlar-jacketed cable led from the package into a hole drilled in the ice. Short of trying to dig it out, which Gunny's team was *not* going to attempt, there was no way to know how long the Kevlar cable was, or what might be wired to its other end. The cable probably penetrated all the way through the ice, and into the unfrozen water below. Gunny assumed that the remote triggering device, whatever that might be, was hanging at the submerged end of the cable. There wasn't really any way to test that assumption, but it seemed logical, and no one else on the team could suggest an alternative.

Of more immediate importance, Gunny hadn't found any booby traps anywhere around the charges or the initiator package. No motion sensors, no proximity detectors, and no anti-tamper devices. Whoever had planted these explosives had apparently depended on secrecy and the remote location for protection. It would have worked too, Gunny figured, if some intelligence bubba hadn't gotten his hands on the rough coordinates of the devices. Somebody with inside knowledge had talked.

Myers and Hicks finished the Mk-26 sweep, and backed away from the device until they were well clear of the danger area. Then they made their way across the ice to Gunny's position, Myers still carrying the L-shaped magnetic sensor.

The wind wasn't blowing very hard, but it had a whistling quality that made conversation difficult, so Myers leaned in close and spoke loudly. "Secondary recon is complete, Gunny. No big surprises. I count six shaped-charges of roughly thirty pounds each. Cyclohexyl-based plastic explosives. The Fido samples called out cyclic nitramine with high mercury content. Looks like Russian military-grade RDX to me."

Gunny nodded. He'd gotten the same readings. "Continue."

"All six charges are wired to a central initiator, enclosed in an insulated housing. On the RTR-4, it looks like a couple of blocks of electronics, connected to each other, to the charges, and to a cable that runs down through the ice."

Gunny nodded again. The report matched his own assessment.

"No signs of any anti-tamper devices," Myers said. "I didn't spot any proximity detectors, no motion sensors, no tripwires. Nothing." He shrugged. "I don't want to jinx anything, but I think our render-safe procedure is going to be pretty simple. I say we take out the initiator with the *PAN*, and use *Niffers* to cut all six pairs of firing wires simultaneously."

The PAN, short for *Percussion-Actuated Non-electric Disrupter*, was a specialty tool of the EOD trade. Consisting of a long stainless steel barrel attached to an adjustable metal frame, the PAN used blank 12-gauge shotgun shells to fire specially-designed slugs into bomb components, destroying key circuits or mechanisms, and making the bomb inoperative.

Niffer was the common pronunciation of the abbreviation NFR, which stood for *Nonvolatile Fast-Response Wire Cutter*. A Niffer was a tube-shaped device—about the size of a fountain pen—that could be attached to a small bundle of electrical wires, and sever them on command. Unlike the PAN, which had been invented specifically for Explosive Ordnance Disposal, Niffers had been adapted from the American movie industry, where special effects technicians used them to remotely control pyrotechnic charges for action films.

"Good plan," Gunny said. "That's about what I was thinking. But I want to take out that Kevlar cable at the same time." He jerked a thumb in the direction of the device. "Odds are, that cable leads to a remote trigger. We'd probably be okay if we left it in place. But I don't want to gamble if we don't have to. So we take it out of the equation, just to be on the safe side."

Staff Sergeant Myers nodded. "Understood. How do you want to cut the cable? It's too heavy for the Niffers, and we're already using the PAN to disrupt the initiator package."

"Let's pop it with detonating cord," Gunny said. "The cable is Kevlar, so it's going to be resistant, but a couple of loops of det. cord ought to do the trick."

"Roger," Myers said. "I should have thought of that."

Gunny Armstrong slapped him on the shoulder. "You will next time."

Myers gave him a thumbs-up, his hand almost cartoonishly large in the thick cold weather glove. "Roger that," he said.

The Staff Sergeant looked out across the grubby surface of the ice, in the direction of the device. "Is it just me? Or is this turning out to be too easy?"

"Don't count your chickens," Gunny said. "When we've finished the render-safe procedure on this site *and* the second site, you can tell me all about how easy this all was while we're riding home in that raggedy-ass chopper. Until then, make sure you keep eyes in the back of your head, Marine."

Myers nodded. "Will do, Gunny." He turned and walked toward the team's pile of equipment, to select the gear they'd need to safe the explosives.

Gunny Armstrong watched the younger Marine go without speaking. He was feeling it too: the nagging suspicion that this mission was proceeding just a little too smoothly. EOD jobs *never* went this easily, not even in training exercises.

He kept wondering if they had forgotten something, if all four members of his team had overlooked some critical detail. But as hard as he wracked his brain, he couldn't think of a thing.

Then again, maybe it wasn't something they'd missed. Maybe it was a premonition.

The idea brought a grunt of disdain. Gunnery Sergeant Thomas Armstrong did not believe in premonitions. That crap was for the Psychic Hotline; dial *1-800-Mystic-Bullshit.*

He shook his head. It was just a case of the heebie-jeebies. His best bet of getting out of this in one piece was to forget about premonitions and focus on doing the job safely and correctly.

He picked his way across the ice, toward the spot where Staff Sergeant Myers was breaking out the gear. Gunny spoke to himself as he walked, his voice swallowed up by the whistling wind. It was an unconscious thing; he wasn't even aware that he was doing it. "This ain't gonna work," he said to himself. "It ain't gonna fucking work."

⚓ ⚓ ⚓

But it *did* work. Despite Gunny Armstrong's growing sense of foreboding, his team rigged their equipment without incident. When everything was set, they all pulled back to a safe distance, and he gave Myers the *go* signal.

Myers flipped up the protective cover on the remote trigger, and gave the button three quick squeezes. On the third squeeze, the disrupters all triggered at once. All six of the Niffers rammed their metal pistons home, shearing six pairs of firing wires with a noise like the slamming of several car doors. At the same instant, the long-barreled PAN fired a ceramic-tipped steel slug into the center of the initiator package, punching through the insulated housing to shatter the modules of electrical circuitry inside. The det cord ignited simultaneously, the little knot of chemical explosive parting the Kevlar cable with a bang not much louder than a firecracker.

In an instant, the job was done. The small quantities of smoke from the PAN disrupter and the det cord were snatched away by the brisk Siberian wind, and the single echo bounced off the face of the ice and faded to silence.

Gunny felt his unease relax half a notch. One job down, and everybody still had their fingers and toes. If the second device went as smoothly as this one, they might make it home after all.

He glanced at Myers. "We'll start packing up the gear," he said. "You get on short-comm and inform the chopper that Response Element Two has completed Site Charlie, and we're standing by for transport to Site Delta."

Staff Sergeant Myers acknowledged the order, and began digging in the side pocket of his parka for the new hand-held battlefield phone known as *short-comm*.

Gunny Armstrong turned toward the other two Marines, and he was getting ready to issue further instructions when he caught a flash of movement out of the corner of his eye. He looked up and saw a helicopter flying toward his team, keeping low to the ice and moving fast. For a couple of seconds, it flew in apparent silence, and then he began to hear the throp of the rotors: barely audible at first, but quickly growing louder as the chopper closed on their position.

Gunny's brain processed three thoughts in rapid succession. *First ...* The helicopter shouldn't be here yet. It was supposed to stand off to the south until the team called for it, which Myers hadn't done yet. *Second ...* It was the wrong kind of helicopter. And *third ...* He was watching the evidence of his premonition brought to life.

He didn't know what he'd been expecting. An accident, maybe, or a misstep, or a booby trap. But not this.

He pursed his lips and whistled sharply, to grab instant attention. "Hit the deck!" he yelled. "That's not our chopper!"

As the words left his mouth, he threw himself forward, hitting the ice hard, his body plowing through several inches of grubby snow. The impact with the ice knocked the breath out of him, but there was no time to worry about that. He reached behind him, his hands scrabbling to find the M-4 carbine slung barrel-down across his back.

His right hand made contact with the collapsible stock of the rifle, gloved fingers groping for purchase on the smooth carbon plastic of the butt. He got a hold on his weapon and hauled it around into a two-handed shooting grip.

The helicopter was still getting closer, the sound of its rotors growing from a rumble to rhythmic thunder.

Out of the sides of his eyes, Gunny took inventory of his men. They had followed his lead. They were all prone on the ice, with weapons drawn and tracking the inbound chopper.

Hopefully, hitting the deck made them smaller targets, but it damned sure didn't hide them. The greens and browns of their woodland camouflage were a sharp visual contrast to the dirty whites and grays of the ice.

Bulldozer in a fucking bathtub, Gunny thought again.

He was getting a better look at the helicopter now. The bulbous nose of the aircraft had two bubble-shaped cockpits, one atop the other and set slightly aft. Angled weapons pylons stuck out from the right and left sides of the fuselage, like stubby wings. Gunny recognized it as a Russian HIND-D. A gunship, well armored against small arms fire. Practically a flying tank, with enough guns and rockets to chew his men to ribbons.

The Soviets had used HINDs in Afghanistan in the nineteen-eighties, and they'd wreaked a vicious toll on the Afghani fighters until President Reagan had authorized the shipment of shoulder-launched *Stinger* missiles through back-door channels in Pakistan.

A Stinger could take down a HIND gunship. A rocket-propelled grenade might manage it too, with a lucky enough shot. But the EOD team didn't carry Stingers, or even RPGs, and there wasn't a chance of punching through that armored Son-of-a-Bitch with the 5.56mm NATO rounds from their M-4 carbines.

The only spots vulnerable to small arms fire were the helicopter's rotors and the tail boom, both of which were difficult to hit. It was the only choice they had, so Gunny flipped a mental coin. It came up *tails*.

"Go for the tail!" he shouted. "You can't get through the armor with M-4s. We gotta shoot the fucking tail off of this thing!"

His Marines answered with two grunts and an *Ooh-rah*. Gunny grinned to himself. Stupid Jarheads. Goddamn, they were good men.

He thumped the base of the magazine with the heel of his hand to make sure that it was seated in the mag well, slapped the bolt release to jack a round into the chamber, and flipped the fire selector from *safe* to *burst*. The weapon felt clumsy in his gloved hands.

Like the rest of his team, Gunny wore BlackHawk/HellStorm ECW Winter Operations gloves from U.S. Cavalry. They weren't as cumbersome as the Marine Corps-issue cold weather gloves, but he knew from experience that they would still affect his accuracy. He couldn't risk shooting bare-handed, because his M-4 had been exposed to the open air for hours. The metal parts of the weapon would be cold enough to stick to his skin.

He glanced at the elevation setting of the rear sight, decided that it was close enough, and sighted in on the helicopter.

The HIND's gunner opened fire, just as Gunny Armstrong was slipping his index finger into the trigger well of his M-4. The turret beneath the helicopter's chin swiveled in the direction of Gunny's team, and the four-barreled Gatling gun cut loose with a sound like a high-speed jackhammer.

A swarm of 12.7mm machinegun bullets slammed into the ice a few yards to Gunny's left, spraying showers of snow and ice fragments into the air. The Marine paid no attention. His focus was riveted on the tail of the gunship.

He popped off a three-round burst of bullets, corrected his aim, and popped off another burst, and then another. The M-4 shuddered in his hand, the shortened stock thumping hard into his right shoulder with each recoil. From somewhere to his left, he heard a scream as the helicopter's minigun found one of his men.

Gunny rolled onto his back as the gunship passed directly over him, not more than thirty feet above the ice. The right edge of his parka hood scooped up a handful of snow as he turned, forcing it under the insulated fabric where it was jammed against his cheek and ear. The downdraft from the chopper lifted snow from all around him and sucked it into the air like a dirty mist. The sound of the rotors reached peak volume, but it wasn't loud enough to drown out a cry of pain from one of his Marines. It sounded like Travers, but Gunny couldn't be sure.

He could smell cordite now, and blood, and the burnt kerosene odor of the gunship's engine exhaust. He continued firing at the helicopter's tail rotor, his weapon bucking in his hands as he unleashed one burst after another. His shell casings fell around him, the hot brass sizzling as it tumbled across the ice.

He saw a trio of holes appear in the tail boom of the helicopter, as someone's bullets found their mark. His weapon locked open on an empty magazine, and then the chopper was past his team, banking hard to starboard and coming around for another pass.

It took the HIND a few seconds to align itself for the next attack run. Gunny used the time to eject the spent magazine from his M-4, scramble for a fresh one, and jam it into the mag well. He hit the bolt release to chamber the first round, and then sighted in on the helicopter again, watching for any sign that the bullet damage to the tail was affecting its airworthiness. The damage didn't seem to be catastrophic, as the HIND kept right on flying.

Gunny braced himself for the next pass, but it didn't come. The gunship came to a hover about fifty yards away, its nose pointed in the direction of the EOD team's position.

A pair of rockets leapt from under the outboard pylon on the starboard wing, shrieking toward Gunny's people on thin trails of gray smoke. Before they were even clear of the airframe, a second pair of rockets leapt from the outboard pylon on the opposite wing.

Gunny's brain instinctively solved a dozen complex geometric calculations in the space of two heartbeats, and he knew that one of the rockets was headed straight for him. With a launch velocity not much lower than the speed of a bullet, the rocket crossed the distance in an instant, but somehow he saw it coming the entire way.

His finger yanked repeatedly against the trigger of his weapon, pumping bullets toward the gunship as rapidly as the M-4's rate of fire permitted—hoping blindly to bring down the helicopter even as it killed him.

He never found out if his final wish was granted. The rocket struck the ice less than a meter from his right elbow. He had only the briefest impression of unbearable light, and heat, and sound. There was a split-second flare of pain, and then there was nothing.

CHAPTER 52

OPERATIONS COMMAND POST #2
OUTSIDE PETROPAVLOVSK-KAMCHATSKI, RUSSIA
THURSDAY; 07 MARCH
1340 hours (1:40 PM)
TIME ZONE +12 'MIKE'

"Comrade President?"

Sergiei Mikhailovich Zhukov wiped a trace of *gorokhovye* broth from his lips with the rough weave of a homespun napkin, and looked up from his lunch. His chief assistant, Maxim Ivanovitch Ustanov, was standing a few meters away from the table. The man was visibly shaking.

Zhukov did not permit himself to frown. The overt nervousness of his assistant was almost certainly a sign of bad tidings, but Zhukov went to considerable effort to avoid directing his temper toward the members of his trusted inner circle. He kept his voice carefully casual. "What is it, Maxim Ivanovitch?"

"Comrade President," his assistant said again, "there is news. I am afraid that it is not good."

Zhukov laid the napkin on the table top next to his brown earthenware bowl. Gorokhovye—pea and onion soup, seasoned with pork—was a traditional Russian dish, dating back to the times before even the Tsars. It was simple, but filling and delicious. A common man's meal, and Zhukov ate it with thick black bread, as was also the tradition.

He waved to a chair. "Please, my old friend. Sit down. Tell me this news that has gotten you so upset."

Ustanov did not take the offered chair. "Comrade President, one of our patrol helicopters has encountered and destroyed a team of United States Marines on the ice pack, in the Sea of Okhotsk."

Zhukov spent several seconds absorbing this news. "Special Forces," he said finally. "They are looking for *me*. They hope to decapitate our revolution by assassinating its leader."

Ustanov shook his head. "I do not think so, Comrade President. These men ... these American Marines ... were ..." His voice trailed off.

"They were *what*?" Zhukov asked quietly. "It is alright, Maxim Ivanovitch. You can tell me. What were these Americans doing?"

Ustanov cleared his throat. "They … ah … They were disarming the explosives at the northeastern *zashishennaja pozicija*."

"*What?*" The word was practically a roar. Zhukov stood up so rapidly that he jarred the table, causing gorokhovye to slosh over onto the table cloth.

Ustanov flinched, and took a half-step backwards.

Zhukov regained control quickly. He lowered himself into his chair, picked up his napkin, and began dabbing at the spilled soup. As he worked at the small task, he concentrated on slowing his breathing and leveling his demeanor.

He had a reputation for being as fierce in protecting those who were loyal to him as he was in punishing those who were disloyal. He dealt harshly with underlings who didn't meet his expectations, but he did not attack his close supporters and confidants.

When he spoke again, his voice was more measured. "Forgive me," he said. "Your news took me by surprise. I hope you can understand my alarm." He laid the napkin down again with movements of almost supernatural delicacy. "The ice pack conceals and protects our submarine, but it also prevents us from firing. We *must* maintain the ability to launch attacks at-will. If the K-506 cannot launch, we lose both our leverage, and our deterrence against retaliation."

He pushed the bowl away from himself. His appetite was gone. "How many of our launch positions have been compromised?"

Ustanov opened and closed his mouth several times, like a fish suddenly snatched from the water.

Zhukov's stomach tightened. Judging from his assistant's demeanor, the situation was even more dire than he had initially feared. "Come," he said. "This knowledge will not improve with waiting. Tell me, Maxim Ivanovitch, how many of our zashishennaja pozicija have been compromised? How many of our precious launch positions have the Americans destroyed?"

Ustanov's reply came out as a hoarse whisper. "Three, Comrade President."

Sergiei Zhukov felt the blood pounding in his temples. "*Three?*"

"Yes, Comrade President."

"Three? You are certain?"

Ustanov nodded. "Yes, Comrade President. When I received word that enemy forces had been spotted near one of the launch positions, I ordered our technicians to conduct remote circuit tests of all launch positions. The equipment at three of the positions failed to respond. Only the southeast launch position passed the remote test."

Zhukov fought to keep his voice even. "Are we certain that the explosives at the southeast launch position are functional?"

Ustanov nodded rapidly, apparently grateful to be delivering at least one piece of good news. "Yes, sir," he said. "I believe the American Marines had completed the destruction of three positions, and were awaiting transportation to the fourth, when our attack helicopter discovered them."

He paused for several seconds, as though unsure whether or not to continue.

Zhukov gave a short beckoning wave with two fingers.

Ustanov followed the signal, and pressed on. "I suggest a change of strategy, Comrade President. We have been operating from the assumption that air cover over the launch positions would draw the attention of our enemies to locations that we wish to keep secret. For much the same reason, we have minimized our remote testing of the launch positions. Frequent use of the satellite communications link may invite unwanted attention to both our methods and the locations of our launch positions."

He raised his hands and dropped them. "Despite our plans, secrecy and concealment have obviously not protected our zashishennaja pozicija. In view of this, I suggest we abandon secrecy, and deploy direct protection over the remaining launch position. With your permission, I will order continuous coverage of the southeast position by attack helicopters, supplemented by frequent over-flights by MiG fighters."

Zhukov nodded. "A wise recommendation, Maxim Ivanovitch. Give the order. Also, send out demolitions teams to prepare six or seven new launch positions, as well as eight or ten decoy positions."

He brought the fingertips of both hands together. "The Americans have evidently seen past that particular deception. We should give them plenty of new possibilities to keep their minds occupied."

Zhukov was thinking rapidly. How *had* the Americans found out? Could it be satellites? The United States had impressive spy satellite capabilities, to be certain, but the launch positions had been prepared nearly two weeks ago—long before the U.S. intelligence community had found a reason to point their expensive surveillance assets in the direction of a backwater province like Kamchatka. He was confident that the Americans had neither noticed, nor cared about a few old helicopters hopping around on a bit of worthless and deserted ice pack to the south of Siberia.

Could one of Zhukov's own people have talked? That didn't seem likely. With the exception of three senior officers aboard the submerged submarine, only a dozen people had ever learned the coordinates of the launch positions. Of that dozen, more than half had been eliminated to avoid just this sort of security breach.

The demolitions personnel who had rigged the explosives were now dead. So were their helicopter pilots, and the old courier, Grigoriev.

So, how had the Americans ferreted out the locations of the launch positions? Could they be using some new and hyper-sensitive technology? Zhukov didn't know.

He decided to treat this unsolved mystery as a not-too-gentle reminder that the Americans could still surprise him. And that thought raised the next question. How could he turn this around? How could he regain the element of surprise?

It was time to do something that America was not expecting. Something that *no one* would expect. He needed to punish the Americans for sending their filthy Marines to invade the sovereign territory of his new Russia. And he needed to teach the entire world that Sergiei Mikhailovich Zhukov was prepared to wield power at a level completely beyond their experience. He was not afraid to step boldly into the land of nightmares, where the other so-called leaders of the world feared to tread.

He regarded his assistant, still standing quietly, no doubt waiting to be dismissed. "Maxim Ivanovitch, refresh my memory. The K-506 is currently following a slow counterclockwise circle, is he not?"

"Yes, Comrade President," Ustanov said.

"When will he pass within communications range of the southeastern launch position?"

Ustanov glanced at his watch. "Approximately 11:50 PM our time, sir. Or 10:50 PM *his* time, as the submarine is operating one time zone west of us."

"Excellent," Zhukov said. He made eye contact with his assistant, and held it. "When the submarine reaches communications range, order the Kapi'tan to carry out *Strike Option 7*."

Ustanov stared. "Comrade President, Strike Option 7 calls for nuclear missile attacks against …"

"I know what the order entails," Zhukov said. "The Americans still wish to play games with us. It's time to teach them, my old friend. This is *not* a game. And *we* make all the rules."

CHAPTER 53

"The update should be coming through the link any time now," Captain Bowie said. He pointed to one of the giant Aegis display screens in Combat Information Center.

Ann Roark and Sheldon Miggs stood among a group of officers and enlisted personnel, waiting for the captain to outline the latest tactical developments.

Ann suppressed a yawn. She was exhausted all the time, now. She didn't sleep well on ships to begin with, and for the past few days, her dreams had been invaded by the faces of dead Russian sailors. Of course, the sailors on that submarine weren't actually dead yet, but Ann and the other people gathered in this room were trying pretty damned hard to change that.

She wondered for the thousandth time how she had gotten caught up in a situation where she was actively plotting to kill other human beings. How had her ethical view of the world shifted so dramatically?

It *hadn't*, she reminded herself. She didn't pretend that killing the crew of the Russian submarine was an acceptable course of action. Her personal decision to carry out the plan was a hideous thing, that burned and fumed like acid at the edges of her conscience. Killing those men was an act of evil. But it was not as evil as the alternative: allowing millions of innocent people to perish in nuclear fire.

Ann was caught in a dilemma so ancient that it had become a cliché in nearly every human culture. She had been forced to choose between the lesser of two evils.

The yawn she was battling decided that it was not going to be denied, so Ann gave in to it. When it had released her from its grip, she turned her eyes back to the big tactical screen.

The display was centered on a large two-color map of the Sea of Okhotsk and its surrounding land masses: Kamchatka to the east, Siberia to the north, the Russian mainland to the west, and the Kuril Island Chain to the south. The water was a strangely fake-looking shade of blue that Ann had only ever seen in video games and computer maps. The land was depicted as an almost equally unnatural shade of greenish-brown.

On the screen five rectangular symbols appeared, each with a large dot in the center, topped by a nestled pair of inverted V-shapes, like a round head wearing two dunce-caps—one cap worn on top of the other. All five of the rectangular symbols were red. Four of them were crossed out by thick diagonal lines, also in red. The fifth rectangle, at the lower right, was not.

The new symbols made no more sense to Ann than any of the rest of the strange markings on the tactical screens. They probably didn't mean much to Sheldon either, but everyone else in the little crowd seemed to nod in response.

"This information comes to us via the Third Marine Expeditionary Force on Okinawa," Captain Bowie said. "They're just sharing it with us now, because these coordinates were provided by a human intelligence source, whose identity is extremely sensitive. Until a few hours ago, this information was too highly classified to transmit via the link, even with full encryption and security protocols. It's still classified above *Secret*, but it's been downgraded far enough for transmission via link, so we're getting it now."

One of the female officers, Lieutenant Somebody-or-other, spoke up. Ann couldn't remember the woman's name, but she'd been Tactical Action Officer during the MiG attack, a couple of days earlier.

"What happened to downgrade this info, Captain?" the lieutenant asked. "Once the big dogs decide to play poker, they're usually pretty stingy about letting us little dogs see their cards. Do we have any idea what prompted them to let the warfighters into the game, sir?"

Captain Bowie raised an eyebrow. "Succinctly put, as always, OPS. I don't know the whole story, but I do have some idea of how the people at flag level were thinking."

He turned toward the big display screen. "We've suspected for some time now that the submarine has been using pre-staged explosives to blow shooting holes in the ice pack. We assumed that Mr. Zhukov's rebels had prepared these positions by planting explosives in the ice at various locations around the Sea of Okhotsk."

The captain smiled ruefully. "It turns out that our assumptions were correct. Intelligence has confirmed that there were *five* of these sites, which they refer to as '*launch positions*,' prepared at different locations on the ice pack."

He leaned over and rested his fingers on the trackball of one of the Aegis consoles. He rolled the ball, and a cross-shaped cursor scrolled across the screen to rest above the northeastern most of the rectangles. It was one of the four symbols crossed out by diagonal lines.

"This launch position no longer exists,' he said. "The submarine used up the explosives at this location when it launched the nuclear missile attack toward California."

The captain rolled the trackball again, bringing the cursor to hover briefly above three of the other rectangles, all of which were also crossed out by diagonal lines. "These three launch positions were destroyed earlier today, by a pair of U.S. Marine Corps EOD teams, flown up from Okinawa. The Marine CH-53 helo we refueled a few hours ago was the transport bird for one of these teams. The helo for the other team refueled aboard USS *Albert D. Kaplan*. Each of the EOD teams was assigned to locate and disarm the pre-staged explosives at two of the launch positions."

A short move of the trackball put the cursor over the top of the fifth rectangle, the only one not crossed out by diagonal lines. "One of the EOD teams completed both of its sites, and was extracted on schedule. The other team finished disarming their first position, but they were detected by a helicopter gunship and killed before they could move to their second assigned position."

The captain continued talking, but Ann had tuned him out. That one word shot through her guts like a jolt of electricity. *Killed*. They had been *killed*. She suddenly wanted to sit down.

"How many of them were there?"

It took Ann a half-second to realize that it was her own voice. She had asked the question, although she couldn't remember deciding to speak.

Captain Bowie stopped. He had obviously moved past that part of the conversation. "How many of *who*?" he asked. "Or *what*?"

"The Marines," Ann said. "The ones who were killed by the helicopter. How many of them were there?"

The captain spoke softly. "Four," he said. "The team consisted of four Marines, from the Third Explosive Ordnance Disposal Company."

His brown eyes somberly regarded Ann for several seconds. "If it helps any, Ms. Roark, we *do* know their names."

Ann shook her head. "I'm sorry. I just thought ..." She stopped, unable to remember what she'd been about to say. "It just seemed ..."

She shook her head again, and felt suddenly like she might cry. "It seemed *important.*"

The captain nodded. "It *is* important," he said. "It's of the utmost importance."

His brow creased slightly, not in anger or annoyance, but as though he was searching for the right words to express whatever was on his mind.

"I never met Gunnery Sergeant Thomas Armstrong," he said. "Nor Staff Sergeant Scot Myers, or the other two Marines on the EOD team. Chances are, no one else on this ship has met any of them either. But if we get out of this, I'll go to their funerals. I'll thank their families personally, and I'll offer my help and my respect in whatever form the families will accept. And if I know my crew as well as I think I do, I won't be alone when that day comes."

He glanced toward the display screen, and then back to Ann. "Today, we have to finish the job those men started. The time will come for mourning our losses, but now is not that time."

Ann nodded slowly. "I'm sorry. I didn't mean to interrupt."

Bowie looked at the cursor, hovering above the last rectangular symbol. "The fifth launch position remains intact," he said. He pressed a button on the console, and an irregular white line appeared, cutting across the lower quarter of the Sea of Okhotsk at a mostly horizontal angle. "This is the estimated southern edge of the ice, based primarily on satellite imagery."

He rolled the trackball in small circles, causing the cursor on the screen to orbit the fifth rectangle. "As you can see, the remaining launch position is close to the boundary of the ice pack. We may be able to maneuver the ship within torpedo range of this position, depending on how accurate the satellite pictures are, and the density of the drift ice near the edge of the pack. If we're lucky, we might get in close enough to get a shot at the submarine."

One of the junior officers raised a hand. "Two questions, Captain."

Bowie nodded and smiled. "You don't have to raise your hand, Dennis."

The young officer reddened slightly, but plowed on. "Sir, you said that one of the Marine EOD teams disarmed both of its assigned positions before being extracted. Why wasn't that team redirected to finish the remaining site? I'm sure they would have needed to refuel their helo, but we've got plenty of gas. They could have vectored down south, rendezvoused with us for refueling, and then flown back up to handle the last launch position. Why didn't Third Marine Expeditionary Force modify their orders to make that happen?"

"Good question," the captain said. "I imagine that the higher-ups realized the cat was out of the bag when hostile helicopter gunships started showing up. An EOD team is too small and too lightly armed to shoot it out against major opposition, especially air-to-ground forces. Their only chance of pulling it off was to sneak in, do the job, and sneak out. They were depending on stealth, and complete secrecy. That may be why they didn't let us untrustworthy Navy types in on the plan until the hard part was already over."

The corners of the captain's mouth came up slightly. "Everybody knows squids can't keep their mouths shut. But the fifth launch position has constant air cover now: HIND-D attack helicopters, with frequent over-flights by MiG fighters. There's not much chance of sneaking another EOD team in there now, and the bad guys are on to the plan. So the Marines must figure that it's finally safe to tell the Navy."

He smiled at his own joke. "What was your second question, Dennis?"

"Well, sir," the young officer said, "we know where the last launch position is, and Zhukov *knows* that we know. He knows we'll be watching that spot closely. What makes us think he'll let his submarine get anywhere *near* there? It seems to me that his smartest move would be to plant some new launch positions, and keep his sub as far as possible from the one that we already know about."

"He might well do that," Captain Bowie said. "If he does, we'll have to figure out an entirely new way to go after his submarine. But COMPACFLEET thinks our Mr. Zhukov is going to want to demonstrate to the world that he's still in the game. And they think he's going to want to do it quickly. They're expecting something *big*, and they're expecting it *soon*."

The captain looked around. "Any other questions?"

No one spoke.

Bowie checked his watch. "Alright," he said. "We've already turned north, toward the ice. We'll be crossing through the Kuril islands just after sunset, a little over two hours from now. We're going to run quiet and dark—full stealth mode, and full EMCON. We know there are MiGs and helicopter gunships operating just north of our planned search position."

He turned to one of his officers. "Your show, XO."

The man he had addressed cleared his throat. "Thank you, Captain."

Ann had forgotten the man's name, but she knew that he was the ship's Executive Officer.

"As the CO mentioned," the Executive Officer said, "we'll be operating in close proximity to hostile air cover. And because we'll be in stealth mode, we're going to be using passive sensors *only*. We won't have any radar to spot the bad guys, or to dodge ice floes, for that matter. We're going to need as many topside lookouts as we can muster, because we're going to be depending on human eyes and ears to identify threats to this vessel. Have representatives from your divisions hoof it up to the Boatswains Locker and draw cold weather gear from our UNREP stash for anybody who needs it. It's going to be freezing up on deck, and I don't want any of my Sailors getting hypothermia because they don't have the proper clothing."

Heads nodded around the small group.

"As the Captain just told us, we've got about two hours until sunset," the XO continued. "We're going to use that time to strip any unnecessary fittings from the topside of this ship. We're obviously going to leave the radars, antennas, and weapons alone, and don't mess with the life lines. We'll need them when we've got Sailors standing up there in the dark. Anything else that's not vital or protected by PCMS gets unbolted and goes below decks. Fire extinguishers, the J-Bar davits, line handling equipment, whatever. Bring it inside the skin of the ship, and find a temporary place to stow it. We're going to shave every fraction off of our radar signature that we can."

He rubbed his chin. "We'd better leave the life rafts alone too. I hope like hell we don't need them, but things might get ugly tonight, so let's not take a chance on that."

"Try to think like ghosts," he said. "Think of anything you can to make this ship invisible and undetectable. Because if we get caught, those bastards are going to do their best to turn us into ghosts for real."

He scanned the assembled faces. "Any questions?"

"Yes, sir," one of the female chiefs said. "What if we've got topside gear that won't fit below decks?"

"If it's not something we're going to need immediately, we may have to toss it over the side," the XO said. "If you're in doubt, ask your Department Head. Make sure you get the serial number off of anything that goes in the drink. We're going to have to account for that stuff later."

If there is a later, Ann thought.

The XO looked around again. "Any more questions?"

No one spoke.

The XO clapped his hands. "Alright, people. Let's get to it."

CHAPTER 54

MOUSE (MULTI-PURPOSE AUTONOMOUS UNDERWATER SYSTEM)
SOUTHEASTERN SEA OF OKHOTSK
THURSDAY; 07 MARCH
2139 hours (9:39 PM)
TIME ZONE +11 'LIMA'

It began with a single frequency. The sound was weak at first, hovering right at the detection threshold for Mouse's passive sonar sensors, so the robot tagged the tonal, and began sending frequency and bearing information to its onboard acoustic processors for evaluation. The signal was very close to one of the frequencies listed in the robot's library of mission data. It was one of the tonals that Mouse's target was known to generate. But the signal strength was only fractionally higher than the ambient noise level under the ice pack. It was too weak and intermittent for tactical exploitation, and there were no corroborating frequencies to make further identification possible.

Mouse's onboard computer labeled the lone frequency as *"Investigatory Signal #1,"* and assigned a confidence factor of 02.1%. Mouse was 2.1% certain that Investigatory Signal #1 was the target the robot had been programmed to find.

The mission was only a few hours old, and Mouse still had most of the search grid left to cover. The computer weighed this knowledge against the low confidence factor it had assigned to Investigatory Signal #1, and decided not to deviate from the search grid to pursue the weak signal. Instead, it would monitor the frequency, and reevaluate later if the circumstances changed.

The robot continued on its course, gliding slowly but quietly toward the next waypoint in the search grid. It cruised past ice keels, which it identified only as navigational hazards, and through swarming schools of under-ice krill, which it recognized only as a source of non-target noises. Mouse was neither interested in these things, nor distracted by them. Despite a high-degree of functional autonomy, it was a very single-minded machine. It had been programmed to carry out a task, and anything not directly related to that task was irrelevant.

As Mouse followed the search grid, the strength of Investigatory Signal #1 began to fade. The robot's computer noted the waning signal strength, but decided that the priority of such a low-confidence tonal was too low to justify turning away from the search program.

Mouse reached the next programmed waypoint, and turned thirty-five degrees to starboard, to begin its transit toward the waypoint after that. Almost immediately after the robot made the turn, the strength of Investigatory Signal #1 began to increase.

It was slow at first, the signal growing stronger by tiny increments. After three minutes on the new course, the signal strength began increasing more rapidly.

The robot detected a second acoustic frequency, on the same bearing as Investigatory Signal #1. The second signal was routed to acoustic processing, and was identified as another tonal that Mouse's target was known to generate. The computer tagged the new frequency as Investigatory Signal #2, and noted that the strength of both signals were increasing now.

To say that Mouse became excited would be both an overstatement, and a misnomer. The robot had no emotions whatsoever. It neither liked, not disliked anything. It had no preferences, or fears. Nevertheless, an examination of the machine's electronic mission records might have easily led an unknowing person to make that mistake.

The electrical activity inside the robot increased dramatically. Mouse's computer began loading and activating additional subroutines and library function calls as it continued to evaluate the signals that its sonar sensors were tracking. The confidence factor rose to 12.7%, and then 25.8%, and then 33.2%.

Based on signal strength and bearing drift, the computer decided to deviate from its programmed search grid. It was not a large enough deviation to affect the integrity of the search, but a small one that could be easily compensated for if the signals did not turn out to be the target of interest.

The robot turned seven more degrees to starboard, and was almost instantly rewarded with a third acoustic signal. Another search of the mission library revealed that this new frequency, Investigatory Signal #3, was also one of the tonals that the target was known to generate.

More significantly, this third tonal was one of the designated *class identifiers*. Unlike the first two frequencies—which might have originated from many underwater sources, including Delta III class submarines—this new frequency was known to come *only* from Delta III class submarines. There were no other known underwater sources for this particular frequency.

In the world of passive sonar, a class identifier is the acoustic equivalent of DNA evidence. It's as close to positive identification as the physical limitations of the audio spectrum will permit.

The robot's mission library included the acoustic class identifiers for the target Mouse had been programmed to find. Based on the newly-detected frequency, the computer elevated its confidence factor to 98.2%. Mouse was now 98.2% certain that it had located the assigned target.

This new confidence level was more than high enough to justify abandoning the search plan to pursue the source of the frequencies. Mouse shifted from *search mode* to *autonomous mission mode*, so it could carry out the next phase of the mission. And that's when the problem occurred.

The mode shift triggered a bug in Mouse's core operating program. If the code had functioned as its programmers intended, a subroutine would have recorded the nature of the mistake for future correction, and then bypassed the error to allow the robot to continue functioning. But the software glitch got in the way.

Instead of bypassing the error, the faulty program activated Mouse's emergency maintenance routine, falsely informing the robot that it had suffered crippling damage, and ordering it to return to its point of launch to surface for repairs.

The robot noted the damage alert immediately, and prepared to terminate the mission and head for the launch and recovery coordinates.

But Ann Roark's software patch was installed and at work. As with the rescue of the *Nereus*, the software workaround had four elements: one conditional statement, and three commands:

```
(1) <<<< IF [emergency_maintenance_routine = active]
    (2) CANCEL [emergency_maintenance_routine]
    (3) RESUME [normal_operation]
    (4) INVERT [last_logical_conflict] >>>>
```

The first line of code triggered the workaround the instant that Mouse's computer kicked into emergency maintenance mode. The second line canceled the order for emergency maintenance mode. The third line ordered the robot to ignore the error and continue operating as if no fault had been reported. The last line of the workaround inverted the logical conflict that had triggered the original error.

The Mouse unit had responded to a false report that it had sustained critical damage. Ann's code patch inverted the logical state of the

erroneous report, switching "CRITICAL DAMAGE = YES" to
"CRITICAL DAMAGE = NO" in the robot's memory.

The conflict was eliminated.   The computer determined that all
conditions had been met for the autonomous phase of the mission to
commence. The robot made a five degree starboard turn to improve its
angle of approach, and began moving toward the target.

Mouse had no idea of the nature of its quarry, or the ultimate purpose
of its mission.   It thought only in terms of waypoints, frequencies,
obstacles, and manipulator functions.

Two hundred feet beneath the ice pack, in a body of water that most
people couldn't find on a map, a small unarmed robot glided through the
darkness toward a 13,000-ton nuclear missile submarine.

CHAPTER 55

USS TOWERS (DDG-103)
SOUTHEASTERN SEA OF OKHOTSK
THURSDAY; 07 MARCH
2206 hours (10:06 PM)
TIME ZONE +11 'LIMA'

Ann Roark was looking the other way when the icon popped up on the display of her laptop. When she looked up, the computer showed only the ship's position indicator and a silhouette map of the Sea of Okhotsk. She glanced back down, perhaps a second later, and the triangular green symbol was burning bright on the screen.

Ann had the laptop speakers muted, so the arrival of the icon came without sound or commotion, but it startled her just the same. Something heavy clunked inside of her, as she realized that the next scene of this crazy little drama was about to play itself out.

She thumbed the trackball, scrolling the computer's cursor over the green triangle. A small block of alphanumerical data appeared to the left of the icon. Ann read the little status report twice, to be certain that she was interpreting the situation correctly.

Then she leaned back in her seat and glanced around. None of the Navy people happened to be standing nearby at the moment, so she stood up, stretched, and walked briskly over to the Tactical Action Officer's station.

She didn't know the man in the TAO chair, but she recognized from the silver bars on his collar that he was a lieutenant. The Navy guys called those bars *railroad tracks*. She was starting to learn this stuff. She wasn't sure if that was a good thing.

She tapped the TAO on the shoulder. The man recoiled at her touch, and Ann felt a tiny hint of satisfaction at having startled one of the warrior types. Obviously, she wasn't the only person feeling the pressure.

When the man looked up, Ann pretended she hadn't noticed his flinch. "I don't have a headset, so I couldn't call you on the net," she said. "My robot has found your submarine."

The man sat up straighter. "What? Are you sure?"

Ann looked back toward her laptop. "Yeah. That's what Mouse is telling me, anyway."

The man keyed his microphone, and spoke into his headset. "USWE—TAO. Can you step over to my station, Chief? I need to talk to you."

The redheaded Sonar Technician, Chief McPherson, appeared at the TAO's chair a few seconds later. The cord of a disconnected headset was draped around her neck. "What's up, sir?"

The TAO inclined his head in Ann's direction. "Ms. Roark's robot has detected the target."

Chief McPherson raised her eyebrows. "You've got high-confidence classification on the contact?"

"Yeah," Ann said. "Mouse detected three frequencies consistent with a Delta III submarine. One of them is flagged as a class identifier."

The chief gave a thumbs-up gesture. "Excellent! We need to get a tactical feed to Fire Control immediately."

Her face took on a thoughtful expression. "We can't hook your laptop into CDRT or Fire Control, so we'll have to do this old school. I'll station a phone talker over your shoulder. He'll relay the data to us, and we'll punch it into the system manually."

Ann held up a hand. "Whoa there, cowboy. I can get you a recent position for the sub, but I can't give you real-time information."

Chief McPherson's eyebrows narrowed. "Why not?"

Ann struggled to keep the frustration out of her voice. "Because your captain told me to lock out the acoustic modems," she said. "Remember that strategy meeting in the wardroom? You guys decided to restrict Mouse's communications to low-power UHF, so the submarine can't detect him. He can't transmit or receive UHF when he's under the ice. Every time he needs to make a report, he has to break off his track of the submarine and come out to open water, where he can drive to the surface. With transit time and everything, our first fix is already nearly twenty minutes old."

Chief McPherson grimaced. "Damn! I forgot about that. What about the beacon? Did he attach it to the submarine's hull?"

"Yes," Ann said. "Your beacon is in place, and waiting to be triggered."

"That's one piece of good news," Chief McPherson said.

"We need to bring the Captain in on this," the TAO said. "Get whatever information you have punched into the CDRT so I can call it up on the screen. Then we can try to figure out the best way to tactically exploit this situation."

The chief nodded. "Aye-aye, sir." She looked at Ann. "Let's go see what you've got."

⚓ ⚓ ⚓

Five minutes later, they were gathered around the TAO station again, joined by Captain Bowie and the Executive Officer.

The big Aegis display screen depicted a highly-magnified view of the tactical situation. The water and landmasses were shown in the same weird shades of blue and brown, and the ice appeared in white.

Seen at this scale, the southern border of the ice pack appeared to be carved and fissured with irregular inlets, like the fjords of Norway cast in ice. Some of the larger passages wound and twisted for miles into the ice, before ending suddenly in blind cul-de-sacs. Ann knew that the ice fjords had a name, but she couldn't remember what it was. Polly-something. *Pollyanna*? That couldn't be right.

The display showed a red rectangular symbol representing one of the submarine's prepared launch positions. The rectangle was not crossed out by diagonal lines. This launch position hadn't been used up, or disarmed. It was still active. The other four launch positions, all now defunct, did not appear on the map at its current resolution.

A few inches to the left of the rectangle was a red circle, enclosing a downward-pointing arrow. This was the *datum* symbol: the last known position of the submarine. In this case, that amounted to the last place Mouse had seen the sub, prior to breaking off contact to transit out from under the ice.

Mouse's green triangular icon was south of datum, an inch or so below the border between ice and water. A half inch below that was the circular green symbol that represented the ship.

Captain Bowie's eyes were locked on the screen. "This is not an easy call to make," he said. "We can't prosecute the contact if all of our reports are twenty minutes time-late."

"Or more," Ann said. "Every time he breaks off contact to report to us, Mouse is going to have to search for the submarine again. He's smart enough to calculate an intercept point, based on the sub's last observed course and speed, but that's only valid if the submarine doesn't maneuver between search runs. Mouse may not always find the contact easily."

The captain nodded gravely. "For that matter, there's no guarantee that your robot will reacquire the submarine at all."

"That's true," Ann said. She didn't voice the other thing on her mind. Every time Mouse had to go through the search and acquire process, he would have to make the shift from *search mode* to *autonomous mission mode*. Her software patch was only a temporary fix for a bug that she hadn't even identified yet. The patch wasn't bulletproof. Every time the mode shift occurred, there was a risk that her little robot would lose his freaking mind, software patch or no software patch.

The Executive Officer frowned. "I understand that we need real-time tracking information. But as Ms. Roark has reminded us, no one has actually verified that her acoustic transponder system is covert. Which means there's a chance that the submarine will detect our signals."

"It's a risk," Ann said. "I can't pretend that it's not. You just have to decide if you need real-time data badly enough to take the chance."

"Captain, we need the tracking data," Chief McPherson said. "I don't see how we can prosecute this submarine without it."

"We don't have a lot of choice," Captain Bowie said. He pointed toward the screen. "The target is heading for the launch position. If COMPACFLEET is right, the sub is going to shoot as soon as he gets there."

The Executive Officer nodded without speaking.

The captain looked at Ann. "Enable your robot's underwater transponder system, and try to get him into an intercept position *before* the submarine reaches the launch position."

He turned to the Executive Officer. "Nick, I want you to go up to the bridge and assume the Conn. You're the best ship driver I've got." He pointed toward the Aegis display. "See that big polynya, to the southeast of the launch position?"

Ann followed his finger to a winding passageway that led miles into the ice. *Polynya. That* was the word.

"Get us as far up in there as you can," the captain said. "We need to get within torpedo range of the submarine, or all of this is for nothing."

The Executive Officer studied the screen. "Sir, there's not going to be much room to maneuver in there. If we need to run, we'll probably have to *back* out. There's not enough fairway to turn around."

"I know," the captain said. "And you'll be sailing in the dark, without radar. So use the infrared cameras on the mast-mounted sight, and make sure your forward lookouts have night vision goggles."

"We're going to bump some ice, Nick," he said. "No way to avoid it. But try not to hit too much of it, and try not to hit it too hard." He smiled. "I don't think our ship's band knows how to play *Abide With Me*."

Ann registered the last sentence as a joke, but she didn't get the reference. Maybe it was some Navy insider thing.

The captain turned to Chief McPherson. "Chief, we can't use ASROC in there, so make sure we've got port and starboard torpedo tubes prepped for urgent attack. We don't know when we're going to get a shot, and I don't want to miss our window."

He looked at the TAO. "We've been operating just across the fence from those MiGs and helicopter gunships all night. We've been lucky so far, but now we're going to climb over the fence and go right into their backyard. Sooner or later, they're going to notice us and start shooting. When that happens, the jig will be up. Forget about EMCON, and forget about stealth. Get the radars up as fast as you can, so we can shoot back. Engage inbound missiles first, and *then* worry about hostile aircraft."

Finally, he turned to Ann. "I appreciate your assistance," he said. "We couldn't do this without you."

Ann nodded, and felt her stomach take a turn. She wondered if this might be a good time to throw up all over Combat Information Center again.

The captain regarded the little group. "Any questions or suggestions?"

No one had any.

"You've all got your orders," he said. "Let's go."

CHAPTER 56

USS TOWERS (DDG-103)
SOUTHEASTERN SEA OF OKHOTSK
THURSDAY; 07 MARCH
2243 hours (10:43 PM)
TIME ZONE +11 'LIMA'

Seaman Apprentice Richard Melillo—better known to his shipmates as *Rich Man*—raised the binoculars to his eyes again and resumed scanning the star-flecked Siberian sky. "It turns out," he said, "that *bondoc* is the Tagalog word for *mountain*. So these American Soldiers who fought in the mountains of the Philippines during World War II were fighting in the *bondocs*. Only the GIs didn't pronounce it correctly. They called it the *boondocks*, or the *boonies*. And that's where the term comes from."

Somewhere to his right, Seaman Dreyfus summoned up a measure of phlegm, and hocked it over the lifeline. "Where do you learn all of this crazy shit?" he asked.

Melillo panned his binoculars slowly to the right, methodically taking in small sections of sky at a time, the way they'd taught him during lookout training. "I just pick it up here and there," he said. "I read. Watch the History Channel. Stuff like that."

"Yeah," Dreyfus said. "But how do you *remember* it? Half the time, I can't remember where I put my shoes. How do you remember all this history junk? I bet you'd kick total ass if you ever went on *Jeopardy*."

Melillo smiled to himself. "I guess," he said. "Maybe." In truth, he though he probably *would* kick ass on Jeopardy. But it didn't seem right to say so.

Dreyfus hocked another one over the rail, and followed it up with a nasty sounding snort. "This cold is killing me," he said. "My feet feel like they're frozen to the deck plates, my damned nose won't stop running.

He stomped his feet several times, to get his circulation moving. "Damn," he said. "It's cold enough to freeze the balls off a brass monkey."

299

Melillo grinned. "Yeah it is," he said. "Hey … Do you know where that saying comes from? About freezing the balls off a brass monkey?"

"Get the hell out of here," Dreyfus said. "You really know where that comes from?"

"Yeah," Melillo said. "It goes back to the days of sail, when they used to stack cannonballs on deck, ready for use—next to the cannon. You know, in little pyramids, like you see on pirate movies. Well cannonballs are round, right? So they had to come up with a way to keep them from rolling all over the deck …" He paused, his binoculars held motionless as he listened intently.

Dreyfus got tired of waiting for him to finish. "Yeah?"

"Be quiet for a second," Melillo said. "I'm listening."

"Listening for what?" Dreyfus asked.

"Shhhhhhhh!"

Seaman Apprentice Melillo shifted the earphone of his headset to free up his right ear, and pulled the cold weather hood out of the way. The air was insanely cold against his exposed skin, but he stood without moving, straining to recognize a sound near the very bottom end of his hearing.

There it was. Yeah. It sounded like …

His binoculars came up again, sweeping the sky in the direction of the sound. After a few seconds of searching, he found what he was looking for: a cluster of black shapes, silhouetted against the starry sky. He calculated a couple of quick angles, and grabbed the push-to-talk button on his headset.

"Bridge—Starboard Lookout. Multiple helicopters, bearing zero-four-zero. Position Angle thirty-three. Moving from left to right very rapidly."

Even as he was listening to the reply from the bridge, he saw the helos turn toward the ship. He had a better look at them now, and the sound of their rotors was now easily distinguishable. He keyed his headset again. "Bridge—Starboard Lookout. I have three helicopters, I say again *three helicopters*, bearing zero-four-five. Position angle thirty-three. Helos have turned towards own ship, and they are inbound. I say again, *helos are inbound*."

The phone talker on the bridge said something in reply, but Melillo's attention was focused on the helos now. Through his binoculars, he saw several brief flashes of light in the night sky.

"Incoming missiles!" he shouted into his headset. "Missiles inbound, from the starboard bow! Bearing zero-four-five!"

Again there was a reply from the bridge, but it was drowned out by the bark of an amplified voice from the ship's topside speakers. "This is the XO from the bridge. We have inbound Vipers! This is *not* a drill! All topside personnel get inside the skin of the ship, *now!* All hands brace for shock!"

The announcement was immediately followed by the raucous whoop of the missile salvo alarm.

Melillo and Dreyfus were nearly knocked over by another Sailor, running past them through the darkness. They made it into the starboard break, clambered through a watertight door, and were dogging it behind themselves when they felt the ship shudder with the first launch of outbound missiles.

As the roar of the missiles was fading, Seaman Apprentice Melillo said, "We're getting our birds up there. They'll knock down the inbounds."

The last word was overpowered by a prolonged metallic burp from the forward Close-In Weapon System, as the defensive Gatling gun hurled a thousand or so 20mm projectiles at the inbound missiles. The sound was followed by two muffled explosions, not very many yards from the ship. The CIWS growled again, pumping out another stream of 20mm tungsten bullets, but it was a fraction of a second too late.

⚓ ⚓ ⚓

S-24 Rocket (mid-flight):

Even as two of the S-24 rockets were shredded by the ship's Close-In Weapon System, a third flew toward its target, unaware that it had escaped early destruction by a margin of less than five meters.

The 240mm Russian-built rocket was only marginally more intelligent than a rifle bullet. It had no sensors, no guidance package, and no processing capability of any kind. It knew only how to ignite its solid fuel engine, how to spin its airframe for flight stabilization, and how to detonate when its arming circuit was completed.

It could not be fooled by chaff, or diverted by jamming. It could only fly in a straight trajectory, and explode on cue, but it did these simple things very well.

Ten meters from the target, the rocket's simple proximity fuse triggered the warhead. One hundred and twenty-three kilograms of RDX-based high explosive erupted into a directed cone of fire and shrapnel.

USS *Towers*:

The rocket struck the destroyer near the centerline of the 5-inch gun, blowing through the wedge-shaped carbon laminate faring, and ripping the large-bore naval cannon from its mount as easily as a child snapping a wishbone.

The concussion heeled the destroyer several degrees to port. The ship immediately rolled back to starboard, and then righted herself as the kinetic energy of the exploding rocket was transmitted down through the keel, and passed from the steel hull into the icy water of the Russian sea.

Broken and burning wreckage from the gun carriage tumbled down into the carrier room beneath the gun, spilling fire, fragments of scorched metal, and scalding hydraulic fluid on the Gunners Mates below. The Gunnery Officer, Ensign Kerry Frey, was killed instantly.

Automatic fire suppression systems kicked on in the carrier room and the 5-inch magazine, limiting the cascade of damage. Two main electrical junction boxes and a breaker panel were shorted out by penetrating shrapnel. Electrical power failed, plunging the carrier room and magazine into darkness. The few surviving battle lanterns came on automatically, casting yellow circles of light over the injured and dying members of the 5-inch gun crew.

⚓ ⚓ ⚓

About sixty feet aft of the gun, Seaman Apprentice Melillo and Seaman Dreyfus were thrown bodily against a lagged steel bulkhead by the explosion. Melillo felt his nose crunch as he collided face-first with the lagging, and then bounced to the deck. He lay there for a few seconds, too dazed to move.

The forward missile launcher fired again, and there were explosions in the distance, somewhere away from the ship.

We're not the only ones getting hammered tonight, Melillo thought groggily. He wiped blood from his nose, and staggered to his feet. A wave of pain and dizziness swept over him, and he stumbled against the bulkhead for support.

The lighting was different now. Electrical power had failed in this section of passageway, and the emergency battle lanterns were on.

Dreyfus lay on the deck, eyes open but not moving.

Melillo looked down at his shipmate. "Hey, Carl? Are you okay?" His words sounded strange, partly because his ears were still ringing from the blast, and partly because he couldn't breathe through his nose, which was already beginning to swell.

Dreyfus lay on the deck without speaking.

Melillo tried to lean over his buddy, and instantly regretted the move, as a rush of nauseous pain surged through his head and nose. He staggered again, but didn't fall.

He nudged Dreyfus with the toe of one steel toed boot. "Carl, are you alright?"

Dreyfus looked up at him, blinking slowly. He seemed to be recovering his senses. "Yeah," he said finally. "I ... I think so." He extended his hand. It trembled at first, but steadied down as Dreyfus began to regain control of his stunned muscles.

Melillo grasped the outstretched hand, and helped his friend climb painfully to his feet.

There was another rumble of launching missiles. Melillo could smell something burning, and people were shouting somewhere at the far end of the passageway.

A voice came over the 1-MC speakers. "This is the Damage Control Assistant, from CCS. All available personnel report to the nearest repair locker." The announcement was immediately repeated.

Melillo looked at his buddy. They were both pretty beat up. But their ship was in trouble, and he knew that some of his shipmates were probably in much worse shape.

"Let's go, dude," he said. "They're playing our song."

⚓ ⚓ ⚓

In the semi-darkness of Combat Information Center, Ann Roark was doing her best to tune out the battle. She swallowed, and took a deep breath. *Don't pay any attention. Let the Navy people worry about their business. Take care of your robot, and leave the other stuff to them. Watch the screen. Just do your job.*

After a few minutes, she had honed that last sentence down to a mantra. *Just do your job. Just do your job. Just do your job.* She repeated the words over and over again in her head, unaware that she was rocking back and forth in her seat as she recited the mental litany. *Just do your job. Just do your job.*

She knew from the reports bouncing around that some of the crew members were dead, and at least part of the ship was on fire. She wondered where Sheldon was. She had to fight the urge to jump up and go looking for him. Not that she thought she had a chance of finding him in this metal maze. Her brain just wanted her to be up and moving, probably because that was as close as she could manage to running away. *Just do your job.*

Another report came through the overhead speakers. "TAO—Air, splash Bogie Number Three. All Bogies are down. All Vipers are down."

There was no cheering this time. The helicopters had been destroyed, and the inbound missiles were all gone. But the ship was wounded and there were MiGs out there somewhere.

Just do your job. Just do your job.

A hand touched her shoulder, and Ann nearly screamed.

It was Sheldon, looking rumpled and tired, but otherwise intact. "How are you holding up, Princess Leia?"

Ann tried to smile. "I haven't thrown up yet."

"Me either," Sheldon said. "But that's not really a problem for me. When the missiles start flying, I'm more worried about peeing my pants."

Ann nodded. "I've been thinking about doing that, myself. I'm trying to figure out if it's an acceptable alternative to yakking all over CIC. I mean, it *might* be alright. But I don't know enough about Navy regulations. Peeing my panties might turn out to be a major breach of military protocol."

"We can always *ask*," Sheldon said.

"*You* ask," Ann said. "I'm not good with that kind of thing."

Sheldon nodded absently. "We're running out of missiles," he said softly.

Ann could tell instantly from the expression on his face that he hadn't meant to say that out loud. She sat up. "What?"

Sheldon blinked, but didn't say anything.

Ann lowered her voice. "We're running out of missiles?"

"Yeah," Sheldon said. "The ship was doing training work-ups when they got tapped for this mission. The *Towers* wasn't scheduled to deploy for several more months, so the ship wasn't fully outfitted for deployment yet. When they got the order to come here, they were only carrying about half of their normal missile load."

He raised an eyebrow. "Between the fight with those MiGs yesterday, and the helicopters tonight, we're running out of missiles. And the 5-inch gun was wiped out by that rocket hit."

Ann felt her jaw muscles tighten. "Why are you telling me this? I was already scared out of my wits. Now you've got to dump all this on me?"

"I'm sorry," Sheldon said. "I thought you'd want to know the truth."

"Not when I'm trying to decide whether to pee my pants of throw up," Ann said. "I don't want the truth right now. I want to hear that everything is fine, and we're all going to make it home alive."

"We're going to be okay," Sheldon said.

Ann cocked an eyebrow. "It's too late for that now, asshole."

"Just take care of Mouse," Sheldon said.

"That's what I was trying to do when you came flitting in like the freaking Bad News Fairy," Ann said. "I was trying to keep my mind on the job. Take care of my little robot."

Sheldon shook his head. "No. I mean *now*. Take care of Mouse, *now*." He reached over and tapped the screen of Ann's laptop. "ET is trying to phone home."

Ann turned her head. Mouse's little green triangle was blinking. The data in the block to the left of the icon was updating every few seconds.

Ann examined the readout carefully. "Go tell Chief McPherson that Mouse is tracking her submarine."

⚓ ⚓ ⚓

Chief McPherson stood near the Computerized Dead-Reckoning Tracer, and looked down at the horizontally-mounted flat-screen digital display that formed the CDRT's entire upper surface. Five feet wide and almost six feet long, it was essentially an electronic map table, with a viewing area nearly as large as the big Aegis display screens. But unlike the Aegis screens, which could tap into feeds from any sensor or weapons system, the CDRT was optimized for Undersea Warfare. It had been designed specifically for hunting and killing submarines.

Near the center of the display was the circular green symbol that signified USS *Towers*. The ship was surrounded by the white of the ice pack, broken only by the irregular ribbon of blue that represented the channel of open water they had sailed into. The ship was close to the northern end of the polynya, where the waterway constricted even further, and then narrowed to a close.

A voice crackled in the left ear of the chief's headset. "USWE—Tracker, testing Net One One."

The chief was currently the ship's *USWE*, short for Undersea Warfare Evaluator. Her job was to coordinate the actions of the ship's USW team, and direct the efforts to detect, classify, and destroy hostile submarines.

Tracker was the temporary watch station ID she had assigned to STG3 Mooney, the Sonar Technician she had appointed to stand behind Ann Roark's chair, and relay contact information from the civilian's laptop.

Because the sensor in question was an underwater robot, Mooney had tried to talk his chief into designating the new watch station as *AquaDroid*, or *RoboGuy*, or *SubSlayer 2000*. The Chief had settled on *Tracker*. It was simple, efficient, and she wouldn't feel like an idiot every time she had to call him over the net.

She keyed her mike. "Tracker—USWE. Read you Lima Charlie. How me?" (Lima Charlie was net-speak for Loud and Clear.)

"USWE—Tracker. Read you same."

"USWE, aye. Break. UB—USWE, what's the status of your torpedoes?"

The Underwater Battery Fire Control Operator keyed into the net. "USWE—UB. Port and starboard torpedo tubes are prepped for firing. I'm ready to shoot as soon as I get a valid firing solution."

"USWE, aye. Break. Sonar—USWE, are you standing by to trigger the beacon?"

The Sonar Supervisor's voice came back at once. "USWE—Sonar. Affirmative, Chief. We're queued up for a single active transmission, Frequency F2, with upward FM ramp. Standing by to transmit on your mark."

"USWE, aye. Give me a ping, Vasily. One ping only, please."

The Sonar Supervisor's voice came back again. "USWE—Sonar. Say again your last."

Chief McPherson smiled to herself. "Never mind, Sonar. It's a line from a movie. One of the good ones, about chasing a Russian missile sub."

The Sonar Supervisor chuckled. "If you say so, Chief. Must be some of that old-school stuff."

The chief keyed her mike. "It *is* old-school, Sonar. I'll tell you about it when you're old enough."

Then, before the Sonar Supervisor could respond, Chief McPherson keyed up again. "All Stations—USWE, stand by to go hot. Break. Tracker—USWE, start feeding me ranges and bearings."

STG3 Mooney's voice came through the left ear of her headset. "USWE—Tracker. All bearings and ranges to follow are from the robot. Stand by... Mark. Bearing three-zero-three, range two thousand four hundred yards."

The chief keyed her mike. "USWE, aye."

She laid her hand on the CDRT's track ball, and scrolled the cursor until it was poised over the green triangular symbol that represented the Mouse robot. She punched a button to give the symbol an electronic tag, and then used the CDRT's keypad to quickly type in the range and bearing information she had just received from Mooney.

When she finished the entry, the red V-shaped symbol for hostile submarine appeared on the screen at the coordinates she had punched in.

There was a red dot at the center of the symbol, but no speed vector. With only one range and bearing fix, the computer couldn't yet begin to calculate the contact's course and speed.

The positional information was all referenced from the Mouse robot, which was currently tracking the submarine using a combination of passive sonar and laser-based LIDAR imaging. The chief selected the new hostile submarine symbol, and used the CDRT's offset tracking function to recalculate all target ranges and bearings from the position of USS *Towers*.

A new data block appeared, containing the requested information. The submarine was outside of the ship's torpedo engagement envelope, by almost eight hundred yards.

Under ordinary circumstances, she would have recommended a port turn to close the range. But the narrow confines of the polynya didn't give the ship enough leeway for the turn. If they made the turn, they'd collide with the ice pack. Their only choice was to wait for the submarine to come closer.

She tagged the new data block, typed in a manual designation, and pressed the button to transmit it to the Fire Control Computers. Then she keyed her mike. "UB—USWE, I'm sending you range and bearing updates for new contact, track number zero-zero-one, designated *Gremlin Zero One*. Start your track, and stand by on port side torpedoes."

"UB, aye!"

The chief keyed her mike again. "TAO—USWE. We're receiving track data from the Mouse robot, but contact is currently outside of our torpedo engagement envelope. Request batteries released for contact *Gremlin Zero One* as soon as target comes within torpedo range."

The off-going Tactical Action Officer had just turned over the watch. The new TAO was the Operations Officer, Lieutenant Augustine, again. Her voice came back immediately. "USWE—TAO. Copy all. Stand by for batteries released."

"USWE, aye."

Chief knew that Lieutenant Augustine would discuss the request with the captain before rendering a decision. For reasons of safety, permission to launch weapons was usually withheld until the last minute, to give the Commanding Officer and the TAO as much time as possible to ensure that the target was valid, and that no friendly or neutral ships or aircraft would be endangered.

It was unusual to grant permission to fire ahead of time, so Chief McPherson rarely requested it. But this engagement—if it happened at all—would be extremely short. Except for a turn directly toward Towers, which only an utter idiot would do, nearly any sort of evasive maneuver would put the submarine outside of torpedo range very quickly. The opportunity for a shot would be brief, and it probably wouldn't happen twice.

The chief continued to receive updated ranges and bearings from STG3 Mooney. She punched them into the CDRT as they arrived, and watched the hostile submarine symbol move slowly across the screen toward the red rectangle that represented the missile launch position.

After two updates, the Underwater Battery Fire Control Operator's voice came over the net. "USWE—UB. I have a trial solution on contact *Gremlin Zero One*. Course zero-three-two, speed four knots. Contact is seven hundred yards outside of torpedo engagement range.

"USWE, aye."

The computer now had enough track history to give the hostile submarine symbol a speed vector. A stubby red line appeared at the center of the V and extended a short distance to its upper right. The speed vector was a visual representation of the target's predicted course and speed. The line was short, because the target was moving slowly. It pointed up and right, because the target was moving in a northeasterly direction.

Chief McPherson punched another command into the keypad, and a green ring appeared on the display. It was several thousand yards in diameter, and centered on the symbol for the *Towers*. The ring was a projection of the ship's torpedo engagement envelope.

The chief noted that the rectangular symbol for the submarine's prepared launch position was just inside the border of the green ring. If the submarine truly intended to launch, it would have to cross into the ship's torpedo engagement envelope to do so, but just barely. They might get a shot at the sub, but it would be at the extreme effective range of their torpedoes, and it would probably end up in a tail chase. The sub might well be able to outdistance their torpedoes. This tactical situation was not really looking good.

These not very pleasant thoughts were interrupted by the Sonar Supervisor.

"USWE—Sonar. I'm getting passive narrowband on the same bearing as *Gremlin Zero One*."

The report struck Chief McPherson as strange. It wasn't in standard sonar reporting format, and it had come over the net. Initial sonar reports were supposed to be made over the 29-MC announcing circuit. It wasn't like her sonar teams to be that sloppy.

She keyed her mike. "Sonar—USWE. If you've got sonar contact on the submarine, call it away over the 29-MC."

There was a short pause before the Sonar Supervisor responded. "USWE—Sonar. Understood, Chief. If these were target-related tonals, I would have called them away. But we're tracking biologics."

That took the chief by surprise. Biologics? "Sonar—USWE, what *kind* of biologics?"

"USWE—Sonar. It sounds like frying bacon, Chief. Maybe a really big swarm of shrimp, or krill."

This was really getting strange. Why was the sonar team suddenly so worried about krill? She keyed her mike. "Sonar—USWE. There are a lot of krill under the ice pack. This is a favorite feeding ground for krill."

Again the reply was slow in coming. "USWE—Sonar. Understood. But this signal is *loud*. Much higher signal strength than we usually get from biologics. And it's tracking right on the bearing for *Gremlin Zero One*. Unless there a few million krill accidentally swimming in perfect formation with our target, that strikes me as a little odd."

The chief was about to ask a question when the Sonar Supervisor keyed up again. "USWE—Sonar. I'm getting a second passive narrowband signal, bearing two-niner-zero. Sounds like the exact same kind of krill, and it's *loud*, just like the first signal."

Chief McPherson looked at the CDRT display. Bearing two-nine-zero ran through the exact center of the rectangular symbol that marked the submarine's prepared launch position. Two exceptionally loud swarms of krill? One centered on the submarine, and the other centered on the submarine's intended launch position? The chief tugged at her lower lip. That *couldn't* be coincidence.

A new voice came over the net. "TAO—EW, I'm tracking one L-band emitter, bearing two-niner-zero. Classification unknown."

"EW—TAO, can you give me a little more to go on? What are the possibilities? What transmits in the L-band?"

"TAO—EW. The signal is right at 1.52 gigahertz, very weak. I think it's directional, and we're only picking up side lobe or back-scatter. Could be a satellite phone, ma'am. Pointed straight up at the sky, so that all we're catching is the bleed-over."

Chief McPherson felt the understanding click into place in her brain. It *wasn't* coincidence. She knew what the krill sounds meant, and she knew where the satellite transmissions were coming from.

She was reaching to key her mike button when another voice came over the net.

"TAO—Air. We've got party crashers, ma'am. SPY is tracking six Bogies inbound from the northeast. Looks like three flights of two. No modes, no codes, and no IFF." The Air Supervisor paused for a second and continued. *"Flight One* bears zero-two-eight. *Flight Two* bears zero-four-three. *Flight Three* bears zero-seven-one."

The chief looked up in time to see six unknown aircraft symbols pop up on the Aegis display screen.

"Air—TAO. Copy your six Bogies, bearing zero-two-eight, zero-four-three, and zero-seven-one. What are their flight profiles?"

"TAO—Air. They're coming in high and fast, ma'am. I think those helicopters we shot up might have called for the cavalry."

"TAO, aye. Break. EW—TAO. Are you tracking any emitters on these Bogies?"

The Electronic Warfare technician responded quickly. "TAO—EW. That's affirmative, ma'am. Bogies have just lit off their radars. I'm tracking six I-band emitters, in three pairs. Zaslon S-800 series phased array radars, on the bearings reported by Air. Looks like MiG-31s. EW concurs that Bogies are grouped in three flights of two. Request permission to seed early chaff."

"EW—TAO. Permission granted. Launch chaff at will."

Several rapid thumps announced the firing of five or six chaff pods.

Chief McPherson took advantage of a two-second lull to key her microphone. "TAO—USWE. Sonar is tracking unusual passive narrowband signals on the bearing of *Gremlin Zero One*, and on the bearing of the submarine launch position. One of those signals corresponds to the bearing of the L-band emitter detected by EW. Be advised target may be using acoustic transponders to relay communications to a satellite phone. The signal may be modulated to simulate biologics. The target submarine could be receiving tactical orders via satellite phone right now. Recommend you have EW try to jam that L-band transmission if possible."

Lieutenant Augustine's voice came in rapid response. "USWE—TAO. Copy all. Break. EW—TAO, jam all L-band transmissions."

Before the Electronic Warfare tech could respond, the 29-MC speaker roared to life. "All Stations—Sonar. Loud underwater explosions, bearing two-niner-zero. No secondaries."

Chief McPherson looked down at the CDRT. She knew exactly what had just happened.

Ice Pack, Southeastern Sea of Okhotsk:

All six charges detonated simultaneously. Ninety kilograms of ex-Soviet military-grade RDX explosive erupted into an expanding shock wave of heat and overpressure. A thirty-meter circle of ice was instantly obliterated, blasting water vapor and shards of ice into the Siberian night. The fragments and mist rained back down to earth, leaving a large circular opening in the ice pack.

The last *zashishennaja pozicija* was ready for action.

⚓ ⚓ ⚓

USS *Towers*:

Lieutenant Augustine's voice came over the net. "Weapons Control—TAO, you have batteries released on all Bogies, and any Vipers. There are no friendly contacts in this area. Engage and destroy at-will. Shift to Aegis ready-auto. Set CIWS to auto-engage."

The instant the Weapons Control Officer acknowledged the orders, the Tactical Action Officer was on the net again. "USWE—TAO. You have batteries released. Kill contact *Gremlin Zero One* as soon as the target enters your engagement envelope."

Chief McPherson keyed into the net. "USWE, aye."

The air was split by the rumble of launching missiles. "TAO—Weapons Control. Six birds away, no apparent casualties. Targeted one each on the inbound Bogies."

Chief McPherson's eyes were locked on the hostile submarine symbol. The target was now only three hundred yards outside of torpedo range. "Come on," the chief said softly. "Just a little closer. Just a *little* closer."

She keyed her mike. "Sonar—USWE, contact is three hundred yards outside of torpedo range, and closing. Stand by to trigger the beacon. Break. UB—USWE, what's the status of your solution?"

"USWE—UB. I hold a firm fire control solution on contact *Gremlin Zero One*. Standing by to engage on your order."

The Chief keyed her mike again. "All Stations—USWE. We're only going to get one crack at this. Let's make it a good one."

Another report came over the net. "TAO—Air. Splash two Bogies! SPY is tracking four inbound missiles, in two flights of two. Bearing zero-four-niner, and zero-seven-five. I say again, four inbound Vipers, bearing zero-four-niner, and zero-seven-five."

The report was immediately confirmed by the Electronic Warfare technicians, but Chief McPherson was no longer listening. The hostile submarine was now less than two hundred yards outside of weapons range.

The Sonar Supervisor's voice rumbled out of the 29-MC speakers. "All Stations—Sonar has hydraulic transients bearing two-eight-five."

"Shit!" Chief McPherson said to herself. "He's opening his missile hatches."

She keyed her mike. "TAO—USWE. *Gremlin Zero One* is opening his missile tube hatches. Submarine is preparing to launch ballistic missiles."

There were three muted explosions in the distance, followed by the roar of more outgoing missiles.

"TAO, aye. How long until you can kill the sub?"

The chief eyed the screen and keyed her headset. "TAO—USWE. Target is one hundred yards outside of my torpedo envelope. At the current rate of closure, I can engage in approximately one minute."

Her report was punctuated by a prolonged blast from the forward CIWS mount. The ship rocked from the concussion of an explosion, not aboard, but *very* close.

On the CDRT, the V-shaped hostile submarine symbol crept across the green ring of the ship's torpedo envelope.

The Underwater Battery Fire Control Operator keyed into the net. "USWE—UB. Contact is at the very edge of my torpedo engagement envelope. UB holds a firm firing solution. Request permission to engage."

"UB—USWE. Copy all. Stand by. Break. Sonar—USWE, go active now!"

"Sonar, aye."

There was a brief pause, and then, "All Stations, Sonar is active."

From Combat Information Center, the transmission was barely audible, but Chief McPherson was listening for it carefully. She caught it: a single shrill warble, nearly lost beneath the noise in CIC.

The Sonar Supervisor's voice came over the net again. "All Stations, Sonar is passive. The beacon has been triggered, and is transmitting. Sonar is tracking acoustic transmissions from the beacon. I say again, the beacon is hot."

The chief keyed up. "UB—USWE. Kill contact *Gremlin Zero One* with over-the-side torpedo."

"UB, aye. Going to *Standby*. Going to *Launch*. Torpedo away—now, now, NOW!"

A blue friendly torpedo symbol appeared on the CDRT, followed an instant later by the Sonar Supervisor's report.

"USWE—Sonar. We have weapon start-up."

Chief McPherson was dimly aware of a report that three more Bogies were down, but she had eyes and ears only for the submarine. She stared at the screen, her eyes begging the blue torpedo symbol to lock onto the hostile submarine. "You can do it," she whispered. "You can do it. Come on ... You can do it."

"USWE—Sonar, torpedo has acquired. Estimated impact in four minutes."

The chief heard CIWS fire again, but this time it was the aft mount. The last Bogie was either bugging out, or trying to attack from a different angle.

There was another close-aboard explosion, and the screen of the CDRT flickered, went dark, and then flared back to life. The chief heard several operators cry out in frustration as their own consoles went down, and apparently did not come back on line.

The ship shuddered as another set of outbound missiles tore off into the night sky.

The blue torpedo symbol continued to close on the submarine, but the sub was making no effort to avoid the attack. The submarine *had* to hear the torpedo. Why wasn't it running away? Why wasn't it coming to flank speed and turning to evade? Why wasn't it launching its own torpedoes in retaliation?

A chilling thought shot through the chief's mind. Could this be a mobile decoy? Had they been suckered? With literally *everything* on the line, had they somehow been seduced into going after the wrong target?

The hostile torpedo symbol crossed the edge of the rectangle that marked the launch position, and suddenly the chief understood. The sub was already committed to the launch cycle. The commanding officer had decided to complete his mission, regardless of the cost to his boat.

The Air Supervisor's voice came over the net. "TAO—Air. Splash Bogie number four. All Bogies are down! All Vipers are down!"

The report was followed quickly by the report from the Weapons Control Officer. "TAO—Weapons Control, our missile inventory is *one*. I say again, we have *one* missile in the box."

"Talk about cutting it *close!*" someone said aloud.

Someone else cut loose with a whistle.

But chief was still watching the screen. It was a race between symbols now. The red submarine symbol and the blue torpedo symbol, on an iconic rendezvous with destiny.

"Get him," Chief McPherson said to the torpedo symbol. "Kill the bastard *now*."

The 29-MC speaker rattled with the voice of the Sonar Supervisor. "All Stations—Sonar has multiple launch transients bearing two-niner-zero!"

The chief's heart froze in her chest as she saw two hostile missile symbols appear on the CDRT.

"Oh God," she said. "Oh my *God...*"

⚓ ⚓ ⚓

Ice Pack, Southeastern Sea of Okhotsk:

The water at the center of the hole roiled and frothed, and the ice began to tremble madly. A final surge of expanding gas ruptured the surface of the water, and riding in its midst came the blunt-nosed profile of a Russian-built R-29R ballistic missile.

The 35-ton machine rose above its watery launching cradle, and the instant that it cleared the surface, the rocket engines of the missile's first stage screamed to life in an orgy of burning fuel and manmade thunder.

The missile climbed toward the heavens on a pillar of silvery fire and smoke.

The displaced water had not even fallen back to the surface of the ice when the performance was repeated. Again the water at the center of the hole churned, and a second Russian nuclear missile leapt toward the stars in the black Siberian sky.

In seconds, both missiles were climbing faster than rifle bullets, and still accelerating rapidly as they roared away into the night.

⚓ ⚓ ⚓

USS *Towers*:

The captain's voice was a shout, and it didn't come over the net. "Weapons Control this is the Captain. Kill those missiles! Kill them now!"

The ship shuddered once in instant reply, and a friendly missile symbol appeared on the Aegis display. "One bird away," the Weapons Control Officer reported. "No apparent casualties."

For the first time, Chief McPherson lost track of the submarine. That was it. The missile cells were empty. There were two nuclear missiles streaking toward their targets, and only one missile to go after them. There were no more. The cupboard was bare.

A deathly quiet descended over Combat Information Center, broken only by the hum of cooling fans and the muffled sobbing of an unseen Sailor.

The spell held for several long seconds, until it was shattered by an amplified voice from the 29-MC speakers. "All Stations—Sonar. Loud underwater explosions with secondaries, bearing two-niner-zero. I think we just killed us a submarine."

For the half-second before the Sonar Supervisor released the microphone button, the cheering of the Sonar team came faintly through the 29-MC. They had done their job, and they were celebrating. But they didn't know what the CIC team knew.

On the Aegis display, three missile symbols rushed toward the sky—two of them red, the other blue.

Chief McPherson felt her eyes well with tears as she watched the writ of Armageddon play itself out in a dance of colored icons.

Someone behind her spoke. It was a man's voice, but she didn't turn to see who it belonged to.

"And the seventh angel poured out his vial into the air," the man said. "And there came a great voice out of the temple of heaven, from the throne, saying, 'It is *done.*'"

As the last word died down into silence, two symbols merged on the screen. A half second later, the Air Supervisor shouted. "Got one! We got one of the bastards! Splash one ballistic missile!"

Someone clapped the Air Supervisor on the back, but no one cheered. On the screen, the remaining missile symbol moved with increasing rapidity as the real ballistic missile gathered speed out there somewhere in the night. Already, it was beginning to edge to the east, toward the United States.

"We're done here," Captain Bowie said. He turned to the TAO. "Call the bridge. Tell the XO to take us home."

He looked away from the screen. "If there's any home left to go to."

CHAPTER 57

"My God," the president said. "I can't believe this is happening again."

On the wall-sized geographic display screen, a curving red trajectory line arced up from the Sea of Okhotsk toward the United States.

National Security Advisor Gregory Brenthoven sat at the briefing table. "I know, Mr. President," he said. "But we can take a little comfort in knowing that this is the last one. USS *Towers* destroyed Zhukov's submarine. That nutcase is all out of nuclear missiles."

As he spoke, the curving red line on the screen flashed and grew longer. The unfinished end of the arc crept toward the U.S.

"One missile is enough," the president said. "Last time, he was aiming for the ocean, and one of the warheads got past us. This time, I guarantee you he's not aiming at the water."

Brenthoven nodded. "I'm sure you're right about that, sir."

⚓ ⚓ ⚓

30th Space Wing, Vandenberg Air Force Base (Santa Barbara County, California):

Hydraulic pumps moaned, and the armored covers slid aside from four of the missile silos. The reinforced concrete silos were octagonal pits of shadow under the dark pre-dawn sky.

Billows of smoke boiled up out of each silo, and four Lockheed Martin booster rockets blasted into the air on snarling trails of fire.

More than 2,000 miles northwest of Vandenberg, three more interceptor missiles climbed away from the Army missile complex at Fort Greely, Alaska, and hurtled toward the fringes of space.

⚓ ⚓ ⚓

EKV:

Seventeen minutes later, and more than a thousand miles to the west, Exoatmospheric Kill Vehicle #1 collided with the first reentry vehicle at 25,000 miles per hour. Millions of Newton-meters of kinetic energy were translated instantly to several hundred megajoules of thermal energy.

With a flash that would have dazzled the eyes of any human observer, the EKV and its target were annihilated.

⚓ ⚓ ⚓

U.S. Strategic Command (STRATCOM), Offutt Air Force Base, Nebraska:

A hundred and fifty miles below, and four time zones to the east, the morning watch team in the Command and Control, Battle Management, and Communications Control Center witnessed the destruction of EKV #1 and its target on the tasking screens of their consoles.

Less than ten seconds later, EKV #4 killed another warhead, followed almost immediately by another successful kill as EKV #2 performed the task for which it had been built.

The Air Force personnel held their collective breath. They needed a miracle. And maybe … just *maybe* … they were going to get one.

A dozen or so seconds later, EKV #5 scored a bull's-eye, bringing the score to a perfect four out of four. Just two more successful intercepts, and the nightmare would be over. Just *two* …

EKV #6 slammed home, and another of the Russian reentry vehicles disappeared in a flare of thermo-kinetic destruction.

If the unfolding situation had been an Ian Fleming movie, James Bond would have clipped the red wire at the last possible instant, staving off the threat of nuclear desolation until the super-spy's next on-screen adventure. If it had been a Tom Clancy novel, President Jack Ryan would have ridden out the attack aboard a guided missile cruiser, lending moral support to the crew and cadging cigarettes as the plucky Sailors blotted the falling warhead from the sky.

But this was not a movie, and it wasn't an adventure novel. EKV #3 missed its target by less than ten meters. It might as well have been ten million miles.

⚓ ⚓ ⚓

R-29R:

The last reentry vehicle fell tail-first into the atmosphere, streaking across the darkened sky like a shooting star.

Within the fat little cone of the heat shield, a relay clicked open, routing electrical power to the ring of high-voltage capacitors that encircled the core of the warhead. The capacitors began ramping up to full charge as the Soviet-built nuclear warhead armed itself for detonation.

⚓ ⚓ ⚓

Latitude 21.37N / Longitude 157.95W:

As the warhead fell past the 3,000-meter mark, ninety-six electrical initiators fired simultaneously, detonating ninety-six trapezoidal charges of high explosive encapsulating a hollow sphere of plutonium 239. Driven inward by the implosion, the shell collapsed toward its own center, super-compressing an envelope of tritium gas and triggering the secondary stage of the bomb.

The local time was 2:38 AM and seven seconds. Dawn was still four hours away, and a yellow three-quarter moon was just climbing above the horizon, when the air above Pearl Harbor, Hawaii was shattered by a flash more than ten times as bright as the sun.

Every eye that happened to be looking toward that portion of the sky was instantaneously blinded. Tourists taking moonlight strolls on Waikiki beach saw an instant of unbearable brilliance and then their vision went dark as their retinas were cauterized. Cab drivers, homeless people, college students, dogs, and seagulls were struck blind without warning. There wasn't even a sound yet, as the nuclear flash traveled at the speed of light, but the noise of the explosion was limited to the speed of sound, which was many thousands of times slower.

The aircrew of a Qantas 737 were facing directly toward the detonation as their plane was on climb-out from Honolulu International Airport. The sightless captain scrambled to set the automatic pilot by touch, while his First Officer made frantic mayday calls over the radio. Their efforts were useless. The electromagnetic pulse from the detonation fried every microchip and transistor on the plane.

Without computers and flight controls, the 737 ceased to be an aircraft, and became a hurtling collection of unflyable parts. It tumbled out of the air and plowed into a suburban neighborhood, gouging a flaming path of destruction through the homes of the sleeping residents. The aircrew, their eighty-five passengers, and the occupants of the mangled and burnt houses became the first human victims of nuclear attack in nearly three-quarters of a century. But the carnage was just beginning.

The atomic bomb that had devastated the Japanese city of Hiroshima in 1945 had yielded an explosive force of 13 kilotons. The warhead that struck Oahu on the morning of March the 7th was more than fifteen times as powerful.

Two hundred kilotons of nuclear energy were converted to nearly a billion megajoules of radiant heat. Thermal radiation burst outward from ground zero in an expanding wave that burned people, buildings, animals, plants, and vehicles with equal efficiency. The firestorm swept through Naval Station Pearl Harbor, and the surrounding communities of Pearl City, 'Aiea, and Waipahu, searing everything and everyone in its path.

Gamma rays, neutrons, and x-rays shot out from the center of the chain reaction, bombarding everything in the area with lethal ionizing radiation.

Less than a second behind the thermal front came the shock wave, lashing out with the explosive force of 440 million pounds of TNT. Anything not already incinerated by the firestorm was ripped apart, or pulverized by the monstrous overpressure of the mechanical wave front.

Again the Naval Station and the surrounding cities were hammered by a destructive force that nothing and no one could withstand. Miles upon miles of buildings were crushed into powder or torn into minute fragments. Vehicles fluttered through the air like leaves in a hurricane. Roofs were peeled away; walls imploded; steel melted; stone shattered; and concrete crumbled. Airplanes and helicopters were swatted out of the air. Telephone poles, mailboxes, guardrails, fence posts, bodies, dirt, and broken window glass all became part of the roaring maelstrom of debris.

At two-thirty in the morning, the manning level of the naval base was at its low point. Slightly less than a thousand civilians and military personnel were on the base when the bomb exploded. Not one of them survived.

Eighty-percent of the residents of Pearl City, nearly 30,000 people, were dead or dying within five seconds of the blast. The adjoining towns of Waipahu and 'Aiea were burned to cinders and smashed flat, killing another 40,000 people within seconds.

The hypocenter of the explosion occurred over the harbor itself. Thousands of tons of water were flash-vaporized, forming steam and radioactive water droplets that recondensed and drizzled from the sky like poison rain.

The rapid formation of super-heated low-density gases at low altitude created a Rayleigh-Taylor instability. An enormous volume of hot gas rose rapidly, causing turbulent vortices to curl downward along the outer perimeter of the rising column. Fire, smoke, dirt, debris, and water vapor were drawn upward by the same principle of physics that causes hot air to rise up a chimney.

The column of gas and debris became the stem of the infamous cloud formation. It continued to rise until it reached an altitude where the surrounding atmospheric pressure became lower than the pressure inside the column. The gases ballooned outward, forming a bulbous cap at the top of the column.

For the third time in the history of the species, the mushroom cloud rose above the cities of man.

CHAPTER 58

"The casualty figures are coming in now, sir," the Secretary of Homeland Security said. Becka Solomon looked much older than her thirty-nine years. She was immaculately dressed, as always, but her face was haggard and the circles under her eyes were deep. Hers was a tough job during the most peaceful of times. It was a nightmare now.

Her political career wouldn't survive this, President Chandler knew. And there was no justice in that. She was doing a good job of coping with the emergencies that had been tossed into her lap, and her advanced planning had been excellent. She was intelligent, forward-thinking, and genuinely dedicated. She was also not afraid to admit her mistakes, which was a rarity in political figures of any stripe.

Of course, the critics would ignore all of that. When the witch hunt started, if it hadn't started already, the political opposition would scream that she hadn't been prepared for Pearl Harbor, or the panic on the West Coast. As though *anyone* could have foreseen events that far outside the scope of human experience.

The president's eyes were drawn to the wall-sized geographic display screen. It was blank now. No curving red trajectory lines. No incoming nuclear missiles. No escalation to doomsday. And yet, the damage had been quite awful enough.

He nodded. "How bad is it?"

"It's pretty bad, Mr. President," Secretary Solomon said. "The initial estimate is about 70,000 dead, about 20,000 injured, and an unknown number of cases of radiation exposure. We're working with FEMA and the National Weather Service to calculate fallout footprints. We'll be issuing radiation warnings in the affected areas, and we'll need to initiate quarantine protocols. That will help us save some lives, but it's still going

321

to be ugly. If we handle everything properly, we'll see something like 140,000 more deaths over the next five years from leukemia, cancer, and various long term side effects of radiation. If we mismanage the casualty response and cleanup, it'll be a lot worse than that."

Becka Solomon sighed. "The hospitals are overwhelmed, of course. The Secretary of the Navy is calling in the hospital ships USNS *Mercy* and USNS *Comfort*. The *Mercy* is fairly close; she'll be on station in a couple of days. The *Comfort* is in the Caribbean so she'll take several more days. In the meantime, the Coast Guard is …"

Her voice trailed away as she apparently realized that she didn't have the president's attention.

He was staring at the blank screen again.

"You've got a full Homeland Security briefing scheduled at one o'clock, Mr. President. We can go over the rest of this then. I just wanted to get you the early casualty figures."

The president nodded. "Thank you, Becka."

He was still looking at the screen when she left the room, but that wasn't what was on his mind. He was thinking about the Single Integrated Operational Plan again.

Like it or not, he was going to have to order a retaliatory nuclear strike against Kamchatka. There really wasn't any other option. America's allies and enemies were both watching carefully, waiting for the U.S. response. If he allowed a foreign leader to nuke an American city and didn't retaliate, the credibility of the nation's nuclear deterrence would evaporate. He might as well declare open season. Every nutcase on the planet would decide that America was too weak or too frightened to defend herself.

That could not be allowed to happen. He had to stop the next punch *before* it was thrown. And that meant sending an unambiguous message to the enemies of the United States that America could not be attacked with impunity.

He *had* to answer Zhukov's attacks with a nuclear response. But he had absolutely no desire to actually do it. Owning the keys to the nuclear arsenal was not the same as wanting to use them.

And he wasn't entirely sure that *could* he use them, without triggering another nuclear conflict. Kamchatka was a Russian province, after all. Now that Zhukov's missile submarine had been eliminated, would the Russian government tolerate a retaliatory strike from the United States? Could he expect them to sit on their hands, while America launched nuclear missiles at targets on Russian soil?

The answer to those very questions walked in the door, in the guise of Gregory Brenthoven. The national security advisor nodded as he pulled out a chair and sat down. "Good morning, Mr. President."

The president stared at him without speaking.

"Okay, poor choice of words," Brenthoven said. "It is most definitely *not* a good morning. But I have a piece of news that you might find useful, in light of your current dilemma."

The president turned his gaze back toward the blank display screen. "What have you got, Greg?"

Brenthoven laid a black diplomatic pouch on the table. "I've just finished up a meeting with Ambassador Kolesnik. He hand-delivered a very interesting proposal from President Turgenev. It's counter-signed by Prime Minister Primakov, and a solid majority of the Russian Federal Assembly."

"What are our Russian friends proposing?" the president asked.

Brenthoven leaned back and made a steeple of his fingers. "They suggest that the United States and the Russian Federation carry out joint retaliatory strikes against Kamchatka. They recommend that we act in concert, and that we hit Kamchatka *hard*."

President Chandler looked around. "What? I think you must have misunderstood…"

Brenthoven shook his head. "No, sir. There's no misunderstanding. Ambassador Kolesnik was extremely direct. The Russians want to divide the target list. They nuke Petropavlosk and the surrounding volcanoes. We hit Yelizovo and as many of the local geographic features as we want."

The national security advisor raised an eyebrow. "That last part is only to give us an even bite of the candy bar. The Russians want to go after the volcanic peaks surrounding Petro, because that's where they think Zhukov is hiding. They're offering us a chance to nuke a few volcanoes too, so we won't feel like we're getting left out of the party."

"That's crazy," the president said. "Why on earth would they agree to such a plan?"

"It's not all that crazy, sir," Brenthoven said. "From the Russian perspective, it solves three different problems at one stroke."

"How is that?"

"Well, sir … *First*, it allows them to demonstrate to us, to the world, and to their own people that they absolutely are *not* afraid to play hardball with any would-be republics who try to break away and take part of the Russian arsenal with them. A demonstration this powerful will go a long way towards keeping some of their more troublesome territories in line. Especially places like Chechnya, and Ingushetia. *Second*, this plan allows the Russians to save face. They *know* we're going to retaliate against Kamchatka. If they just sit back and take a punch in the face from another nuclear superpower, they look weak and foolish. On the other hand, if they line up shoulder-to-shoulder with the U.S. and we *both* retaliate, they get to play the part of the avenging hero."

The president nodded. "I can see some logic in that. What's their third reason?"

Brenthoven half-smiled. "We knocked a lot of their warheads out of the sky, Mr. President. We didn't intercept them all, but we got *most* of them. From the Russian point of view, that casts serious doubt on the credibility of their nuclear arsenal. This plan gives them the chance to demonstrate the power of the Russian nuclear forces in a way that leaves no room for doubt. It's sort of a public renewal of their ticket to the Nuclear Superpower Club."

The president frowned. His advisor's words were flippant, but the underlying idea seemed to have some merit. The Russian attack plan wasn't pleasant or humanitarian, by any stretch of the imagination. But it might actually do the nasty job that needed doing.

"I think Russians division of targets is pretty shrewd," Brenthoven said.

"How so?"

"They know we have a national aversion to killing civilian populace, so they're offering us Yelizovo as a primary target. It has a population of about 42,000 people. *Their* primary target, Petropavlovsk, is closer to 200,000 people. This plan gives us a significant enough target to demonstrate that we're not afraid to retaliate, while allowing us to reduce civilian casualties by about seventy-five percent."

"That's a good point," the president said. "But 42,000 is still a *lot* of people."

"You're right, sir," Brenthoven said. "It *is* a lot of people. But Zhukov nuked about twice as many of our people at Pearl Harbor."

He spoke more softly. "No matter how we do this, it's going to be hideous, Mr. President. But compared to what's been done to our citizens, this response is almost merciful. And I suspect that it's just about the minimum retaliation we can get away with, and still salvage the credibility of our nuclear deterrence."

"What about radiation?" the president asked. "The prevailing winds are from West-to-East. Are we going to have a fallout cloud over Alaska, Washington, and Oregon?"

"The western states will get some residual radiation, sir. But not as much as you might think. The Pentagon has run fallout projections for just about every conceivable strike scenario. The results are in Appendix G of the SIOP. If we hit Yelizovo, the major fallout footprint will extend about seventy miles downwind from the blast. After that, radiation levels will taper off dramatically."

"*How* dramatically?"

"Five hundred miles east of the blast, the contamination level won't be much higher than the normal background radiation we experience every day. Most of it will blow out to sea, where it will be absorbed and diluted by the ocean."

"Which isn't going to do the environment any good," the president said.

"No, sir, it won't," Brenthoven said. "But it's been done before. Back before the Limited Test Ban Treaty, the Russians tested a lot of nuclear weapons in the Pacific ocean, and so did we. If we attack Yelizovo, the environmental impact shouldn't be any worse than the old tests at Bikini Atoll, or Johnson Island, or Enewetak."

"That's not particularly comforting," the president said. "We still don't know the long-term environmental impact of Bikini, or any of those other tests. We haven't even figured out how to accurately measure the damage they've caused to the ocean eco-systems."

"That's true, Mr. President," the national security advisor said.

President Chandler didn't speak for nearly a minute. At last, he took a deep breath and let it out slowly. "I'm sorry, Greg. I'm just trying to figure out how to make this omelet without breaking any eggs."

"I don't think it can be done, sir," Brenthoven said.

"Neither do I," the president said. "But that doesn't stop me from wishing."

He looked at his national security advisor for several seconds. "Let's talk this over with State and the Joint Chiefs. If our people can't offer any compelling reasons to the contrary, I'm going to take the Russians up on their offer."

He turned back to the blank display again. One way or another, in a few hours there would be missile trajectories painted on that screen again. But this time, they'd be pointed in the other direction.

CHAPTER 59

Sergiei Mikhailovich Zhukov checked his watch for the twentieth time. What was keeping that accursed helicopter? It was time to be away from this place—*past* time. Didn't these fools understand that?

It was all arranged; the Chinese treasury bills were safely hidden in three banks on Grand Cayman. Zhukov and his senior advisors would evacuate to the Caribbean islands, submerge beneath the never-ending flow of tourists, and calculate the most effective way to leverage the Chinese money into another opportunity.

Zhukov was not abandoning the plan. This was only a change of tactics. He was still dedicated to restoring the Rodina to her rightful glory.

The Russian people were yearning for a return to their proper place in the world. He could feel the undercurrent of their hidden desire coursing through the streets and alleyways like the flow of an invisible river.

It was his destiny to make the secret dream of his people into a reality. This battle was lost, but the war was far from over. This was a setback—nothing more. He would study his errors, and learn. And then, he would begin again.

He took some comfort in the knowledge that even Vladimir Ilyich Lenin had suffered failures and reversals of fortune in the early days of the great revolution. Lenin had become a hunted man. He'd gone into hiding, to elude his pursuers, and to gather his forces. And he had returned, to triumph over the enemies of the people, to forge the great Soviet empire.

Zhukov would follow that magnificent example. He would form a covert government in exile, operating quietly from the shadows until he was ready to strip away the veil of secrecy, to reveal the reborn revolution. By his hand, *Novaya Rossiya*, the New Russia, would be molded from the very ashes of this failure.

326

If only that damned helicopter would arrive …

"Comrade President?"

Zhukov's head snapped around, his eyes quickly locating the source of the voice. His chief assistant, Maxim Ivanovitch Ustanov, stood at the door.

"Yes," Zhukov said. "Is it the helicopter? Has it finally arrived?"

Ustanov's face was a mask of exhaustion. "I'm sorry, Comrade President. No helicopter. Not yet. There is a meteor shower."

Zhukov felt the frown form on his face. "A *meteor shower*?"

"Yes, Comrade President," Ustanov said. "You asked to be notified of anything out of the ordinary. There is a meteor shower."

Zhukov swallowed the urge to shout at this idiot, for bothering him with such trivial matters as meteor showers. He reached for his coat.

Three minutes later, he stood at the entrance to the cave, staring up into the darkness. It *did* look like a meteor shower. Trails of flaming brightness were streaking down out of the sky.

Zhukov's heart went cold. Those were *not* meteors. They were …

The air above Koryaksky mountain, 1,000 meters directly over Zhukov's head, was shattered by a flash more than ten times as bright as the sun.

It was the last thing that Sergiei Mikhailovich Zhukov ever saw.

CHAPTER 60

The cargo was divided between the two ships. Strapped to steel cradles on the lower vehicle decks, each of the 20,000-ton Roll-on/Roll-off vessels carried the warhead section of an ex-Soviet R-29R nuclear missile—the unofficial (and unacknowledged) payment for China's support of Sergiei Mikhailovich Zhukov's short-lived revolution.

As true owners of the nuclear warheads, the Russian Federation had not authorized their transfer to the People's Republic of China, but the transfer was taking place nonetheless. In the bowels of two innocent-looking merchant ships rode the technology that would finally transform China into a nuclear superpower. The balance of world power was poised to shift suddenly and (perhaps) irrevocably toward Communist Asia.

In the years to follow, no one would ever be able to prove the details of the illegal transaction taking place on a lonely stretch of shipping lanes in the Western Pacific Ocean. Despite a mountain of suspicion, and an avalanche of circumstantial evidence, no investigative body would ever manage to formally verify the link between the Central Committee of the Communist Party of China and Zhukov. No court would ever bring official charges against the Chinese government or the People's Liberation Army.

Unconcerned by the growing controversy in Russia, the United States, and Japan, the Motor Vessel *Shunfeng* and the Motor Vessel *Jifeng* made twelve and a half knots of steady headway against a brisk easterly wind. When they made landfall in their home port of Zhuhai, the masters and crews of both ships would all become very wealthy men, as well as national heroes of the People's Republic of China. And they would all take pride in having elevated their great nation to its rightful place as the dominant military force of the new millennium.

328

The West would rattle and rail, but the sluggish mechanisms of the international courts would move far too slowly to have any real effect. By the time the self-important fools had finished wrangling with themselves, the deed would be done.

⚓ ⚓ ⚓

They came from the northwest: six Mitsubishi F-2A fighter jets, screaming through the darkness in three flights of two, afterburners trailing streaks of translucent blue flame less than 1,000 meters above the wave tops. Although no one aboard the *Shunfeng* or *Jifeng* would ever see them, each plane had the 'rising-sun' roundel of the Japan Air Self-Defense Force emblazoned on its wings and fuselage.

The attack was sanctioned by no court. It was recorded in no log book, and it was not formally authorized by any agency of any recognized government.

Officially, the attack never occurred at all. Unofficially, it happened quickly and without mercy.

Twelve jewel-like flashes announced the launch of a dozen Japanese ASM-2/Type 93 Air-to-Ship missiles. The dart-shaped weapons locked onto the heat signatures from the two unarmed merchant vessels and hurled themselves toward their respective targets.

The darkness was shattered by a dozen simultaneous explosions, as the Motor Vessels *Shunfeng* and *Jifeng* received Japan's unofficial answer to China's unofficial bid for nuclear supremacy. The fragments of the broken R-29R nuclear warheads tumbled to the bottom of the ocean, accompanied by the wreckage of two ships and the bodies of their crews.

The fighter planes circled the area until the demands of fuel consumption forced them to turn back toward the waters of their own country.

When the sun finally straggled above the horizon, the location was marked only by a scattered field of floating debris, and the rainbow smudge of an oil slick from the ruptured fuel tanks of the *Shunfeng* and *Jifeng*.

There were no survivors.

EPILOGUE

Whoever it was, would not stop knocking.

Ann Roark grabbed the remote for her stereo and wound up the volume another few clicks. Johan Sebastian Bach fairly flew out of the speakers, the buoyant violins filling the living room of her condo with the brightness and promise that were totally lacking from her life.

The knocking grew louder.

"Go away!" Ann said. She fingered the remote again, and Bach swelled to maximum volume.

The scars on her wrists were fading now, just thin white lines where the razor blades had cut their tracks through her skin. She wondered when she'd have the courage to try again. Maybe she'd get it right this time. And maybe that would finally end the dreams. Maybe she'd stop seeing the fireball in the sky over Pearl Harbor. Stop seeing the faces of the dead strangers she hadn't been able to save.

The knocking on the door continued unabated.

She would wait them out, whoever it was. She wasn't going to answer the door.

But the knocking continued, pausing only for brief intervals every now and then, as the unwanted visitor changed up and began knocking with the other hand.

The Bach CD ran out, and the stereo restarted it automatically. Ann wondered if the persistent asshole at the door would still be pounding away when the disc restarted the next time.

She sighed and stood up, trudging to the door as though the weight of the world was on her shoulders. And, in a way, it was.

She left the security chain on, opening the door only as far as the short length of chain would allow. She glared at the dark-haired man outside her door. He looked familiar, but she couldn't quite place him.

330

"What?" she said. "Can you *not* take a freaking hint? Are you too freaking dense to see that I don't want visitors?"

The dark haired man smiled, and suddenly Ann recognized him. It was Bowie. *Captain* Bowie, from the *Towers*. She'd never seen him in civilian clothes before. He looked different. Like a regular guy.

"I realize that you don't want visitors," he said. "But you know how captains are. We get spoiled. We're accustomed to having things our own way."

"So I remember," Ann said.

Bowie looked through the gap of the partially-opened door, past Ann into her living room. "Brandenburg Concerto Number 3, right? One of my favorite Bach pieces, but I don't usually listen to it quite this loud."

Ann turned far enough to point the remote toward the stereo. She brought the volume down.

"Are you going to invite me in?" Bowie asked.

Ann made a face. "Do I *have* to?"

Bowie smiled again, and she saw again that he really was a decent looking guy, in a Boy Scout sort of way.

"It's not an order, if that's what you mean," Bowie said. "And I don't really need to come in. I actually came to take you out. Let's go have a drink, okay?"

The request took Ann completely by surprise.

Bowie must have caught the expression on her face, because he waved a hand. "I'm not trying to pick you up," he said. "I promise."

He crossed his heart. "I'm happily engaged. But even if I weren't attached, I wouldn't shoot my career in the head, by hitting on a civilian contractor. This is completely innocent. Scout's honor."

Ann nearly snorted. The damned Eagle Scout thing again. "What about that girl in every port thing?" she asked. "No mistress on the side?"

Bowie's smile widened into a grin. "I've got the sexiest mistress in the world," he said. "She's five hundred and twenty-nine feet long, and she's made of steel."

"I've seen her," Ann said. "You can *keep* her."

Bowie leaned against the doorframe. He was evidently going to make himself comfortable, whether Ann invited him in or not. "Come have a drink with me," he said. "I want you to meet some people. Sort of friends of mine."

He shrugged. "I just met them a few days ago, but I think we're going to be friends. I hope so, anyway. They strike me as good people."

Ann frowned. "I'm not really into meeting people," she said. "That's Sheldon's department. I'm more of a hardware type of girl."

"I understand that," Bowie said. "But these people want to meet *you*. In fact, they're pretty excited about it."

"Why do they want to meet me?" Ann asked.

"They're a couple," Bowie said. "Charlie Sweigart, and Gabriella Marchand. They just got engaged. They want to meet you, so that they can thank you in person."

Ann recoiled. "Thank me? For what?"

"For saving their lives," Bowie said. "They were aboard the submersible *Nereus*. They would have died down there if it hadn't been for you and Mouse."

Ann tried to look past him. "Are they here?"

Bowie shook his head. "No. I didn't want to spring them on you. I know you're not a people person. And I know you're having a rough time lately."

Ann felt her cheeks go warm. "Did Sheldon tell you that?"

"Yeah," Bowie said. "Sheldon and I chat sometimes. He tells me you're having dreams."

Ann didn't like where this was going. "Everybody has dreams," she said.

Bowie cocked his head a few degrees to one side. "Not these kinds of dreams. Sheldon says you're having nightmares about Pearl Harbor. About the people we didn't save."

"Sheldon talks too much," Ann said.

Bowie smiled again, but it was a different kind of smile. "Would it help any if I told you that I'm having nightmares too?"

His question surprised Ann. "You *are*?"

"Of course," Bowie said. "Believe me, I'm no stranger to bad dreams. It goes with the territory."

"What territory?" Ann asked.

"With saving part of the world," Bowie said.

"*Part* of it? What does that mean?"

Bowie's strange little smile disappeared. "In the comic books, Superman gets to save the entire world. But we're just mortals, and this is not a comic book. We can only save *part* of the world. And even doing *that* much takes a hell of a lot of luck, and more sacrifice than I care to think about."

"What about the parts you can't save?" Ann asked. "What do you do about the people who die because you can't do your job well enough to save them?"

Bowie slid his hands into his pockets. "I try to remind myself that every doctor, and every firefighter faces that exact same question. Nobody wins every time, Ann. We just do the best we can."

He paused for a couple of seconds. "And things get worse the minute we stop trying."

Ann felt her throat beginning to constrict. "I screwed up," she said. "When I was programming Mouse to go after the submarine, I screwed up. I forgot to reinstall the software patch."

"You made a mistake," Bowie said. "It happens. You're fallible, just like the rest of us."

"But you could have killed that sub the first time," Ann said miserably. "Mouse had the submarine located. If my programming glitch hadn't driven Mouse off task, you could have destroyed the submarine a whole day earlier. *Before* it had a chance to launch its missiles."

Her voice was shaky now. "It's my fault," she said. "Those people didn't have to die. If I had done my job properly, they'd still be alive."

Bowie rubbed his chin. "Can I share an observation with you? It's a bit of wisdom that I picked up from a very intelligent person."

Ann gave a half-hearted jerk of her head, not particularly interested in whatever comforting platitude that Bowie was about to trot out.

"You're full of shit," Bowie said.

His words stopped Ann cold. *"What?"*

"You're full of shit," Bowie said again. "That's what you said to me that day in the wardroom, when you reminded me that you had crammed two days worth of programming into a few hours. You were working under incredible pressure, busting your ass to get the job done, and trying your hardest to do it right, and you missed something. You didn't do it on purpose; you didn't try to cover it up; and you fixed your mistake the minute you found out about it."

Bowie laughed. "You stood right there on my own ship, and told me that I was full of shit," he said. "And you were absolutely right. Now you want to go back and judge yourself by the same screwed up standards? I'm sorry, but you're just as full of shit *now*, as I was *then*."

"But those people," Ann said. "They didn't have to ..."

Bowie cut her off. "We couldn't have gotten that submarine without you, Ann. If you need to fixate on something, try focusing on *that*. You saved millions of lives. Not hundreds. Not thousands. *Millions*."

Ann didn't respond.

"Come on," Bowie said. "Let's go meet Charlie and Gabriella. We'll have a drink, and blow off some steam. And you'll get a chance to meet some of the people you *did* save."

He gave Ann a serious look. "It helps," he said softly. "It won't make all of the doubts and the bad dreams go away, but it really does help."

"Where's the other guy?" Anne asked.

"What other guy?"

"The third guy from the submersible," Anne said. "There were three people on the *Nereus*, right? You want me to meet with two of them. What happened to the other guy?"

She stopped, as a horrid thought crossed her mind. "Did he ..."

"The other guy is fine," Bowie said. "His name is Steve Harper. He won't be here today."

"Why not?"

Bowie grinned. "Mr. Harper is gearing up to sue NOAA, and the Navy, and the manufacturer of the submersible, and probably the Easter Bunny."

"You're joking," Anne said.

"Nope," Bowie said. "Mr. Harper is suing everything in sight. I guess he doesn't want to be seen fraternizing with potential defendants."

"Is he suing *me*?" Anne asked.

"Not as far as I know," Bowie said. "But don't be surprised if he gets around to it. That's part of the down-side of saving the day. Not everyone is grateful."

Ann felt herself reach a decision on some unconscious level. She pushed the door closed, just far enough to release the chain. "I don't guess I can pass up the opportunity to have a drink with my co-defendants."

She opened the door and stepped back, finally allowing Bowie into her living room. "Have a seat, while I get changed."

Bowie stepped through the door. "Thanks."

Ann headed for the hall. Just before she left the room, she stopped and turned around. "I'll go with you to meet these people," she said. "But it's only fair to tell you up front. I *still* don't like you."

Bowie nodded. "I know," he said. "That's why you're buying."

AUTHOR'S NOTES

As students of oceanography or climatology will note, I've taken a few liberties with the ice formations in the Sea of Okhotsk. I've described the location and geography accurately, and the surface topography of the ice is every bit as rugged as I've depicted it, but the density and coverage of the winter ice pack are not as heavy as my story suggests. From late February through early March, the ice in the Sea of Okhotsk is often 30 to 50 inches thick, but less than half of the sea will freeze over during a typical winter.

These exaggerations were strictly for dramatic purposes. The Soviet Navy actually did hide ballistic missile submarines under the ice pack in the Sea of Okhotsk during the Cold War, and the practice may still continue under the new Russian Navy. I didn't invent the strategy. I simply embellished the size and thickness of the ice pack to make the task of going after the rogue missile submarine a little tougher for the crew of USS *Towers*.

I've also exercised a bit of artistic license in my portrayal of the Defense Intelligence Agency. The real world mission of the DIA is to provide timely, objective, and cogent military intelligence to warfighters, defense planners, and national security policymakers.

DIA agents don't generally conduct the kind of field operations that I've written about in *The Seventh Angel*. They are unlikely to stash wounded foreign intelligence operatives in U.S. military hospitals, and they don't customarily threaten to shoot people for breaches of security protocol. If such extreme actions ever become necessary, the DIA will probably not be called upon to handle the dirty work. I thought it would be fun to let a couple of DIA agents do some cowboy stuff, even if only in the pages of a novel.

I'm sorry to report that I did *not* invent or exaggerate the tragic condition of the Russian Federation's nuclear forces. The Russian military has fallen into an advanced state of decay, and the Russian news media has stated openly on several occasions that the integrity and security of the massive post-Soviet nuclear arsenal are in serious jeopardy. In 2007, the Russian government began a series of major military funding initiatives that are supposed to halt and (eventually) reverse this dangerous trend. At the time of this writing, I'm seeing no compelling indications that the budget increases are having the desired effect. They may well be too little, too late.

335

Personally, I hope the Russians do manage to turn the problem around. As strange as it sounds, I believe that a stable and capable Russian military is better for global security than one on the verge of disintegration. If the Russian military collapses, the thousands of remaining nuclear weapons in the Russian stockpile will not magically evaporate. Every one of those warheads will ultimately fall into someone's hands. We cannot predict who will gain control over those weapons, or what their agendas will be.

In the writing of this book, I've deliberately created tense situations. I'm a thriller writer, and there are no thrills without a sense of danger and dramatic tension. But I didn't invent many of the scariest parts of this story. I simply looked at the current climate of world affairs, and wrote what I saw.

— Jeff Edwards

Award-winning novelist

JEFF EDWARDS

delivers another cutting-edge naval thriller
from the pages of

the Sea Warrior Files...

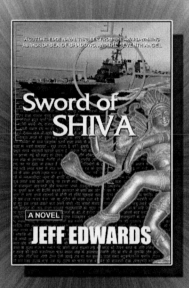

SWORD OF SHIVA

Coming in 2011, from Stealth Books.

CPSIA information can be obtained at www.ICGtesting.com
Printed in the USA
LVOW061630190911

246946LV00006B/1/P